Praise for

CANDACE CAMP

"Camp has again produced a fast-paced plot brimming with lively conflict among family, lovers and enemies."
—*Publishers Weekly* on *A Dangerous Man*

"Romance, humor, adventure, Incan treasure, dreams, murder, psychics—the latest addition to Camp's Mad Moreland series has it all."
—*Booklist* on *An Unexpected Pleasure*

"Entertaining, well-written Victorian romantic mystery."
—*The Best Reviews* on *An Unexpected Pleasure*

"A smart, fun-filled romp."
—*Publishers Weekly* on *Impetuous*

"Camp brings the dark Victorian world to life. Her strong characters and perfect pacing keep you turning the pages of this chilling mystery."
—*Romantic Times BOOKreviews* on *Winterset*

"From its delicious beginning to its satisfying ending, [*Mesmerized*] offers a double helping of romance."
—*Booklist*

CANDACE CAMP

Promise Me Tomorrow

HQN™

If you purchased this book without a cover you should be aware that this book is stolen property. It was reported as "unsold and destroyed" to the publisher, and neither the author nor the publisher has received any payment for this "stripped book."

ISBN-13: 978-0-373-77269-8
ISBN-10:   0-373-77269-6

PROMISE ME TOMORROW

Copyright © 2000 by Candace Camp

All rights reserved. Except for use in any review, the reproduction or utilization of this work in whole or in part in any form by any electronic, mechanical or other means, now known or hereafter invented, including xerography, photocopying and recording, or in any information storage or retrieval system, is forbidden without the written permission of the publisher, Harlequin Enterprises Limited, 225 Duncan Mill Road, Don Mills, Ontario M3B 3K9, Canada.

This is a work of fiction. Names, characters, places and incidents are either the product of the author's imagination or are used fictitiously, and any resemblance to actual persons, living or dead, business establishments, events or locales is entirely coincidental.

This edition published by arrangement with Harlequin Books S.A.

® and TM are trademarks of the publisher. Trademarks indicated with ® are registered in the United States Patent and Trademark Office, the Canadian Trade Marks Office and in other countries.

www.HQNBooks.com

Printed in U.S.A.

**Other newly released classics from
Candace Camp and HQN Books**

A Stolen Heart
No Other Love

Other books by Candace Camp

A Dangerous Man
An Independent Woman
An Unexpected Pleasure
So Wild a Heart
The Hidden Heart
Swept Away
Winterset
Beyond Compare
Mesmerized
Impetuous
Indiscreet
Impulse
Scandalous
Suddenly

**Watch for Candace Camp's newest historical
romance series, The Matchmakers, beginning this
September with *The Marriage Wager***

Promise Me Tomorrow

PROLOGUE

THE CHILD LIFTED HER HEAD SLEEPILY AND looked at the man across from her in the carriage. She blinked, then scowled.

"You're a bad man."

The man glanced at her and sighed. "Hush. We're almost there."

His face was shadowed in the dim light. He was almost skeletally thin, and he fidgeted constantly. Marie Anne knew that Nurse would have snapped at him to sit still and behave himself.

"I want to go home," she said plaintively. *Everything was so confusing. It had been for weeks.* She missed John, and she missed the baby. Most of all, she missed Mama and Papa. She remembered That Night and the way her mother had hustled her out the door and along the dark, scary street. She remembered the familiar scent of Mama's perfume as she squeezed Marie Anne to her chest, whispering "Take care, ma chérie." Mama had been crying, and Marie Anne knew that it was the bad people in the streets who made her cry.

"I want to stay with you!" Marie Anne had wailed, clinging tightly to her mother. That had made the baby cry, too, and try to scramble out of Mrs. Ward's arms and back to their mother. Only John had stood stoically silent and still.

"Oh, *chérie!* If you only knew—I wish you could, too, but it isn't safe." Her mother, more beautiful than any other woman in the world, had wiped the tears from her cheeks and tried to smile. "You must go home to England. To your Mimi and Granpapa. You will like that, won't you? Mrs. Ward will take you. You know Mrs. Ward. She's Mama's *ami,* and she will take good care of you. She'll see that you get to Mimi's house in the City. Papa and I must stay here and get *Granmama* and *Granpere* to leave. But as soon as we do, we will join you at Mimi's house."

"Promise?"

"I promise, my little love. I promise."

"Where's Mama?" Marie Anne asked now, turning to her companion accusingly, "You said we were going to see Mama." She had cried and kicked when he'd carried her from her bed earlier, until finally he had told her to be still, that he was taking her to her mother.

"We are almost there," the man repeated glancing out the window.

Marie Anne looked out the window, too, and saw that they were approaching a large building. But it was not their home, nor even Mimi's large house in the country or the tall white one in the City. It was a huge squat block of gray stone, far too ugly, she knew, to be anyplace where Mama was. Tears filled her eyes.

"That's not Mimi's." For a little while, she and her brother John had been at Mimi's home in the City. Mrs. Ward, Mama's friend from Paris, had taken them there, and at first Marie Anne's sad heart had lifted joyfully, thinking that she was going to get to see her beloved grandmother. But then That Woman had whisked them away, taking them outside and to another house, where the Awful Man was. She had seen him before, but he was not the sort who spoke to children, and she wasn't sure who he was.

Then That Woman had fed her something and tried to give John something, as well, but he was too sick. She had left them in a room, with John twisting and turning on his bed, sweating and shaking. It had scared Marie Anne to see him like that; it had scared her to be there without any grown-up. But it was even scarier to be away from her big brother, traveling through the dark night with this stranger. *Why had Mrs. Ward left them with That Woman? Why had she taken the baby, but not John and Marie Anne? Where was Mimi?*

She began to cry, although she did not want to in front of this odd, jittery man whom she did not know at all. "I want Mimi," she said, her voice trembling. "I want Nurse. I want Mama!"

"Later, later." His voice was impatient, and he barely waited for the carriage to stop before he unlatched the door and jumped down. He reached for her, but Marie Anne backed away, her heart thumping. The ugly building loomed outside, and she was certain she did not want to go there.

"No. No!" The word ended in a shriek as he wrapped one arm around her and dragged her out.

She screamed and began to struggle. "Mama! Papa!"

He carried her inexorably up the front stairs to the door and banged the heavy knocker. It was some minutes before the door was opened by a scowling servant, and some time more before a large, stern-looking woman swept into the entryway, a dressing gown wrapped around her and a nightcap on her head.

The sight of her was enough to freeze Marie Anne's sobs in her throat. She stared at the woman, ice forming in the pit of her stomach. The woman was tall and heavyset, with none of the beauty and warmth that lived in Marie Anne's mother and grandmothers. This woman's eyes were pale and cold as metal, and her face was grim, dominated by a predatory beak of a nose. She looked at Marie Anne as though she knew every naughty thing the girl had ever done.

"I found her," the jittery man was saying. "She was on the side of the road, obviously abandoned. I didn't know where else to take her."

His words were enough to jolt Marie Anne out of her fear, and she cried out indignantly, "That's a lie! I wasn't on the side of the road!"

The woman clapped her hands together so loudly that both Marie Anne and the man jumped. "Enough!" Her voice cracked like a whip. "Don't presume to correct your betters, child. You will soon learn that here you speak only when spoken to, and you do not contradict an adult."

Her tone made Marie Anne's heart thump inside her chest, but she squared her shoulders and thrust out her chin. She was not the sort to knuckle under without a fight. She thought of the way her father would ruffle her hair and chuckle, calling her his tiger.

"But I wasn't by the side of the road," she insisted.

The woman's eyes narrowed. "I can see that you are going to be stiff-necked. Redheads are always trouble."

"I am sure she will settle down," the man said quickly, panic tinging his voice. "Once she has been here awhile, she will be all right."

"Don't worry, sir," the woman replied with a faintly sardonic smile. She looked at him as if she, too, knew what he was thinking, Marie Anne noticed. "We shall take her. I am not one to turn away a soul just because she is obviously in need of improvement. We shall straighten her out soon enough." The woman's eyes sparkled with anticipation.

The man let out a sigh of relief and set Marie Anne down. "Thank you."

He turned and hurried toward the door. Little as the girl had liked him, it frightened her to see him leave. Even he was better than this hard-faced woman.

"No! Wait!" Marie Anne shrieked, turning to run after him, but the woman hooked a hand in her sash and jerked her back.

"Stop it! Stop that behavior this instant!" The woman accompanied her words with a stinging slap to the back of the girl's legs, bare below her skirts.

Marie Anne, who had never been struck in her life, whirled and gaped at the woman. The man hurried out the door, closing it after him.

"That's better." The woman nodded approvingly. "The children of St. Anselm's do not act that way, as you will soon find out. The children of St. Anselm's are quiet and obedient. Now..." Satisfied that she had set this unseemly child on the proper path, the woman looked her over. "How old are you?"

"Five," the girl responded promptly, rather proud of her age.

"And what is your name?"

"Marie Anne."

"That is scarcely a proper name for a child of your sort. No doubt you are that gentleman's by-blow. Just plain Mary will do fine for you. Do you have a last name?"

Marie Anne stared at her. "I—I'm not sure. I am just Marie Anne."

"Do you have a father?"

"Of course I do!" Marie Anne responded indignantly. "And he will come here and get me! And he will make you sorry!"

"No doubt," the matron said dryly. "There are many children waiting for their fathers to come. In the meantime, we shall have to give you a name. Now, what do people call your father?"

"Chilton," she answered.

"All right. Mary Chilton. That is your name. I am called Mrs. Brown. I am the matron of St. Anselm's."

"But that's not my name," Marie Anne protested indignantly.

"It is now. Do not contradict me. I told you before that that is not acceptable behavior."

"But you're wrong!"

Mrs. Brown's hand lashed out and slapped Marie Anne sharply across her ear. "You will *not* speak to me that way. Do you understand?"

Stunned, Marie Anne nodded, her hand going up to her cheek. Never in her life had she been treated in such a manner. Even during the past few harrowing weeks, rocking about the countryside with Mrs. Ward and John and the baby, running from those bad people and having to pretend that they were Mrs. Ward's children—even during all that, no one had ever raised a hand to her or talked to her in this way. Tears pooled in her eyes, and for a moment she wavered on the edge of bursting into tears. But years of aristocratic breeding came to her rescue, and she stiffened her back, gazing up at the woman coolly. Mama would say that this woman was déclassée, she decided. Papa, on the other hand, would say that what she had done was "bad form." She clung to the words, hearing her parents in her head.

"Answer me when I speak to you," Mrs. Brown snapped.

"Yes, Mrs. Brown," Marie Anne responded dutifully, but her voice was chilly and carried all the humility of a duchess.

The older woman looked at her sharply but could not quite put her finger on what it was in the girl's tone that raised her hackles. Finally she turned away, saying crisply, "Follow me."

She led her up the stairs and down a hallway barely lit by a few sconces on the wall. The candlelight flickered and flared, casting strange shadows. Marie Anne felt fear rising up in her throat, but she pushed it back down. She could hear her Mimi's voice the time she had gone running to her in tears when John and the boys were teasing her with scary stories: "Head up, my girl. Never let them know you're afraid. It would give them far too much pleasure."

Mrs. Brown stopped at a cupboard and opened it, pulling out a thin blanket and a folded brown dress. To the top of the pile she added a white petticoat, faded through many washings, a pair of rough lisle stockings, darned in several places, and an overly large nightgown. She handed the stack to Marie Anne.

"Here are your clothes and a blanket for your bed."

Marie Anne looked doubtfully at the ugly brown dress. "But I have clothes. I like my dress better."

The older woman cast a scornful glance at Marie Anne's attire. "Your clothes are completely inappropriate. Far above your station. You are at St. Anselm's now, and you will wear the dress I gave you."

Remembering the stinging slap, Marie Anne decided not to argue. She merely hugged the stack of her new possessions tightly to her chest and followed Mrs. Brown into the room beyond the cupboard.

It was a long room, lined with narrow beds along either side. Beside each bed was a small chest with three drawers. In each bed lay a girl. Marie Anne had never seen so many people sleeping in one room before. *Was she expected to sleep here, among so many other children? Where was* her *room?* She thought with longing of the nursery at home, with her own snug little room, and John and Nurse and the baby all in their little rooms across the schoolroom from her.

Some of the children slept, but most of them awoke at Mrs. Brown's entrance. In the glow of the woman's candle, Marie Anne could see wide-open eyes peeking out from beneath their blankets. Mrs. Brown turned to Marie Anne.

"Now, I want you to undress and get into bed. Tomorrow you will be introduced to the other children and assigned your duties."

"Duties?"

"Of course. Everyone earns their keep around here." The woman turned and started away.

"But—what about the light?" Marie Anne asked, unable to completely hide the tremor in her voice at the thought of being left here in the dark. "How can I see to undress?"

"There is plenty of light from the windows," the matron answered, indicating the tall, curtainless windows that lined either side of the room. "I don't allow children to waste candles."

With those words, the woman strode out of the room. Marie Anne watched the flickering light of her candle recede. Tears welled in her eyes, and her chin began to wobble, no matter how hard she struggled to keep it still. She had never felt so alone in all her life, even the night her mother had handed them over to Mrs. Ward, then hurried out the door, sobbing. At least then she had had

John and Alexandra, and she had known Mrs. Ward, who was a kind, soft-spoken woman. But now—now she was utterly alone and abandoned.

A small hand slipped into hers, and a soft voice whispered, "'Ere now, don't cry. It'll be better tomorrow, you'll see."

Marie Anne turned to see a girl about her size, but with a face much older than hers. She looked at the girl curiously, her tears slowly subsiding. She wiped them away with her hand and said, "Hullo. Who are you?"

"I'm Winny," the girl responded with a shy smile. "I'm eight. Wot's your name?"

"Marie Anne. But that woman said now I must be Mary."

The little girl nodded. "She likes plain names. 'Ow old are you? Would you like to be my friend?"

"Aw, don't be daft, Winny." A rough voice spoke from the bed on the other side of them, and an older girl swung around to sit on the side of the bed, facing them. She had curly dark hair poorly suppressed into braids, and a round, pugnacious face liberally sprinkled with freckles. "'Oo'd want to be friends with the likes o' you?"

"I would," Marie Anne told the other girl stoutly. "Winny seems very nice."

"'Winny seems very nice,'" the other girl mimicked in a high voice, striving to imitate Marie Anne's precise diction. "'Oo're you, a bleedin' princess?"

Marie Anne lifted her chin. "No, but I shall be a duchess one day, if I want. Mimi said so."

"A duchess!" This statement afforded the other girl much amusement, for she slapped her thigh and rocked with laughter. "Lookee 'ere, everybody, we got a bleedin' duchess among us."

Marie Anne frowned at her. "You shouldn't use such

words. Nurse says it's wicked and—and low class. Beside, I'm not a duchess now. But I will be, if I want to. Mimi said I could—and she's a countess!"

"The Duchess of St. Anselm's," the other girl pronounced, still chuckling.

"Never mind her," Winny whispered. "Betty don't like anyone. I think you look like a duchess." She touched the sleeve of Marie Anne's dress admiringly. "But you'd best get into your nightgown now. Miss Patman will be coming through shortly. She comes every hour to check on us, and she'll punish you if you're out o' bed."

Marie Anne sighed. She didn't want to take off her clothes and put on the rough nightgown, but she *was* dreadfully tired. And perhaps if she went to sleep, she would wake up the next morning and find herself back in the nursery with John and the baby, and Nurse waking them up with a cheerful hello and a cup of hot chocolate.

She unbuttoned her dress with Winny's help, pulled it off and reached for the nightdress to put it on.

"'Ere! Wot's that?" Betty, still watching her, leaned forward now and reached for the locket around Marie Anne's neck.

Marie Anne stepped back quickly, her hand closing around the precious locket. Mimi had given it to her last Boxing Day. It was gold and opened to show a cunning little portrait of her mother on one side and of her father on the other. The front was inscribed with an ornate, looping *M* for Marie. Mimi had given one just like it to the baby, with an *A* on the front for Alexandra. Of course, the baby was too young to wear it, only two, but Marie Anne had put hers on and never took it off .

"Give it to me," Betty demanded, getting up and coming around the bed toward her.

"No! It's mine! Mimi gave it to me."

Betty's face lit with a wicked glee. "It's mine now."

Her hand lashed out and grabbed Marie Anne's smaller fist. She jerked it toward her, and the chain of the locket bit painfully into Marie Anne's neck. All the anger and fear of the past few weeks exploded now in Marie Anne, and she let out a feral shriek and sank her teeth into the other girl's hand.

Betty jerked back her hand, letting out a yowl. She drew back her other fist to hit the smaller girl, but Marie Anne was on her like a wild thing, hitting and kicking and biting. Finally, laughing, the oldest girl in the room came over and hauled Marie Anne off the bully and set her on her feet. Betty sat up, hunched over, trying to nurse both her injured hand and her bleeding nose, and gasping for air from a blow that had landed square in her stomach.

"I think you met your match, Bet," the fourteen-year-old said in an amused voice. She made a mocking bow toward the little girl standing beside her, still rigid with fury. "Pleased to make your acquaintance, Duchess. I'm Sally Gravers."

"Thank you. I'm pleased to meet you, too," Marie told her, giving a little curtsy, just as Nurse had taught her to do when she met important adults. Sally Gravers wasn't an adult, but she looked the most important person in this group, so the gesture seemed appropriate.

The older girl grinned, further amused. "You're all right." She turned toward Betty and scowled. "You leave 'er alone now. You 'ear me? That trinket's 'ers."

"All right, Sally," the bully replied in a surly voice, shooting Marie Anne a venomous look.

"Right now. Let's get some sleep," Sally went on. "I, for one, ain't lookin' forward to getting up at five and scrubbin' floors on no sleep."

Marie Anne gaped at the older girl, scarcely able to believe her ears. *Had she somehow become a maidservant?* But, given the topsy-turvy events of the last few weeks, she knew that anything was possible. She scrambled into her nightgown, tucking the locket protectively beneath it.

Winny, still beside her, whispered, "She won't steal it now—she's too afraid of Sally. But the matron will take it if she sees it. She'll say it's above you. I've got a 'idin' place. No one's ever found it. I'll show it to you, and you can 'ide it there."

Marie Anne nodded gratefully as she and Winny spread the blanket over the narrow mattress. Then she crawled into bed, remembering with a sigh the deep feather mattress of her bed at home and the layers of thick, warm blankets that Nurse would tuck around her at night. The thought led her to memories of her mother coming in to kiss her good-night. Sometimes she would be already dressed to go out, her elegant brocade dress spreading out wide beneath her narrow waist, her hair powdered and towering in a confection of curls, decorated with jewels or feathers. Other times, she would still be in a dressing gown, and her thick black hair would be tumbling down around her shoulders in a curling cloud. She would bend over Marie Anne and whisper that she loved her. Marie Anne could smell again the orris root of her powder mingling with the scent of her perfume.

Tears seeped out of her eyes, and she lifted the locket out from beneath her nightgown, her fist closing around it. *Why hadn't Mama come for them?* She had told them that she and Papa would join them as soon as they could. A horrible lonely feeling welled inside Marie Anne as a wicked voice whispered that Mama and Papa no longer wanted her.

But that wasn't true! Marie struggled against the engulfing horror. She knew her mother and father loved her. They would come and get her, and they would find the baby, too, and John—and he wouldn't be sick anymore. She just had to hold on, she told herself, and someday they would come for her. *Someday her family would find her, and she would be happy again....*

CHAPTER ONE

MARIANNE DREW A DEEP BREATH AS SHE surveyed the glittering crowd. She had never been to a party this large, nor one filled with so many titled people. She wondered what they would think if they knew she was plain Mary Chilton from St. Anselm's Orphanage, not the genteel widow Mrs. Marianne Cotterwood.

She smiled to herself. The thing she enjoyed the most about her pretense was the idea of pulling the wool over the eyes of the aristocracy, of conversing with some blue-blooded member of the *ton*—who would have been horrified if he had known that he was speaking to a former chambermaid as if to an equal.

The thought settled her nerves somewhat. This might be a larger and more cosmopolitan set of people than she had deceived in the resorts of Bath and Brighton, but essentially they were the same. If one spoke as if one were genteel, and walked and sat and ate as if one had been trained to do so from birth, people assumed that one belonged. As long as she kept her lies small and plausible and was careful never to pretend to be someone more than the minor gentry, it was doubtful that anyone would sniff out her deceit. After all, most of the people here were too self-absorbed to spare much thought for anyone else, for good or ill. That was one of the traits which made it so easy to prey upon them.

Marianne regarded all members of the ruling class as her natural enemies. She could still remember the days at the orphanage, when the grand ladies would come on their "missions of mercy." Well-fed and warm, they would stand in their elegant dresses that cost more than would be spent on any of the orphans in a year and look at them with pitying contempt. Then they would go away, feeling vastly superior and quite holy for their charity. Marianne had stared at them with anger burning in her heart. Nothing that happened to her after the orphanage had lessened her contempt for them. She had been sent into service at Lady Quartermaine's house when she was fourteen, and there she had worked as a housemaid, emptying ashes from the fireplace, hauling water for baths, and cleaning, all for less than a shilling a day, with only Sunday afternoons off— and woe to her if anything was deemed ill-done or amiss. Of course, even that did not compare to what else had happened to her at Quartermaine Hall....

"It's a lovely party," Marianne's companion said, and Marianne turned to her, firmly shoving aside her thoughts.

Mrs. Willoughby was a fluttery woman, so proud of her invitation to Lady Batterslee's rout that she had simply had to invite someone along with her to witness her glory. Marianne was glad she had been the person with Mrs. Willoughby the day she received her invitation.

A party at the elegant Batterslee House was an opportunity that did not come along every day, and Marianne had seized upon it, even though it meant suffering Mrs. Willoughby's stultifying conversation all evening.

Not, of course, that she meant to stay by Mrs. Willoughby's side. She would stay with her long enough not to appear obvious—and to meet as many people as

Mrs. Willoughby could introduce her to, for the chance to
mingle with this many people who might invite her to other
parties was almost as important as examining the treasures
of the house. But as soon as she reasonably could, she
meant to slip away and spend the evening exploring.

They were almost at the front of the receiving line now,
just beyond the doorway of the ballroom. It was the sight
of the ballroom filled with people whose clothing and
jewelry cost more than most people would earn in a
lifetime that had given rise to Marianne's jitters. The room
was enormous, all white and gilt and filled with mirrors.
A small orchestra played on a raised platform at the far end,
but the noise from the crush of people was so great that
Marianne could barely make out a tune. The walls were
lined with spindly-legged chairs, as white and gold as the
room, except for the red velvet of their cushions. Tall can-
delabras were filled with white wax candles, and more
such candles blazed in the chandeliers, setting off bright
rainbows in the prisms that dangled beneath them.

It was a glittering, extravagant scene, made even more
vivid and beautiful by the wealth of jewels that gleamed
at the women's ears and throats and wrists, a bounty of
diamonds, rubies, sapphires and emeralds, as well as the
subtler shimmer of pearls. The men were uniformly clad
in the black-and-white elegance of evening wear, but the
women's gowns covered a vibrant spectrum of colors. Silk,
satin and lace abounded, and—despite the warmth of the
August evening—even velvet. Looking at the rose silk of
the woman in line before them, the peacock-blue satin
trimmed with black lace of the woman in front of *her,* and
the white tissue embroidered with gold thread that adorned
their hostess, Marianne began to wonder if her own simply

cut ice-blue silk evening dress was elegant enough. It had done very well in Bath, but here in London…

Marianne glanced around, hoping to assure herself that she was not out of place here. She stopped as her gaze fell upon a man leaning against one of the slender columns of the ballroom, only twenty feet away from her. He was watching her, and when she noticed him, he did not glance away embarrassedly, as most would have. He continued to gaze at her steadily in a way that was most rude.

He was tall and lean, with the broad shoulders and muscled thighs of a man who had spent much of his life on horseback. His hair, cut rather short and slightly tousled, was light brown, streaked golden here and there by the sun. His eyes, too, were gold, and hooded, reminding her of a hawk. His cheekbones were high, his nose straight and narrow; it was an aristocrat's face, handsome, proud and slightly bored, as if all the world did not hold enough to retain his jaded interest.

The man's gaze unsettled her. She felt unaccountably warm, and it was hard, somehow, to move her eyes away from him. He smiled at her, a slow, sensuous smile that set off a strange, tingling reaction somewhere in the area of her stomach. Marianne started to smile back, but she caught herself in time, remembering what he was and how she felt about his sort. Besides, a genteel widow did not stand about smiling at strangers. So she kept her face as cool and blank as she could, and raised one eyebrow disdainfully, then turned pointedly away from him.

Their hostess was only two people away from her now, expertly greeting her guests and sliding them along. She greeted Mrs. Willoughby with no sign of recognition on her face, then nodded to Marianne with the same polite, measured warmth. It was such a huge party that Marianne was sure there were many people there whom Lady Batterslee barely knew, which made it a perfect opportunity for Marianne, and silently she thanked her companion for inviting her to come along despite their casual acquaintance.

There were so many people, it was difficult to work their way through the crowd. Marianne did not see how anyone could find room to dance to the orchestra gamely playing at the other end of the room. Finally they reached the wall and were able to find two empty chairs. Mrs. Willoughby plopped down in one, fanning her flushed face, and looked around with all the enthusiasm of a career social climber.

"There's Lady Bulwen—I'm surprised she's here. They say she is only a step away from debtor's prison, you know." She shook her head, clucking her tongue in apparent sympathy, then plunged on, "That's Harold Upsmith. Do you know him? An excellent gentleman, everything that's proper—not like his brother James. An absolute wastrel, that one."

"Indeed," Marianne murmured. It took little effort on her part to keep the conversation going, only an occasional nod or comment to assure her companion that she was listening. It was her great good fortune that Mrs. Willoughby was a perfect combination of social climber and inveterate gossip. Before this evening was through, she would know as much about the *ton* as if she had been a member for years.

After a few moments, however, her attention was distracted by the imperious tones of a woman sitting to her right. "Don't slouch, Penelope. And do try to look as if you're having a good time. It is a party, you know, not a deathwatch."

Curious, Marianne glanced to the side. The voice

belonged to a large woman clad in an unfortunate shade of purple. Her bosom jutted forward like the prow of a ship, and her chin had a matching forward thrust. She, too, was watching the crowd like a predatory bird, interspersing comments about this or that eligible bachelor with commands to her young female companion. The girl in question sat between Marianne and the older woman, a plain slip of a thing in a white dress. White, Marianne knew, was considered the only appropriate color for an unmarried girl at a ball, but it was not a color that did anything for this particular young woman, merely emphasizing the colorlessness of her face. Nor was her appearance enhanced by the glass spectacles that perched on her nose, hiding her best features—a pair of warm brown eyes.

"Yes, Mama," Penelope murmured in a toneless voice, her fingers clenched together in her lap. She reached up to adjust the spectacles that sat on her nose, and her fan, lying in her lap, slid off and hit the floor, bouncing over and landing on Marianne's toe.

"Really, Penelope, do try not to be so clumsy. There's nothing so unattractive as a clumsy female."

"I'm sorry, Mama." Penelope flushed with embarrassment and bent toward her fan, but Marianne had already retrieved it.

She handed it to Penelope with a smile, sympathy for the girl rising inside her. It must be bad enough to be sitting here against the wall, not being asked to dance, without having her mother carping at her the whole time.

"Thank you," Penelope murmured softly, giving Marianne a shy smile.

"You're quite welcome. A dreadful crush, isn't it?"

Penelope nodded emphatically, causing the light to

glint off her spectacles. "Yes. I hate it when there are so many people."

"I'm Mrs. Cotterwood. Marianne Cotterwood," Marianne told her. It was not proper to introduce oneself, Marianne knew, but she suspected that Penelope was not the sort to mind. Others, like Penelope's mother, would meet such boldness with a rebuff.

But Penelope smiled and said, "I am Penelope Castlereigh. It's very nice to meet you."

"The pleasure is all mine. You must think me bold to introduce myself, but in truth, I find it excessively silly to sit here not talking because there is no one around at the moment who knows both of us to introduce us."

"You are absolutely right," Penelope agreed. "I would have introduced myself if I had more nerve. I'm afraid I am the veriest coward."

At that moment, Penelope's mother, who had been droning away the past few minutes, finally realized that her daughter was not listening to her and turned to see what she was doing. At seeing the girl engaged in conversation with a strange woman, she scowled and brought her lorgnette up to her eyes to peer disapprovingly at Marianne.

"Penelope! What *are* you doing?"

Penelope jumped a little, and a guilty look flashed across her face. She turned back to the older woman, saying brightly, "I was just talking to Mrs. Cotterwood. I met her at Nicola's last week."

Quickly, before her mother could inquire more deeply into the matter, she introduced Marianne and her mother to each other. Her mother, Marianne learned, was Lady Ursula Castlereigh.

On the other side of Marianne, Mrs. Willoughby leaned

forward, saying with delight, "Oh, do you know Lady Castlereigh, Mrs. Cotterwood? Mrs. Willoughby, Lady Castlereigh. If you remember, we met at Mrs. Blackwood's fete, oh, sometime last Season."

"Indeed?" Lady Ursula replied in a voice that would have daunted a less determined woman than Mrs. Willoughby.

"Yes, indeed. I admired the dress you were wearing." Mrs. Willoughby launched into a detailed description of a gown, popping up and moving around the others to plant herself in the empty chair beside Lady Ursula.

Marianne seized the opportunity to escape both women. "Shall we take a stroll around the room, Miss Castlereigh?"

Penelope brightened. "That would be lovely."

It suited Marianne's purpose to get away from the chattering Mrs. Willoughby, but she knew that she had proposed the stroll partly to help out Penelope, as well. Penelope, despite her social status, touched a responsive chord in Marianne. She could not help but feel for the poor girl, obviously shy, and just as obviously dominated by her dragon of a mother.

Penelope visibly relaxed as they moved away from Lady Ursula's vicinity. Marianne glanced around them as they walked, automatically checking the room. There were few of the valuable items she sought in the large, open room. The only access to the doors was a series of long windows, open to alleviate the heated stuffiness created by the crowd of people. Marianne maneuvered Penelope in the direction of the windows.

"Ah," she said. "It's much more pleasant here."

"Oh, yes," Penelope agreed, following her. "The fresh air feels good."

Marianne casually looked out. They were on the second floor, looking down at the small garden in the back of the house. There were no convenient trees or trellises nearby. Still, Marianne cast a professional eye over the window and its lock before she guided Penelope away.

As they walked, Marianne felt an odd prickling at the base of her neck that told her she was being watched. She turned her head, scanning the room, and after a moment she saw him—the same man who had been watching her earlier. As she looked at him, he sketched a bow to her. Warmth flooded her, a sensation she was unused to. She told herself it was embarrassment.

"Penelope…" She took her companion's arm. "Who is that man?"

"What man?" Penelope stopped and looked around.

"Over there." Marianne indicated him with her head.

Penelope adjusted her glasses, looking in the direction of Marianne's gaze. "Oh. Do you mean Lord Lambeth?"

"The good-looking wretch with a superior smile on his face."

Penelope smiled faintly at the description. "Yes. That's Justin. He's the Marquess of Lambeth."

"He keeps looking at me. It's most disconcerting."

"I should think you would be used to men looking at you," Penelope responded, grinning, looking at her companion. With her red hair, vivid blue eyes and creamy white skin, Marianne Cotterwood was stunning. Penelope had noticed her almost as soon as she had entered the ballroom. Marianne's dress, though simpler than most here tonight, was the perfect setting for her beauty, showing off her tall, voluptuous figure; she had no need for the frills and bows that many women added to their clothes.

"Thank you for the compliment—I think." Marianne smiled back at her. "But that is the second time I've caught him staring at me in the rudest way. And he doesn't seem at all embarrassed by being caught doing it. He just stands there looking...."

"Arrogant?" Penelope supplied. "That's not surprising. Lambeth's quite arrogant. Of course, I suppose he has every reason to be. Everyone fawns over him, especially giddy young girls looking to marry."

"He's a catch?"

Penelope chuckled. "I should say so." She looked at her curiously. "Do you mean you have not heard of him?"

"I'm afraid not. I have spent the past few years in Bath, you see, living rather quietly—since my husband's death."

"Of course. I'm sorry. I don't suppose you would have heard of him. Bath is not the sort of place Lambeth frequents. Not exciting enough."

"He's a carouser, then?"

Penelope shrugged. "I don't know whether he lives a wilder life than most men. But he despises boredom. Bucky says he will go to any lengths to avoid it. Last month, he and Sir Charles Pellingham placed bets on how fast a spider would build its web in the corner of a window at White's."

Marianne grimaced. "He sounds excessively silly."

"Sir Charles is," Penelope admitted frankly. "But Bucky says that Lambeth is a knowing one."

"Who is Bucky?" Marianne asked.

Penelope colored slightly. "Lord Buckminster. He is a cousin of my good friend Nicola Falcourt." She went on hurriedly, "He *is* considered quite a catch."

"Lord Buckminster or Lord Lambeth?" Marianne asked quizzically.

Penelope's blush deepened, "Well, both, I suppose, but

I was speaking about Lord Lambeth. They say he's rich as Croesus, and his father is the Duke of Storbridge, so all the matchmaking mamas consider him fair game."

"I see." *No wonder the man felt no hesitation in staring so rudely. Probably most of the women at the party would be thrilled to have him notice them.* Marianne glanced back in his direction, but he had gone. She and Penelope started their perambulation again.

"But I imagine it's all useless," Penelope went on. "Mother says that there's an unspoken understanding between him and Cecilia Winborne that someday they will marry. It would be a perfect match. Her lineage is as good as his, and there has never been a scandal in her family—they're all terribly priggish," she added confidentially.

Marianne laughed.

Penelope looked a trifle abashed. "I'm sorry. I should not have said that. You must think me terrible. Mother says I am always letting my tongue run away with me."

"Nonsense," Marianne assured her. "I think you are most enjoyable company—and that runaway tongue is one of the main reasons."

"Really?" Penelope looked pleased. "I am always afraid that I'm going to say the wrong thing—and then, when I'm expected to talk, it seems as if my tongue won't even work."

"I have often felt that way myself," Marianne lied kindly. In truth, she had rarely been afflicted with shyness. The matron at St. Anselm's had always maintained that boldness was her worst vice—the first in a long list, of course.

Her words cheered Penelope up, however, for she began to talk again. "Bucky likes Lord Lambeth, says he's a 'fine chap.' But he quite frightens me," Penelope added honestly.

"He is so very proud and cold. Everyone says so. His whole family is that way. His mother is even scarier than he is."

"She must be a terror, then."

"She is. Personally, I think she and Cecilia Winborne are cut from the same cloth. But since Lord Lambeth quite disdains love, I suppose it won't matter to him."

"Mmm. They sound like a delightful pair."

Penelope giggled.

"I say—Penelope!" A male voice sounded behind them, and the two women turned to see a man strolling toward them. He was tall and sandy-haired, with a pleasant face, and he was smiling as he looked at Penelope. "What good luck, to catch you without Lady Ursula around."

Color dotted Penelope's cheeks, and her soft brown eyes lit up. She held out her hand to him. "Bucky! I wasn't sure if you would be here tonight."

"Oh, yes. I left the opera early. Nicola's mother will probably have my head the next time I see her, but I mean, really!" He paused, indignation clear on his face. "There's only so much of that caterwauling a man can be expected to take!"

Penelope smiled. "I am sure Lady Falcourt will understand."

"No," he replied ruefully. "But she won't say much, for fear I won't escort her next time." He turned toward Marianne, saying, "Sorry, frightfully rude of me—"

His words died as he looked into Marianne's face, and the color drained from his cheeks, then came back in a rush. "Oh, uh, I—I say."

It was all Marianne could do to suppress a giggle. Lord Buckminster looked as if someone had hit him on the head.

"Mrs. Cotterwood, please allow me to introduce Lord Buckminster," Penelope introduced them.

"How do you do?" Marianne held out her hand politely.

"Oh. I say. Great pleasure," Buckminster managed to get out, stepping forward to take her hand. As he did so, he stumbled, but caught himself. He took Marianne's hand and bowed over it, then released her and stood grinning down at her foolishly.

Marianne sighed inwardly. It was obvious to her that Penelope had very fond feelings for "Bucky," but the man seemed oblivious to them. It was just as obvious that he was entranced by Marianne. She had had other men react to her this way. Marianne knew that she had the sort of looks that attracted men, although she was not vain about it—most of her life, her vibrant good looks had been the source of more trouble than good fortune.

Usually an infatuated admirer was no worse than a nuisance; she had learned how to discourage and avoid them. This time, however, she worried that Lord Buckminster's open admiration would make Penelope dislike her. She glanced at Penelope, who looked a trifle sad, but resigned, then at Lord Buckminster, who was still smiling vapidly.

"It is very nice to meet you," Marianne said pleasantly to Lord Buckminster, "but I am afraid I cannot stay and chat. I must get back to Mrs. Willoughby, or she will wonder what has become of me."

"Allow me to escort you," Buckminster said eagerly, straightening his cuff and in the process somehow dislodging the gold cuff link. It dropped to the floor and rolled away. "Oh, I say..." The man looked with some dismay at the piece of jewelry and bent to retrieve it.

"Oh, no," Marianne protested quickly. "You must stay here and keep Penelope company. I am sure that you have a lot to talk about."

She slipped away immediately, while Buckminster's attention was still concentrated on his cuff link. Her departure was a trifle rude, she knew, but she felt sure that Penelope would not mind.

Weaving her way through the throng of people, Marianne made her way to the door. Snapping open her fan and wafting it as though the heat of the crowd was what had impelled her to leave the ballroom, she strolled along the corridor past a pair of footmen. She glanced about her in a seemingly casual way, noting to herself the locations of doors, windows and stairs. She paused as if to admire a portrait, and as she did so looked out the window, checking its accessibility from the street. Then she wandered to her right until she was out of sight of the footmen.

She made a quick check to be sure that there were no other guests or servants around, then started down the hallway, looking into each room as she passed it. Every one, she saw, was filled with expensive items, from artwork to furniture, but she was concerned only with those things that were easy to transport and just as easy to sell, such as silver vases and ornamental pieces. She was primarily interested in finding the study, for she knew that it was the most likely place for the safe to be located. Finding the safe and the best entrances and exits was always the focus of her job.

She located two drawing rooms and a music room, but no study, so she turned and made her way back down the corridor. As she neared the wide hallway that crossed this one and led back to the ballroom, her steps slowed to a seemingly aimless walk, and she once again began to ply her fan and to look up at the row of portraits as if she were studying them. She crossed the corridor, glancing down it out of the corner of her eye. She could not see that anyone, either the footmen or the two men standing outside the ballroom door conversing, was paying any attention to her.

Once across the hallway and out of sight, she resumed her investigation, opening doors and peering inside. The second door she opened was obviously the masculine retreat of the house, though it appeared to be more a smoking room than a study. There was no desk, nor were there any books, but the chairs were large and comfortable, and there was a cabinet with glasses and several decanters of whiskey and brandy atop it, as well as a narrow table holding two humidors and a rack of pipes. The drawings on the walls were hunting scenes, full of dogs and horses.

With a smile of satisfaction, Marianne reached into the room, picked up the candlestick on the table beside the door and lit it from the wall sconce in the hall. Then she slipped into the room and closed the door after her. This was the most dangerous part of her mission, as well as the most exciting. There was no good reason for her to be in her host's smoking room, and if someone happened to come in on her, she would be hard pressed to talk her way out of the situation. She could lock the door, of course, but if someone tried to get in, that would seem even more suspicious. The best thing to do was simply to work as quickly as possible and hope that, if she did get caught, a winning smile and a quick tongue would get her out of the situation.

Heart pounding, Marianne set the candle down on the table and began to go around the room, shifting each of the hunting prints aside to examine the wall behind it. The third picture yielded the prize: a safe set into the wall. She leaned forward, examining the lock, which opened with a key rather than a combination.

"I do apologize, but I really cannot allow you to break open my host's safe," a masculine voice said behind her.

Marianne jumped and whirled around, her heart in her throat. Leaning negligently against the doorjamb, one eyebrow raised quizzically, was Lord Lambeth.

CHAPTER TWO

FOR A LONG MOMENT MARIANNE COULD DO nothing but stare at him, her mind skittering about wildly. Finally she managed to paste on a shaky smile and say, "My lord! You gave me quite a turn!"

"Did I?" He grinned, showing even, white teeth. Marianne had the sudden strong image of a wolf. "I would have thought that you had stronger nerves...given your profession."

Marianne drew herself up to her fullest height and put on a haughty face, one she had copied from Lady Quartermaine. "I beg your pardon? My profession? I am afraid I haven't the slightest idea what you're talking about."

"Well done." Lambeth moved away from the doorjamb and came inside, closing the door behind him. "I might almost believe you—if I hadn't just caught you with your hand in the cookie jar."

Marianne's stomach tightened with dread. "What are you doing?" She realized that her voice had skidded up, showing fear, and she forced herself to lower it. "I must insist that you open that door. This is highly improper."

He cocked one eyebrow. "I would have thought that you would prefer we discussed your larceny outside the hearing of the rest of the company. But of course, if you insist on opening the door so that all may hear..."

Lambeth started toward the door, and Marianne stepped forward quickly. "No! No, wait. You are right. Let us clear this up privately."

He smiled in a smug way that made Marianne long to slap him, and crossed his arms. "You have an explanation? Pray, go on. I should love to hear it."

"I see no reason why I should give you an explanation," Marianne retorted hotly.

Her initial spurt of fear over, her normal spirit was returning. The smirk on the man's face goaded her. He was everything she despised in the aristocracy: supercilious, arrogant, utterly disdainful of everyone whom he considered beneath him—which was most of the world.

"Other than the fact that I should turn you over to our host for rifling through his smoking chamber?"

"Don't be absurd! I was simply looking around. There is no harm in that, surely."

"What about the safe?" He nodded toward the picture, still askew, with the safe behind it.

"Safe?" Marianne could think of nothing to do except brazen it out.

His mouth twitched. "Yes. Safe. The one behind that picture. The one you were breaking into."

"I was doing no such thing!" She put on an expression of utmost indignation. "The picture was crooked, and I straightened it."

He let out a bark of laughter. "You are a bold one. I'll give you that. But I have you dead to rights, and you know it." He strolled toward her. "This was a deadly dull party, but it certainly got livelier once you arrived."

"Is that supposed to be a compliment?" Marianne took a step backward. She found his closeness disconcerting.

She disliked him thoroughly; he was her enemy. Yet his smile created the oddest sensation in the pit of her stomach. And when he came near, she could see that his eyes were clear and gold, the color of sherry, darkened by the row of thick lashes around them. She found herself staring into them, unable to look away.

His gaze was knowing and amused, as if he sensed what she was feeling. "Yes, it is. Most young women bore me."

"I am not a young woman," she pointed out. "I am a widow."

"Are you?"

"Yes, of course. What a thing to say!" He was so close now that she could feel the heat of his body. Marianne took another step back but came up against the liquor cabinet and could move no farther. She braced her hands on the cabinet on either side of her and tried to face him down. "You are a very rude man."

"So I have been told. I am not, however, a flat, so I suggest that you try to stop bamming me. I have been watching you all evening."

"I know. I saw you. That was when I first realized how very rude you were."

"I watched you at first because you are devilishly attractive." He smiled and raised his hand, running his forefinger down her cheek.

A shiver ran through Marianne, unfamiliar and delightful, and she twitched away from him, irritated with herself.

"I was wondering how to get an introduction when I saw you with Miss Castlereigh and Lord Buckminster. I knew they would introduce us, but by the time I got there, you were gone. I followed you out into the hall, and that is when I noticed your extremely odd behavior."

"You were spying on me? I find *that* extremely odd, my lord."

"You have the advantage of me. You seem to know who I am—that is twice you have called me 'my lord.' Yet I do not know your name."

"It is scarcely any of your business."

"You may as well tell me. I shall find out from Bucky anyway."

Marianne frowned. "I am Marianne Cotterwood. *Mrs.* Cotterwood."

"Oh, yes, a widow. I forgot."

"I wish you would stop using that supercilious tone. Why should I say I am a widow if I am not?"

"I don't know. Perhaps you are. On the other hand, perhaps it is simply part of your sham."

"I am not shamming. This is a pointless conversation, and I am leaving."

She started around him, but Lambeth reached out and grasped the low cabinet, blocking her exit. "Not until you tell me why you were sneaking up and down this hall, peering into all the rooms. And why you came into this one and proceeded to walk around it, lifting each picture, until you found the one with a safe behind it."

Marianne's throat was dry, and only partly because of her trepidation. Lambeth's body was only inches from her; his eyes were boring into hers. It was hard to breathe, and she felt strangely hot and cold.

"You are a thief, Mrs. Cotterwood," he said in a low voice. "I can think of no other explanation."

"No." Her voice came out barely a whisper. Her lips were dry, and her tongue crept out to moisten them.

Lambeth's eyes darkened, and his hand came up, his

thumb tracing her lower lip. "You are the most beautiful woman I have ever met, but I really cannot allow you to go about robbing my friends." He paused, and a smile touched his lips. "On the other hand, Lord Batterslee is not really what I would call a friend. More an acquaintance, actually."

He leaned closer, his warmth and scent surrounding her. Marianne closed her eyes, almost dizzy from his nearness. Then his lips were on hers, and she jumped slightly in surprise, but she did not move away. The sensation he was creating in her was too sweet and unfamiliar. She relaxed, giving in to the pleasure. She felt the hot exhalation of his breath against her cheek as he sensed her yielding. His arms went around her, and he pulled her closer, his mouth sinking into hers urgently.

Marianne felt as if she were melting, her loins hot and waxen, her whole body shimmering with pleasure. No man had ever made her feel like this. Indeed, she had rarely allowed a man to touch her, not since Daniel. Daniel's kisses, too, had been sweet at first…

Marianne stiffened at the thought of Daniel Quartermaine. Another aristocrat with kisses and soft words—and no thought in his mind except using and abandoning her. Suddenly she realized what Lambeth was about. She jerked away from him, her hand cracking against his cheek in a resounding slap.

He stared at her, surprised, his hand going to his cheek.

"I know what you are trying to do!" she cried.

"It seems fairly obvious," he replied dryly.

"You think that I will bed you to keep you from telling everyone I am a thief!"

His eyebrows sailed upward. "I never said—"

"You didn't have to. As you just said, it is obvious. You

accuse me of being a thief, then start to kiss me. What else would I think?"

"That your beauty distracts me from my duty."

"Please. I am not a fool. Nor am I a whore. You are wasting your time. I won't sleep with you, no matter how you might slander me to everyone you know." Marianne's eyes flashed. She had no idea what an arousing picture she made—her eyes sparkling, cheeks flushed, her lips soft and moist from his kisses.

"A thief with morals, in other words."

The faint amusement in his voice goaded her, and Marianne opened her mouth to reply hotly. But at that moment the door opened, and a middle-aged man stepped into the room. He stopped and gaped at them.

"I say."

"Lord Batterslee." Lambeth nodded to the older man.

Marianne's stomach turned to ice. Now it would come. He would tell the owner of the house that he had found her going through his study, searching for something to steal. Her only hope lay in the fact that she had nothing on her that she had stolen. But the accusation of a duke's son would be enough to bring a constable.

"Oh. Lambeth. What the devil's going on here?"

Lambeth smiled suggestively. "Exactly what it looks like, I'm afraid. I was…ah, seeking a place of solitude to, um, convince the lady of my regard for her."

Heat stole into Marianne's face. He was intimating that they had sneaked off to the smoking room for a romantic interlude. She was torn between relief that he had not turned her over to the authorities and humiliation that he was blackening her reputation.

"A tryst? In my smoking room? Really, Lambeth…"

Lambeth shrugged, and his hand went pointedly to his reddened cheek. "Not a tryst, exactly. As you can see, Mrs. Cotterwood was somewhat averse to my suggestions." He looked toward Marianne. "You needn't turn violent, you know. A simple no would have sufficed."

"Don't speak to me!" The emotion in Marianne's choked voice was real enough. She felt as if she might burst into tears at any moment from all the conflicting feelings that were tearing at her. But she also had the presence of mind to seize the opportunity to flee. Spitting out, "You cad!" to Lambeth, she rushed out the door, skirting Lord Batterslee's rotund form. Lord Lambeth could hardly come running after her with the other man standing right there.

She ran down the hallway to the stairs, only slowing when she came in sight of the other partygoers. It would attract attention to run down the stairs in full view of everyone, but she walked as quickly as she could, her body tensed for the sound of her name or a touch on her shoulder. However, she made it to the front doors without incident, and since there were several hackney coaches in the street in the hopes of catching fares from the party, she was able to scramble into one immediately.

To her relief, the hackney set off at a smart pace. She turned and looked out the window. There was no sign of Lord Lambeth. With any luck, he had gone back to the ballroom, thinking that she would have rejoined the party. Or perhaps he would not care enough to search for her. She doubted that Lord Lambeth had any trouble getting women; he would not need to track down a recalcitrant one. *But why had he lied to Lord Batterslee?* Perhaps he had hoped that he could still blackmail her with his knowledge, given a little more time to persuade her.

Marianne smiled to herself. He was going to find it difficult to see her again. No one there tonight, not even Mrs. Willoughby, knew where she lived. She was always careful to keep her private life separated from the world of what Piers called the "flats." Besides, this was the first time that she had made a foray into the highest society of London. In years past, they had worked on the well-to-do, the Cits and lesser gentry both in London and in other cities. Their quarry had not moved in the highest circles. The last year or two, as sort of an audition, they had spent their time in the resort towns of Brighton and Bath, where she had mingled with the upper crust who were vacationing there. It had been only two months ago that they had decided to try their game among the *ton* of London.

She had spent the time establishing herself in London, calling on the women, such as Mrs. Willoughby, whom she had met in Bath and Brighton and who had encouraged her to visit them if she ever came to London. She had hoped to gradually work her way into their social spheres, meeting ever more people. It had been sheer good fortune that she had been calling on Mrs. Willoughby the day the woman received her coveted invitation to Lady Batterslee's party. Gleeful and wanting someone to witness her triumph, Mrs. Willoughby had impulsively invited Marianne along, thus propelling Marianne higher and more quickly into Society than she had ever dreamed.

Now, of course, she thought gloomily, it was all ruined. Leaning back against the seat, Marianne closed her eyes and gave herself up to depressing thoughts. All their hard work…all the time and effort…all the hopes they had had of making enough money in London to retire from the Game…all was for naught. By the time the hackney stopped in front of her narrow, pleasant house on the fringes of Mayfair, Marianne was thoroughly blue.

Climbing out of the coach, she paid the driver and walked slowly toward the house. Before she could reach for the doorknob, it swung open. Winny stood in the doorway, grinning at her.

"I was watchin' for you," Winny confided, the proper English she had been cultivating for the past few years slipping a little, as it always did when she was excited.

She was still small, though the past few years of decent food had put more pounds on her frame and roses in her cheeks. But nothing could make up for the years of malnourishment in her youth. She and Marianne had been friends for as long as Marianne could remember, growing up as best they could in the orphanage. Winny, older than Marianne, had left St. Anselm's two years before Marianne. She had gotten a job in service at the Quartermaine household, not far from the orphanage. On her rare days off, she had visited Marianne, and when Marianne turned fourteen and left the orphanage, Winny had recommended her to the Quartermaine housekeeper. They had been together ever since, except for the two years after Marianne had been thrown out of the Quartermaine house. But later, after Marianne was established in her new life, she had sent for Winny, and Winny had joined her new "family." She had not had the skills that the rest of the family used to earn their way, but she had contributed by being their housekeeper, work she was well acquainted with.

"Everyone's waiting in the sitting room," Winny went on.

Marianne nodded, her heart sinking even lower. She knew that everyone had been excited about their first foray into the upper reaches of Society, and she hated to face them with her failure. They would be kind, of course; they always were. It was only with these outcasts that she had found kindness. But their very kindness made her feel even worse about letting them down.

She went down the hall into the sitting room, with Winny following her. They were indeed all there. Rory Kiernan, whom they all affectionately called "Da" because he was the oldest among them, was sitting on the couch with his wife, Betsy. Betsy was an expert at cards and at separating the flats from their money, and Da was one of the premiere pickpockets of London, but they were largely retired now. They were the parents of Della, the improbably dark-haired middle-aged woman who was sitting in a chair beside them, and who now sprang to her feet at Marianne's entrance.

"Marianne!" Della grinned from ear to ear and opened her arms wide to embrace Marianne. She was a short, plump woman with twinkling brown eyes and an infectious laugh, and it was clear that she had been a beauty in her day. She was the closest thing to a mother that Marianne had known. It was she and her husband, Harrison, the short, wiry man beside her, who had rescued Marianne when she came to London over nine years ago.

Marianne had been Mary Chilton then, not quite nineteen years old, frightened and alone—and pregnant. Working as a maid in the Quartermaine household, she had caught the eye of the eldest son, Daniel, when he had been sent down from Oxford. To pass the time, Daniel had first flirted with her, then wooed her with seductive words and sweet promises. Naively, she had thought that he loved her, and for a brief time she had been very happy. But when his words of love did not prevail upon her to come to his bed, he had taken her by force. Crushed and heartbroken,

Marianne had gone to the housekeeper, who had told her that she had best keep quiet about the matter or she would only stir up trouble for herself. Daniel would be returning to Oxford soon, the housekeeper reminded her, and in the meantime, she would keep Marianne at work in the kitchen, where she would not have to run into him.

Before long, Marianne had realized that she was pregnant. She wrote to Daniel, putting aside her pride for the sake of her unborn child, and begged him for help, but he never replied. When she began to show, Lady Quartermaine had ordered the housekeeper to dismiss her. Marianne had been unable to get work at any other house in the area. No one wanted a servant with licentious ways. Finally, she had gone to London, hoping that in that impersonal city she would find some job where her pregnancy would not matter. Winny had given her every penny that she had saved, but Marianne could not find work in London, either, and it was not long before all of Winny's meager savings were gone.

Desperate and hungry, she had stolen some fruit from a vendor's stall. She had not been very good at it, and the vendor saw her take it and began to chase her. Della and Harrison, who had been watching the scene unfold, saved her. Harrison neatly tripped the vendor, then helped him up with a great many apologies, insisting on brushing off his clothes and explaining at great length how the accident had come to happen. Della, in the meantime, took Marianne by the arm and whisked her away. She had taken her to their home, a set of rooms in a less fashionable part of town, and had given her supper. Marianne, overwhelmed by her kindness, had collapsed into sobs and told Della her story.

Della's heart had ached for the poor girl, alone in the

world, with no family to help her and nowhere to go, no way to make a living. She knew that the workhouse was the only option left to Marianne, and that was a fate that Della would not have wished on anyone. So, with no fuss, she and Harrison had taken Marianne in.

Marianne knew that they had helped her more than she could ever repay, and she would have done anything for them. When she found out that Della and Harrison were thieves by trade, she had revised her moral standards. Whatever she had been taught in the orphanage about right and wrong, she knew that Della and her husband were good people, whereas the supposedly virtuous Lady Quartermaine and the matron at St. Anselm's were at heart wicked.

Della and Harrison were not common thieves. Harrison was an "upper-story" man, skilled at picking locks, opening safes and breaking into houses without disturbing the occupants. One of the reasons for his success was the work of his partner Della. She spoke and acted like one of the gentry. Her mother, Betsy, had run a gaming hall much of Della's life, and she had taught Della to speak and act genteelly, preparing her for the same sort of life that Betsy had led. After Della met Harrison, they had realized that if she moved among the wealthier classes, she could determine the layout of a house and the location of its valuables, and then Harrison could far more easily get in and out of the house and lighten its occupants of some of the burden of their wealth.

Marianne stayed with the two of them all through her pregnancy and for several months after the baby, Rosalind, was born. She could not help feeling that she was a burden to them, but she also could not see how she was going to support herself and her daughter, as well as raise the child.

The only occupation she knew was being a maid, and she knew that no one would hire her if she had a child with her. But there was no way she could give Rosalind up.

Harrison had come up with the solution to their problem. Marianne, he pointed out, could do the same job as Della. She already spoke rather better than most of her peers, and she carried herself with a natural grace. He and Della, he pointed out, could train her in all the finer points of manners and speech. Dressed like a lady, she would be stunning, and her beauty and youth would help them obtain entré into finer houses—an idea that he expressed with a great deal of tact and circumlocution, until finally Della had chuckled and told him that she was well aware that Marianne outshone her. Indeed, Marianne outshone any woman she knew. Motherhood—and an adequate diet—had made Marianne even more beautiful, giving her skin a luminous glow and adding more curves to her slender body.

Marianne had felt some qualms about entering the world of thieves, but she had suppressed them. She would do anything Della and Harrison asked of her, and, besides, she had a mother's fierce instinct to take care of her child. She was determined to make enough money to give her daughter an easier and better life than she had had. So she had entered into lessons with Della, and they had discovered, somewhat to their surprise, that she picked up the correct speech and manners of the upper class with ease. She was, Harrison declared, a natural, and by the time Rosalind was a year old, Marianne had adopted the name Marianne Cotterwood, making herself a respectable widow, and was making calls with Della.

It was an easy enough job, as long as one had a quick wit and good nerves, both of which Marianne possessed.

In order to pass among the wealthy, one had to dress well, so she had a supply of beautiful clothes. She ate well. She had a great deal of time to spend with her daughter, and when she was not there, Della or Betsy was happy to take care of the little girl. Marianne was also good at what she did. She had a quick eye and a good memory, and without appearing to study a house, she could quickly spot the best entrances and exits, as well as the most expensive and most portable valuables, and carry all the information in her head to give to Harrison. Della readily admitted that Marianne was better than she at what she did, and Della soon slipped into a happy semiretirement, going along with Marianne only when they thought a chaperone was a social imperative.

Marianne had been scouting for Harrison for eight years now, and their fortunes had been steadily increasing all that time. They were able now to rent a fair-size home in a good neighborhood, as well as hire Winny as housekeeper and cook, and two maids to help her. Their "family" had also grown. First, Da and Betsy, growing too old for the Game, had moved in with them. Then Harrison and Della had taken in a stray adolescent who had been scratching out a living as a pickpocket, working for a hard fellow who ran a ring of youthful pickpockets, giving them a place to sleep and some food to eat and taking most of their profits in return. Piers was twenty-two years old now, and Harrison had turned him into a skilled upper-story man.

Now Della hugged Marianne and pulled her toward a chair. "Sit and tell us all about it. Was it terribly grand?"

"The grandest party I've ever seen," Marianne replied honestly. She looked around at the eager faces watching her, from Betsy's wrinkled, powdered visage to Piers' freckled, snub-nosed one.

"I knew it!" Betsy let out a hoot of laughter. "His father used to come to my gaming house, and he was always flush in the pockets—at least when he came in the door. Drunk as a wheelbarrow, of course, but, still, a real blue blood."

"Well, I don't know the color of his blood, but I'd say the son is flush in the pockets, as well. The problem is..." She hesitated, glancing around at them, then sighed. "Oh, the devil! The truth is, I made a dreadful mull of it."

"Don't be daft," Piers said, dismissing her words with a wave of his hand. "You always think you did something wrong."

"He's right. I am sure you did wonderfully," Della agreed.

"No." Marianne shook her head, and tears sprang unexpectedly to her eyes. She blinked them away and went on. "It wasn't just *something* I did wrong. It was everything. I was discovered."

The room fell silent. Marianne dropped her eyes, unable to look at the others.

Finally Harrison started to speak, then had to stop and clear his throat. "Wh-what? How could you have been discovered? You're sitting right here. They couldn't have—"

"He did not turn me in. But he saw what I did. He accused me. Oh, how could I have been so careless? I didn't see him at all!"

"But who—I don't understand." Harrison came forward. "Who saw you?"

"Lord Lambeth. He had been looking at me earlier. But I didn't see him as I left the ballroom. I went up and down the corridor looking for the study because I presumed the safe would be there—although I did see some excellent silver pieces in one of the drawing rooms. Anyway, I found a smoking room finally, and I began to hunt around the walls, looking for a safe. Then *he* appeared."

Della drew a sharp breath. "Oh, no. What did he say?"

"He thought I was about to try to open the safe. Of course I told him that he had misinterpreted the scene, that I was simply straightening the picture, but he didn't believe it. He was sure I was a thief. He had followed me out of the ballroom, you see, and had seen me looking into all the rooms up and down the hallway, and searching behind the pictures for a safe. He knew I was lying."

"But he didn't say anything to anyone? He didn't betray you to Lord Batterslee?"

Marianne shook her head. "No. It was very odd. He was—well, he seemed rather amused by the thought that I was a thief. A most peculiar man. When Lord Batterslee came into the study and found us, Lord Lambeth did not say a word about what I had been doing."

"Thank heavens!" Della replied heartfeltly.

"Yes," Harrison agreed. "But why?"

"Come now, lad." Da spoke up for the first time. "Don't tell me me daughter married a nodcock. Just look at the girl." He winked at Marianne. "Why, any man worth his salt would let such a beauty get away with a little thievery. That's why Della's mother was so successful." He reached over and patted Betsy's hand, his eyes twinkling. "She was so pleasing to the eye, they scarcely noticed the blunt leaving their pockets."

Betsy dimpled girlishly. "Go on, you old charmer."

Harrison ignored his in-laws' byplay and looked at Marianne. "Is that it, do you think?"

Marianne could feel her cheeks coloring. "Well…I think

he was hoping that I would agree to…ah…some sort of arrangement in return for his silence."

"The blackguard!" Piers growled, jumping to his feet, his boyish face dark with anger. In the excitement of the moment, he forgot his careful work on his accent and plunged back into the cockney of his roots. "I ought to draw 'is cork. You mean 'e offered you a carte blanche?"

"Heavens, no. Oh, Piers, do sit down. Don't get in such a taking. He never really *said* anything. It was just, well…" She hesitated, not wanting to tell them about that kiss. Just the thought of it made her go all strange and melting inside. "It was just a feeling I had. Perhaps I was wrong. Because I told him I would not, yet he still did not tell Lord Batterslee."

Piers snorted. "I know 'is type. 'E—I mean, *he*—just didn't want to give up his power over you. He's hoping to wangle his way into your bed, that's what."

"That thought occurred to me. But he is bound to see that that is an empty threat. I am afraid that then he *will* tell Lord Batterslee. Harrison, I'm so worried. I fear I have ruined everything for us. What if he tells Lord Batterslee, and he sets a Bow Street Runner on us? Perhaps we ought to try our luck on the Continent for a few months, as you were talking about last year."

"But what can they prove?" Harrison pointed out reasonably. "You didn't steal anything. He didn't even see you trying to steal something. All he saw was you wandering around, looking at things. That's not proof."

"They don't always need proof," Da put in, his voice tinged with bitterness. "One word from a lord and—" He drew his forefinger across his throat in an ominous gesture.

"Even if he did not tell the authorities," Betsy pointed out, "all he has to do is spread it around that Marianne is a thief, and the Game will be ruined. She won't be received in polite society after that."

"That's true." Harrison rubbed his chin thoughtfully. "But we were on the verge of such opportunity—I hate to throw it away on a mere chance. I think we should wait and see. If we lie low for a few weeks, we might be all right."

"Do you think so?" Marianne brightened a little. She hated to think that she had ruined their plans for everyone.

Harrison nodded. "Some other pretty young thing'll come along to tickle his fancy."

That much was true, Marianne was sure. No nobleman was going to waste his time looking for or thinking about some socially inferior girl. If one was not of their class, there was only one use for a woman, and no doubt he could find other willing participants. Marianne realized that that idea gave her no joy, but she shoved the thought aside. She was, after all, a realist; she had to be.

"He doesn't know where you live, right?"

"No. I left the party, and I am sure that he did not follow."

"If we take nothing from Batterslee House, it will lull his suspicions—or at least give him no proof to back them up."

Marianne sighed. "I am so sorry. I don't know how I could have been so careless."

"It happens to all of us," Harrison assured her kindly. "The main thing is that nothing happened to you."

"Thank you. But it would have been a nice bit of change. They had some beautiful things."

"I am sure it wasn't all a loss. You met some people, didn't you?"

Marianne nodded. "A few. Lady Ursula Castlereigh and her daughter. I talked to the daughter at some length."

"There? That will get you entré into other places. You

see if it doesn't. And if not…" Harrison shrugged. "Well, we'll try the Continent, as you said, or go back to Bath."

Piers groaned. "Not Bath! There's nothing but old ladies there."

Harrison cocked an eyebrow at him. "We aren't there for your entertainment."

"I know. I know." Piers sighed and subsided.

"Well." Della glanced around. "There is nothing else to do tonight. We will just have to wait and see. I am sure Marianne would like a bite to eat and a good night's sleep."

Marianne smiled gratefully at the older woman. "Thank you. I don't think I could eat anything, truthfully. But the thought of sleep is appealing. Hopefully everything will seem better tomorrow morning."

The group broke up, starting up the stairs toward their rooms. Marianne, too, started out of the room, but Winny caught her arm. "Stay for a bit, Mary."

Marianne looked around at her questioningly.

"I—there's something I need to tell you."

"What?" Fear clutched at Marianne's heart. "Is it Rosalind? She's not sick, is she?"

"No. No. Nothing like that. It's just…well, I got a letter today. From Ruth Applegate. You remember her, don't you? She were—*was*—a scullery maid at the Hall."

Marianne frowned. In referring to the Hall, Marianne knew that Winny meant the Quartermaines' house, where they had both worked. The look on her friend's face disturbed her. "Yes, I remember. You were good friends with her. What's the matter? Did something happen to her?"

"No. She knows that I went to live with you. She wrote to warn you. There's been a man at the Hall asking about you. She thinks a Bow Street Runner is after you."

CHAPTER THREE

"A Bow Street Runner!" Marianne gasped. "Sweet Lord, I thought it couldn't get any worse."

Winny reached into her pocket and pulled out a piece of paper, which she unfolded to reveal a pencilled scrawl. "It's very difficult to read. Ruth never learned to read and write very well. What she said, I think, was, 'There was a man—two men at—' I think she means different '—times. They was asking about Mary C. But nobody knows about her, and I didn't tell. I thought I should warn you. Bow Street Runners'."

"Could we have been found out? Has someone—but no. No one I've met the past few years would know I was Mary Chilton or that I worked for the Quartermaines."

Winny nodded. "I know. It's got to be someone from the past."

"But who? Why?"

"Do you—do you think it could be your family?" Winny asked tentatively, voicing every orphan's dream. "If they went to St. Anselm's, they'd have told them you'd gone on to the Hall."

"After all this time?" Marianne suppressed the little spurt of hope that had leapt up in her at Winny's words. It was foolish to think that there was family who wanted her after so many years. "I haven't any family, or they would have looked for me years ago. It's been over twenty years."

"Maybe they didn't know. Maybe you were stolen from them."

Marianne smiled. "That's a child's dream. I used to tell myself that that was what had happened, that my parents were still alive, still wanted me, that a wicked person had taken me from them. But that's nonsense. It's the stuff of dramas. Why would someone steal a child and then drop it at an orphanage? Besides, she said 'warn.' There must have been something sinister about the man."

"Well, if Ruth thinks he's a Bow Street Runner, then she would think he's wantin' to arrest you." Winny gnawed at her lip. "It worries me."

"It *is* unsettling," Marianne agreed. "If someone who knew me as Mary Chilton, who knew I was only an orphan and a housemaid, saw me masquerading as a lady, they could have guessed, I suppose, that I was doing something havey-cavey."

"And gone to the trouble of hiring a Bow Street Runner?" Winny asked skeptically. The Bow Street Runners, though they pursued criminals, had to be hired.

"That seems rather absurd, too, doesn't it? The thing is, if it was someone we nabbed a few things from, someone with the blunt to hire a Bow Street Runner, they would know me as Mrs. Cotterwood. They wouldn't send the man to Quartermaine Hall looking for Mary Chilton."

"Maybe it was someone like you said, who saw you and had known you as Mary Chilton." Winny's eyes widened as a thought struck. "Maybe it was someone who had visited the Hall, and when they saw you again, they knew you were a housemaid."

"You think they would remember a maid that well?"

"One that looks like you, they would," Winny replied bluntly. "And then they saw you at a party, say, in Bath."

"And when some things went missing, they suspected me?" Marianne nodded thoughtfully. "That makes sense. But they had been introduced to me as Cotterwood. They would have looked for me under that name. Surely they would not have remembered my name from ten years ago."

"But what if they looked for Mrs. Cotterwood and couldn't find you? What if it was after we came back to London?"

"So they decided to trace me through the Quartermaines." Marianne sighed. "Oh, Lord! As if things weren't bad enough! Winny, what should I do? If I've brought the Bow Street Runners down upon us—" Tears sprang into her eyes. "I'm ruining everything!"

"No, you're not," Winny assured her friend stoutly. "They've all made ever so much more money because of you, and you know it. This is just a patch of bad luck. It happens sometimes. You couldn't help it if someone recognized you." She smiled and added, "Cheer up. Maybe it'll turn out to be your long-lost relations after all. The gypsies took you, and they just now found out where you went."

Marianne smiled. "Perhaps. Well, there's nothing I can do about it now. And apparently they found a dead end at the Hall, so they won't know where to come looking for me." She reached out and hugged Winny. "Thank you. I don't know what I would do without you."

"Don't be daft. It's me who'd a been lost without you. Go on with you, now. You need to be getting to bed."

Marianne nodded and went upstairs, but before she went to her bedroom, she stopped at the small room next door to hers and tiptoed inside. The curtains were open, as

Rosalind liked them, and moonlight cast a pale wash across
the room. Marianne moved to the side of the bed and stood
for a moment gazing down at her daughter. Rosalind's
dark curly hair had escaped from her braid, as was usually
the case, and spilled across her pillow. Long, dark eye-
lashes shadowed her porcelain cheeks, and the little
rosebud mouth was open slightly. She was a handful during
the day, smart and lively, full of questions about everything,
but now she looked like an angel. Marianne reached down
and moved the covers up over her shoulders and brushed
a kiss across her forehead. She might despise the man who
had done this to her, but she had never felt anything but an
intense love for this child. Rosalind was her life, and the
desire to protect her and nurture her was always uppermost
in her mind. Whoever this man was looking for her, and
whatever he wanted, she must make sure that nothing he
did harmed Rosalind.

Finally she turned and left her daughter's room, slipping
down the hall to her bedroom. She undressed quickly and
efficiently, hanging her dress in the wardrobe and placing
her thin slippers in the neat row on the floor of the
wardrobe. She pulled on a plain cotton nightgown, at odds
with the expensive dress she had worn this evening, then
set about the task of taking down her hair and brushing it
out. Before she got into bed, she opened the small japanned
box on her dresser. Inside lay her small assortment of
jewelry. She lifted out a compartment and reached underneath it to pull out a locket. It was a gold locket on a
simple chain, not the chain that had come with it, for that
had long since been too short and she had replaced it. But
the locket itself had been with her since she could
remember; she had kept it through thick and thin, refusing

to sell it even when she was starving. It was all she had of her past life.

The front of the locket was engraved with an ornate *M*, and when she slid her thumbnail between the edges, it came open to reveal two miniature portraits. Marianne sank down on the stool in front of the dresser and gazed at the man and woman pictured inside the locket. She was certain that the couple were her parents, though she could not be sure that she actually remembered them or only thought she did from having gazed at the pictures so many times. Sometimes she fancied she saw a resemblance in her own chin and mouth to the woman in the portrait, but she could not be sure whether it was real or only wishful thinking. Certainly neither one of them had her flaming red hair. Still, she knew they must be her parents—even though a cynic would have pointed out that parents wealthy enough to have miniature portraits drawn for a locket would have been unlikely to have left no provision for their child.

This locket had been her talisman all through the dark, dreary days at the orphanage. She had worn it under her dress every day and even slept with it on. As the years had passed, she had gradually forgotten whatever her life had been before the orphanage. She thought she remembered the woman in the portrait laughing, and she remembered a permeating sense of fear, of running and being so scared she thought her heart would burst. That, she thought, must have been when she was brought to the orphanage. But she could no longer remember arriving at St. Anselm's or who had brought her there, and, of course, the matron had steadfastly refused to answer her questions about the event. She was not even sure if Mary Chilton had been her real name or merely one the orphanage had given her.

Marianne rubbed her thumb over the delicate tracery in an old habit, remembering the stories she had made up about her parents to help sustain her. She had imagined them wealthy and noble and very loving. A wicked man had stolen her from them and taken her to St. Anselm's, but she knew that her parents were still out there looking for her. They would never give up.

She smiled a little sadly and set the locket back into its case. *Children's stories, that was all they were. No one was searching for her to bring her back to her family. Her only family was here: her daughter, Rosalind, and Winny and the others.* Yet, as she climbed into bed and settled down to sleep, she could not quite still the ache in her heart for the family she had never known.

LORD LAMBETH GAZED DOWN INTO THE brandy snifter, circling it idly in his hand, and watched the liquid swirl around the balloon glass. *Marianne Cotterwood. Who the devil was she?*

He found it decidedly irritating that she had managed to slip away from him. Justin was not accustomed to being thwarted, least of all by a woman. Women usually hung upon his every word, smiling and fluttering their lashes, eager to be the one on whom he decided to settle his sizable fortune. He was cynical enough to realize that while his good looks might make the effort more palatable, it was his money that was the real lure. Marriageable girls had been after him since he reached his majority ten years ago. The truth was that he found all of them dead bores, and the thought of shackling himself to one of them for the rest of his life was enough to make him shiver. He supposed that someday, when he could delay it no longer, he would marry Cecilia Winborne, as she and his parents expected. Her family was equal to his in birth—or close enough to it to make the match a good one—and a future Duke had to produce a few heirs, after all. Then, of course, they would go their separate ways, and he would have mistresses to counteract Cecilia's coldness.

Women of lighter virtue, of course, were rather more fun, not bound by the rigid rules of propriety that afflicted their more genteel sisters, but he found them just as vapid, primarily interested in their looks and his pocketbook, with few thoughts in their head. His friend Buckminster sometimes teased him that he should try his luck with a bluestocking female if he was so interested in intelligence, but the truth was that they were as serious and dull in their own way—and usually without the spark of beauty to ignite his interest.

The truth was, he had never met a woman who didn't bore him within a short amount of time—and above all things, Lord Lambeth despised boredom. In fact, tonight he had been just about to leave Lady Batterslee's rout, having judged it deadly dull, when he caught sight of the redhead.

He had had no idea who she was. He had never seen her before; he knew he would have remembered her if he had. She was the most beautiful woman he had ever seen. Just looking at her across the room had sent a thrill of pure sexual desire through him, and his first thought had been that he wanted to see that flaming mass of hair spread across his pillow. Then she had looked at him in that haughty way, lifting her chin, and had turned away, snubbing him. It was a reaction he was not used to receiving from a woman, and his interest in her had heightened. Nothing that had happened afterward, from discovering that she was an apparent thief to kissing her in Lord Batterslee's study, had lessened his interest.

He smiled faintly to himself, his lips softening sensually as he remembered their kiss. He rubbed his thumb over the smooth glass of the snifter, wishing it were her skin. This was a woman, he thought, who could hold his interest longer than most. She was somewhat infuriating, of course… Unconsciously, he raised a hand and rubbed it along the cheek that she had slapped. The sting had been well worth it, given the kiss that had preceded it. Her mouth had been soft and sweet, and there had been a certain awkward naïveté to her kiss that had been curiously arousing. It had left him wanting a good deal more—and he intended to have it.

The only problem, of course, was that he hadn't the slightest idea where to find her. He knew only her name— if she had not been lying to him about that, which was a distinct possibility. Thieves, in his experience, rarely balked at lying. However, she was scarcely the usual thief. She spoke and acted like a gentlewoman. *Was she a lady who had fallen on hard times and chosen this way to keep herself afloat?* It seemed absurd. More likely she had been blessed with good looks and learned to imitate the upper classes—*a lady's maid, perhaps?* Then she had somehow managed to worm her way into Society. But whatever her background, it seemed to Justin a particularly daring and unusual thing for a woman to do. He certainly could not fault her for her courage.

Damn that fool Batterslee for barging in when he did! If only he had had a few more moments with her, Justin was sure that he could have wormed more information out of her, could even have convinced her that he did not intend to use his knowledge of her illegal activities to bludgeon her into coming to his bed. As it was, she thought him the basest of men and had fled without a trace.

He was not without resources, however. He had seen her with Penelope Castlereigh and Lord Buckminster. Perhaps they knew who she was and where she lived. He would make it a point to drop in on Bucky tomorrow and pump him for information. However long it might take, he was determined that he was going to find that girl.

RICHARD MONTFORD, THE SIXTH EARL OF EXMOOR, leaned back in his chair, contemplating the man standing in front of him. "Well, well... It's been a while since we have talked, hasn't it? Sit down, sit down." He waved toward the chair facing his desk. "No need to stand there like a gapeseed."

The other man shook his head, frowning. He was younger than the Earl, and there was only a hint of gray in his hair yet. He was conservatively dressed, though his clothes were well-tailored, and his features were attractive but not memorable. He was the sort of man one might pass on the street and never notice, but anyone who met him would immediately classify him as a gentleman.

"What is this all about, Montford?" he asked, his voice rough with irritation and something else, perhaps a touch of apprehension. "We are scarcely what one would consider friends any longer."

"No. One would hardly recognize in you the flamboyant youth I once knew."

"Flamboyant? Hardly. In a haze of opium and alcohol, more like. But as we both know, I have put that life behind me. I cannot conceive why you should wish to speak to me."

"It is not so much 'wish' as necessity, dear chap. You

have heard, I presume, the gossip about this American heiress who married Lord Thorpe, Alexandra Ward?"

"Of course. The Countess's granddaughter whom everyone thought was dead. Is that what you called me here for—to rehash yesterday's gossip?"

Richard did not answer except to give him a thin, tight smile that conveyed the opposite of amusement. His visitor looked at him for a moment, trying for an air of unconcern, but the tapping of his fingers against his thigh gave him away.

Finally, when the Earl said nothing else, he burst out, "What the devil does it have to do with me? She is your cousin, not mine."

"Ah, but your past is intertwined...."

"Not with hers! I never saw the child. You said she was dead."

"So I believed." Exmoor's hazel eyes hardened in his thin, almost ascetic face. "The damned woman lied to me!"

"I don't know why you care. You had nothing to do with *her* disappearance. From what I heard it was her mother— her *supposed* mother—who pretended that she died."

"Yes, but Alexandra's return alerted them to the fact that the other two children did not die in Paris, either. The Countess knows that this Ward woman brought them to Exmoor House."

"But you were not implicated, surely. I thought their disappearance was blamed on this woman who confessed, the Countess's companion, and she is dead."

"The Countess suspects me. She knows that I am the only person who would benefit from the boy's death. For all I know, that fool Miss Everhart told her I was involved."

"But she cannot prove it, or surely she would have by now."

"Yes, and I don't want her to be able to prove anything in the future. She won't drag the Exmoor name through the mud for no reason, but if she were able to prove that I was involved, even the fear of scandal would not hold her back."

"How could she possibly prove it? The Everhart woman is dead, and I certainly am not going to say anything. I have as much to lose as you."

Again the Earl's lips curled up in a cruel smile. "I know. That is why I sent for you. The Countess is looking for the girl, Marie Anne."

The other man stiffened, his fidgeting hand going still. After a long moment, he cleared his throat nervously. "She cannot find her."

"They've put a Bow Street Runner on it. I understand that he has tracked her down to the orphanage."

"St. Anselm's?" Sweat dotted the man's lip.

"I'm surprised you remember."

"How could I forget?" His mouth twisted bitterly. "Not all of us are blessed with your lack of conscience."

Richard raised one eyebrow. "It wasn't your boringly pedestrian morality I questioned. Frankly, I'm surprised you remember anything from that time."

The other man pressed his lips together. "It was a sobering experience."

"That was what caused you to give up your old life?" Richard's voice was tinged with amusement.

"Yes. When I found myself standing in my room holding a pistol to my head."

"How very dramatic."

"I am sure the scene would have afforded you a great deal of amusement. But I realized then that I had to die or

I had to change. I could not go on as I was. I chose to give up my vices. God knows, there were moments in the weeks that followed when I wished that I *had* pulled the trigger."

"I, for one, am glad that you did not. I have a task for you."

"A task?" He looked astonished. "You think that I am going to do something for you? I paid my debt to you when I took those children for you. I wouldn't lift a finger for you again."

"Ah, but what about for yourself?"

"What are you talking about?"

"I am not the only one who would suffer if certain details from the past came to light."

"How could it? The older one, the boy, didn't even live, did he? He was at death's door when I left him."

"The boy is dead," Richard replied curtly. "That is not the problem. It is the girl."

"She can't have been more than five or six. She couldn't remember."

"Perhaps not. But if she saw a face—the face of the man who had ripped her from her brother, say, who had taken her to an orphanage and placed her in that hellhole—who is to say that she might not remember then?"

"Surely—you're not telling me that they have found her."

Richard shrugged. "I doubt it. Not yet. But I sent a man to St. Anselm's, too, when I heard that the Countess was looking for the chit. They told me where she went when she left there."

"Where was that?" The words seemed pulled from him, as if he did not really want to know, yet could not stop himself from asking.

"She went into service with one of the local gentry. Family named Quartermaine."

"Good God!" He paled a trifle. "The daughter of generations of earls, a maid."

"Mmm. Ironic, isn't it?"

"Tragic, I would say."

"She was cast out of the Quartermaine house—pregnant."
The other man closed his eyes. "God forgive me."

"God may, but I doubt the polite world would."

"I did not want to!" he lashed out, goaded. "You know
I tried to argue you out of it. Sweet Jesus, when I handed
the little thing over to that dragon of a matron, and she was
kicking and screaming and crying…." His hands clenched
into fists at his sides.

"Yet you did it."

"You made me! It was the only way I could wipe clean
my debt to you. You kept giving me the money, urging me
to take it, and I couldn't stop myself. I had to have that
sweet oblivion."

"I hardly forced it on you. You begged me for the money,
shaking and sweating, the color of a corpse. What else
could a friend have done? As I remember, at the time you
praised me for my generosity."

"I did not know then why you did it! How you got
people in your debt and made them do wicked things! How
you twisted and crushed them into monsters scarcely recognizable as themselves."

"Really. Dear fellow…do you think you would have
done it if you hadn't had it in you already? You could have
refused, you know."

"I know." Self-disgust filled his voice. "I was weak."

Richard did not comment. He could have pointed out
that the man was still weak or he would not have come in
answer to his summons. But there wasn't any point in an-

tagonizing him unduly. It might put his back up enough to give him some spine.

"Do you think that will help you any? If people know that you took Chilton's daughter from her family and put her in an orphanage because you had to have money for opium? For gambling and drinking and whoring? Do you think they will feel any sympathy for you?" Richard asked. When the other man glared at him, he went on, "Quite so. You and I both know what would happen to this exemplary little life that you have built up if the *ton* knew what you had done. Oh, no doubt some people with long memories still can recall that you were wild in your youth—so many men are, and then sober up and become responsible citizens. But none of them know about *this*."

"What are you threatening? To tell everyone what I did? It will only implicate you!"

"Oh, no, I shan't tell…not unless I am forced to. But if the Countess's man finds the girl…if she tells everyone what happened, and I am brought down because of it, I promise you, I shan't go down alone. I will take you with me."

"You are disgusting."

"What has that to do with the matter at hand? And just think, what if this girl identifies you? You are the one who took her there, you know, the last face she saw. It is you she will remember best."

"I tell you, she won't remember! You forget the things that happened to you when you were a child."

"Even something that changed your life forever? I don't know. It seems to me to be something she might remember. Or say she chanced to meet you and at the sight of your face those long forgotten memories came back? But if you are willing to risk it…" He shrugged eloquently.

"Damn you! What is it you want of me?"

"I want you to make sure that the Countess's man doesn't find her."

"And how am I supposed to find her?"

"That will not be so very hard. All the servants disclaimed knowledge of her whereabouts, but one of the grooms pulled him aside and told him some interesting facts—for a price, of course. The world is so venal. It seems that little Mary Chilton—yes, that is what she called herself—had a special friend among the other servants, another maid named Winny Thompson. A couple of years after Mary left, this Winny apparently came into some good fortune. She received a letter, and promptly after that she quit her job and took the stage to London. He says the rumor was that Mary had found some means to support herself and had invited her dear friend to come live with her. My man paid him to keep the information to himself, and then he tracked this Winny Thompson to London. It seems that one of the maids gets letters from her every so often, and the housekeeper has seen the most recent address."

"So he found...Mary?"

"I think so. He found Winny Thompson, in any case. She is the housekeeper for an apparent family, one of whom is a 'widow' with a nine-year-old daughter. That is the right age for Mary Chilton's 'delicate condition.' The supposed widow's name is Marianne Cotterwood. She is in her mid-twenties, and her hair is a bright red."

The other man groaned.

"Yes. It sounds very much like the girl we seek."

"If your man has found out so much, why don't you have him keep her away from the Countess? He sounds quite competent."

"Oh, he is. He is. But there are two problems. One is that I would like to make sure that Mrs. Cotterwood really is the woman I seek. The other is that I do not like to hire someone for an operation as delicate as this. A paid servant of that type can so easily turn around and gouge more money from you for being silent, you see. You, on the other hand, could scarcely extort money by threatening to break your silence. That is why I realized that you would be the perfect man for the job."

"What is it you want me to do—pay her to leave London before the Countess's man can find her?"

"An easy solution, of course, but too unreliable. I find that people so rarely keep their word."

"Then what am I supposed to do?" he asked, his patience obviously wearing thin.

"It's quite simple. This woman appears to a gentlewoman, not a former maid. She moves in your sort of circle. You could easily meet her and ascertain whether she is, in fact, the woman we seek. Then…"

He paused and fixed a gaze of pure iron on the man. "Then you will kill her."

CHAPTER FOUR

MARIANNE SMILED DOWN AT HER DAUGHTER. One of her favorite things was teaching Rosalind, who had a quick mind and a ready wit. At nine, Marianne thought she was approaching the age where she would need a tutor. The Quartermaine girls had had a beleaguered governess, a round little brown wren of a woman over whom the three girls had run roughshod. Though Marianne's knowledge was adequate for the basic subjects she had been teaching up until now—and she could still, with her extensive reading, do a passable job of teaching literature and history—she knew that to be educated as a lady was, she needed someone who could teach music and drawing adequately, as well as mathematics, French, and possibly Latin, as well. Marianne had always thirsted for knowledge. Though the orphanage had seen to it that they were able to read, write and do figures, they had been given no opportunity to venture into the upper realms of education. Most of what Marianne had learned she had gotten from books, which she had read over and over at every opportunity.

They were in the kitchen, books and tablets spread out on the table, deep in a lesson combining vocabulary, spelling and handwriting. Across the table from them, Betsy was enjoying a late morning cup of tea, while Winny, with help from Della, was beginning to prepare dinner. Rosalind, tongue firmly between her teeth, was carefully writing with the stub of a pencil.

"Beautiful," Marianne encouraged her, watching the copperplate writing slowly unfold. "Now what is that word?"

"S-p-e-c-u-l-a-t-e. Speculate."

"Very good. Do you know what it means?"

Rosalind looked at her, her big blue eyes, so like her mother's, serious in her small face. "Mmm. Is it like speculation?"

"Yes. Speculation is the noun form of the word. Speculate is the verb. Do you know what speculation is?"

Rosalind nodded, pleased that she knew the answer. "Yes. Gran taught me yesterday evening when you were gone."

"Gran?" Marianne turned toward Betsy, who was the only grandmother Rosalind had ever known. Betsy, who had only a rudimentary education, hardly seemed the type to engage in vocabulary lessons.

Betsy gazed back at her guilelessly, her hand halting with the cup of tea halfway to her lips. Marianne's eyes narrowed. "All right, Roz. Exactly what is speculation?"

"Well, it's where you ante up a certain amount of money. Gran and I did a ha'pence. Only the dealer antes up double. Then he gives everyone three cards, and—"

"A card game?" Marianne swung to Betsy. "You were teaching her a card game?"

Betsy shrugged. "Just a simple one, to pass the time."

"It was fun, Mama, and I even won!" Rosalind said excitedly. "Gran says one day she'll teach me loo, but that takes five people, and we couldn't get the others to play. They're always too fidgety when you're at a party."

"Betsy, I told you about teaching Rosalind to gamble!"

"She has a natural gift," Betsy protested. "It's a shame, it is, to waste it. I never met anyone who caught on faster."

"Rosalind is not going to be a cardsharp."

"Of course not. But it never hurts to be able to pick up a little pocket money when you need it."

Marianne groaned and closed her eyes. She heard a muffled snort and looked over to see Winny and Della smothering their laughter.

"Go ahead and laugh, all of you," Marianne grumbled.

"I'm sorry, Mary," Winny said, still smiling. "It's just—she looked so cute, sitting there, holding those cards and dealing them like a professional."

Marianne could well imagine it, and even her own lips twitched at the thought. "Honestly, Betsy," she said, trying to remain stern. "She is only nine years old."

"I know. That's what makes it so amazing. I'd 'a thought she was much older, the way she played."

Marianne smiled. "Well, in the future, please, could you teach her something besides gambling games? And don't teach her any of your tricks, either."

Betsy widened her eyes innocently. "Tricks? Why would I teach the child any tricks?"

"You taught me one last week," Rosalind pointed out. "You know, about how if you prick the ace with a pin, you can feel it as you deal, but it doesn't show, and—"

"Betsy! That's exactly what I'm talking about."

Betsy shrugged. "Well, of course, if that's what you want. But it seems to me that a girl can always use a leg up, if you know what I mean."

Shaking her head, Marianne resumed the lesson. It was useless, she knew, to try to get Betsy to understand the desire she had for Rosalind to lead a normal life. She didn't know how she was going to achieve it, but Marianne was determined that Rosalind grow up not knowing poverty and want and lack of love—or the fear of living outside the law.

The rest of the lesson passed without incident, for Rosalind wanted no delays for her afternoon treat: Piers had promised to take her to fly kites. Promptly after dinner, they set off, and Marianne, faced with the prospect of an afternoon free, decided to visit the lending library.

It was one of her favorite things to do. She loved to read, a habit that everyone else in the house found a trifle odd. She was used to that attitude. All the children in the orphanage had found it even stranger. She had hidden her reading from everyone at the Quartermaine house, sneaking books out of the library in the Hall and spending her entire afternoon off reading in a special place she liked to go down by the brook. When she moved to London and started living with Harrison and Della, she had discovered the joys of a lending library.

So she tied her bonnet beneath her chin and set off. When she was a half block from the lending library, she saw a young lady walking toward her, trailed properly by her maid. As she drew closer, she recognized the young woman's features.

"Miss Castlereigh!" Marianne was surprised by the quiet leap of pleasure she felt upon seeing the woman she had met the night before.

Penelope, who had been walking along with her eyes down, glanced up, and a smile lit her face. "Mrs. Cotterwood! What a pleasant surprise."

"Yes. Isn't it? I was just on my way to the lending library." Marianne looked at the book Penelope carried. "It looks as though that is where you have been."

"Yes, it is." Penelope's smile grew wider. "Do you enjoy reading, too?"

"Oh, yes," Marianne confessed. "It is my favorite pastime."

"Really? Me, too." Penelope looked delighted at finding a fellow bibliophile. "Mama calls me a bookworm. But books are so much more…exciting than real life. Don't you think?" Her eyes shone behind her spectacles. "I am quite addicted to the gothic sort of books, with mad monks and haunted castles and evil counts. One never finds that sort of thing in real life."

"No." Marianne dimpled. "Though I expect we should not enjoy it so much if it really happened to us."

"I'm sure you are right." They stood for a few minutes, chatting about their favorite books. Then Penelope reached out a hand impulsively and touched Marianne's arm. "Do come visit me, won't you? We can talk about books and such. I would love for you to meet my friend Nicola, as well. I am sure you would like her." She hesitated uncertainly. "I—I hope I'm not too forward."

"Goodness, no. I would be delighted to come." It was an opportunity that Marianne would not dream of passing up, but she knew that she would have agreed even if it had helped her not at all. She liked this shy girl, and it was an unusual pleasure for her to get to talk to someone about books.

"That's wonderful." Penelope told her where she lived, a tony Mayfair address that confirmed Marianne's initial impression of her mother's social standing.

Behind Penelope, the maid stirred and said warningly, "Miss…"

"Yes, I know, Millie." Penelope smiled apologetically at Marianne. "I wish we could talk longer, but I am supposed to meet Mother at my grandmother's house, and I don't want to be late."

"Then I won't keep you." Marianne felt sure that the fierce Lady Ursula would ring quite a peal over her daughter's head if she inconvenienced her.

"But you will come to see me?"

"I promise." Marianne said her goodbyes and continued on her way to the lending library.

PENELOPE TURNED AND HURRIED OFF toward her grandmother's house. She knew that her mother would not be well pleased at her making friends with someone she barely knew, and she did not want to make it worse by arriving late.

Rushing into the drawing room of her grandmother's house, however, she found her mother in a pleasant mood. Lady Ursula smiled at Penelope, saying, "There you are, dear. My goodness, you look quite flushed. These girls…" She flashed a coy look across the room at the two men who had stood up when Penelope entered the room. "Always running about, looking at frills and geegaws."

Penelope, following her mother's gaze, understood Lady Ursula's mellow attitude. Lord Lambeth and Lord Buckminster had come to call on her grandmother, the Countess of Exmoor, and while Lady Ursula dismissed Bucky as a "fribble," she, like most of the other women in Society, was dazzled by Lord Lambeth. Penelope groaned inwardly. Frankly, Lord Lambeth made her a trifle ill at ease, and she was certain that he had absolutely no interest in her, despite her mother's fond hopes regarding London's most eligible bachelor. Though he was polite to her, the only reason he called on them was because he was friends with Bucky.

"Actually, I was getting a book from the lending library," Penelope corrected her.

Lady Ursula frowned at her horribly. "Now, dear, you don't want the gentlemen thinking you're a bluestocking, do you?"

"I'm sure I don't know why she should care." The Countess spoke up for the first time. "Any man worth having admires a woman with a brain. Isn't that right, Lord Lambeth?"

"But of course, my lady," Justin replied smoothly. "After all, look how much you are admired."

The Countess laughed. She was a tall, regal woman whom age had bent only a little, and it was clear that she had been a beauty when she was younger. "You are such a flatterer, Lord Lambeth. Fortunately, you are quite good at it." She turned to her granddaughter. "Come here, child, and give me a kiss and show me what book you got."

Penelope did as she was bid, kissing the Countess's cheek and dropping onto the low stool beside her chair. While the Countess took her book from her hand and examined it, Penelope decided that it was better to get her news out now while her mother's protestations would be tempered by the fact that Lord Lambeth was present.

"I met Mrs. Cotterwood while I was out," she began.

Both Buckminster and Lambeth straightened at her announcement.

"Did you?" Buckminster asked admiringly. "By Jove, I might have known you would be the one who'd know how to find her. You always were a downy one."

At his words, Lambeth turned and looked at him consideringly. "Were you trying to find her, then?"

"Well, I—that is—" Color rose in Buckminster's

cheeks. Finally he said, "Thought Nicola would probably want to invite her to her little soiree on Friday. You know. Have to send an invitation."

"Ah. I see." Justin thought that he did see, indeed. It was rare for his friend to be so interested in a woman. *That certainly complicated the matter a bit.* He glanced over at Penelope and saw that she, too, was watching Bucky, a wistful look on her face. He wondered what she made of it.

"Who?" Lady Ursula demanded. "Who is this Mrs. Cotterwood?"

"You know, Mama, the lady we met last night at the party. That woman you know, Mrs. Willoughby, introduced us."

"I scarcely know Mrs. Willoughby—encroaching woman! I doubt that any friend of hers is someone we want to know."

"Perhaps she is no more a friend of Mrs. Willoughby's than you are," Penelope suggested.

Her mother's eyes narrowed, somewhat suspicious that Penelope in her quiet way was making game of her. But Lord Buckminster said seriously, "There you go. Probably Mrs. Willoughby was encroaching to her, too. Mrs. Cotterwood is perfectly respectable, I'm sure."

Lady Ursula's pursed mouth made clear her opinion of Lord Buckminster's ability to judge respectability. She turned toward Lord Lambeth. "Is she known to your family, Lord Lambeth?"

"Oh, yes," Justin replied easily. "I've been acquainted with Mrs. Cotterwood for some time."

Penelope shot him a grateful look as Lady Ursula remarked, somewhat reluctantly, "I suppose that she is all right, then."

"I invited her to call on us," Penelope went on, pressing her point.

"Without asking me first?"

"Well, you were not there," Penelope pointed out reasonably, "and I quite liked her."

"Are you going to call on her, Pen?" Lord Buckminster asked, blithely unaware of Lady Ursula's disapproving look at his use of Penelope's nickname. "I would be happy to escort you."

"I'm afraid I cannot. I don't know where she lives," Penelope confessed. "She did not tell me, and I didn't think to ask."

Buckminster's face fell so ludicrously that Lambeth had to smother a laugh.

"Who is she?" the Countess asked. "Have I met her?"

"I don't think so, Grandmama. She is very nice—and she's beautiful, as well."

"Ah. A rare combination, to be sure." Lady Exmoor smiled at her granddaughter.

"Yes. But that isn't even the best part. She likes to read. We had a nice chat about books. She had read this one I borrowed, and she said it was thrilling. In fact, that's where I met her. I was coming from the lending library, and she was going to it."

"I hope I shall meet her." The Countess looked across at Lord Buckminster, who seemed to have sunk into a gloom, and Lord Lambeth, whose attention was focused on a tiny piece of lint he was picking from his trousers. "But I am afraid we are boring our visitors. Lord Buckminster came to see if we had had any word from Thorpe and Alexandra."

"Oh! And have you?" Penelope's interest was diverted.

"Yes. I got a letter from Alexandra this morning. They are still in Italy on their honeymoon—Venice now, it seems. She waxed quite ecstatic over the beauty of it, but she did say that they planned to come home shortly."

"Good. I shall like to see her again."

"Yes. I say, that will be bang-up," Lord Buckminster agreed, abandoning his glumness. "Thorpe's a good chap." He paused. "Lady Thorpe, too, of course—well, what I meant was, not a chap, of course, but still—though I don't know her all that well—I mean—"

"Yes, Bucky," Lady Ursula stuck in blightingly. "I feel sure we all know what you meant to say."

"Er—yes. Quite." Buckminster subsided.

"I feel sure you will be very glad to have Lady Thorpe back, Lady Castlereigh," Lord Lambeth said blandly to Ursula, observing her through half-closed lids.

The Countess smiled faintly and carefully avoided looking at her daughter. Lady Ursula colored. Most people in the *ton* knew how little she had believed that Alexandra Ward was her long-lost niece when the American heiress had arrived in London a few months ago, and how vigorously she had fought against the Countess's accepting her as such. When finally it had been proved, she had given in with ill grace.

"Of course I will," she told Lord Lambeth, reproof tinting her voice. "Now that I am sure that Alexandra is really Chilton's child, I am fond of her, as I am of everyone in my family."

"Naturally." Given the fact that he had never seen any evidence of true fondness from Lady Ursula toward her daughter or son, Lambeth supposed that perhaps she was as fond of Alexandra as she was of others in her family.

He did not know all the facts of the case, not being close friends with the family or Lord Thorpe. However, ample gossip had passed around the *ton* this Season for him to know that the Countess's son, Lord Chilton, and his French-born wife had been visiting in France at the outbreak of the revolution twenty-two years earlier. They and their three children had been reported dead, killed by the mob. This spring, at the beginning of the Season, an American woman had shown up in London and had somehow proved that she was in reality Lord Chilton's youngest child. It had ended with the long-lost heiress marrying Lord Thorpe. The whole story, in Lambeth's opinion, sounded like something out of a lurid novel of the sort Penelope professed to enjoy.

Lambeth's purpose in persuading Buckminster to call on Penelope and her family had been accomplished. He had not found out the secretive Mrs. Cotterwood's location, but he had discovered all that was to be gotten out of Penelope. It would be enough, he reasoned. A book lover—not what he had expected of that redheaded temptress—would return to the same lending library. A servant set to watch the place would soon find out where she lived.

Accordingly, Lambeth took his leave, having no wish to endure Lady Ursula's presence any longer than was absolutely necessary. As soon as the front door closed behind him and Lord Buckminster, Lady Ursula turned on her daughter, scowling.

"Really, Penelope! Did you have to go on about those silly novels? One would think you could have made a little effort to impress Lord Lambeth."

"Oh, Mama, Lord Lambeth has no interest in me," Penelope replied, flushing with embarrassment. "I wish you would not say such things."

Lady Ursula sighed. "Sometimes I quite despair of you, Penelope. Any other girl would have at least made a push to be appealing."

"What nonsense, Ursula," the Countess put in. "Lord Lambeth and Penelope would not suit at all. I wonder you can even think of such a match."

"Would not suit? How could a marquess with a family back to the Invasion and barrels full of money possibly not suit?"

"I am sure *I* would not suit *him,* Mama. Everyone says he will eventually marry Cecilia Winborne, and even if he did not, well, I am sure that I am hardly his style."

"Who a man flirts with and who he marries are two entirely different things," Lady Ursula said pedantically. "Our family is as old and genteel as one could hope to find—the equal of Lord Lambeth's and certainly better than the Winbornes, I should hope."

Penelope gave up the struggle. She had found out long ago that it was useless to try to make her mother see reason. Her grandmother spoke quickly to forestall Ursula, who was gathering herself for another attack.

"Of course we are," Lady Exmoor said. "Indeed, I wonder that you should think a Montford should marry an upstart like the Duke of Storbridge's son."

Ursula turned a startled gaze to her mother, then grimaced as she saw the twinkle in the Countess's eyes. "Really, Mother, this is scarcely something to joke about."

"I think it is precisely the sort of the thing to joke about. As if Penelope would want to marry Lord Lambeth. Do let us stop talking such nonsense." She turned back to Penelope. "I have had a report from the Runner I set on finding Marie Anne."

"Did he have any luck?" Penelope asked eagerly.

Lady Exmoor sighed. "Partially. I had told you that he found an orphanage outside London where a child named Mary Chilton had been taken, and it was the right time. When he went there, he found that the matron was retired, but one of her assistants still worked there, and she remembered the child. 'Redheaded spitfire,' was the way she put it." A smile trembled on the older woman's lips, and Penelope saw moisture in her eyes. "That sounds like Marie. He managed to worm out of them where the child went when she left the orphanage."

The Countess paused and swallowed hard before she could continue. "She went into service at a local house."

"Oh, no!" Penelope cried, reaching out and taking her grandmother's hand. Lady Exmoor squeezed it hard, pressing her lips together to stop their trembling. "That's awful! I mean, well, to think of my cousin having to scrub and clean."

"Yes. For nobodies like those Quartermaines," Lady Ursula added, her indignation roused by the slight on the family. "I've never even heard of them."

"Local gentry," Lady Exmoor explained. "Still, I don't suppose it really matters who they are. The real problem is that she left there a few years later, and no one seems to know where she went. The trail just vanishes."

"So that's the end of it?" Penelope asked, disappointed.

"The housekeeper told him that she was friends with another maid. But that girl is gone from the house, too. The servants and family seem to be an unusually reticent lot. The Runner is inclined to think that there was perhaps some scandal involved in her leaving."

Penelope's eye widened. "This is terrible."

The Countess sighed. "Well, at least the other man would have had no better luck, I guess. That's the only bright side."

"What other man?"

"There had been someone else at the Quartermaine house asking questions about Mary Chilton before my fellow came. The housekeeper remarked on it, wondering why so many people were suddenly interested in her."

"And you think this other man is from—the Earl?"

Lady Exmoor's mouth tightened. "I am sure of it. Who else would be looking for her? He knows I suspect him of having gotten rid of Marie Anne and Johnny—oh, if only that wicked woman had lived!"

Penelope knew to what woman her grandmother referred. It was her grandmother's cousin and former companion, Willa Everhart. Recently, on her deathbed, Miss Everhart had confessed that twenty-two years earlier, she had conspired against the Countess to keep her grandchildren from her. During the dark days in Paris, after the storming of the Bastille, the Countess's son, Lord Chilton, and his wife had been killed by the mob, who had mistaken them for French aristocrats. The reports that had come back to London had said that Chilton's three children had been killed, as well. But in fact they had not died, but had been smuggled out of France and brought to London by an American friend of Lady Chilton's, Rhea Ward. Mrs. Ward, lonely and unable to bear a child herself, had taken the baby, Alexandra, as her own and raised her in the United States, but she had brought the older two, John and Marie Anne, to the Countess's home.

The Countess, prostrate with grief over the deaths of her son and the supposed deaths of his children, had taken to her bed and refused all visitors, so Miss Everhart had been the one who spoke to Mrs. Ward and took the two children from her. Mrs. Ward then left the country, thinking the children safe with their grandmother, but Miss Everhart had played the Countess false. Desperately in love with Richard Montford, the distant cousin who had become the Earl of Exmoor upon the death of Chilton and the supposed death of his son John, the true heir, she had taken the children to Richard instead. The existence of the boy John, she knew, would mean that her lover would lose the title and estates, and she counted on his gratitude for what she had done to tie him to her. The boy, Willa had told them as she lay dying, had been very sick with a fever and had died. The girl Marie, however, had been taken to an orphanage.

The Countess had immediately hired a Bow Street Runner to investigate Marie's whereabouts, but she had realized that there was little she could do about Richard's treachery. Willa had died immediately after telling them her story, and they had no proof or witnesses to show that the present Earl of Exmoor was the villain they all knew he was. He, of course, had denied the story and claimed that Willa was a madwoman who had undoubtedly acted on her own—if there was any truth to the story in the first place. Since the boy John was dead, even though not at the time or place they had thought, Richard was still the legal holder of the title. To accuse him of kidnapping the children and murdering John, as the Countess suspected, would do nothing but involve the family in an enormous scandal.

"But why would Richard be searching for her?" Lady Ursula asked, puzzled. "Richard doesn't give a whit about her. I would think he would just as soon she stayed lost."

"I am sure he does," the Countess agreed dryly. "I think

it is precisely for that reason that he is searching for her—to make sure she stays lost."

Penelope sucked in a startled breath. "You mean…you think that he will kill her?"

"It's not something I would put past him. I am sure he is desperate to maintain the lie that he has lived all these years. At the very least, he will put her on ship and send her off to America or India or some other remote place where I cannot locate her. She was five when it happened, after all. There might be some hope that she would remember what happened to her—or who had turned her over to the orphanage. She might even remember what happened to her brother."

"Oh, my. I certainly hope that *he* doesn't find her, then. Is there nothing further we can do?"

"Mr. Garner—that is the man whom I hired—says that he will try to track down this friend of Mary Chilton's, Winny something-or-other. The housekeeper did know that she moved to London, though no one had any idea where she lived. Another one of the maids was friends with her but told Garner that she did not know where this Winny was now—even after Garner offered her money. But even if he finds the friend, I hold little hope that she will know where Mary Chilton is. After all, it has been over nine years since Mary left the Quartermaine house."

None of what she had told them sounded good, Penelope thought, but she tried to put the best face on it that she could. She patted her grandmother's hand. "Don't worry, Grandmama. I am sure she will turn up just as Alexandra did. We Montfords are a trifle hard to do away with, you know."

Lady Exmoor smiled at her. "Thank you, dear. I am sure you are right. We will find her."

"Let us only hope it is before Richard does." Lady Ursula, as always, had to have the last word.

MARIANNE LAID DOWN HER CARDS WITH a sigh. "You win—as usual, Betsy."

"Hmmph." The old lady narrowed her eyes. "It was easy enough. What's bothering you, child? You played even more poorly than you normally do."

Marianne smiled a little ruefully. "Nothing. It is just anxiety…not knowing, you see, whether Lord Lambeth will forget about me or go to the authorities. I don't like this inactivity."

In truth, she knew it was more than that, though she did not want to tell Betsy about her vague insecurities. The odd letter from Winny's friend had disturbed her more than she cared to admit. Over the past few days, her thoughts had kept returning to it. *What could this stranger want with her?* It had stirred up memories, too, things from her days at the orphanage and at the Hall that she would just as soon forget. She kept thinking of that day when Daniel Quartermaine had cornered her in his bedroom as she was dusting his room, of the way he had begun to kiss and caress her, not letting her go when she told him no. She had finally begun to struggle, frightened, and it was then that he had slapped her and thrown her down on the floor beside the bed. His eyes had lit with a fierce, wild glow that she had not seen there before, and it had terrified her. She remembered the fear and disgust as his hands had moved over her and his tongue had thrust deeply into her mouth.

She could not help but think how differently she had felt the other night when Lord Lambeth kissed her, how her whole insides had turned to melting wax and her blood had hummed in her veins. Lambeth would have turned to force, too, if he had had the chance, she told herself. He was, after all, even more arrogant than young Quartermaine. No doubt he, too, thought that all women ought to feel honored to receive his advances. It did not mean anything that he had released her when she pulled away, or that he had not made a move toward her when she slapped him. It had been merely surprise that she would oppose him that had kept him rooted to the spot.

She remembered his golden eyes darkened with lust, his well-cut lips sensually full and soft, and she felt again that clenching deep in her loins that was both delightful and dissatisfying. It annoyed her that she continued to think about him.

Worse than the thoughts that had been plaguing her, however, was the strange sensation she had felt yesterday as she was walking home from the lending library, where she had gone to return the book she had borrowed two days earlier. As she strolled along, she had begun to have the oddest feeling at the base of her neck. She had stopped and turned, but she saw nothing out of the ordinary, just another person or two walking along as she was. All the way home, she had been unable to get rid of the impression that someone was watching her. Feeling foolish, she had looked around again, but this time there had been no one on the block but her. Still, thinking about the tingling along her spine made her want to shiver.

"Mrs. Cotterwood." One of their two maids stood hesitantly at the door. "There's someone here to see you. I—he's in the foyer."

Marianne looked at her, surprised. No one ever came to visit her. She eschewed any sort of intimacy with the

Society flats. It occurred to her now that a visitor was so rare that the maid wasn't even sure what she should do with the fellow.

"Thank you, Nettie." She rose, glancing over at Betsy, who looked back at her with as much puzzlement as Marianne felt. *Had the man who had been inquiring after her at the Hall managed to find her? Was it he watching her yesterday when she had felt those odd sensations?*

Suppressing her fears as best she could, Marianne rose and went out into the hallway. She stopped cold when she saw the man standing in the foyer, hat in hand, smiling down at her daughter.

Lord Lambeth had found her.

CHAPTER FIVE

"MY LORD," MARIANNE SAID FAINTLY.

Lambeth looked up at Marianne and smiled, a faintly vulpine curving of his lips that seemed as much a warning of danger as a greeting. "Mrs. Cotterwood."

"Rosalind, what are you doing here? I thought you were in the kitchen with Winny, working on your studies."

"I came out to see who was here, Mama," Rosalind replied pragmatically. "Nettie came into the kitchen and said, 'Lor' but there's a 'andsome devil out there.' So I wanted to see."

Lambeth chuckled. Marianne couldn't see that the disclosure discomfited him much. He probably expected everyone to find him handsome.

"But he doesn't look like a devil to me," Rosalind went on seriously.

"Bless you, child." Lambeth grinned. "Just for that, I'll take you up with me one of these days in my curricle."

"Would you?" Rosalind turned to him, eyes sparkling. "Where everybody could see?"

"Indeed. What would be the point otherwise?"

A sunny smile spread across her daughter's face. "I'd enjoy that ever so much."

"Rosalind, I think it's time you went back to your studies, don't you?"

"Yes, Mama." She turned and started away, then turned, asking Lambeth gravely, "You won't forget, will you?"

"I swear it." Lambeth laid his hand over his heart dramatically.

Rosalind grinned and skipped away. Marianne watched the child leave, then turned back to Lambeth, irritated at the easy way he had won her daughter over.

"How did you find me?" she asked bluntly.

His eyes lit with laughter. "Were you hiding from me?"

"Of course not." Irritation stiffened her spine. "But I gave you no permission to call on me."

"I know. I am far too bold. I've been told so before. However, I felt sure that if we had not been so rudely interrupted, you would have given me your direction."

"You take rather a lot upon yourself." *This was an awkward situation.* If they were to stay in London, as the others wanted, she needed somehow to deflect this man's suspicions. She could not simply turn him away, for that would only increase his doubts about her. But she knew that if he were to meet any of her supposed family, it would likely do the same thing. While most of them spoke rather genteelly, she knew from being around the *ton* that they would not pass any discerning eye—and this man's eyes were more discerning than most.

"I felt sure I could depend on your good nature." Lambeth's eyes were laughing at her again, and Marianne felt as though she could cheerfully shove him out the front door. It was especially irritating that the twinkle of those sherry-colored eyes made her insides jangle in a most disturbing way.

"Won't you come in, then?" she asked, assuming as gracious a voice as she could muster, and extended her hand toward the front drawing room, the most formal room in the house. She spared a glance toward the sitting room, which she had just left, and caught sight of Betsy's curious face peering around the door.

She closed the door to the drawing room behind them. It was a thoroughly indelicate thing to do, and God knew what Lambeth would think of her for it, but she hoped that the closed door would send a message to the rest of the "family" to stay out.

"Now, would you tell me why you came here?"

"Why, to see you. Why else?"

"I don't know. That's why I asked. I though perhaps you came to renew your absurd allegations."

"My dear girl." Lambeth put on a wounded expression as he took her hand in his and raised it to his mouth. "I came to apologize for offending you."

His lips brushed her skin like velvet, and Marianne felt it clear down to her toes. She struggled to keep her breathing even. "A note would have done as well."

"Ah, but then I would not have had the pleasure of looking at you while I threw myself on your mercy."

"Don't talk nonsense. I don't think you are in the slightest sorry."

"Indeed, I am. I am very sorry that you slipped away last night before we had finished our conversation."

"There was nothing further to say. Somehow you got the wrong impression of me, and I don't know how I can change your mind."

"I would not be at all averse to your trying."

"Lord Lambeth, you are very presumptuous." He was still holding on to her hand, and it took some effort for her to pull it from his grasp. She walked away from him, sitting down in a chair and gesturing him toward the sofa opposite her.

"Mmm. No doubt. I have found that it usually serves me well." Lambeth took the chair beside her instead.

"Was it you following me yesterday?" she asked bluntly.

"No, I assure you." He smiled. "I knew that if you saw me you would flee immediately. I sent one of my servants instead—and a cursed clumsy job he must have made of it if you spotted him."

"I didn't spot him. It was just a feeling."

"I apologize if he alarmed you." His voice sounded sincere, and Marianne felt unwillingly warmed by it. "I wanted very much to see you again—that is my only excuse for such behavior. You say that I got the wrong impression of you the other night at Lord Batterslee's. I fear that you received the wrong impression of me, as well."

He was leaning closer to her, his dark-lashed eyes gazing into hers. Marianne's breath caught in her throat, and her eyes went involuntarily to his mouth. He caught the glance, and his eyes darkened. His hand came out to cup her chin.

"You are a very desirable woman, and I will admit freely that I want you. But I would not coerce you into my bed with threats, madame."

His face loomed closer, and Marianne knew that he was going to kiss her. She also knew that she ought to pull away, but she found it terribly difficult to move. Her eyes drifted closed.

The door snapped open behind them, and they jumped, pulling back from each other and whirling around to face the door. Piers stood there, scowling suspiciously. Marianne's heart sank. She had been afraid that Betsy would join them, but Piers was even worse. He had taken a dislike to Lambert last night from her story. She only hoped that he would not get some silly idea in his head and confront the man.

"Piers. How nice to see you." Her voice rang false.

"Marianne." He looked pointedly at Lambeth.

"I'm sorry. Lord Lambeth, this is Piers Robertson."

Lambeth rose politely and shook the man's hand. "Are you Mrs. Cotterwood's brother?"

"No," Marianne answered.

"Yes," Piers responded at the same time.

Lambeth's eyebrows rose.

Marianne glared at Piers, then turned back to Lambeth, smiling woodenly. "Piers is actually my cousin, but we have always been as close as brother and sister. I—he—his parents raised me. Mine died when I was quite young."

"I am sorry to hear that."

"It was a long time ago. I don't remember them." *That much, at least, was true.*

Lambeth's eyes went from Marianne back to Piers. "Do you live in London, Mr. Robertson?"

"I live *here.*" Piers' feet were spread apart, his jaw thrust forward, his whole attitude bespeaking a readiness to fight.

"Ah. I see."

"My whole family lives here," Marianne put in hastily. "Piers, why don't you sit down?"

Piers consented to move to the couch, still regarding Lambeth pugnaciously.

"I don't believe I saw you last night at the Batterslees'," Lambeth went on coolly. "Did you accompany your… *cousin?*"

"No. Piers never attends such things." Marianne jumped in before Piers could answer. Piers' rudeness was obviously making Lambeth's distrust worse. "He finds them dead bores, don't you, dear?"

"Yes. Though perhaps I should attend, if fellows are going to be making advances to you." He glared meaningfully at Lambeth.

"Piers!"

A faint smile touched Lambeth's lips, but his eyes were as cold as metal. "Yes. Perhaps you should. Not quite the thing to leave a lady unprotected."

"I am well capable of taking care of myself," Marianne put in crisply, forestalling Piers' reply with a dagger look. "I don't need a keeper."

"Indeed. I suspect it is more the gentlemen who need protection from you," Lambeth replied, turning away from Piers, the amusement back in his gaze.

"What the devil does that mean?" Piers demanded, starting to rise.

Lambeth turned a bland face toward him. "Why, only that Mrs. Cotterwood's beauty is so great, it is we gentlemen who are in danger of losing our hearts."

"That would be a prettier statement if I thought you had a heart to lose," Marianne said tartly.

Justin let out a surprised bark of laughter. "Touché, my dear."

Piers' jaw clenched, and Marianne tensed in fear of what he might say. At that moment Betsy breezed into the room, followed by her husband. Marianne noticed that Betsy had used the time since Lambeth had arrived to fluff white powder on her face and rouge her cheeks and lips. Though she had given in to modern styles of dress and hair, she refused to give up the makeup worn twenty or thirty years before, with a result that was startling.

"Oh, my!" the old woman exclaimed in a girlish voice. "I didn't realize you had company, Marianne."

"Yes, *Grandmama*," Marianne said pointedly. "Lord Lambeth has honored us with his presence."

She had no choice but to introduce Lambeth to the other couple, explaining that they were her grandparents.

"It's too bad that Harrison and Della aren't here to meet you," Betsy said, dimpling at Lambeth.

"My parents," Marianne explained. "That is, I mean, *Piers'* parents. The people who raised me."

"Of course."

She had thought that the situation could get no worse, but she was wrong, for at that moment the maid appeared in the doorway and said nervously, "Lord Buckminster, madam."

Marianne shot to her feet. Even Lord Lambeth looked stunned. He rose, also, turning toward the doorway where Lord Buckminster's amiable countenance appeared behind the maid.

"Bucky!"

"Lambeth. I say." Lord Buckminster smiled. "Didn't expect to see you here."

"Nor I you." Lambeth regarded his friend thoughtfully. "I didn't realize you knew Mrs. Cotterwood's address."

"And so I didn't," Bucky admitted cheerfully. "But I set my valet on it. Clever chap, Wiggins, always knows just what to do. When I told him what Penny said the other day about meeting Mrs. Cotterwood, he went right out and came back with the address."

"Mmm. Yes, I see."

Lord Buckminster advanced toward Marianne, catching his toe on the edge of the rug and stumbling forward. He managed to stop just before he crashed into the back of

Lambeth's chair, but he dropped his hat when he grabbed at the chair, and it rolled across the floor. Buckminster chased after it and caught it before it went under the sofa, managing to crack his shin on a stool as he did so. All the others watched numbly, unable to tear their eyes away. Buckminster straightened and grinned, his cheeks flushed.

"I say. Not usually so clumsy. My feet seem to get all tangled up around you, Mrs. Cotterwood."

"Sure, now," Da told him comfortingly, coming forward to shake Buckminster's hand. "Isn't unusual at all. My granddaughter has that effect on a number of men. Let me introduce myself. Rory Kiernan's me name, and this is me wife, Betsy."

"How do you do, Mr. Kiernan? Are you from Ireland? I have lands there, you know."

"Faith, and do you now?" Da's eyes twinkled merrily, and he gestured Buckminster toward a seat, sitting down beside him and launching into questions about Buckminster's land.

"Now, Rory," Betsy cut through the lilting flow of his words. "Stop all that talk about Ireland. If it was so wonderful, I can't imagine why you left it. I am sure Lord Buckminster didn't come here to discuss the 'old sod.'" She smiled at Bucky, and for a moment one could glimpse the charm that had once enchanted more than one poor card player.

Buckminster smiled back. "Actually, I came to bring Mrs. Cotterwood an invitation to my cousin's ball." He reached inside his jacket, frowned, and stuck his hand into the other side of his jacket. "That's odd. I would have sworn I put the invitation in here."

He patted his outside pockets, then returned to the inner one.

"Is this what you're looking for?" Da asked, reaching behind Buckminster and pulling out a white envelope.

"Why, yes." Buckminster looked delighted and reached out to take the envelope from him.

"Must have fallen out of your pocket when you sat down," Da suggested.

"How fortunate you found it," Marianne said stiffly and glared at Rory.

"Yes, isn't it?" Rory agreed blandly.

Lord Buckminster rose and took the invitation to Marianne. "Nicola is most hopeful that you will come."

"Nicola?"

"My cousin Nicola Falcourt. It is her mother's party, but of course Nicola is the one running it all. I told her all about you, and she is dying to meet you. It's Friday. Sorry about the short notice. I do hope you are not already engaged."

"Why, no, I'm not."

Marianne opened the invitation and glanced over it. Across the bottom was a note written in an elegant hand: "I am so looking forward to meeting you. Bucky has told me all about you. Nicola Falcourt."

"I do feel a trifle odd about going, however," Marianne went on. "Since I don't know your cousin."

"Oh, Nicola don't stand on formality," Buckminster assured her.

"But what about her mother? Won't she mind?"

"No. She doesn't think about things like that. She's only interested in dosing herself. Lady Falcourt's invalidish."

"The woman's a walking infirmary," Lambeth added dryly. "Don't let her get you in a corner, or you'll hear nothing but complaints all night."

"That's true. Spent an hour telling me about her heart

palpitations one evening. Made me dashed queasy, I can tell you." Lord Buckminster paled at the memory.

Marianne stifled a chuckle. "I will be sure to avoid her, then. Thank you. I should love to come. I will send my acceptance to your cousin this afternoon."

"Splendid. You will enjoy it better than the Batterslee affair the other night."

"I'm sure I will." Marianne glanced involuntarily at Lambeth and found him watching her enigmatically.

"Perhaps you will join us one evening, Lord Buckminster," Betsy said brightly. "We live quietly here, but we could get up a little game of cards now and then."

Marianne's eye widened in alarm. "I am sure that Lord Buckminster would not be interested in the sort of low stakes we play for."

"But I would," Buckminster hastened to assure her. "An evening of cards sounds delightful."

"Wonderful. Then next Tuesday, say?"

"I am afraid I have something to do that evening," Marianne said quickly. "Why don't we discuss this later, Grandmama?" She cast a stern look at Betsy, who shrugged and subsided.

Lord Lambeth, who had watched this byplay with interest, started to speak, but Buckminster jumped in first. "Mrs. Cotterwood, if I may be so bold…hope you will also consider…I am having a few people out to my country house in a fortnight. It would give me a great deal of pleasure if you would join us."

Lambeth glanced at his friend sharply. Marianne looked stunned.

"Uh—I'm not sure. I mean…"

"Sorry. I hope I'm not being too forward. Just thought—

as I was having it, you see—that you might like to come. Nothing fancy, of course. Just a week of ruralizing. I am sure Mother will insist on having a dance one night so she can invite the locals, but that's all. Just country entertainments. Nicola and Penelope will be there. You'll like Nicola."

"I—I'm sure I will."

"Well, no need to answer now. Just say you will think about it."

"Yes, certainly."

"Splendid!" Buckminster's open, pleasant face beamed. "Oh. I suppose it must be time to leave." First calls were not supposed to last more than fifteen minutes. Buckminster went to the small pocket in his vest to pull out his watch, then stopped, amazed, lifting up the dangling chain. "I say. I must have dropped my watch, as well."

"Odd, that," Justin commented.

Marianne stiffened. "It certainly is. We'll help you look for it. *Da…*" She sent a steely glance the old man's way.

"What? Oh, oh, yes. A watch. Let's see here." He began to look around the couch, then rose and circled around behind their chairs. "Aha!" He bent over and straightened up, holding a gold watch up triumphantly. "Here it is, behind this chair."

Buckminster's face cleared. "Yes, that's it. So glad you found it."

"Strange that it should have wound up clear over there," Justin remarked dryly.

"Yes, isn't it?" Rory Kiernan replied blandly.

Buckminster agreed pleasantly, with the air of a man who often encountered mysteries beyond his understanding. "Yes. Good thing you thought to look over there, sir."

"Probably fell off and rolled," Piers suggested helpfully. "Tricky things, watches."

"No doubt." Lambeth reached into his vest pocket to check his own watch. "You're right, Bucky. It is getting late. I will walk out with you."

Both men rose and took their polite leave of the company. Marianne walked them to the door and shut it behind them, then sagged against the wood in relief. All the others came bustling out of the drawing room, grinning.

"Ah, yer a rare one, me girl," Da pronounced. "Two lords calling on ye, full of invitations."

"Just think what you can do with a whole week at Buckminster's estate," Piers added eagerly, his distrust of Lord Lambeth apparently vanquished by the prospect of a new job.

"Oh, aye, that one's a bird just ripe for plucking," Da agreed, rubbing his hands together gleefully.

"No!" The thought of stealing from Lord Buckminster appalled her. He was so pleasant and friendly, such a simple, likeable man. It made her queasy to think of lying to him, of accepting his friendship and hospitality, then taking things from him. The others looked at her oddly. "I mean…well, it would be too dangerous. I would be staying there, and the constables would come and question us, and—"

"Lord love you, Marianne, have some sense," Piers said with a smile. "We wouldn't do it while you were there. Harrison and I would wait—weeks, even months—before we went in there. They wouldn't have any reason to connect it with you. The thing is, you would have a whole week to get the layout and locate the safe and the other valuables."

"Aye, and that one's rich. Did you see the diamond pin in his cravat?" Betsy added.

"But I would be stuck in a house with those people for

a whole week!" Marianne protested. "I couldn't keep up my disguise for that long."

"Why, sure you can," Da assured. "Ye shouldn't be so hard on yerself, girl. Nobody'd ever know you weren't a lady. Besides, that one's so google-eyed over ye, he'd not notice if you spat and swore."

"Maybe not, but he won't be the only one there. There will be lots of others, and I will have to talk to them at length. They will talk about things I don't know and people I have never met. I would be sure to make a misstep. Lord Lambeth will be there, too, no doubt, and he's no fool. He already thinks I'm a thief. And you can bet he wasn't fooled by that watch story of yours, either, Da. I could see it all over his face. He knew you stole Lord Buckminster's watch. The invitation, too! What were you thinking of?"

"Just wanted to see if I still had me touch," Rory replied cheerfully. "I didn't know it was only an invitation or I'd never have bothered with it."

"If Lord Lambeth already thinks you're a thief and hasn't said anything, he's not likely to," Betsy pointed out. "If nothing else, everybody would wonder why he hadn't spoken up earlier."

"That's right. He won't be trying to catch you out in your story. All he would do is watch you to make sure you don't steal nothing, and since you won't be taking anything, there won't be any problem," Piers added.

"'Sides," Da went on, "that Lambeth fellow's sweet on ye, too."

Marianne could feel herself blushing. "I don't think you could exactly call it that."

"What else would you call it?" Betsy said reasonably. "The man came to call on you, didn't he? He had to go to all the trouble to track down where you lived, too. He's just better at hiding it than Lord Buckminster."

"He may be interested in me," Marianne admitted tartly, "but not in the way that Lord Buckminster is."

"That may be, but as long as he thinks that he can persuade you to accept a carte blanche, he won't be turning you in."

"Betsy! Is that what you think I should do? Encourage that man to think that I would—would *sell* myself to keep his mouth shut?"

Piers scowled. "Absolutely not. I won't permit it. Neither would Harrison."

"I'm not suggesting you *do* anything," Betsy protested. "Just don't absolutely turn him down. A little flirtation never hurt anyone."

"You don't know Lambeth if you think that is all it would be."

Betsy shrugged. The older woman belonged to a more licentious age, and Marianne suspected that she thought an affair with Lord Lambeth would not be such a terrible thing. Marianne, thinking of his kisses, knew that it would be all too easy a thing to do; that was one reason why she was so against going any farther along this path.

At that point Della and Harrison came in, and the entire afternoon had to be recounted to them, and all the arguments for and against her attending the parties hashed over once again. Finally, after much discussion, Della and Harrison came down on the side of the rest of the family.

"Go to this party of Miss Falcourt's and the one in the country," Harrison said, stroking his chin thoughtfully. "Get the layout of both places, and we will write it all down, just as we did the other day with the Batterslees, but we won't do anything. Then later, after your young lord has been lulled into complacence, we'll do all of them, one right after another. Then we'll have enough swag to last us for a long time. We'll hie off to the Continent, and they'll never catch us."

Marianne gave in. She could not ruin it for the others just because of her own qualms, which she was sure everyone else would regard as foolish. These people were her family, the only ones to whom she owed loyalty. Buckminster was a nice man, but he was still a member of the class that she hated; if he knew the true story of her origins, he would doubtless be appalled. He probably had so much wealth that he would scarcely notice anything was missing. If his heart came out a little bruised, well, there was nothing she could do about that. As for Lambeth, his heart, of course, would never be in danger of getting hurt. And she would make sure that her own heart was well protected.

LORD LAMBETH GLANCED OVER AT his companion as they strolled along. Lord Buckminster was humming tunelessly, a smile upon his lips. Justin hesitated, then said, "You seem rather taken with Mrs. Cotterwood."

Bucky turned to him, beaming. "Yes. You know, Lambeth, I believe I am in love. Never had it happen, you know. Rather delightful, actually."

"I wouldn't know. But don't you think that you are, perhaps, being a trifle too hasty? I mean, you scarcely know the woman."

His friend's behavior worried him. Justin had never seen Bucky act this head over heels in love with a woman—and Buckminster would be easy prey for anyone given to larceny. Why, Bucky hadn't a clue that Mrs. Cotterwood's little "family" was a ring of crooks, or that her grandfather had deftly lifted both his gold watch and the invitation right out of his pocket. He would be easy pickings for a group like that.

"I know enough." Bucky's grin was jaunty. "Trying to scare off a rival? I'm not that easy, old chap."

"Bucky, think. You don't know anything about her—who she is, where she came from, what she's doing here."

"Doing?" Bucky looked puzzled. "What should she be doing? She is here for the Season, just like the rest of us."

"How do you know that she is not an adventuress?" Justin asked bluntly.

Bucky chuckled. "Don't be absurd. Besides, you vouched for her."

Justin groaned. "That was to Lady Ursula, and I only did it because I can't abide that woman. I don't know Mrs. Cotterwood any better than you do. Why did she suddenly appear here in London? The Season is almost over, you know. And why have I never heard her name before?"

"You can't know everyone," Bucky pointed out mildly. "I believe Penelope said that she had been living in Bath. Perhaps she's been in seclusion since her husband's death."

"That's another thing. Precisely who was *Mr.* Cotterwood? When did he die, and of what?"

"Really, Justin, you go too far. One can scarcely ask a widow questions like that."

"No doubt that is what she counts on."

Buckminster looked at his friend askance. "Whatever are you implying?"

"That she could be something other than what she seems."

"Nonsense. Anyone can tell that she is a lady just by talking to her. She is as beautiful on the inside as on the out."

Justin scowled. He could not let his friend be taken in

by Mrs. Cotterwood. He knew he should tell him what he suspected about her, yet somehow, the words stuck in his throat. Bucky probably wouldn't believe him, anyway, the mood he was in. "And when did this party at your estate come into being?"

Buckminster laughed. "About ten minutes before I asked her. I shall have to remember to send Mama off a note post-haste to let her know she will be having guests." He glanced at his friend and noticed the black look on the other man's face. "I say, you aren't upset because I fancy Mrs. Cotterwood, too, are you? I mean, it isn't the first time we've pursued the same female. There was Frances Wallesford."

"Oh, Lord. Thank heavens Ferdy beat us both out on that one."

"I know. A narrow escape. And there was that bird of paradise, what was her name? You know, the black-headed girl with—"

"Lizzy. Yes, I know. I'm just not sure it's the same thing this time."

Buckminster looked at him in some surprise. "You mean to say you're serious about Mrs. Cotterwood?"

"Me? No." Justin shook his head. "Lord, no. I don't know that I've ever been serious about a woman. Certainly not Mrs. Cotterwood."

"Good. Then there's no problem, is there? You will come to my house party, won't you?"

"Oh, yes," Justin promised. "Believe me, I will be there." And, somehow, he would find a way to keep Bucky out of the beautiful Mrs. Cotterwood's web.

CHAPTER SIX

ON FRIDAY AFTERNOON, A BOX CONTAINING a corsage was delivered to Marianne's door. The flowers were from Lord Buckminster. An hour later, another cluster of flowers arrived with an accompanying note from Lord Lambeth, asking if Marianne would allow him the privilege of escorting her to Nicola Falcourt's ball that evening. Marianne could not keep a smile from stealing across her face as she inhaled the scent of the rosebuds. It meant nothing, of course, she told herself, but she sat down immediately and penned a note giving him permission to pick her up. Della and Winny came in to admire the posies.

Just as she was putting them back into the box, the front door opened, and Rosalind tumbled in, followed by Nettie. "Mama!" Rosalind cried when she saw the women standing in the front hallway. "We saw someone at the park!"

Marianne turned. "What? What do you mean you saw someone? Who?"

"I don't know. But he was asking about you." She bounced to a stop in front of Marianne, her chest puffed up with importance.

"What!" A cold chill ran through Marianne, and she looked over at the maid. "Nettie?"

The maid nodded. "Yes, madam. 'E did. 'E asked if we lived in this 'ouse."

"What did you say?"

"I didn't say nothin'. I told 'im 'e was impudent, but then 'e asked if I knew Mary Chilton, and I said no, 'cause I don't know nobody by that name. 'E said she was a maid 'ere. Then 'e said she 'ad red 'air."

She paused significantly, and Rosalind jumped into the silence, "So I told him my mama had red hair!"

"Oh."

"I'm sorry, madam," Nettie said apologetically. "I told 'im that you were not Mary Chilton, though, so I thought 'e 'ad the wrong place."

"What did he say to that?"

"Not much, madam. 'E asked your name, an' I told 'im it wasn't any of 'is business." She paused, then added, "But I reckon 'e'll be able to find out easy enough from somebody else around 'ere."

"Yes, no doubt." Marianne looked from the maid to Winny, who stared back at her in consternation.

Della looked back and forth between the two of them, confused. "What is it, dear? Who is this man? Why is he looking for you?"

"I don't know!" She glanced down at her daughter, who was looking at her worriedly.

"Did I do wrong, Mama?" she asked.

"Well, you should not engage in conversation with strange men in the park, even when Nettie is with you. But there was nothing wrong with what you said today." She smiled at Rosalind lovingly. "Why don't you run up and wash your hands and comb your hair? Then come back down and you can help decide which flowers I shall wear."

Rosalind smiled and tore off up the stairs, Nettie following her more slowly. Marianne turned to Winny.

"Is he the same man, do you think?" Winny asked, frowning.

"What are you two talking about?" Della asked, growing concerned.

Marianne quickly told her the story of Winny's letter and the men who had been looking for her. Della was just as puzzled about the matter as the two of them had been.

"But didn't she say that she didn't tell them about you or Winny?" she asked.

"Yes. But I guess he might have found out from another servant or someone in the village, and she just didn't know about it. Everyone knew that Winny and I were friends, so they could have suggested he try to find her. But who would have known Winny's address except her friend?"

"But somehow he must have found out. Surely there could not be two different sets of people looking for you."

"I wouldn't think so. I can't imagine what they want, and it scares me!"

"Me too," Della agreed. All of them had a deep distrust of outsiders, born of years of evading the law, and an even deeper distrust of someone asking questions about them. "I know you don't want to go to that house in the country next week." She chuckled at Marianne's quick look of surprise. "Oh, I'm not blind. I can see the way you look whenever anyone brings it up. But I think it might be a very good thing for you to get away from here for a few days right now."

"You are probably right." Marianne still hated the idea of spending a week at Lord Buckminster's house. Every time she thought about it, it made her cringe. But she could see the point in what Della said. No one would find her at a lord's estate in the country.

"And if he comes to our door asking questions, we'll send him on his way fast enough. In the meantime, you cover up your head any time you leave this house."

"I will."

Of course, she couldn't cover her hair with a hat that night, not with it coiled elegantly around her head and a ribbon to match her dress wound through it. She could only hope that in the dark, and with Lambeth's carriage blocking the doorway, the man, if he was watching, would not be able to get a good glimpse of her.

She wore a gown of peacock-blue satin that turned her eyes to sapphires. The neckline was low, off her shoulders and skimming across the tops of her breasts. She wore Bucky's wrist corsage, even though she liked Lambeth's better. Lambeth, after all, must not feel that he had everything his way. For the same reason, she left him standing five minutes after he arrived, even though she was ready to go.

Taking her wrap of silver tissue and her small reticule, she went downstairs. The widening of Lambeth's eyes was enough to tell her how she looked, even though he followed it up with a pretty compliment. Then his eyes went down to her wrist and saw the flowers that he had not sent, and his mouth tightened.

"From Bucky?" he asked, extending his arm to her.

"Yes. They matched the dress better," she explained.

"Ah. I see." From the dance of amusement in his hazel eyes as he mentally compared Buckminster's white camellias to his white rosebuds, she thought that he did indeed see the real cause of her ploy. "Then I hope that you will at least grant me the honor of the first waltz of the evening."

She agreed graciously, tucking her hand through his elbow, and they started out the door. Marianne felt nervous and happy and a little excited. Maybe the others were right, she thought; everything would turn out all right. It was easy to believe that in the warmth of the August night, Lambeth's strong arm beneath her hand, the scent of camellias wafting up to her. She looked up at him and found his eyes on her, and excitement began to dance in her stomach. Perhaps he did have feelings for her.

He handed her up into the carriage, a sleek black affair with the ducal crest of his family in gold on the door. This was what it was like to be a person of privilege, she thought, pampered and cosseted, clothed in the finest of garments and seated on the plushest of cushions, no thought on one's mind but the evening's pleasures. It was no wonder the aristocracy were arrogant.

Lambeth settled into the seat across from her, and the carriage started off slowly. Marianne was a trifle shy with him, closed up in this small space. She remembered his eyes as they had been a few moments before as he gazed down at her, hot and yearning; she remembered the feel of his lips on hers, the strength of his arms around her, the dizzying heat that had enveloped her when he kissed her. His kiss had aroused her as no other's ever had, and she could not help but feel a faint flowering of hope within her chest. Perhaps he meant it when he said he would not coerce her. He had, after all, not turned her in to the authorities. He was right now escorting her to a party as if she really were a lady. She shifted a little on her seat and wondered what he was thinking. His face was shadowed, and she could not make out his expression.

"I want you to leave Buckminster alone," he said, his voice harsh in the darkness, shattering Marianne's thoughts.

She simply looked at him, too startled even to speak.

"He is a good man, too naive for one such as you, and I will not see him hurt," Lambeth went on, crushing the tendrils of soft emotion that had risen in her moments earlier.

Marianne realized with a rush of shame that while she had been dreaming of his kiss, he had been thinking only of keeping her from his friend. She swallowed hard, forcing the tears from her voice. "I scarcely see how this concerns you, my lord."

Marianne was pleased to hear that her voice came out tart.

"Bucky has been my friend all my life, and he is a good fellow. I have no intention of letting him get his heart broken by a conniving adventuress."

His words sliced through her like a knife. He had no interest in her, she knew. Indeed, his voice held nothing but contempt.

"You think that I would set out to hurt him?" She could not completely hide the tremor of emotion in her voice, but he did not seem to hear.

"What else should I think? He is a very wealthy man and obviously head over heels in love with you. You, on the other hand, are a thief."

"How can you say that? I have not stolen anything!"

"I have not seen you take anything with my own eyes," Lambeth conceded. "But it was obvious that you were up to something. If I needed any confirmation, I think it was amply provided by your 'family.'"

"How dare you!"

"How dare I what? Speak the truth? Your kin are as fine a set of criminals as any I have ever seen. Your 'da' picked Bucky's pocket neatly, and your grandmother seemed inordinately eager to involve him in a game of cards. I am not sure whether you actually steal things from people's houses or are just a lure to bring wealthy men into the circle of your family, where they can fleece them thoroughly. But whatever your scheme, you are clearly an adventuress. You certainly are not going to pass up a golden opportunity like Buckminster. You will get every cent you can out of him and leave him heartbroken."

"I wonder, then, that you should soil yourself by being with me. It seems most odd that you come calling and send me posies when my soul is so black. One would think that you would want nothing to do with me."

"There is a world of difference between Bucky and me," he replied flatly. "Bucky is naive and trusting, easily taken in by a schemer. I, on the other hand, know you for what you are, and I can handle you without getting my heart broken."

"As if you had a heart to break!"

"That is precisely what I mean," he said, his smile flashing whitely in the darkness. "I can enjoy your charms without losing myself. Buckminster cannot."

Marianne was swept with a sick fury. *How could she have been so stupid? How could she have thought even for an instant that he might have feelings for her?* He was like Quartermaine, interested in nothing but his own gratification. She was not a person to him, but an object of contempt to be used and discarded, to be kept away from his more vulnerable friend for fear she might contaminate him.

Almost shaking with rage, she leaned forward, her voice a fierce rasp, "I will do what I want with Buckminster, and there is nothing you can do about it."

Lambeth's eyes flashed, and his jaw tightened. "By God, I'll tell him the truth about you."

"Go ahead." Her tone was contemptuous. "Tell him I am wicked. He will not believe you, he will only think you are jealous and want me for yourself. I will make him fall in love with me so hard and deep that he will never recover. If you make your slimy accusations about me, it will serve only to make him dislike you. And if you make him believe the worst about me, he will not thank you for it. He will hate you for being the person who destroyed his dreams. So you see, you are in my power as securely as he, and you would have done better not to order me away from him."

They had reached the Falcourt house and were drawn up in the line of carriages waiting to reach the front door. Marianne wrenched open the door and scrambled out of the carriage, ignoring Lambeth's furious command to stop. He reached out for her arm, but she twisted away from him and jumped down to the ground. She heard his muffled oath behind her, but she did not look back, only hurried up the street, ducking around the knot of people emerging from the carriage at the head of the line, and joined the group of guests moving up the steps to the front door.

When she stepped through the front door, she saw Bucky standing on the landing of the staircase, where it split and went up on either side. He was scanning the crowd, and when he saw her, a broad smile curved his lips. He hurried down the steps to her.

"Mrs. Cotterwood!" He managed to make it to her side without knocking into more than one fellow. "I am so glad to see you."

Marianne, sure that Lambeth was somewhere behind them, observing the greeting, turned a dazzling smile on Buckminster. "I am so glad you are here," she said, tucking her hand confidingly into the crook of his arm. "I feel quite alone. I know no one here."

He patted her hand reassuringly. "I will introduce you to everyone."

The line of guests moved forward at a good pace. Lord Buckminster stayed at Marianne's side, and she flirted shamelessly with him for Lambeth's benefit. She felt a momentary qualm for Buckminster's sake. He really was a nice man, and it was cruel to raise his hopes. It was also unkind to Penelope, whom she liked, and whom she suspected was more than fond of Lord Buckminster. Later, she told herself, she would somehow make it up to the two of them. She would think of a way to turn Buckminster's affection away from her, and perhaps she could even manage to direct it toward Penelope.

Bucky introduced her to his cousin Nicola, who stood at the head of the receiving line, along with her mother, a middle-aged woman of faded beauty and a die-away voice. Nicola was a beauty of the most English type: pale blond hair, cornflower-blue eyes and a rose-and-white complexion. There was a fragile look to her that was belied by her firm handshake. She smiled at Marianne, her eyes curious. Marianne suspected that she was assessing her.

"I am very pleased to meet you," Nicola said in a friendly manner. "Bucky has told me so much about you that I feel almost as if I know you already."

Marianne smiled, guilt piercing her once more at the woman's open, friendly manner. "Thank you. I am equally delighted to meet you."

There were others behind them, so they could not linger to talk. Lord Buckminster led her farther into the room.

Buckminster found, to his bemusement, that practically every young gentleman of his acquaintance came up to talk to him, angling for an introduction to his lovely companion.

"Confounded fellows," he grumbled, making an abrupt right to avoid another young man headed toward them. "They're like gnats. A fellow can't have a decent word alone with you."

"Well, I can't speak very many words alone with you, anyway," Marianne pointed out, "or it would be quite unacceptable."

"Yes, I know. Don't see why they have to spoil my time with you, though. Oh, there's Penelope. Shall we go see her? Looks like her mother's in full voice."

She was indeed. Lady Ursula was holding forth at some length and great volume about some perceived mistake of Parliament to a square-set man whose dark eyes had taken on a rather glazed look.

"Hallo, Pen," Buckminster said in a friendly manner to her daughter, who had turned away as far as politely possible from her mother's conversation.

Penelope smiled, her face lighting up. "Bucky! And Mrs. Cotterwood. How nice to see you again."

"Thank you. But please, call me Marianne."

"So I shall. And you must call me Penelope."

Lady Ursula broke off her tirade to turn to see who had joined her daughter. She was less than pleased to see Lord Buckminster and the redheaded woman with him, but she was obliged to make introductions. The man turned out to be a Mr. Alan Thurston, who was standing for Parliament, and the pale woman beside him was his wife, Elizabeth. Thurston looked relieved to have someone divert Lady Ursula's attention. The talk soon turned to Lord Buckminster's house party, to which Mr. and Mrs. Thurston had been invited, as had Penelope's family.

Penelope looked distressed at the very mention of the party, and it did not take long to learn why, as Lady Ursula boomed, "Sorry, Lord Buckminster, but I am afraid that I cannot get away on such quick notice. I had promised to go to my son's during his wife's confinement, and I received word yesterday that I was needed. I will be leaving first thing Monday morning."

"I am sorry to hear that," Buckminster replied, looking anything but regretful. "But don't worry about Penelope. We shall take good care of her."

Lady Ursula looked shocked. "But Penelope cannot go alone! Unchaperoned!"

At that moment, Nicola Falcourt came strolling up, her hand on the arm of Lord Lambeth. Marianne looked toward him, and their eyes met and held for a long moment. His eyes, she noticed, were as cool and blank as a sheet of gold. It took an effort to tear her eyes away.

"What?" Nicola cried, turning to Lady Ursula. "You are not allowing Penelope to go to Bucky's party? But that will quite spoil it."

"I find such hyperbole unnecessary, Nicola," Lady Ursula said in a disapproving tone. "Her absence will scarcely 'spoil' the party, as you say. I am sure that Penelope will be disappointed, but—"

"But why can she not come?" Nicola protested, cutting across the woman's words. Lady Ursula pressed her lips together at this bit of impertinence, but repeated to the newcomers what she had just said to the rest of the group.

"But I will be there," Nicola pointed out. "We can share a room, and I will look out for her. I promise."

"The presence of another unmarried girl Penelope's age is scarcely what I would call proper chaperonage," Lady Ursula told her. "Really, Nicola, you know better than that. I wonder your mother is allowing you to go by yourself."

"But my aunt, Bucky's mother, will be there," Nicola pointed out. "Surely she counts as an adequate chaperone."

"Lady Buckminster?" Lady Ursula sniffed at the idea. "Far be it from me to criticize your mother, Lord Buckminster, but everyone knows that Adelaide is far more interested in her horses than in her guests. Besides, a hostess cannot adequately watch a young girl. She needs someone who can be with her all the time."

"But Penelope doesn't need constant watching over," Nicola protested, drawing herself up and facing the older woman pugnaciously. "I have never met anyone who behaved better than Penny."

"Of course Penelope would behave herself," Lady Ursula said, as though the thought of her doing anything else was ridiculous. "But it is the appearance that counts. An unmarried girl simply cannot be hanging about at a house party without a chaperone."

"I say, Lady Ursula," Bucky protested. "That's hardly fair." He cast a troubled glance at Penelope's sad countenance. "It won't be the same without Penelope."

Penelope cast him a pathetically grateful look, strengthening Marianne's suspicion that the girl had a *tendre* for him. Marianne wasn't sure what prompted her to do it. Perhaps it was Penelope's woeful face. But suddenly she found herself saying, "My lady, I would be more than happy to act as a chaperone for Miss Castlereigh."

Buckminster beamed. "There you have it. Mrs. Cotterwood can be Penny's chaperone."

"Yes!" Penelope cried out, her face brightening. "That would be wonderful. Oh, thank you, Mrs. Cotterwood. That is very sweet of you."

"Yes, isn't it?" Lord Lambeth drawled, looking enigmatically at Marianne.

Marianne lifted her brows and gazed back at him coldly. *No doubt the man thought she was trying to advance some underhanded scheme by offering to help Penelope. Well, let him think what he would.*

Lady Ursula swept Marianne with a look that clearly said she did not measure up to her standards as a chaperone. "But you are just a girl yourself."

"Thank you for saying so, my lady, but that is hardly the case. I am a widow and a mother."

"There, Mother, you see? That settles it, doesn't it?" Penelope asked eagerly, and even the redoubtable Lady Ursula's face softened as she saw the pleasure in her daughter's eyes.

"We don't really know Mrs. Cotterwood, though it is certainly a gracious offer."

"But we settled that the other day," Buckminster reminded her cheerfully. "Remember? Lambeth said he was acquainted with her family. I have met them, too. Very pleasant people."

Lady Ursula ignored Buckminster's endorsement, but her eyes went questioningly to Lord Lambeth.

"Oh, yes," he told her blandly. "I know Mrs. Cotterwood's family. You needn't worry about Penelope."

"Well…I suppose it is all right then, Penelope. You may go."

Penelope let out a squeal of delight, her face almost pretty in her happiness. "Thank you, Mother. Oh, thank you."

"There, now, girl, remember where you are," Lady Ursula said dampeningly.

The orchestra at the other end of the room started up, and Lord Lambeth turned to Marianne, sketching a bow. "Ah, the first waltz of the evening. I believe that you promised this to me, Mrs. Cotterwood."

Marianne would have liked to refuse him in no uncertain terms, but she hardly could, given the fact that only moments before he had approved her and her family to the rest of them. She smiled stiffly. "Yes, I believe I did."

She put her hand lightly on his crooked arm and let him lead her out onto the floor. He swept her expertly into the dance, his hold light and impersonal.

"I am surprised, my lord," Marianne began, "that you should wish to keep your waltz with me—and even more surprised that you recommended my family to Lady Castlereigh, given your opinion of me and my relatives."

"I did not recommend them precisely. I said that they were known to me, which is true. My suspicions about them I prefer to keep to myself. I encouraged Lady Ursula to rely on you as a chaperone entirely for Penelope's sake. That poor mouse of a girl would benefit greatly by escaping her mother for a while. And since I know that Penelope is a woman of excellent character, I know that she really has no need for a chaperone. She would not think of doing anything foolish or wrong. Therefore I had no qualms about endorsing you."

"Oh, I see. What you are saying is that Penelope is so wonderful a person that anyone, even a hussy off the street, would do for a chaperone." Marianne could not quite keep the tremor of anger from her voice.

Lambeth merely glanced at her and did not reply.

He knew that he had handled it all wrong earlier this evening. He had not meant to say anything about Bucky. His plan had been to charm Marianne into a liaison with him. He had wanted her from the moment he saw her, and an affair with her would both satisfy his desire and keep her from swindling Bucky. Bucky's heart would be bruised for a time, but he would get over it much more quickly than if the woman drew him deeper and deeper into love with her and then betrayed him.

It never entered his head that Marianne might not be wooed into an affair. The kiss they had shared had made it clear that she was a woman of passion—even if she had been so infuriated that she had slapped him. She had a child, so she was experienced. And it seemed unlikely that she would have any moral qualms. After all, she was an adventuress, not a lily-white damsel. Meeting her family had only reinforced his suspicions about her actions at the Batterslee house. They were an entertaining lot, but clearly a set of rascals. He supposed it was possible that she really was a widow, but he suspected that it was only a pose to explain the absence of a husband. Such a woman, he thought, would be quite willing to enter into a mutually satisfying relationship. It was, after all, not as dangerous as stealing or swindling.

But, somehow, when he had arrived at her house this evening and seen her wearing Bucky's corsage instead of his, he had felt such a fierce surge of anger that he had lost sight of his objectives and blurted out the first thing that came into his head. He had quickly realized, of course, that he had done the wrong thing. He had only made her angry and determined to spite him. But by then, he was well into it, and so furious at her that he could not stop.

He was under control now, of course, and he was determined to rectify the matter. "I must apologize for my remarks earlier," he said, irritated at how stiff his words sounded. "I did not act as a gentleman should."

Marianne lifted an elegantly curved eyebrow. "Indeed, you did not."

This was not going as he had planned, either, he realized. With an oath, he whirled her off the dance floor and guided her toward the bank of long windows, opened onto the night air. The windows, tall and reaching almost to the floor, were easy enough to step through, and then they were out on the back terrace of the house, which overlooked the small garden.

"What do you think you're doing?" Marianne snapped. "This is highly improper behavior."

"No one saw us," he said shortly, walking across the terrace and down the steps into the darkness of the garden. "I want to talk to you in private."

"What if I don't want to talk to you? You are an insufferably arrogant man, Lord Lambeth."

"No doubt. I still intend to have a private conversation with you."

"If you are planning to resume your earlier arguments, I can tell you that—"

"No," he said impatiently, turning down a narrow graveled path that ended at a small fountain. He turned toward her. "I regret what I said earlier. I've already told you that. I was concerned for my friend, and it led me to speak hastily. But it was not what I wanted to say."

Marianne looked at him curiously. His face was immobile, even stern, in the pale wash of the moonlight. With his eyes shadowed, she could not even make out the expression in them. There was an odd feeling in her chest, something shivery and hopeful. *He said he regretted what he said. Perhaps it wasn't what he really felt, only a cruelty that he had spoken out of anger.*

"What I meant to say was—well, I have a proposition for you. I am offering you my protection."

"Your protection?" she repeated faintly, not sure she had heard aright. "You mean, you want...?"

"Yes. I am asking you to be my mistress."

CHAPTER SEVEN

MARIANNE'S FACE DRAINED OF COLOR. "I—I beg your pardon?"

"It is far better for you." Lambeth realized immediately that he had spoken too bluntly and clumsily, and now he rushed to explain. "I would set you up in a house, of course and give you an ample allowance. You would want for nothing, and there would be none of the dangers inherent in your present occupation. You would not have to pretend love with me as you would with Bucky, so it would be far easier. And we would, I think, enjoy each other." His face softened slightly on those last words, and his voice turned husky. His hand touched her arm softly.

Marianne jerked back. She felt as if he had hit her in the stomach. *To him she was nothing but a whore!* She had thought his words in the carriage had been painful, but they had not cut her as this did. *To think she had foolishly almost believed him when he apologized!*

"Don't touch me!" she cried out in a low voice, shaking with rage. "How can you think that I would let you near me? It would not be hard to love Bucky, but it would make me *ill* to endure your caresses!"

Justin's face hardened. Marianne rushed on.

"What makes you think I would settle for being any

man's mistress—yours *or* Lord Buckminster's? He thinks I am a woman of gentle birth, and as smitten as he is with me, I see no reason why I cannot look forward to being Lady Buckminster."

Justin's eyes flamed, and his face flushed with fury. He took a quick step forward. Marianne backed up hastily, thinking that he meant to hit her. She bent, lifting her skirt up to her knee, and whipped out the small knife she kept in a scabbard on her calf. She faced him defiantly, her knife at the ready.

Lambeth's eyes widened, and he looked from the knife to her face. A sneer touched his well-cut lips. "I am not the sort of man you are accustomed to, my dear."

His hand lashed out and clamped around her wrist, cutting off her circulation. Marianne tried to pull away, infuriated by how easily he had thwarted her, but he held her fast and reached up with his other hand to pull the knife out of her grasp.

"Let go of me!" she panted, twisting and tugging. Her cheeks were flushed, her eyes hot with fury. His gaze fell to her breasts, swaying with her movements, the nipples brazen points beneath the material. He stood for a moment, gazing at her, his eyes glittering, his chest rising and falling rapidly.

Then he jerked her forward so that she slammed into his chest, their bodies flush all the way up and down. Marianne's eyes widened, and her breath rushed out as she felt the imprint of his desire against her, hot and imperative. She gazed up into his fiery eyes, her lips parted slightly. She could not remember what she had been about to say. Her flesh tingled at every point where their bodies touched, and the sensations spread out so that every part of her was suddenly alive.

Justin's face loomed closer. Then his lips found hers. His mouth was greedy, consuming her. A shudder ran through Marianne, and she sagged against him, her arms going around his waist. A groan escaped him. He wrapped his arms around her, pulling her up into his body. The small knife fell unheeded to the ground.

Marianne clung to him, trembling. She had never felt like this before, so wild and out of control. Even when she had thought herself in love with Daniel Quartermaine, his kiss had not excited her as this man's did. Justin kissed her again and again, as if he could not get enough of the sweet taste of her mouth. His tongue twined around hers, exploring, teasing, demanding. His hands roamed up and down her back, pressing her into him, curving over her buttocks. His fingers dug into the fleshy mounds, pushing her pelvis up hard against his, so that the hard ridge of his desire pressed into her. It was not enough for Marianne, however, and she twisted closer, her loins blossoming with hot desire.

He mumbled something she could not understand, his lips leaving hers to trail down the soft column of her throat. One hand came up to cup her breast, his thumb caressing the nipple through the cloth of her dress. Her breasts were full and aching, alive to his merest touch, and her nipples hardened eagerly. His arms went around her, hard as iron, lifting her up, and his mouth roamed downward, nudging aside the cloth of her dress to press into the soft curve of her breast. Marianne let out a sound almost like a sob, digging her fingers into his hair.

Justin jerked away from her with a heartfelt oath. "We can't—not here," he panted. His eyes were bright and feral, his face flushed, and his chest rose and fell in quick bursts. "We—I—my house is nearby."

It had been all Marianne could do not to cry out at the loss of his clever hands and mouth. Now she stood staring at him, trying to make sense of his words. It took a moment before their meaning sank in: he was suggesting that they retire to his house, where this moment of passion could reach its natural conclusion. It was what all her senses wanted to do, but her mind was at last working again, taking in the full import of what had just happened. He had offered her a position as his mistress as coldly and calculatedly as if she had been a merchant discussing wares with him, and when she had turned him down, he had ignored her wishes and kissed her, assuming like all the aristocracy, that he could have whatever he wanted.

It was both humiliating and infuriating that she had given in so easily, responding like the trollop he took her to be. Anger washed through her, as much at herself as at him, and it stiffened her spine. Steadfastly ignoring the sensations that still raged through her body, Marianne faced him, crossing her arms over her chest.

"No!" Her voice was filled with disgust, though she was not sure whether she was more disgusted with him or with herself. "I am no man's property. You cannot purchase me."

Justin let out a string of lurid oaths. "Bloody hell, woman, I do not want to buy you, I want to make love to you."

Everything in him cried out to have this woman. His fingers itched to grab her and drag her back against him and kiss her into submission. *How in the hell had he let this happen?* He had, once again, bungled what he had set out to do, exhibiting a clumsiness and gaucheness that were foreign to him. She had the most unsettling effect on him.

"Love?" Marianne asked scornfully. "I doubt you know the meaning of the word. This is only your base attempt to 'save' Lord Buckminster—or to best him. I'm not sure exactly what your aim is."

"My aim is to keep him out of the clutches of a heartless tease such as you," he retorted, desire, frustration and anger blending in a roiling maelstrom inside him.

"A tease? You force your kisses on me, and then you have the audacity to call me a 'tease'?"

"There was no force involved." Justin's lip curled. "You were as hot for me as I was for you."

Tears welled in Marianne's eyes, and she had to swallow hard to keep from bursting into sobs. The contempt in his voice matched her own contempt for herself. She whirled and hurried away.

Justin took a step after her, his hand going out. He thought he had seen a flash of tears in her eyes as she turned away, and guilt pierced him. He stopped as he heard Bucky's voice calling Marianne from the terrace. His hand curled in on itself, and he turned and walked away.

"I—I'm here, my lord," Marianne called back, forcing her voice to sound calm, even cheerful, as she hastily smoothed her hair and clothes into place. She hoped her lips did not look as tender and well-kissed as they felt.

Bucky trotted down the steps to the garden to meet her, his brow creased in concern. "You should not be out here all alone, Mrs. Cotterwood."

"Oh, I do not think there is any danger." Marianne smiled. "I—I was feeling a trifle ill. It was so close inside. So I came out for a breath of air, hoping it would make me feel better. Would you—do you possibly think you could take me home, Lord Buckminster?"

His lordship was more than happy to do so, though he expressed a great deal of concern over Marianne's health.

It was not until they were in his carriage and headed toward her home that it occurred to her that she had not made even the smallest attempt to discover the layout of the house in which the party had been held or what treasures it might contain. She closed her eyes, letting Buckminster's inconsequential chatter flow unnoticed.

It was all Lord Lambeth's fault, of course. He had her in such a state that she could not even think straight, let alone look for safes and entry routes and easily portable, expensive items. She burned with anger and a tremendous desire for revenge on Lord Lambeth. Somehow he had slipped under her guard and aroused feelings and sensations in her that she had thought were long dead. She was a fool, she told herself, for letting herself be lured into passion by another nobleman. All they cared about was themselves and their own desires, and the people of the lower classes might as well be animals for all they thought about them. Lambeth was just like the others: he desired her, but he felt contempt for her. He thought she could be paid for like an object in a shop, and no doubt just as easily used and discarded.

Hatred seared through her. She wanted to hurt Lambeth…to humiliate him as he had humiliated her tonight. It would be wonderful beyond all things, she thought, if she could make him fall in love with her. She imagined his face as he poured out his heart to her, telling her that he could not live without her. And then, of course, in this delightful vision, she would scorn him, crush his heart beneath her heel. That would satisfy her burning resentment.

Unfortunately, she admitted to herself in the next instant, sending the dream crashing to the ground, such a thing would never happen. Lambeth was incapable of falling in love with anyone; he had no heart.

She could hurt him through Bucky, of course. Marianne glanced at Bucky's amiable face. Lambeth would be furious if she actually did as she had threatened and encouraged Bucky to love her. However, she knew that she could not do that. Buckminster, even if he was a lord, was too nice a man for her to purposely set out to hurt him. It was one thing to taunt Lambeth with the idea and make him worry and stew over it, but she hadn't the heart to actually do it. Besides, it was obvious to her that Penelope was in love with Lord Buckminster, and it would break her heart to see him in love with another woman. She could not do that to Penelope, either.

The only other idea she could come up with was to steal something precious to Lambeth. Perhaps at the party she could learn what he really valued, and then she could arrange for Harrison and Piers to take it from him. The problem there would be that she would be the first person he would suspect, and she doubted that he would have any compunction about sending the constabulary after her and her friends. The only reason he hadn't done so already was because he was hopeful of getting her into his bed.

Her house was ablaze with lights when they approached. Marianne knew with a sinking heart that everyone would be awaiting news of the house she was supposed to have checked out this evening. *How was she to explain to them that she had not done it?*

It was something of a relief when she walked into the house after bidding Lord Buckminster a quick, platonic goodbye, to find that the house was in a commotion and no one even asked what had happened at her party.

No one was at the door to greet her, and when she

tracked them down by the noise of their excited babble, she found them in the kitchen, all gathered around a young woman who sat at the table, a snifter of brandy on the table before her. She was a pretty girl, with fair skin and red-gold hair, dressed in a severe gray dress ornamented by a white apron that looked like the uniform of a maid. She had obviously been crying, for there were tear tracks staining her cheeks, and her eyes were red, her lashes stuck together starrily. Piers was standing beside her looking fierce, and everyone was talking at once, listening to no one else.

"What is going on?" No one turned toward her, and Marianne had to repeat her words in a louder voice.

Della swiveled around and saw her. "Marianne! It's just dreadful!"

"What is? What happened? Who is this?"

The girl looked up at her, her face a trifle awed by the picture of a grand lady that Marianne presented in her ball gown. "Oh, Miss. I'm sorry."

She started to rise, but Marianne motioned the girl back down. "What's the matter?"

"This is Iris," Winny explained. "She lives down the street. She's a ladies' maid at the Cunninghams'. Someone attacked her on the street!"

"What? Here?" Marianne was astounded. Theirs was a very respectable, quiet neighborhood, not the sort of place where people were attacked on the street.

"You mean someone tried to—"

"He tried to strangle me, Miss," the girl exclaimed. "Right outside."

"Outside of our house?"

The girl nodded emphatically. "Right in front of the house next door. I had just left here, and he jumped out of the bushes right at me and put his hands around me throat. I was that scared, I'll tell you!"

"I should imagine so. What happened?"

Iris turned toward Piers, her eyes shining. "Piers saved me."

"I should have walked you home," Piers said, guilt written plain on his face.

Iris took his hand and held it to her cheek. "No. It wasn't your fault. I didn't want you to walk me home—the master and missus wouldn't like it."

"So you were here at this house."

"Yes, I was…talking to Iris just outside the back door," Piers said, a faint flush rising in his cheeks.

Flirting was more like it, Marianne thought, but she said nothing. This obviously wasn't the time for levity.

"I heard her cry out a moment after she reached the front of the house," Piers continued, "so I ran out and found them. I punched the scoundrel, of course, and he dropped her and ran off." He scowled at the memory. "I wish I'd caught the devil, but I couldn't run after him and leave Iris lying there."

"Of course not," Della agreed.

"How awful!" A shiver ran through Marianne. It shook her to think of something like that happening here. It could have happened to any of them just as easily. First that man asking the maid and Rosalind about her, and now this… Her home no longer seemed a safe haven.

"Do you think it could be the same man?" she asked Winny the next morning, sitting at the kitchen table and sharing a cup of tea with her old friend.

"The same man as who?" Winny asked, looking at her in some surprise.

"The one who spoke to Nettie and Rosalind in the Park yesterday."

"What?" Winny's eyebrows went up.

"Didn't you know? They were talking about it yesterday afternoon when they came in." Marianne went on to describe the encounter between the stranger and her daughter in the Park. By the time she finished, Winny was scowling.

"That sly boots!" Winny exclaimed. "Nettie somehow 'forgot' to mention that to me. I've warned her about talking to strangers—and letting them talk to Rosalind! I'll have a little talk with her she won't soon forget."

"But do you think that's the man who attacked Iris last night?"

"Why would he attack Iris?" Winny pointed out. "It's you he's after, isn't it?"

"Yes, but doesn't it seem awfully coincidental that he's there, talking to Nettie and Rosalind, asking them about Mary Chilton, thinking she's a maid, and then that evening a maid leaving our house gets attacked?"

"Either one of them's odd," Winny said. "It does seem reasonable to think that they're connected, but—why attack Iris?"

"What if he only wanted to question her, but she took it wrong, got scared and started to scream, and then he just tried to silence her? Or…"

She hesitated and glanced at Winny. "This may sound a little far-fetched, but—did you notice the color of Iris's hair, that red-gold hue?" Winny nodded. "Well, what if in the dark, it looked more red than gold? What if you were after someone with red hair and knew where they lived, but didn't really know what they looked like?"

"You mean, what if he thought Iris was you?"

"It's possible, don't you think?"

Winny's gaze was troubled. "But why? Why would someone who doesn't even know you be looking for you? And then try to kill you?"

"I don't know! It doesn't seem very likely, does it? Yet..."

Winny nodded. "I know. It is suspicious." She sighed. "I don't like it."

"How do you think I feel?"

"Mama! Mama!" Rosalind ran into the room, her face flushed with excitement.

"What is it?" Marianne jumped up from her seat in alarm.

"I saw him!"

"Who?"

"The man who asked about you yesterday! Come here." She started from the room, gesturing impatiently. "Come here."

Marianne followed her daughter out of the kitchen and up the stairs, Winny right behind them. Rosalind led them to Della and Harrison's room at the front of the house. Della was standing at the window, but well back, looking out. She turned at their approach.

"He's still there," Della said, frowning. "Who could he be?"

"I was in here with Aunt Della," Rosalind explained, "and I looked out the window, and I saw him! He was just standing there."

She took her mother's hand and led her to the window. Della stepped back to make room for them, and Marianne looked out. The street looked much as it usually did, except that there was a short, rather rotund man standing across the street, leaning against the fence of the house opposite them.

"He walked up the street and back once, but the rest of

the time he just stands there and looks at our house! What does he want, Mama? Is he a bad man?"

"Yes, I am afraid he might be, sweetheart. Until we know for sure, you stay well away from him. Do you understand? I don't want you to leave the house—ever!—without Piers or Harrison with you. Not even with Nettie."

"All right, Mama, I won't." Rosalind nodded solemnly.

Marianne studied the man. She had never seen him before. He was not a fearsome-looking sort, just a plain man in an ill-fitting suit. But it sent a chill of fear through her to know that he was watching her house.

"Shall I go down and give him a piece of my mind?" Winny asked pugnaciously.

"No. I think it's best if we pretend that we don't see him. We want him to lose interest, and that would only stir it up. I will just take care not to let him see me, and no one will go out alone, as we discussed."

Just at that moment, the door of the house across the street opened, and a dignified butler came out and approached the man. He spoke sharply to the loiterer, and after a brief conversation, the watcher reluctantly moved off.

Marianne chuckled. "Perhaps the neighbors will take care of him for us."

"It's a good thing you're going to that fellow's party in a few days," Winny said, moving up beside Marianne. "If someone is after you, they won't know to look there."

Marianne turned around. "I can't go now! How could I leave Rosalind here in danger—or you and the others, either! How could you think I would?"

"*We* are not in danger," Winny pointed out. "If you are right, the only reason Iris was attacked was the color of her hair, and none of us would ever be mistaken for you.

Indeed, if you are not here, we would probably be safer, for he wouldn't injure one of us trying to get to you."

"Oh." Winny's argument did have a certain sense to it, Marianne had to admit. Perhaps she was endangering the rest of her "family" by being here.

"If he hangs about outside somewhere waiting for a redhead to emerge, then he will have a very long wait," Della put in. "And I promise you that I will not let Rosalind out of the house with anyone unless Piers or Harrison goes, too, to protect them."

"Don't any of you go out alone," Marianne added. "At least go in twos, and preferably with Piers or Harrison along."

Winny nodded. "We will. And if he has the nerve to come up to the door and ask about you, I shall tell him that you don't live here anymore." She paused, then grinned. "But first I'll ask him why he's looking for you."

Marianne smiled in response. "All right. That will make me feel easier about going to Buckminster."

It would be impossible to feel entirely easy, of course, what with Lord Lambeth being there. But Marianne was determined to put aside these foolish feelings she had been having. She would approach the country party as a purely business opportunity. She would diagram the house and check out the location of the valuables so well that it would make up for the fact that she hadn't even investigated Nicola Falcourt's home last night. It was the height of stupidity, she told herself, for her to worry about Bucky or Penelope, or to feel guilty about using them. They would spurn her if they knew who she really was. As for Lord Lambeth...well, she did not even want to think about him. She would avoid him as much as she could. Surely, in a large house party, that would be possible. And once she got through this party, hopefully she would never have to see the obnoxious man again.

THE EARL OF EXMOOR'S CARRIAGE STOPPED, and the man who had been standing on the street corner got in. He took off his hat, shaking the droplets of water from it, and settled himself on the seat across from Exmoor.

"You failed," the Earl commented without preamble. His face was impassive, but one who knew him could have seen the signs of bad temper in the compression of his lips and the tightening of his nostrils. "Not only did you not finish the job, you didn't even get the right person."

"I told you that you should have used a professional," the other man pointed out with some irritation, looking away from the Earl. "I am not in the habit of murdering people."

"I believe I explained to you why I do not wish to involve any person in this for money. I will allow no man to have that sort of hold on me."

"The sort of hold you have on me, you mean?"

The faintest of smiles moved across the Earl's lips. "Precisely." He paused, then continued. "You will have to try again."

"I cannot continue hanging about, hoping that a red-headed woman will walk out the door!" the man burst out.

"Fortunately, I have learned that our friend Mrs. Cotterwood is planning to attend Lord Buckminster's country party next week. That empty-headed fool dropped in this morning to inquire after my wife, and he was kind enough to invite Lady Exmoor and me to several of the larger functions during the visit. Our country seat is near Buckminster, and Lady Exmoor is his cousin. I suppose that I will have to return to the country so that I can go to them."

"Then you can do the job yourself," his companion suggested.

"Out of the question. I cannot appear to have anything to do with it. I shall spend my time creating unshakable alibis for myself. No. What you need to do is get yourself invited to Buckminster's party. That shouldn't be too difficult. You know the fellow, don't you? Bucky's a lamentably friendly soul, it shouldn't be hard to wangle an invitation."

"It's absurd. We don't even know if it's the right woman."

"Oh, it's the right one all right—the similarity of names, a child of the right age, the red hair. But I will meet her and make sure of it. I am sure I can see if there is any family resemblance."

"I am not a killer," the other man ground out. "I cannot do it. I had the shakes for hours afterward last night, and I didn't even kill that girl. It's utterly impossible."

"Stop being such a sniveler. Of course you can do it if the stakes are high enough. You are the sort who can do all manner of base acts if you are in danger. And, believe me, you are in danger."

"I would rather take my chances on them finding her and her remembering what I did."

"And do you want to take your chances on details of your past life being made available to certain persons?"

"You wouldn't. You can't tell anyone without implicating yourself."

"I wasn't speaking of getting rid of the children. I was referring to your consumption of opium. Your gambling and drinking and whoring. Oh, Society knows you were a trifle wild in your youth, but I don't believe anyone is aware of the depths of degradation to which you sank." A smile played across his lips.

"You enjoy this, don't you?" his companion burst out. "You like destroying people! You get pleasure out of making them squirm."

"It does alleviate the boredom. Well, sir, what is it to be? Are you going to do the job—correctly this time—or will certain people be receiving packets of information about your former activities?"

"All right! I'll do it, damn you!"

"Excellent. I was sure you would see the light." Richard tapped with his cane on the roof of the carriage, and it came to a halt.

With a low growl, the other man bolted out the door, and the carriage rolled off again.

CHAPTER EIGHT

MARIANNE LEFT THE NEXT WEEK FOR Buckminster Hall, traveling in a carriage with Penelope and Nicola. Lord Buckminster and Lord Lambeth accompanied them, riding their horses beside the carriage. Both Lord Buckminster and Lord Lambeth had come to call on her during the intervening days, but Marianne had left strict instructions to tell them that she was out. She spent most of her time with Della and one of the maids, making sure that all her best clothes were mended, cleaned and packed for the long visit. She needed several different gowns, for there would be all sorts of activities, from a ball held for the guests and the local gentry, for which she would need an elegant gown, to riding, archery, hiking and dinners, which would require evening dress only slightly less fancy than a party. Even her nightdress and dressing gown needed to be of the finest quality and style, since she would be spending several nights there, and there was even the possibility that she might have to share a room with Penelope in order to meet Lady Ursula's strict chaperonage requirements.

Marianne took care of the mending, sewing on ripped flounces and replacing tired-looking ribbons with something brighter, adding flowers to a neckline or a new sash to a dressing gown, or a bit of embroidery to a cotton chemise to make it more elegant. Della, who was rather good with a needle, and Winny, worked fast and furiously at sewing two new walking dresses, while the talented seamstress who usually made Marianne's gowns did a rush job on a sky-blue riding habit and a stunning new ballgown of deep emerald green velvet. There was also a good bit of shopping to do, for there were gloves, stockings, ribbons, hats and other necessities to buy in order to be ready for continuous scrutiny by the gentry.

Marianne's mind had been busily at work while she went about her tasks, devising a plan to rid Buckminster of his infatuation with her. She told herself that she was not doing it to help poor Penelope; it would only be a hindrance to have Lord Buckminster always around, dancing attendance on her. She would hardly get a chance to explore the house.

As for Lambeth…well, she dreamed up and discarded plan after plan for delicious revenge. None of them seemed quite adequate, somehow. Only Justin down on his knees, begging, would satisfy her, and no matter how pleasant the daydream, her mind always seemed to balk before she could reach that image.

Penelope had invited Marianne to ride to Buckminster with her and Nicola. However, it was something of a shock when she walked out the door and saw Lambeth and Buckminster waiting outside, as well. Both men had dismounted and stood holding their horses' reins, and they bowed to her. Marianne acknowledged Lambeth's bow with a cool, slight nod, but she gave a warm smile and her hand to Buckminster. She watched Lambeth out of the corner of her eye but could see no change of expression at her friendliness with Bucky.

Bucky solicitously handed her up into the carriage, where Nicola sat waiting, and Lambeth gave Penelope a hand up. Nicola greeted her with a certain coolness, Marianne thought. Nicola had seemed friendly enough the other night at the party. Marianne wondered if something had happened since then to make her wary. Could Lord Lambeth have revealed the truth about Marianne to her? Marianne squirmed inside at the thought.

Buckminster bid Marianne goodbye with a sappy grin, waving a casual hand to Nicola and Penelope, then closed the door, and the two men mounted their horses. The carriage rumbled off down the street.

"Bucky is quite smitten with you," Penelope said, and Marianne shot her a quick glance.

She wondered if Penelope was angry with her, but one look at the girl's face dispelled that notion. She was trying valiantly to look pleased at the idea, but her smile had a telltale tremble.

"Men are always chasing after a new female. It rarely lasts, I find. I have no interest in Lord Buckminster."

"Really?" Nicola drawled. "I thought you were quite friendly toward him."

So that was what made Nicola cool toward her. The fact raised her in Marianne's estimation. Penelope was too self-effacing to be angry with her about Bucky, but her friend resented it on her behalf.

"Oh, that…" Marianne waved a hand. "I am friendly for the moment. It is part of my plan, you see."

"What plan?" Penelope asked.

"Why, to end his lordship's crush," Marianne explained. Nicola's eyebrows rose, and Penelope looked astounded.

"What—what do you mean?" she asked.

"I wasn't sure what to do at first," Marianne began. "I mean, Lord Buckminster obviously has no real affection for me. He hardly knows me. He is suffering from the sort of calf-love that men seem to fall into now and then. And I have no interest in him. It is just as obvious that Penelope is the perfect one for him. He simply has not realized it yet."

Penelope stared at her, a blush rising in her cheeks. "Oh, no. Bucky doesn't care for me—I mean, well, yes, he cares, but in the same way that he cares for Nicola or—or for a sister. He is quite kind to me."

"I think it is more than kindness. Why, think of the fuss he made the other day when your mama wasn't going to let you come. If he was merely being kind, he might have made a token protest, but he would have dropped it. After all, he is rather awed by Lady Castlereigh, I think."

Nicola was surprised into a snort of laughter. "Terrified is more like it."

Even Penelope had to smile. "Yes, he is, rather. Mother can be pretty terrifying."

"Then he must have been quite concerned about your not coming if he risked a dressing-down from your mother for interfering."

"Do you really think so?" Penelope could not keep the hope from rising in her voice. Nicola was watching Marianne consideringly.

"Yes, I think he is very fond of you. But, as I said, he simply has not awakened to it yet." Marianne found herself warming to her subject. It was not difficult to do, with Penelope gazing at her with such rapt attention. Penelope was such a sweet little thing, it was impossible not to like her. "Therefore we have to help him realize it."

"And how do you propose to do that?" Nicola asked, but Marianne noticed that the faintly cynical tone was missing from her voice now.

"Well, I thought if I am icy and rejecting, he is all too likely to go mooning about and fancying himself still in love with me and suffering unrequitedly."

"That's true." Nicola nodded. "Bucky is not as romantic as some, but when he gets his head set on something, he is hard to turn."

"The only thing to do, then, is to make him fall out of love with me. Then he will be heart-whole, ready and able to fall in love with Penelope. It will be even better if, along the way, we can also throw him together with Penelope."

"But how do you intend to accomplish that?" Penelope asked, wide-eyed. "I have never seen Bucky so head over heels."

"I intend to be heartless, domineering and demanding. I shall blow hot-and-cold, a heartless flirt. I shall whine and complain. I shall demand that he dance attendance on me—especially when there is something else he would far rather do."

"Hunting," Nicola supplied. "The men always go hunting at these things."

Marianne smiled at her conspiratorially. "Hunting it will be, then. Before long, I suspect that Lord Buckminster will be thoroughly sick of me and looking for some other fellow to take me off his hands."

"Capital!" Nicola clapped her hands together, grinning. "I will be happy to help in any way I can."

"Wonderful. Then you can engage me in conversation around him that will show what a thoroughly shallow person I am. We can work out just what to say."

"Yes, and if we could do it so that Penelope, on the other hand, looks compassionate and kind and wonderful…"

"Exactly."

Nicola and Marianne smiled at each other in perfect agreement. All traces of reserve had fled from Nicola's manner now. Her blue eyes sparkled, and her cheeks were high with color.

"This is a perfectly marvelous idea," Nicola told her.

"Thank you."

"That's very good," Penelope said uncertainly. "I mean, I can see how it would be easier on Bucky if he could be led to believe that you are not a nice person, instead of his suffering unrequited love for you. But how is that going to make him fall in love with me?"

"Ah, but that is the beauty of it. You are going to be right there, precisely where and when he needs you. When he wants to talk, you will be there to listen and sympathize, to give him loving support."

"But that is not enough to make him love me," Penelope told her softly. "I am sure if I were someone like you, it would be. But, well, look at me. I am not beautiful. I am not enchanting. I have tried to make myself over. Nicola has lent me dresses and tried to teach me how to flirt, but I was no good at it."

"Don't make yourself over," Marianne told her firmly. "That is your first mistake. You see, Bucky already likes you for who you are. He just needs to see that that person is the one he is really in love with. You shall be so refreshingly the opposite of me. Where I will be cruel and uncaring, you will be warm and sympathetic. I will be shallow, you will be kind. I will be interested in talking about nothing but myself, you will listen to whatever he wants to say. How can he help but warm to you? Nicola and I shall see that he will have every opportunity to be thrown together with you and to see what a wonderful contrast you are to me."

Penelope smiled. "Well, if you think so…"

"I definitely do. As for your looks—a different hairstyle would help."

"I can do that," Nicola said confidently. "And you have no idea how much it improves your looks to be away from your mama, Pen. You just brighten up all over. A new hairdo, pinch your cheeks a little…"

"And I can lend you some of my dresses," Marianne offered. "White washes you out."

"I know. Mother insists I wear it—she says it's the only appropriate color for a young girl. I keep telling her I'm not so young anymore."

"I can also see that the kind of pastels that look beautiful with Nicola's blond coloring would still leave you…a trifle dull. But I have some deeper blues and greens that I think would look quite good on you—and rose, definitely rose."

"I believe you're right," Nicola agreed. "Even at the time, I wished that my pinks and blues were not so…icy. She's right, too, about being yourself, Penny. What good would it be if Bucky fell in love with some person you are pretending to be? He must fall in love with you as you are if you expect to be happy the rest of your life."

They spent the rest of the trip happily chattering away, making plans for their charade and wandering off along intersecting paths concerning clothes, hair and men. At some point Lord Lambeth entered the conversation.

"Now there is a handsome devil," Nicola commented.

"Very," Penelope agreed, and grinned mischievously at

Marianne. "I would say that he has definitely had his eye on you, too."

"True," Nicola agreed, but added warningly, "However, they say that he will marry Cecilia, and I am sure that's true. That family never marries for love. He's the sort who will break your heart."

"I know. I have no intention of falling into his *trap*."

"But, oh, those eyes!" Penelope sighed dramatically, and the other two women laughed.

"Yes. Damn those eyes."

By the time the carriage pulled into an inn a few hours later to change horses, the ladies emerged from the vehicle fast friends. True to her stated intention, Marianne largely ignored Bucky and flirted outrageously with Lord Lambeth. His lordship looked faintly surprised at the first languishing look she sent him from under her lashes as she stretched out her hand to take his to descend from the carriage, but after that he kept up his end of the flirtation. He flattered her and made outlandish compliments as they made their way into the inn and sat down to a light luncheon, all the while watching her in a lazy, cynical way that made it clear that he did not take her seriously for a moment.

"Doing it rather too brown, aren't you?" he commented under his breath as she took his arm to be escorted back out to the carriage.

Marianne looked at him with faint disdain. "I am sure I don't know what you are talking about."

"This little attempt of yours to make Bucky jealous by flirting with me."

"It never crossed my mind."

"Mmm. I am sure it did not. Well, it's working rather well. He looks positively green."

"Personally, I've never cared for green gentlemen."

His brows rose a little. "Mrs. Cotterwood! I am shocked. Was that a double entendre?"

"What? No. What are you talking about?" Marianne blurted out, surprised. Then understanding of the sexual undertones that could be applied to her statement dawned on her, and she flushed. "No! I had no such intent."

The warm laughter in his eyes made her blush all the more. Marianne scowled at him. "You are a rude, crude man, and I cannot imagine why I have been wasting my time talking to you."

She pulled her hand away and stalked off to the carriage by herself. Bucky hastened to help her up into the vehicle, and she smiled at him.

"Thank you, my lord. At least some men are *gentlemen*." She flashed a dark look at Lord Lambeth, who was standing a few feet away and smiling at her in a most irritating way.

THEY SPENT THE NIGHT AT AN INN IN the country, where Nicola, Penelope and Marianne had to share a room. As the public room of the inn was filled with locals drinking and there were no private rooms downstairs, the women also took their meal on trays in their bedchamber. Marianne was relieved not to have to spend the evening with either Lambeth or Buckminster, who joined the locals downstairs. The next day, the carriage rumbled on through the countryside to Dartmoor.

It was late afternoon when they arrived at the Buckminster estate, a large, rambling building of yellowish stone, warmly lit by the setting sun. Grooms came running to take Bucky's and Lord Lambeth's horses. The front door was

thrown open by a footman, and a dignified butler came out
to greet Lord Buckminster. He was followed by an older
woman, comfortably round, who met Buckminster with
considerably less restraint. She threw her arms around the
young man and kissed him soundly on both cheeks,
babbling and crying all the while. Marianne would have
taken her to be his mother by her actions, but she knew
from the woman's plain dress, rolled up to the elbows to
reveal red, work-hardened hands, that she could not be
Lady Buckminster.

Nicola looked out at the scene and smiled. "Ah, I see
Nurse is still here. Whenever Bucky comes home, she cries
as if he had been away at the wars instead of living in
London for a few months."

Lord Lambeth came over to help the women down from
the carriage, since Buckminster was more than occupied
by the greetings of the servants, whose number had now
grown to include the housekeeper and the gamekeeper,
who came up from the kennels with a variety of dogs
frisking around him and adding their voices to the din.

A woman's voice boomed across the yard, rising above
the babble. "Bucky! Egad, boy, bring your guests in, then.
Don't leave them standing out in the sun."

Marianne looked up to see a middle-aged woman
standing on the steps, a whole brood of toy spaniels spilling
out the door after her and tumbling around her skirts. Dis-
regarding the fact that she had just told them to come inside,
she came down the steps toward the new arrivals, her plain,
weathered face wreathed in smiles. Lady Buckminster was
a large woman, built along the lines of her son, and she was
obviously no slave to fashion. She was dressed in boots and
a riding habit of a rust-brown color and a cut at least ten

years out of date. Her iron-gray hair was braided and wrapped around her head in a simple coronet, and her skin was not the soft white of most ladies, but tanned and wind-burned, with deep lines scored around her eyes and mouth.

She gave Buckminster a buss on the cheek, then moved on to the carriage and shook Lambeth's hand in a jovial, no-nonsense manner. "Good to see you again, Lambeth. Carter's promised me a decent hunt. Too early for it, of course, but we shall make the best of it, won't we?"

She turned to the women. "Nicola, my girl. It has been far too long since we've seen you here. You're looking thin, girl. We shall have to fatten you up, eh, Mrs. Waterhouse?" She threw the comment over her shoulder toward the housekeeper. "And, Penny, child, so glad you could come."

"Thank you. I am sorry Mother could not make it, but she had pressing—"

Lady Buckminster waved away the rest of the statement, declaring bluntly, "You will have a far better time without her. I always tell Ursula she's got you on too tight a rein. But then, she always was cowhanded—horses, and people, too." She turned toward Marianne. "And you must be Mrs. Cotterwood. Bucky's note was full of references to you, though half the time I couldn't make out what he meant. Boy has a terrible scrawl at the best of times. My, but you're a pretty chit. I can see what caught my boy's eye. Welcome to Buckminster. Do you ride?"

"When I get a chance," Marianne equivocated. She had taken lessons a few years ago and had managed to ride decently, but she never had a chance to practice. "I am afraid that I don't maintain a stable."

"Hard to, in the City," Lady Buckminster sympathized. "Terrible place. Never go there myself. Don't worry. We shall put you up on a good mount. Have you riding like Penelope here in no time." She grinned at the slight girl beside Marianne. "You wouldn't think it, but Penny can ride like a centaur. Course, she always stays well away from the kill. Ha!"

She whipped around and strode off toward the house, calling, "Come inside, then. No point in standing around out here like a bunch of ninnies. Might as well have tea."

They trooped in after her. Penelope looped her arm through Marianne's and said in a quiet voice, "Don't worry. She shan't force you to ride if you don't want to. Lady B is horse-mad, as you have no doubt guessed, but she is quite kind, as well. She feels pity for those who don't like to ride, but she doesn't get angry with them."

"I don't mind riding. I just haven't much experience. I mean, well, of course I rode when I was younger, but I have lived in London—or Bath—for the past ten years, and it is rather difficult to keep a stable there."

"I know. We don't, either, except for Mother's carriage and the team that pulls it."

"Aunt Adelaide is a dear," Nicola said warmly. "She's been very kind to me. After my father died, Mama and I moved in here with them. Our house, you see, was entailed, and I had no brother. It went to my cousin, whose wife and Mama did not get along. Later Mama got a house in London, but I stayed with Aunt Adelaide and Bucky. I was very happy here." She smiled reminiscently, but Marianne thought there was a certain sadness in her eyes, as well.

Inside they found that two of the other guests had already arrived. Lady Buckminster introduced them as Sir George Merridale and his wife Sophronia. Sir George was a plain, quiet man in his early forties, with blond, thinning hair and the sort of beaky, bony face that bespoke his ancient Norman heritage. His wife, though equally plain, was his opposite in every other way. Where he was tall and thin, she was short and plump, dark to his fair, and incessantly talking. By the time Marianne had known her ten minutes, she knew that they had three children— Alice, Frederick and George, Jr., whom they called for some unknown reason Wiffy—and that only George, Jr., was old enough to go off to school, the others being at home with their governess; that Lady Merridale had a terrible servant problem; and that she was thinking of hiring French help.

When the woman asked Marianne her opinion, she was at a loss for words. "Well...I'm not sure. I have never employed anyone French."

To her relief, Nicola intervened, "I feel sure, Lady Merridale, that French servants would probably be no better than English ones, I'm afraid."

"Do you think so?" the woman asked worriedly. She lifted a beringed hand to her head and pushed back a strand of hair.

Marianne had noticed, having nothing better to do while the woman jabbered, that Sophronia Merridale was dripping with jewels. She wore three rings on one hand and four on the other, each one set with some sort of stone, the largest being a flashing diamond. A bracelet of emeralds shone on her wrist, along with a jangling set of bangles, and matching emeralds dangled from her ears, surrounded by a circle of tiny diamonds. It was, Marianne noted, one of the gaudiest displays of wealth she had ever seen, particularly given the more austere style of the present day.

She felt a movement by her side, and a masculine voice whispered in her ear, "Contemplating the removal of some of Lady Merridale's jewelry?"

She looked up into Lambeth's dancing golden eyes. She couldn't keep herself from smiling. "I think it would be an improvement, don't you?"

"Oh, I agree. Perhaps we could plan it together."

Marianne had to remind herself that she disliked this man. *How could he be so charming one moment and so despicable the next?*

"I was hoping you would do me the honor of letting me show you around the grounds," Lambeth went on, his lips curving in a way that did odd things to Marianne's insides. "They are quite lovely."

"Why, yes," Marianne acquiesced. At this moment she thought she would have agreed to a stroll with the devil to get away from Lady Merridale's incessant chatter. "It would be nice to stretch my legs."

"What a splendid idea!" Lady Merridale cried, hearing him. "Why don't we all go? George, dear…"

Marianne cast a sideways glance at Lambeth, who was gazing at Lady Merridale in a frozen way. He glanced back at Marianne, and she had to hide a smile.

"I believe that I will stay here and catch up with Aunt Adelaide," Nicola said, not bothering to hide her mischievous grin.

The others went out to the garden, for Lord Buckminster obviously was determined to go wherever Marianne went, and Penelope could not keep herself from following Lord Buckminster. Marianne took Lambeth's arm, however, leaving him to squire Penelope.

"I am afraid that I am used to rather brisk walks, my

lord," Marianne said loudly as they walked out the side door. "I find it beneficial to the constitution."

"I shall endeavor to keep up," Lambeth assured her gravely.

She matched her words by striding off as fast she could go, leaving Sophronia and the others behind. They rounded a hedge several feet in front of the rest of the party, and Lambeth pulled her off the path.

"This way," he said, taking Marianne's hand and starting across the grass almost at a run. They rounded the end of the hedge before the others appeared and stopped to catch their breath, hiding behind the greenery.

They listened to the sound of Sophronia's voice as the others followed the path in the opposite direction. Marianne let out a sound of relief, part sigh and part laugh.

"Thank heavens! I was afraid they had seen us," she said, unfurling her fan and beginning to ply it. "I feel terribly guilty for leaving poor Penelope with her, but I could not take it a moment longer."

Marianne's cheeks were flushed, and her eyes sparkled, and strands of her hair had slipped free from their pins in her rush and were curling damply around her face.

Lambeth's eyes darkened as he gazed down at her, and the teasing words he had been about to speak died on his lips. He reached up and brushed his knuckles down her cheek, his mouth growing softer and wider. "You are beautiful."

Marianne stepped back quickly. "Sir! You have gotten the wrong idea. I did not come to the garden to be secluded with you. I meant what I said to you the other night. If you mean to badger me—"

"No. I assure you. I did not misunderstand. I am quite aware that it was only desperation to leave Lady Merridale that drove you to run away with me. I did not mean to say that. The words just slipped out, as truth has a way of doing. I will not say anything else about it."

As if to show his good intent, he held out his arm formally for her to take, and when she did so after a brief hesitation, he set off toward the small rose garden a few yards away from them.

Justin was no fool, nor was he unaware of the ways of women. He knew that he had stumbled badly in his dealings with Marianne at Nicola's party last week—not once, but twice. He had been entirely too blunt, even gauche. Obviously warning her away from Buckminster had gotten her back up, and then his proposal to put her under his protection had been delivered with a lack of polish that confounded him. He could not remember when he had mishandled an affair so badly. There was something about Marianne that seemed to bring out the worst in him, that turned him into a callow youth again.

He was still convinced that the best way to keep her from getting her clutches on Bucky was to win her favors himself, a goal that also conformed to his own desires. If he exercised better control over himself, he thought, he could still bring it off. But first, he knew, he would have to make amends to her. That it would not be an easy process was clear from the wary look in her eyes.

"Mrs. Cotterwood, I must apologize for my actions the other night, the things I said. Clearly I was mistaken as to your character."

"Clearly." Marianne gave him a sideways look that held little belief in his sincerity.

"I said things I should not have. No doubt you think me a fool or a villain."

"Or both," Marianne added pleasantly.

He glanced at her in surprise, then lapsed into a grin. "I can see you have no intention of making this easy for me."

"I see no reason why I should."

"I understand." He sighed. "Please accept my heartfelt apology, Mrs. Cotterwood. I spoke precipitously. I see now how wrong I was."

"Do you?" Marianne asked cynically. "And what caused this great transformation in your thinking?"

He hadn't expected her to ask him this, and for a moment Justin was set back. "Well…it was the anger with which you rejected me. I realized that I had missaid your character. Obviously your principles were much higher than I had thought."

"That would scarcely be difficult," she pointed out dryly. "Since you thought me a thief, an adventuress and a prostitute."

"I would not put it that way."

"What other way is there to put it?" Marianne drew to a halt, so that he had to stop, too, and turned to face him. "Lord Lambeth, it is clear that you still take me for a goosecap. Do you expect me to believe that you have actually changed your opinion of me on the basis of nothing more than a few days' reflection? You accused me of stealing. You accused me of setting out to defraud your friend Bucky. Next you asked me to accept a carte blanche from you. It is obvious that you thought my virtue was for sale. And now you have decided that I am none of those things?"

"You *were* stealing," Justin was spurred to defend himself. "I walked in on you looking at the safe!"

"Did I take anything?"

"Of course not. I caught you before you could."

"Really, Lord Lambeth, what do you think I was going to do, stick the family plate under my skirts and walk out? Or would I just have stuffed it all in a pillowcase and slung it over my back? It is absurd."

"You could easily have taken a few pieces of jewelry. Or perhaps you were doing something else—examining the place for your friends, say. Once I met young Piers and the others, I realized that you probably were operating as part of a ring of thieves. What do you do—use your beauty and apparent refinement to get inside the houses of the wealthy? Then you can locate the valuables, including the safe, for your less elegant friends to break into the house some night and swipe? Rather a nice plan, actually. I can see how it would be of great benefit—makes for a quick in and out, less opportunity of discovery. What I can't decide is whether you have picked up the mannerisms and speech of a lady in order to play the role, or whether you were brought up as such and have since then fallen."

"It really doesn't matter to me what you think. But I wish you would stop trying to bamboozle me into thinking that you hold me in some esteem. The truth is that you think I am the lowest sort of person, that I would have no qualms about selling my body. As if the nobility were the only people who had any sort of morals!"

"I know that there are many good, honest people who are not noble or wealthy. But I would scarcely classify a thief or a pickpocket or a cardsharp as one of those!"

"At least you are being more honest. I realize what you think of me. Just don't try to gudgeon me into thinking that you regard me in any other light. Your only interest in me is to keep me from fixing Lord Buckminster's interest, and you would do almost anything—including plying me with flattery—to achieve that. Your tricks won't work, sir. Now, if you will excuse me, I believe that I will go back inside and see if someone will show me to my room."

She turned on her heel and strode away from him.

CHAPTER NINE

As MARIANNE STARTED DOWN THE STAIRS to join the others for supper, her eyes went to where Lambeth stood, chatting with another man, a few feet away from the door to the drawing room. He turned as she watched him and looked up at the stairs. Marianne quickly turned her head away, feeling a tell-tale blush creeping up her neck and hoping that he was too far away to see it. He would think that she had been looking for him—and, of course, she had to admit to herself that she had been, which made it even worse.

She glanced around the large entryway below, looking for Penelope or Nicola. Her stomach was dancing with nerves; she had never had to play her role in a situation like this, where she was with the people she was trying to deceive all the time. She could not let down her guard for even an instant. Her accent and carriage were second nature to her now; she wasn't really afraid of making a slip in that regard. But she knew it would be all too easy to let loose a statement that, while uttered in perfect tones, would reveal that she had not been raised a lady at all. An opinion that did not match that of an aristocratic woman, or the relation of an experience that a lady would not have had, or the expression of some sort of knowledge that would be forever out of the ken of a well-bred woman—any of those things could sink her.

Worst of all was the fact that she knew nothing about most of the people that they knew. It would not be strange not to know the people of this "set," of course, but they would know many people outside that group, and their names would come up in conversation, especially the prolonged sort of conversations that must take place at an extended party. It would look odd if she had to admit time and again that she did not know this person or that. She could pretend to know them, of course, but then, if somehow her lie came out, it would look even worse. The possibilities made her feel quite ill. So she looked for the comfort of a friend, not even noticing that she was regarding Penelope as a friend.

As she strolled across the entryway, she caught sight of Nicola and Penelope inside the drawing room itself, chatting with Lord Buckminster and a few other people. Penelope, she saw with some satisfaction, was looking much better tonight. That afternoon, she and Nicola had helped Penelope dress. Marianne had picked out a dinner gown in a dark, yellowish green that had suited Penelope's coloring. Its simple style did not overwhelm the girl with frills and furbelows, as most of the clothes her mother chose did. When Penelope was dressed, Nicola and her personal maid arranged Penelope's hair in a soft, pleasant style, pulled back to the crown of her head and falling in a few fat curls. Both the dress and the hairstyle suited her. But, Marianne thought, watching her, it was the increased color and animation in Penelope's face that really enhanced her looks, and that, Marianne felt sure, was largely a result of being out from under the watchful, censorious eye of her mother.

Marianne started toward the drawing room to join them, watching Lord Lambeth from the corner of her eye. Her heart speeded up as she wondered if he would intercept her before she reached the door, not quite sure whether she hoped that he would or would not. But then Buckminster came striding out the door, ending her speculation. He came toward her, beaming, and Marianne, aware of Lord Lambeth's gaze on her, returned the smile, holding out her hand to him.

"Lord Buckminster," she said gaily, as if she had not seen him in ages, as he bowed over her hand. Then she tucked her hand into his arm, leaning cozily in toward him. "Shall we walk a little?"

Buckminster was of course pleased to acquiesce to this desire, and they took a slow stroll around the wide central hall. It occurred to Marianne that she might as well begin her role-within-a-role. It wasn't really something she wanted to do, but she knew that it was the best way to quash Buckminster's infatuation with her.

She smiled up at him archly. "I am sure Miss Castlereigh must be fuming."

Bucky looked surprised. "Penelope? Why?"

"Why, because I have lured you away from her."

"Penelope? Oh, no. She's a good girl, Penelope, friend of mine for years."

Marianne let out a tinkling laugh and gave him a pitying look. "Oh, really, Lord Buckminster. The girl is in love with you."

It would do him good to be shaken up a little, Marianne thought. His way of thinking of Penelope as a chum was an impediment to his thinking of her as a woman he could love. Besides, Marianne had often noted that if a man discovered that someone had an interest in him, it often made him realize that perhaps he had an interest in her.

Buckminster looked at Marianne in astonishment. "No, you can't be right."

He turned to look back into the room at Penelope as if seeing her suddenly with new eyes. Then he shook his head firmly. "I am sure you are wrong."

Marianne shrugged coolly. "Of course she tries to hide it. She knows she hasn't a chance. Poor thing…it must be quite dreadful to be plain."

"Penelope isn't plain!" Lord Buckminster protested in shocked tones. He looked at Marianne in pained surprise. "I thought Penelope was your friend."

Marianne chuckled. "Why, Lord Buckminster, didn't you realize that a plain woman is the very best sort of friend for a woman to have? She is such a nice foil…and one never has to worry about her stealing your beaux."

Buckminster gaped at her, his pleasant face stamped with shock. Marianne sighed inside. She hated having to make the man dislike her. They strolled on for a moment, and a troubled frown replaced the shock on Buckminster's face.

After a moment, he said firmly, "I am sure you don't mean that, Mrs. Cotterwood."

"Heavens no, just a little jest," Marianne replied. She had not really expected Bucky's feelings to change in an instant, but she knew that her callous words would be like a worm inside him now, eating away at his regard for her. She began to flirt assiduously with him again. They were drawing close to Lambeth.

Lambeth and the other man bowed as they approached, and Buckminster stopped to introduce Marianne to the other man. He was Sir William Verst, one of Bucky's and Lambeth's friends, a horse-mad sort whose conversation primarily consisted of discussion of horses he owned and horses he was thinking of purchasing, with a few comments sprinkled in about horses someone else possessed.

Several other guests had arrived, and by the time they removed to the dining room for the meal, she had been introduced to most of them. Alan Thurston and his wife, Elizabeth, were there. Marianne had met them at Nicola's party the week before, and she remembered that he was standing for Parliament. He had brought his secretary with him this time, a Reginald Fuquay. Marianne wondered whether it was because he had so much political business to attend to that he could not spend even a week without working or without his secretary—or because he simply wanted to appear to be that harried and busy. Fuquay, Marianne thought, looked much more like a distinguished statesman than Thurston, who was short and balding. Fuquay, on the other hand, was tall and elegantly slim, with dark hair. He was also, Marianne thought, a more interesting conversationalist.

Besides Sir William, there were two other unattached males who were friends of Lord Buckminster. The two were invariably together and made an amusing contrast. Lesley Westerton was short and slightly pudgy, with thinning, overly long blond hair. He spoke at length and with an often biting wit. Lord Chesfield, on the other hand, was dark, tall, thin and almost disconcertingly quiet. Both, Lord Buckminster assured her, were "bang-up fellows," though he had to admit with some embarrassment that Westerton was not much of a rider. This, Marianne took it, was a flaw that loomed large with Bucky.

Rounding out their guest list were Edward Minton and his wife, an older couple who apparently had been invited by Bucky's mother, and the couple whom they

had met earlier in the afternoon, Sir George and Sophronia Merridale. Buckminster was quick to steer
Marianne away from them.

"Took me an hour to get free of them this afternoon,"
he confided sotto voce. "That woman talked so much it
made my ears hurt. Thank God Penelope was there, too."

He steered her in the direction of Penelope, who was
talking with the tandem of Lord Chesfield and Lesley
Westerton. Marianne, as soon as she was introduced to the
group, proceeded to flirt like mad with both men, though
it was Westerton who produced most of the banter. She
could sense Bucky's growing dismay beside her, but she
steeled herself to do the job. Subtly she edged away from
Buckminster, turning toward the other two men. After a
moment, she expressed an interest in viewing a certain
painting across the room, and obligingly Westerton offered
her his arm. Chesfield, of course, came with them.
Marianne resolutely kept her gaze away from Lord Buckminster as she left him to Penelope's sympathetic care.

Westerton, she suspected, was more interested in their
wordplay than he was in her, which fit her plans perfectly.
She had no desire to add another swain to complicate
matters. He was also, she found out, a great gossip. Sir
George Merridale, he informed her, had married the
voluble Sophronia for her fortune.

"Really?" Marianne turned speculative eyes on the pair.
Now there *was someone she would not feel any qualms
about taking possessions from.*

"Oh, yes," Westerton went on chattily. "Her grandfather
was a Cit, you know. He bought his daughter's way into a
marriage with some sort of minor gentry—fourth son of a
daughter of a baronet or some such thing. Went one better

with the granddaughter and hitched her to Merridale. Sir George was penniless, I hear."

"What about Mr. Thurston and his wife?" Marianne asked.

Westerton shrugged. "As far as I know, he is rather average in most ways. Decent family, decent money. I have heard he sowed a few wild oats when he was younger— who hasn't? But now he is a rather dull fellow. His secretary, now, comes from an old family, but no money. Intelligent fellow—I've talked to him. Then there's Verst— good gad, don't get him started on horses—though I suppose there's little else he's able to talk about."

Marianne chuckled. "You are rather hard on your fellow guests, aren't you?"

"I wouldn't say a word against Lambeth," Westerton protested, then added with a twinkle in his eyes, "Wouldn't dare. Fellow's dashed handy with his fists."

"Well, *I* think he is far too proud for his own good." Unconsciously she glanced across the room to where he lounged, elbow on the mantelpiece, talking to Lady Buckminster. He laughed at something the older woman said, his face alight with affection, and Marianne was aware of a twist of pain in her chest. *What would it be like to have Lambeth look at her like that?*

Westerton arched a brow. "My, my, what do we have here? Has the future Duke of Storbridge made a misstep with you? Usually he's a favorite with the females."

"Not this female. I found him rude and arrogant."

"What did he do? I am all agog."

Marianne made a dismissive gesture with her hand. She had revealed too much by her statement. The last thing she wanted was for the gossipy Westerton to start trying to ferret out information about her and Lord Lambeth.

"He is rather proud," Lord Chesfield said suddenly, startling them both. "Whole family is. It's the duke thing."

Westerton's lips quirked at one corner, and he said seriously, "No doubt you're right, Ches."

At that moment Lord Lambeth turned his head, and his eyes fastened on their little group. He glanced from Marianne to Chesfield, then over to Westerton, his gaze as hard as stone.

"Oh, my," Westerton murmured. "It appears I have made an enemy of *two* lords tonight." He flashed a humorous look at Marianne. "Buckminster is one thing, but I'm not sure I want to incur Lambeth's wrath even for your fine eyes."

"Don't worry. I doubt his anger is directed at *you*. Lord Lambeth and I…have had a few disagreements."

"Mmm." Westerton's voice was noncommittal as he raised a hand in greeting to Lord Lambeth. "I wouldn't be so sure, dear girl. The man looks positively proprietary."

"He is rather set on owning things, I've noticed," Marianne retorted, gazing at Lambeth with what she hoped was hauteur. "Pity he hasn't realized that it doesn't extend to people."

Westerton's eyes glowed with interest. "My dear Mrs. Cotterwood, pray tell me what Lambeth has done to inspire such enmity. I confess, you have me fairly twitching with curiosity. Should I challenge him for your sake?"

His words touched Marianne's ready sense of humor, and laughter bubbled up from her throat. "No. I don't think that's required."

"Good," Chesfield commented. "Wouldn't want to have to be your second, old chap."

Lambeth said something to Lady Buckminster, then levered himself away from the mantel and started across the room toward them. The butler entered the room at that moment, however, and announced that dinner was served. Lambeth frowned, but stopped and returned to Lady Buckminster to do his duty, as the highest ranking man in the room, of escorting her to dinner. Marianne took Westerton's arm with relief, and they made their way out of the room, well behind Lord Lambeth.

MARIANNE WAS UP EARLY THE NEXT morning, as were most of the other guests, for the evening before, after supper, Lady Buckminster had announced that they had planned an expedition to White Lady Falls this morning. It was a ride of some distance, with a picnic served at the Falls itself, so they would have to get an early start. Marianne intended to use the trip and her own lack of riding skills to further her plan with Bucky. His mother had said that Penelope was an excellent rider, and, knowing Bucky's interest in riding, Marianne hoped that the contrast between the two of them would show Penelope to advantage.

Before they started, she made sure to remind Lady Buckminster that she required a placid, preferably slow mount. The woman gave her a faintly pitying look, but Marianne saw with satisfaction that while Penelope was mounted on a splendid bay mare, her own horse was a pudgy, docile pony. Lord Buckminster gave her a leg up, and she managed to mount as clumsily as she could. He manfully stayed with her at the back of the party, matching his own spirited steed's pace to her plodding one, but she could see that he shot envious glances from time to time ahead of him, where Nicola and Penelope rode with Verst, Lord Lambeth and the other young men. Only Westerton, an admittedly poor horseman, stayed back with them, irritating Buckminster further by vying with him for Marianne's attention.

Lady Buckminster was right, Marianne saw. Penelope did ride well. Her trim little figure was almost one with the horse. Her riding habit suited her, for even Lady Ursula could not advocate an insipidly pale riding suit, and the warm brown set off her hair and eyes well. Her face was flushed with happiness, and her eyes sparkled, and Marianne noticed that Verst was paying a good deal of attention to her.

"It seems a dreadfully long way to go by horseback," Marianne whined. "Why couldn't we have gone in carriages?"

"Yes, a curricle would have allowed one to enjoy the air just as much," Mr. Westerton agreed, happy to have found an ally among his horse-mad friends.

"You have to travel cross country," Buckminster explained with a smile to Marianne and an irritated glance at his friend. "Why, even the wagon that the servants and food are taking can't make it all the way to the falls. They will have to carry it the remainder of the way."

Of course these people would think nothing of making their servants trek across rough terrain with baskets and blankets and such for their convenience, Marianne thought sourly.

"It sounds dreadful," she said, allowing a touch of petulance to creep into her voice. "Is it really worth all the trouble?"

"Oh, the Falls is a beautiful sight," Lord Buckminster assured her. "The waters fall a hundred feet. You have to see Lydford Gorge to appreciate it. I know you'll find the beauty well worth the trek."

Marianne set her mouth in a pout. "I certainly hope so.

It is so hot already. I do hope that I won't turn brown." She touched her pale cheek with concern.

She saw doubt creep into Bucky's eyes, but then he dismissed it and smiled at her. "You look beautiful," he assured her stoutly.

Marianne smiled back. She definitely thought she was making some inroads on his infatuation.

After a few miles, they saw three other riders approaching them: two men and a woman, all mounted on excellent animals. Lady Buckminster hailed them with a hearty shout and wave.

"Who is that?" Marianne asked curiously.

"Oh. That's the Earl of Exmoor. He has guests staying with him, and they're joining us today. Miss Cecilia Winborne and her brother, Fanshaw." Buckminster's tone was colorless, and Marianne glanced at him sharply. She had the strong suspicion that he did not like one or more of the approaching group.

"Miss Winborne—she is the one who is going to marry Lord Lambeth, is she not?" she asked, keeping her voice carefully casual.

"They're not engaged," Buckminster replied almost sharply. "People say that, but Lambeth's never offered for her."

"I get the impression that you are not fond of Miss Winborne."

Bucky's stiff face relaxed, and he smiled at her. "You are too sharp for me, Mrs. Cotterwood. The Winbornes are a cold lot, I think. Good family and all, but…well, *I* certainly wouldn't want to marry her."

"I am sure Lord Lambeth will not mind," Marianne replied frostily.

On the other side of her, Westerton chuckled. "I wouldn't be so sure. Everyone's been pushing the match for years, but Justin's not been very forward with his suit, I must say."

The two groups came together, and Marianne surveyed the others with interest. Lord Exmoor was a man approaching fifty, with streaks of silver running through his brown hair at the temples. His features were rather sharp and not unattractive, except for his mouth, which was thin and had a rather sneering set to it. He was tall and still fit for a man his age, and he sat his horse well. On either side of him were Cecilia Winborne and her brother. Cecilia's hair was jet black, and her eyes were a cool gray. She would have been quite attractive, Marianne thought, if her features had not been stamped with such hauteur. Her brother, though much older, looked enough like her to be a twin.

"Lady Buckminster," the Earl said, sweeping off his hat and bowing to the older woman. "Pleasure to join you on this outing."

"Lovely day for it, eh?" Lady Buckminster countered jovially. "Hallo, Cecilia, Fanshaw. Glad you could join us."

Cecilia responded politely to Lady Buckminster, but Marianne noticed that her eyes sought out Lord Lambeth. He nodded toward her, but Marianne could see no sign of affection in his face. Beside him, Nicola urged her horse forward so that she faced Lord Exmoor.

"Where is Deborah?" she asked, and Marianne was surprised to see that Nicola's face was white and set and her eyes blazing.

"Your sister could not join us," the Earl replied smoothly, startling Marianne even more. Nicola had not said a word about her sister living nearby. "She is indisposed, I'm afraid. You know that she is a trifle invalidish."

"She never was before she married you," Nicola snapped. The air around her fairly crackled with antagonism. Everyone else in the group looked at them with interest.

"Oh, dear," Bucky muttered under his breath. He cast an apologetic glance at Marianne and said, "Excuse me, Mrs. Cotterwood."

He urged his horse forward to form the third point of a triangle with Nicola and the Earl of Exmoor. "Good morning, Exmoor. Sorry Deborah could not be here. Nicola was so looking forward to seeing her. Weren't you, Nicky?"

He reached out and closed his hand around her wrist, looking into Nicola's eyes. For a moment Marianne thought that Nicola was going to jerk her wrist away and launch into a speech, but she relaxed and gave her cousin a tight smile.

"Yes. I was." She did not look at Exmoor.

"Please send Deborah our best wishes," Buckminster added to the Earl, who nodded.

"Better get going," Lady Buckminster boomed. "Wasted enough time already.

Bucky urged his horse forward, positioning himself between Nicola and Exmoor. He talked quietly to Nicola as they moved ahead of the rest, and Penelope joined them. The Earl fell back beside Alan Thurston, while Cecilia and her brother mingled with Lambeth, Verst and the other young men. Cecilia twisted around in her saddle, looking behind her, and her gaze fell on Marianne. She looked at her for a moment without expression, then turned forward again.

Marianne watched the group from her perspective

behind them, her mind only half on Mr. Westerton's chatter. Cecilia had taken up a place beside Lord Lambeth, but after a while Lambeth dropped back to talk with Lady Buckminster's friends, the Mintons, leaving Cecilia with Verst and Lord Chesfield. After a few more moments he left the Mintons and pulled off to the side, waiting with an air of patience until Marianne and Mr. Westerton pulled close to him.

Lambeth swept off his hat and bowed toward her. "Mrs. Cotterwood. Mr. Westerton." He directed a meaningful gaze at the other man. "I'm surprised to see you are not riding with your friend Chesfield and the others."

"Lambeth, really, you know my skill on horseback. I wouldn't even have come today except that her ladyship insisted."

"Mmm. Too bad. Miss Winborne was asking about you."

Westerton's brows shot up in disbelief. "Cecilia Winborne? She thinks I'm an impertinent fool, you know that."

"Still, scarcely polite of you not to greet her, don't you think? I am sure you would find it more enjoyable riding there." He looked at Westerton blandly, one brow cocked, until finally the other man sighed.

"Yes. All right. I will yield the field to you, Lambeth. Mrs. Cotterwood, if you would excuse me?" He bowed toward her and urged his pony into a trot.

Marianne watched him ride, bouncing madly, up to the group that included his friend. Marianne cast a jaundiced look at Lord Lambeth. "You certainly have a way with people."

"Yes." He did not look at all abashed. "'Tis one of my many charms."

They rode along in silence for a moment, then Lambeth gestured toward where Buckminster rode with Nicola and Penelope. "It looks as if you have lost one of your swains."

"Both of them, actually—thanks to you," Marianne pointed out sarcastically.

"I did help Westerton along," he admitted, "but I can lay no claim to Buckminster."

"What was that all about?" Marianne asked, her curiosity overriding her desire to freeze out Lord Lambeth.

Lambeth shrugged. "I don't know. I'm not even sure if Bucky does. But it is a well-known fact that Nicola despises the Earl of Exmoor." Lambeth's lip curled a little as he said the name.

"I take it you are not very fond of the man, either."

"He is not a man I would call my friend, but I would not classify him as an enemy, either. There is simply something about him…" His voice trailed off.

"But Nicola's sister is married to him?"

"Yes. They've been married for several years now. I suppose the enmity between Nicola and Richard has something to do with the marriage, but I'm not sure what. My guess would be that he is less than an ideal husband. One never sees Deborah anymore. She always stays here in the country, doesn't come to London. Apparently she's rather invalidish; my understanding is that she has had several disappointments concerning heirs."

Marianne took this statement to be a socially approved way of intimating that she had miscarried several times. "Oh. I see. Poor woman."

Cecilia Winborne turned around again to look back at Marianne. There was no expression in her face as she took in the sight of Lord Lambeth riding beside her, but

Marianne had the suspicion that Miss Winborne was not destined to be her friend.

Confirming her guess, Lambeth said, "Miss Winborne has come to protect her investment, I believe."

"Her investment?"

Lambeth flashed a sardonic grin at her. "Don't tell me you have not heard the rumors that she and I have 'an understanding.'"

"Yes. Are they unfounded?"

Again he shrugged. "It is what our families want. What Cecilia wants."

"And you?"

"She is as eligible as any other young woman. And at least she has the advantage of not expecting me to dance attendance on her or spout words of love. She will enter into it in the same manner I do."

"A business arrangement only? No love?"

"That is the way marriage usually is. An alliance with another family. Love does not enter into it."

"For a future duke, perhaps," Marianne conceded. "Not for everyone."

"No doubt you and your husband were a love match," he retorted in a cynical voice.

Marianne stiffened. She had forgotten for a moment her role as a widow. "What Mr. Cotterwood and I were is none of your business, my lord."

"Of course not. But that does not stop my curiosity about the man."

"Well, I am afraid that it shall have to remain unfulfilled. I prefer not to discuss my late husband."

"Mmm. Not even to the extent of saying whether he is actually dead or not?"

"What? How dare you?" Marianne's cheeks flamed, though she was not sure whether it was from anger or embarrassment.

"Come, come, you do not have to dissemble in front of me. I am the one person here who knows that you are a sham, and I frankly do not care, although I sincerely hope that you and your friends will refrain from stripping Bucky's house bare. Lady Buckminster would be quite unhappy to lose her treasures."

"As long as it was not her horses, I'm not sure Lady Buckminster would care," Marianne retorted frankly.

He smiled faintly. "You might be right about that. But we are getting off the subject."

"Which is?"

"I would like to know about you—the person you really are. Rosalind's mother, for instance. A woman of great beauty and passion. But what else? I don't even know if Cotterwood is really your name. Somehow I doubt it."

"This conversation is absurd. If I were the person you maintain I am, why would I admit any of it to you?"

"Perhaps because it might be pleasant to have an honest relationship with someone?"

"I know what sort of relationship you wish with me," Marianne replied, bitterness staining her voice. "I have never heard that it was a particularly honest one."

"Indeed? I think sometimes it is far more honest and real than most marriages. At least it springs from genuine passion."

Marianne cast him a contemptuous look. "On the side of the man, perhaps. After all, he is the buyer. The woman is the seller, and she, like most salespeople, tells him what he wants to hear."

"Ouch. A direct hit." Lambeth chuckled. "You certainly do not try to spare a man."

"What is the point? All relationships to you are business. A wife, a mistress, whatever light-of-love you choose to spend the night with—they are all the same to you, things that you can buy. Are they not? Why should you recoil from hearing that there is no feeling in return?"

"I know there is feeling in you," he said in a husky voice, leaning toward her. "I felt your passion. You cannot deny it, no matter how much you might try. I don't ask for words of love, only the heat that I touched in you. That is the honesty, the truth, I seek."

His eyes bored into hers, fiercely gold, holding her gaze, willing her to respond. Instinctively Marianne moved toward him, her blood warming, as it always did, at his nearness. This man made her feel, made her yearn, as no man had. She had never known what it was like to want something this way, to ache with a hunger that was more than physical. Anger burned very near the surface when she was with him, followed by a flame even hotter and more primal.

A peal of feminine laughter floated back from the front riders to them, thrusting reality upon Marianne. She started and pulled back, the warmth in her face replaced by cool suspicion. She was stung by her own stupidity.

"Honesty?" she asked sardonically. "I doubt you know the meaning of the word. What you 'seek' is to keep me from Lord Buckminster. You have already informed me that that is the reason you wish to make me your mistress."

"Buckminster!" In truth, Lambeth had not given a thought to Bucky the past few minutes, he realized a little guiltily. Marianne had a way of driving all rational thought from his brain. "I don't wish to talk about Buckminster," he told her impatiently. "I want to talk about us."

"There is nothing to discuss," Marianne pointed out coolly. "There is no 'us.'"

"There could be if you would only—" He stopped abruptly, realizing that he was arguing with her. That was scarcely the way to win a woman's heart. "I am sorry. I swore I would not press you."

They rode in silence for a few minutes. Ahead and to her left, Marianne saw an odd structure of wooden timbers, seemingly built into a low hill. "What is that?" she asked curiously, pointing toward the dark opening.

Lambeth looked. "Oh. That is Wheal Sarah. An abandoned mine—I cannot remember whether it was iron or tin. There are quite a few mines here in Dartmoor. Not as many as in Cornwall, of course, but there has been mining in the area since, oh, medieval times. Most of them are still in operation, but that one played out several years ago."

"Why is it named that?"

"It comes from an old Cornish word, *hweal,* meaning mine. They're all named after women."

"Why is that?"

He shrugged and glanced at her with a grin. "Probably because of their allure and their danger."

"Of course. That *is* what a man would say."

He chuckled. "This whole area is like that. My home is in Kent, but I can see the lure of the moor. The streams, the high, rolling land, the stunning beauty of the gorges and waterfalls. But it can be an eerie, benighted place, too, especially when the mist rolls over it. Then you cannot see your hand in front of your face, and the tors loom up at you, great broken slabs of rock. And you never know when you might be setting your foot into one of the quaking bogs."

"Bogs?" Marianne looked at him wide-eyed.

"Oh, yes. The place is rife with them, hidden by grass. It's the kind of place where you can almost feel the presence of the old gods. That's why you have all the stone rows and the rings and such. The ancients lived here. It is no wonder that there are so many legends about the moor."

"Such as?"

"The hellhounds, for one. There was a certain nobleman—an evil fellow, Sir Richard Cabell—and they say that when he died, black hounds from hell raced across the moor to throw themselves at his tomb, snapping and snarling. On beyond Lydford Gorge, where we are going, there is a high point named Gibbet Hill, where they used to hang thieves and other miscreants, in order to set an example to others. It is said their ghosts walk the hill. But most famous of all, of course, is Lady Howard."

"Who was she?"

"A beauty, I suppose, for she lured four men into marriage, but with a black heart—she murdered each and every one of them. They hanged her for being a witch. It is said that some nights, when there is evil abroad, she rides across the moor in her coach made all out of bones and drawn by headless horses, a black hellhound running beside her carriage."

"If you are trying to frighten me, you have certainly succeeded," Marianne snapped, unable to suppress a shiver.

Lambeth laughed. "You'll be all right—as long as you don't get caught out on the moor at night."

"I shall make a point of it."

They continued to ride along, chatting, with Lambeth

pointing out the various sights, until they reached Lydford Gorge. The gorge was deep and verdant with trees, ferns and meadowsweet. The narrow, rock-strewn River Lyd rushed through the center of it, curling around moss-covered boulders. The walls of the gorge rose steeply around them, pockmarked with dark caves. Finally they arrived at their destination, White Lady Falls, where the river roared down a hundred feet in a shining white spray of waterfall.

Here, beside the Falls, the servants had spread out their picnic. Blankets lay on the ground for the guests to sit upon, and servants had laid out covered dishes of food for them. They sat in something of an oval, the older folks seated at one end, mostly on boulders, and the younger set arranged beside the river in an elongated circle.

Marianne was rather surprised when Sir George Merridale spoke. She had scarcely heard his voice, what with his wife's nonstop chatter. But Sophronia's mouth was stopped with food now, and Marianne supposed that Sir George had seized the opportunity to say something.

He gestured toward the high walls of the gorge and said, "You know, a family of outlaws used to live here. Quite feared, they were. Gubbins was their name, and they all had great red beards. Used to pillage the outlying farms and villages, then come back here to hide. They lived up in the caves, you see. It was easy to conceal themselves, and easy to defend, too. Took years to catch them."

"I suspect that no one was overly keen on riding in here to try to drive them out," Lambeth commented, glancing at the narrow, rocky path beside the river, with the cliffs looming above it."

"That was long ago," Bucky said.

"Oh, but there are outlaws here again," Lady Buckminster put in. When everyone turned startled faces in her direction, she chuckled and shook her head. "I don't mean here in Lydford Gorge. Just in the area. No one knows where they hide—or who they are, either. It's a band of highwaymen. Their leader is a well-spoken man. People call him 'The Gentleman.'"

"The devil!" Mr. Thurston exclaimed. "The gall of him! A common thief, claiming to be a gentleman."

"I don't know that he claims to be anything, Alan. They simply call him that because of his manners, you see. He is supposed to be very polite to ladies. It is said that he told one woman that he would not take her necklace because it adorned such a beautiful throat."

Verst snorted. "I doubt that. I never heard of a thief who gave up any of his loot for any reason."

"What do you think, Mrs. Cotterwood?" Lambeth asked Marianne, looking at her with dancing golden eyes.

"About what, Lord Lambeth?" she replied coolly.

"Why, gentlemen thieves—do you think there is such a thing?"

"I am sure there are thieves who act quite as nobly as many gentlemen I know," Marianne responded tartly, goaded by the laughter in his eyes.

Her statement was met by a joking outcry from the men present. Cecilia Winborne, who had maneuvered things so that she sat on one side of Lambeth, placed a hand on his arm in a gesture betokening familiarity. "Really, Justin, you should not tease Mrs. Cotterwood. She does not know you. She won't know how to take these things you say."

The dark-haired woman cast a sidelong look at Marianne, her words and manner emphasizing that Marianne was a stranger to Lambeth and she a dear friend. No matter how much Marianne told herself that it did not matter, that she did not want to be close to Lambeth, she could not help but bridle at Cecilia's words.

"Oh," she replied, with a slow smile, looking straight at Lord Lambeth, "I think I know exactly how to take the things Lord Lambeth says."

Lambeth's teeth flashed in a grin, his eyes locked on Marianne's, and for an instant it was the two of them who were paired in an intimate moment, the rest of the party excluded.

Cecilia rose to her feet. Her voice was brittle as she said, "Well, enough of this talk of highwaymen, or you will frighten me. I think a walk would be in order. Justin…"

The men automatically rose to their feet as she stood up. Lambeth turned toward her. "Yes?"

Cecilia's gray eyes turned even stormier. "I thought you might accompany me."

"Oh. Of course."

Marianne bit her lip to hide a smile at his response, so obviously polite and tepid. She did not think that Miss Winborne could know his lordship's nature very well, despite her implied closeness to him, if she did not realize that the approach she was taking was possibly the one most likely to get the man's back up. Few men liked to be maneuvered or treated proprietorily, and Marianne suspected that Lord Lambeth took to it even less than most.

He crooked his arm politely to take her hand, but as he did so, he said to the party in general, "That sounds a good idea. We should all go exploring. What do you say?"

Most of the young men were quick to agree with him, and soon all the younger members of the party set off together on a stroll alongside the rushing river. They walked more or less in a group, picking their way along a barely defined path. The ground was uneven, broken by slabs of granite and mossy stones, and the vegetation ran wild, so that one had to pick one's way around.

Marianne was watching her feet as she traversed a broken shelf of rock right beside the river, swerving to avoid a sapling. Just as she lifted her foot to step forward, she felt a hard shove in the small of her back, and suddenly she was falling toward the swift, rocky water.

CHAPTER TEN

MARIANNE GASPED AND FLUNG OUT HER arms as she felt herself falling. One hand met a limb of the sapling, and she grabbed it. For a moment she hung out over the water at an angle, holding on to the sapling for dear life. A woman screamed, and there were several shouts. She could feel her grip slipping; she was at too much of an angle to pull herself upright. Then a hard arm went around her waist and she was jerked back to safety. It had all happened in an instant.

She found herself staring into Lord Lambeth's eyes, dark with anger and stark in his white face. "What the devil were you doing?" he barked, his mouth a slash in his face. "Watch where you're going! You might have killed yourself."

Marianne, who had been afraid for a moment that she was about to disgrace herself by fainting, was revived by an answering anger at his tone. "I *was* watching."

She started to add that she had been pushed, but she stopped, looking at the groups of people behind Lambeth, all staring at her in varying stages of shock and interest. She realized how ridiculous her accusation would sound. *Who among these people would try to push her into the water? And why?* She wasn't even sure it would have caused her any great injury. She was a good swimmer, and there were plenty of rocks and vegetation along the bank to grab hold of. Surely she would have been able to pull herself out, and would have suffered nothing worse than the embarrassment of a douse in the river.

Marianne looked into a pair of malicious gray eyes, and she felt reasonably sure who had done it. Cecilia Winborne disliked her, and Marianne had the feeling that the woman did exactly as she pleased. Embarrassing Marianne would have appealed to her very much, especially if it meant getting Marianne away from Lord Lambeth for the rest of the evening. After all, Miss Winborne had no way of knowing that Lord Lambeth's interest in her was not the sort that would affect his marrying Cecilia.

"I—I slipped," she said quietly. There would be no point in saying anything. No one would believe her, and she would only make herself look ridiculous. Besides, she knew a better way to get back at Cecilia Winborne.

She let herself slump against Lambeth with a little sigh. His arm tightened around her, and he swung her up into his arms and carried her back to where the older people still sat. Marianne allowed herself to rest her head against his shoulder, drinking in his warmth and scent, pretending for just a moment that he cared for her, that they belonged to one another.

She heard Lady Buckminster cry out in alarm as they approached, and then Lambeth laid Marianne down on one of the blankets. Marianne opened her eyes and looked up at him. His face was taut and harsh, his brows pulled together into a frown.

"Are you all right?"

Marianne nodded and smiled up at him. "Yes. Just a trifle scared."

His face relaxed a little. Then Lady Buckminster and

Nicola and Penelope were crowding around her, bringing out smelling salts and shooing him and the other men away.

Marianne sat up, pushing away the sharp-smelling bottle that Sophronia Merridale produced and thrust under her nose. "I'm all right. Really. I'm fine."

"What happened?" Lady Buckminster demanded.

"It was silly," Marianne said. "I slipped on a mossy rock. It was nothing, really."

"You could have been killed!" Penelope exclaimed worriedly.

"Oh, no. I can swim and—"

"But the current is terribly strong and fast. It would have swept you right down—and over those rocks! At the very least, you could have broken something."

"Well, I didn't," Marianne reminded her with a smile. "So you needn't look so worried, Penelope."

Nicola, though silent, looked quite white, and she had her arms crossed over her chest, hugging herself tightly. "She's right. It's a dangerous place," she said tersely. A shudder ran through her.

"We had better go back," Lady Buckminster said. "I am sure you don't feel up to continuing."

"Oh, no,' Marianne said quickly. "Please, I don't want to spoil the afternoon. "

"Don't be ridiculous," Lord Lambeth spoke from behind the women. "You should return to the house."

Marianne turned and saw him looming a few feet away, scowling. She frowned back at him and sat up.

"I'm fine," she said staunchly. "Nothing happened. I didn't even get wet. I just slipped, and Lord Lambeth kept me from falling into the river. It was a perfectly minor accident."

In truth, her nerves were still jangling, and she did not

look forward to an afternoon of socializing and being polite, when all the time she was feeling again that surge of panic as she started falling toward the river. However, she wanted even less to be the cause of the whole party having to return to the house instead of enjoying their afternoon in the cool and lovely gorge. And she certainly did not want to give in to Lord Lambeth's demands.

Just as he opened his mouth to speak again, Nicola said quietly, "I will be happy to ride back with Mrs. Cotterwood. That way the rest of you can stay here as we had planned."

"Oh, no," Sophronia protested. "Two young ladies could not go riding all that way without someone with them."

Lady Buckminster looked a little abashed, but hastily agreed. "No, I suppose you're right."

"I will take them," Lambeth spoke up.

"No, it is my responsibility," Lord Buckminster was quick to add.

Nicola sighed. "I am sure we do not need escorts. However, if it is necessary for everyone's piece of mind, Mrs. Cotterwood and I will ride back with the servants' wagon. Surely they will be protection enough for us."

Everyone agreed that they were satisfied with this compromise, though Bucky insisted on accompanying them to the end of the gorge, where the servants were busy packing the remains of the picnic into the wagon. Bucky bid them a protracted farewell and finally left, turning back for a final wave of the hand.

Nicola let out a groan and turned toward Marianne. "Don't you feel sometimes as if you could just scream, the way everyone tries to keep one wrapped up in cotton wool?"

Marianne nodded. It was not something that had ever happened to her much before, but she was beginning to understand that there were some definite annoyances in being raised a young lady. "It is much easier being a widow than an unmarried woman."

"I hope you don't mind traveling with the servants," Nicola said a little anxiously. "It was the only way I could think of to avoid having the men all arguing endlessly about who should escort us."

"No, not at all. It seems a sensible plan, and since my mount is about as fast as the wagon, it won't make much difference to me. You are the one who will suffer, dawdling along. I am sorry to have spoiled your afternoon. It was terribly kind of you to offer to ride home with me."

Nicola shook her head. "Don't worry. Frankly, it was a relief. I should not have gone there."

Marianne glanced at her in surprise and noticed that Nicola's face was drawn and her fine eyes held an almost haunted look. She remembered how white and shaken she had appeared when Lambeth had set Marianne down on the ground.

"Are you all right?" she asked Nicola now in concern. "Are you feeling ill?"

Nicola shook her head, saying, "Only in spirit. I— Lydford Gorge holds strong memories for me. It has been a long time now, and I had hoped that I would be able to bear it, but I found it very difficult. I should have obeyed my instincts and told Aunt Adelaide that I could not go."

It was all Marianne could do not to give in to her curiosity and ask the other woman why, but she managed to preserve a polite silence. She hoped that Nicola would volunteer more, but she did not. Instead, with a wan smile, she turned toward the servants, who were now loading the wagon.

One of the footmen nodded toward her, a broad grin

splitting his face. "Glad to see you home, Miss Nicola. It's been too long."

Around him, the other servants echoed his opinion. Nicola smiled at them. "Why, thank you, Jim. It seems too long to me, too. I miss the moor. How is your sister? Aunt Adelaide tells me she had a bouncing baby boy."

"Aye, that she did, miss. She and Nat are proud as peacocks about it, I'll tell you. She'd be that happy if you'd drop in and see the little 'un while you're here."

"I shall. I had planned to ride out with Aunt Adelaide tomorrow to visit some of the farms. I'll make it a point to see Annie."

Marianne watched the interaction between Nicola and the servants with some astonishment. There had never been this sort of friendliness between servant and employer in the Quartermaine household—except for the oldest son's pursuit of her, of course. The two groups had kept their distance, with no affection whatsoever between them. Marianne doubted that Mrs. Quartermaine had even known all the servants' names, let alone known anything about their sisters, or paid visits to them. Certainly neither Marianne nor any of the other maids or footmen had felt the slightest inclination to welcome Mrs. Quartermaine back from a trip or to tell her of their family's doings.

Nicola glanced at Marianne and saw her studying her. She smiled as she turned her horse and moved in front of the servants' wagon. Marianne followed her. "Do you think I am too familiar with the servants?"

"What?" The question surprised Marianne.

"Do you think that I'm not reserved enough with the servants? My mother does. She tells me that I undermine my authority, and that they will lose respect for me."

"Oh, no," Marianne hastened to tell her, adding truthfully, "Actually, I am quite good friends with my housekeeper."

Nicola grinned almost conspiratorially. "Really? The truth is, I have always felt at ease in the servants' hall. When I was little I used to sneak away from my governess and go down to the kitchen. It seemed much warmer and happier there." She looked a trifle wistful. "And Cook used to tell me about herbs—not just spices for food, but how you could use them to treat illnesses. Everyone in the house used to come to her when they were sick, and she would dose them. I found it fascinating, and I would pester her to show me how she made them."

She made a little face. "That is another way that Mama says I act beneath my station. The staff always come to me with their illnesses, as do most of the people around here. Since Granny Rose is gone…"

She paused, sorrow touching her face.

"Granny Rose?"

Nicola nodded. "She was an old woman who lived on the moor, not far from here. She was known as a healer for miles around. When Mama and I moved to Buckminster Hall, I heard about her, and I went to visit her. She was much more skilled than our cook had been, and I learned a great deal from her. She had more success than most doctors, I'll tell you. And so do I," she added a trifle defiantly.

"I think that's wonderful," Marianne said sincerely. She would never have imagined that a high-born beauty such as Nicola could be so down-to-earth and warm as she was. "I—I don't think I've ever known anyone quite like you."

Nicola chuckled. "I will take that as a compliment."

"It is," Marianne assured her. "I find that most ladies are

not interested in such things. Nor are they concerned about people who aren't—well…"

"Important? No, you're right." Nicola's mouth was set in a hard line. "Most ladies are vapid and self-absorbed." She looked at Marianne and sighed. "Don't get me started. Even Aunt Adelaide is shocked by some of my opinions. I am too egalitarian. Penelope is tender-hearted enough that she agrees about my concern for the poor and the down-trodden—if you could see some of the conditions in the slums that I have seen, it would make you weep!—but I'm not sure that even she agrees with some of my radical beliefs."

"What are they?"

Nicola looked at her. "Are you sure you want to hear? I am afraid it will shock you."

Marianne smiled. "I am not easily shocked, I assure you."

Nicola raised her brows. "Not even if I tell you that I see no reason why a man is any better than another because he is a peer? Frankly, I often find him less so. What difference does it make that you can trace your ancestors back to the Conquest? Everyone's ancestors go back that far and beyond. Why is it so important to know all their names? If you are more honorable or braver or smarter, it is because that is the way you are, the way you have been raised. It is not because your blood is purer. Frankly, I think the Americans have it right—and even the French, though their methods were wicked, God knows."

She paused and glanced at Marianne. "There. I *have* shocked you."

"Oh, no. I mean, well, yes, you have shocked me, but not in a bad way, I assure you. I quite agree with you."

"Really?"

"Yes. But it is rather astonishing to find such beliefs among the aristocracy."

Nicola looked puzzled. "You speak as if you were not an aristocrat."

Marianne realized that she had slipped. She smiled deprecatingly. "Ah, but surely you realize that my family is not the sort that yours or Penelope's are. There isn't a title among my ancestors. Country gentry—that's the stock I come from."

Nicola waved her hand dismissively. "Whether your father was a country squire or a curate instead of a baron, you are still of the same class. It is quite different from your family being in trade or, God forbid, the serving class. What if you had been raised not to follow the genteel pursuits of a lady, but to scrub and sweep? What if you had been told that your lot in life was to be hungry and ill-clothed and uneducated, that you were not as good as the people for whom you slaved or—"

Nicola broke off a little sheepishly. "There. I'm off again. I'm sorry. Once I get started on one of my pet subjects, I am afraid I'm rather didactic."

"No, please. I am impressed by your beliefs."

They continued to talk—about that and several other subjects, including the charities in which Nicola was involved in the City—and by the time they reached the house, Marianne's nerves were long since settled, and she and Nicola had become good friends.

It was with a pang that Marianne realized, as she climbed the stairs to her room, that it was not likely that she and Nicola could continue as friends. Friends, after all, exchanged visits, and Marianne felt sure that Nicola, unlike her cousin Bucky, would immediately see, as Lambeth had, how odd and unlikely her "family" was. Marianne knew that she could not allow another person to become suspicious about her. Given what she did, she could not afford to make friends among the people who were her victims. For the first time she used that word to describe the people from whom she and her group stole things, and it made her feel low to acknowledge it.

Gloomy and tired, she spent the rest of the day in her room, requesting that the evening meal be brought to her on a tray instead of going down to join the others. Penelope knocked lightly on her door in the evening, but Marianne pretended to be asleep and did not answer. In the mood she was in, she did not think that she could face Penelope's sweet countenance. So she lay in bed, morosely considering her options, which seemed to her to be pathetically few, until at last she fell asleep.

SHE WAS IN BETTER SPIRITS THE NEXT morning when she got up and went downstairs. There were only two women in the dining room breakfasting when she went in. Sophronia Merridale of course proceeded to explain that Lady Buckminster, accompanied by her niece Nicola and Penelope, had gone out for a day of visiting their tenants. Most of the men, including Lord Buckminster and Sophronia's own husband, had set out early on a daylong fishing excursion on the River Teign, near Fingle Bridge.

Marianne, foreseeing a long, boring day in the company of Sophronia Merridale and Mrs. Thurston, finished her breakfast quickly and went outside for a stroll through the gardens, hoping that the other two women would remain inside most of the day. Mrs. Thurston had not seemed a great enthusiast of the outdoors; she had not even gone on the expedition the day before. Hopefully Sophronia would decide to stay and assault that lady's ears rather than seek out Marianne.

She had not gone very far along the path before she came upon Mr. Thurston's secretary, seated on one of the benches and enjoying the vista of the sloping lawn, and the lake and land beyond it. He jumped up politely when she approached.

"Mrs. Cotterwood! How nice to see you. Please, sit down and join me."

Marianne did not see how she could politely refuse, so she sat down on the bench beside him. "You did not go fishing with the others, Mr. Fuquay?"

"No. I fear I am not a keen enthusiast of fishing." He smiled, the action lightening his long, rather somber face. "Nor hunting, for that matter. I have a few duties I need to take care of, anyway—correspondence and such."

"Mr. Thurston must be busy indeed, to need his secretary even at a social occasion."

He made a noncommittal gesture with his hands. "There were a few loose ends of business that needed to be taken care of, because Mr. Thurston had not planned to come until the last moment. He is not a close friend of Lord Buckminster's. However, despite the small amount of work, I suspect that he primarily brought me along as a kindness. It is more a holiday for me than work, you see."

Marianne did see. Though, according to Mr. Westerton, Fuquay's lineage was as good as Thurston's, he belonged in a sort of limbo socially. Unable to afford the life-style of his peers, he was forced to work for a living, yet he was of vastly higher social status than a servant or tutor. As a result, he did not really socialize with either group. A weeklong trip to a country estate would allow him to enjoy some of the benefits others of his station enjoyed.

"He sounds like a nice man," she commented.

"Oh, yes, he is. Mrs. Thurston, as well, of course. He is capable, too, of being a great statesman, I think."

"Then I hope that he gets elected."

"Yes. I hope so, as well." He paused for a moment, then suggested, "Would you care to take a turn around the gardens, Mrs. Cotterwood? It is a lovely morning for a walk."

Marianne accepted. Fuquay's company was much more enjoyable than that of Sophronia Merridale. They had not gone far, however, when there was the sound of footsteps crunching on the graveled path behind them, and they turned to see Lord Lambeth approaching.

"Hello. Saw you two walking and thought I would join you," he said cheerfully, leaving Mr. Fuquay with little option except to invite him along.

Marianne gave him a sour look. "I would have thought you would have gone with the other men."

He shrugged. "I had other plans."

"Indeed?"

"Yes." He gave her an enigmatic smile and did not elaborate, merely turned toward her companion. "Did you enjoy the visit to Lydford Gorge yesterday, Mr. Fuquay?"

"Yes. I have never been there before. I am afraid that I have had little occasion to visit Dartmoor."

They strolled through the garden, with Lambeth keeping up polite, meaningless chatter about the Falls, the moor and other general topics, until finally Mr. Fuquay excused himself and returned to the house, saying that he had work he needed to finish.

"I say," Lambeth remarked with an innocent air. "Did I drive the man away?"

"Apparently he found your conversation less than riveting."

"Mmm. I rather suspect it was more that he had hoped to enjoy your company alone," Lambeth retorted with a grin. "And he realized that I intended to stick with you for the duration. He beat a strategic retreat, with the hope of trying again at a more opportune time."

"If you are implying that Mr. Fuquay has any interest in me, I am sure that you are wrong," Marianne retorted, somehow nettled by his words.

"My dear Mrs. Cotterwood, surely you realize that every man at this gathering has an interest in you. He would have to be made of stone not to."

"Very pretty flattery, my lord, but—"

"Do you not think that you could call me Justin? I get very tired of 'my lord' this and 'my lord' that."

Marianne looked up at him. "That would be highly improper."

"Mrs. Cotterwood… Marianne…"

"That is equally improper. We are hardly on the terms to address one another so familiarly."

"Then we shall not do so in front of others. But when we are alone together, what would be so wrong about it?"

"Being alone together is in itself another impropriety," Marianne pointed out.

"Damn propriety," he growled.

"That is easy for you to say. Quite a bit less easy for a woman."

"You are, as always, determined to thwart me."

"I am merely watching out for myself. A woman in my position has to."

He reached out to take her hand and pulled her to a halt. "Let us stop fencing, shall we? I want to talk to you."

"About what?"

"Nothing. Everything. I am not asking for a royal audience. I simply want to spend some time with you." He took her other hand in his, as well, and stood, looking down into her face. "I had Cook fix up a picnic luncheon. I thought we would row across the lake to the summer-house there. Have you seen it?"

Marianne shook her head.

"It is a charming place. And there is scarcely anyone around today. It is the perfect chance to get away."

Marianne set her mouth. "A perfect chance for you to seduce me, you mean."

He smiled. "You are a very suspicious woman. What if I promise that I will not do anything you do not wish me to do?" He put his hand over his heart in a gesture so theatrical that Marianne had to smile. "What would you like me to swear by? On my word as an Englishman? A gentleman?"

"How am I to know what thing you would remain true to?"

"Have I been deceitful with you? Have I done aught but tell you straightforwardly what I think or feel?"

Marianne paused, considering. "I have to admit that you have been decidedly blunt."

"What is there to deceive you about? You know that I desire you." His eyes darkened as he gazed down into hers, and Marianne's loins began to warm in response. "You know that I do not want you with Buckminster. But I promised you I would not force you. I want you freely. I cannot say I would not entice you or flirt with you. But I will not do anything that you do not want me to."

Marianne hesitated. He grinned, his eyes dancing. "Or is it that you are scared not of what I will do but of what *you* will? Perhaps you don't trust yourself not to seduce me."

"Don't be absurd!" Marianne snapped, irritated by his cocky, self-sure attitude. "There is no likelihood of that, I can assure you."

"Then why are you afraid to go to the summerhouse with me?"

"I am not afraid. When are you going?"

"As soon as I can collect our luncheon. We can take a boat from the pier at the foot of the garden."

"I will be there."

MARIANNE TRAILED HER HAND languidly through the water, looking over the side of the boat into the calm lake water. It had taken Justin very little time to fetch a basket of food from the kitchen and meet her at the small pier at the foot of the garden. Indeed, Marianne, who had returned to her room to fetch her hat and a parasol, arrived there after he did. He had loaded the basket into the small boat and handed her in, then untied the boat and taken up the oars, propelling them smoothly across the water.

Marianne turned her head to look at Lambeth, seated across from her in the small boat. His jacket and cravat lay folded between them, and he had unbuttoned the top button of his shirt and rolled up his sleeves in order to row. Marianne's eyes could not keep from going to the strong column of his throat and the triangle of flesh below it, exposed by his opened shirt. She watched the play of muscles beneath the golden skin of his arms, the ripple that his lawn shirt only partially concealed. She could feel warmth blossoming in her abdomen, and it occurred to her that apparently he did not have to *do* anything to stir her senses; it was enough just to look at him.

She turned her face away, looking out over the blue water of the pond to the small white pavilion on the other side, so carved and ornamented that it looked rather like something that belonged on a wedding cake. But in her mind's eye she could still see the smooth, firm flesh, the vulnerable hollow of his throat, where his pulse beat, the bead of perspiration that rolled down his skin and settled in the hollow, glistening. Marianne swallowed, thinking that perhaps she had been foolish to come. *It was all very well to trust Lambeth not to push her, but what if she could not trust herself?*

She glanced at him, hoping he could not read her thoughts. He smiled at her in a slow way that made her suspect that her hope was groundless. Nervously she cast about for some topic of conversation that would take her mind off her treacherous thoughts.

"It seems an inconvenient place for a summerhouse," she said finally. "Having to row across to it."

"There is a path that leads to it from the house. It just takes longer. I think the seclusion was part of its appeal. The Lord Buckminster who built it apparently built it to escape from his wife."

"You mean he used it for trysts?" Marianne looked at him suspiciously. "Is that the purpose of the place?"

"No. I don't think he was a licentious man. According to Bucky, his lady was a shrew with a voice that would shatter glass, and everyone on the estate lived in terror of her. The Fourth Earl used to come here to read in peace, according to Bucky, as did his son. Now Bucky's grandfather, the Sixth Earl, is another story—there is no knowing for what purpose that old roué might have used it. The family tries to ignore his part in their history."

Marianne smiled.

"That's better," he said.

"What is?"

"Your smile. 'Tis far more pleasant than that glower of suspicion."

"I was not glowering."

He said nothing, merely raised his brows and continued the smooth rhythmic pull of the oars. Marianne's eyes went to his hands, large and powerful, curled around the oars. He had not worn gloves; she had noticed that he did not when he rode yesterday, either. She wondered if his palms were callused from such activities and how that roughened skin would feel sliding over her own flesh.

Again desire tingled between her legs, and a blush rose in her cheeks. *Where had all this sudden lasciviousness sprung from?*

The boat glided through the water, and in a few moments they reached the shore in front of the summer-house. Lambeth stepped out into the shallow water and pulled the boat up onto the land. Then he reached down and swept Marianne up into his arms.

She let out a squeak of surprise. "What are you doing? Put me down."

His heat enveloped her. She was only inches from his face. She could feel the thudding of his heart against her own chest.

"Don't worry." He grinned at her. "I am not about to ravish you. The ground is muddy here."

He set her down on higher ground, and she stepped away, straightening her skirts and feeling both foolish and breathless with excitement. He went back to the boat and retrieved the large picnic basket that Cook had sent with him, and carried it into the small white building. Marianne followed him.

The summerhouse was round and enclosed by slatted screens, which Justin folded back to admit the light and air. When all the screens were opened, it gave a lovely view of the pond and gardens and house across the water, and of a verdant meadow and woods beside and behind it. Roses grew on trellises around the base of the house, and their sweet scent filled the air.

"It is beautiful," Marianne admitted, walking around the inside perimeter to take in all the aspects of the view. The heady perfume of the full-blown roses filled her nostrils.

"And comfortable." He gestured at the wide, cushioned window seat that ran around the inside wall, just below the opened screens.

"Yes." Marianne sat down on the edge of the seat, folding her hands on her knees.

At the moment she felt anything but comfortable. The scene was far too conducive to seduction—from the balmy caress of the breeze across the lake to the heavy scent of the flowers to the inviting softness of the cushion beneath her—for her to relax. Despite his protestations to the contrary, she feared that Justin would begin to kiss her. It was not that she feared he would hurt her, for she felt rather sure that he would stop if she insisted. Nor was it that she did not want to feel his mouth on hers, for, if the truth were known, she would like very much to have that happen. But she knew that she could not allow it, and she did not want to have to face that dilemma.

"Let me take your hat," he said, reaching for the wide ribbon tied beneath her chin, and Marianne started, looking at him warily.

"You scarcely need it in here," he pointed out mildly, adding, "I shan't request any other articles of clothing."

She smiled, feeling a trifle foolish, and reached up to loosen the ribbons. She handed the hat to him, and he laid it on the table beside the picnic basket.

"You needn't look so wary," he told her. "I intend only to sit and enjoy the view and talk with you."

He followed his words by sitting down beside her and half turning, so that he was looking both at her and at the lake beyond.

"What did you wish to talk about?" she asked a little primly.

"Whatever comes to mind. I had nothing planned."

"Then tell me about yourself. I know less about you than you do about me."

"All right. But I warn you that my life has been rather dull. I grew up in Kent, a rather unremarkable child, I'm afraid, and did my time at Eton and Oxford. The past few years I have spent doing little but enjoying myself in London. My mother tells me I ignore my responsibilities. I think she means that I should be getting married and producing heirs, but I fail to see the need for haste."

"Surely there must be more to you than that. You have described half the gentlemen in London."

"Probably."

"Yet you are not the same as they. You are not like Bucky or Mr. Westerton or Lord Chesfield."

"Am I not?" His smile was quizzical. "What is different?"

She hesitated. She could scarcely answer that none of them turned her knees to water or made her doubt her own emotions. "There is in you," she began slowly, feeling her way, "a kind of power, I suppose, that I do not see in the others. A sense of...I don't know, danger, perhaps."

"Danger?" He chuckled. "Mrs. Cotterwood, I think you mistake me."

"I think not. You are not a man a person wants to cross."

"You make me sound very forbidding," he responded lightly.

She shrugged. "You require...watching. No one else at that party noticed my actions. No one else followed me."

He gazed at her for a long moment, then said, "Perhaps no one else was as bewitched by you as I."

The glow in his eyes made her a trifle breathless as she said, "I think it was more than that."

"Perhaps it was. I dislike boredom, and curiosity has always been one of my besetting sins. When I see a lovely woman acting as you were, it makes me wonder."

"Why did you not set up a hue and cry when you decided I was a thief?"

Lambeth leaned closer. "Frankly, I was far more intrigued by you than I was concerned about Lord Batterslee's valuables."

"Why?" she asked him bluntly.

"Because I find you quite different, and I like things—and people—that are unusual. You did not seem to know who I was—or care. You defied me. You were...a challenge."

"Ah. I see. The problem with being a challenge is that once the challenge has been met and conquered, it no longer intrigues." Marianne turned away from him, rising to her feet.

He stood up, his hands going to her shoulders to stop her and turn her around. "I am not sure that a man could ever completely overcome the challenge that you are."

Marianne looked up at him, her heart beginning to knock

wildly in her chest. His hands were warm and strong upon her shoulders. As he gazed down at her, his thumbs began a slow, sensuous rubbing. His eyes darkened, and his mouth grew softer, and she knew he wanted to kiss her. The awful thing was, she realized, that she wanted him to do it, too.

"No," she began feebly. "You said you would not."

"I said I would not force you. Or do anything you did not want me to." The implication of his words hung clearly in the air. "I have wanted you from the first moment I saw you. I don't give a damn about what you do at parties or how many treasures you and your 'family' take. And, honestly, at this moment, I don't give a damn about Bucky or how tight a web you weave around him." His eyes flamed with a fierce light, and his voice was low and fraught with desire. "All I want is to kiss you. To take down that blazing hair and let it run over my hands. To touch your skin."

As he said those last words, he touched his forefinger to her cheek, running it lightly down to the line of her jaw and along it. His skin seared her, and she could feel the faint tremor of passion in his touch. She sucked in her breath sharply at the sensations it evoked inside her. *This was what she had feared—this hunger that he could raise in her so quickly and easily.*

"Lord Lambeth..." she began shakily, her hands clenching into fists at her sides—not, she knew, from a desire to strike him, but from fear that if she did not, her hands would go of their own free will to slide across the expanse of his chest.

"Justin," he said hoarsely, his head bending close to hers. "Call me Justin. I want to hear my name on your lips."

"Justin," she complied, raising her face so that she was

gazing straight into his eyes. It was a mistake, she knew: his gold eyes, darkened by desire, bored into hers, seducing her without his ever moving a muscle.

A sound escaped him, part sigh, part groan, and he cupped her face with his hands and bent to kiss her. A shudder ran down through Marianne, and she moaned, leaning into him, her lips hungry on his. Desire lanced through her, shocking in its intensity. She curled her fingers into his shirt, holding on to him as if she might fall if she let go.

CHAPTER ELEVEN

JUSTIN'S ARMS WENT AROUND MARIANNE, pressing her up into him. They clung together, eager and hot, the flame from one stoking the fires within the other, building higher and ever higher. His hands stroked her body, roaming down her back and over her hips, squeezing her buttocks and grinding her pelvis against his. Flames licked through Marianne's abdomen, and she felt frenzied and out of control. She wanted to feel his hands everywhere on her; she hated the cloth that separated them from her flesh. His mouth was desperate on hers, his fingers almost bruising in their hunger.

He tore his lips from hers and began to kiss his way down her neck. Making a noise deep in his throat, Justin lifted her into his arms and carried her in two quick steps to the wide cushioned bench. He laid her down on the cushion and went down on his knees beside her. He kissed the soft tops of her breasts, his lips leaving a trail of fire across her chest, as his hand cupped one breast, his thumb caressing the nipple into a hard bud. Marianne squeezed her legs together, aware of a deep, insistent ache there.

Justin slipped his hand beneath the top of her dress, sliding over her bare skin, caressing the soft flesh, until his fingers found the taut nipple. Impatiently he shoved down the material, freeing one white globe. For a long moment he simply gazed at it, his thumb circling the dark pink bud, making it harden and point. Then he bent and touched the tip of his tongue to it, wetting it with slow, velvety strokes. Expertly he teased the button until Marianne was whimpering and arching up toward him, the fire in her loins raging out of control. Then he took her nipple into his mouth, pulling at the bud with a hot, wet suction that shot delightful pulses of sensation down through her.

Marianne moved restlessly. She felt at once languid and frenzied. She wanted to scream with impatience, and at the same time, she wanted the lazy movements of his tongue and mouth to go on forever. She ran her hands over his back and shoulders and up into his hair, caressing and squeezing, digging her fingers into his flesh whenever some new and delightful sensation shook her.

Justin's hand went behind her, undoing the top buttons of her dress, and he shoved down the neckline of her dress and the sheer chemise beneath, exposing both her creamy white breasts. His mouth began to feast upon them as his hand stole down her leg and up under her skirt. Marianne gasped at the feel of his hand against her skin, separated only by the thin cotton cloth of her undergarment, and she raked her nails down his back.

His fingers slid between her legs and moved upward, easing her legs apart and gliding smoothly up and up until she was almost sobbing with anticipation, assaulted by the dual pleasures of his mouth and hand. Then his fingers found the hot, damp center of her desire, and Marianne let out a groan, arching up against his palm. He stroked her through the cloth, and she grew wetter beneath his ministrations. Involuntarily, Marianne's hips began to circle, seeking satisfaction. She fumbled at the buttons of his shirt, opening the top two, and slid her hands inside, roaming over the bare skin of his chest. His skin was hot to her touch, exciting her even more, and she explored him eagerly, her fingertips caressing the smooth, firm flesh and twining through the curling hairs, touching the hard buttons of his masculine nipples.

The wordless sound he made confirmed his enjoyment of her explorations, and his mouth came back up to take hers once again. He unfastened the tie of her underdrawers and slid his hand beneath the material, delving down between her legs. Marianne gasped and shuddered as his fingers moved expertly in the soft, slick folds, finding the hidden nub of flesh that was at the seat of her pleasure. His finger moved gently, teasingly over it, arousing her with the merest feather of a touch.

Justin kissed his way to her ear, taking the lobe between his teeth and worrying it delicately, and all the while his fingers worked their magic, until she was groaning and clutching at his shoulders, urging him to the completion she sought. His finger tightened on her, and suddenly pleasure crashed through her, blinding in its intensity. Marianne cried out, her legs stiffening, as the pleasure washed through her in waves.

Justin nuzzled against her neck and murmured, his voice rich with satisfaction, "Bucky has never brought you that, I'll warrant."

It took a moment for his words to penetrate the haze of pleasure in which she floated. Languorous and sated, she lay still for a moment, his sentence gradually soaking into her consciousness. "What?"

Ice stabbed through her satisfaction. *Buckminster*

again—always Buckminster! "That is why you did this? To woo me away from Bucky?"

Marianne's voice rose in indignation, and she sat up, twisting away from him. Justin looked at her flashing eyes and realized what a mistake he had made. *Curse his tongue!* "No! That wasn't what I meant at all!"

"No? Then what *did* you mean?"

His mind befogged by the hunger that throbbed within him, Justin struggled to find words to express the primitive male satisfaction that had surged inside him at her cry of pleasure. It was a tangle of pride and possession, sexual need and jealousy, that he barely comprehended himself. "Why, only that—that you are mine. That neither Buckminster nor any other man shall have you."

"Your possession, you mean?" Marianne spat. "How nice for you."

She sprang up, tears clogging her throat, and adjusted her clothing. *How could she have been so stupid? So naive? She had known he wanted to seduce her away from Buckminster, yet she had fallen into his arms like a piece of ripe fruit ready for plucking.*

"You've certainly come out ahead today," she went on furiously, reaching behind her to fasten the buttons he had undone. "You have bested both Buckminster *and* me."

"I wasn't trying to *best* you," Justin protested, rising to face her. "What is so wrong in taking pleasure in giving you satisfaction?"

"How saintly of you! I am sure that you did not have a thought of removing Bucky from my clutches—or of showing me how easily you could control me." Marianne's cheeks flamed with humiliation.

"I wasn't trying to control you," Justin retorted hotly.

"Damn it, woman, how can you accuse me of base motives when I have given you pleasure while I am still damned unsatisfied!"

"Poor thing!" Marianne retorted sarcastically. "Perhaps it will make you think twice next time before you start one of your foolish games!"

She whirled and ran from the room. Justin started after her, then stopped with a low curse. He thought with some pleasure of picking up the picnic basket—and perhaps the table and chairs as well—and tossing it into the pond, but he stopped himself, knowing that he would feel even more the fool after he had done it.

Damn the woman! How did she manage to remain so indifferent to the passion that seemed to rob him of all ability to think? Justin had, in truth, originally conceived of the idea of seducing Marianne in the summerhouse as a way to woo her away from Buckminster, but in the passion of the moment, he had forgotten all about it. All he had been thinking of was making love to her, and his remark about Bucky, if he was honest, had spoken more to jealousy than to any desire to help his friend.

Obviously, however, it was Buckminster and the possibilities he offered her that were uppermost in Marianne's mind, Justin thought bitterly. He reminded himself that he had known from the first that Marianne was a criminal schemer; he knew that he should not be surprised that she gave more importance to money matters than to passion.

The devil of it was that he had given in so to desire. If she was not interested, he should move on. He would have done so long since with any other woman. And that was exactly what he would do now, he told himself. He would stop this foolish pursuit. He would forget about Marianne

Cotterwood—if that was even her name—and find a more pliable female. Buckminster did not need his help; he was a grown man, and quite capable of taking care of himself.

With those pragmatic thoughts uppermost in his mind, Justin grabbed the basket and marched back to the boat. After tossing the basket into the vessel so hard that it rocked, he jerked off the mooring rope and climbed into the small boat. He put his back into his rowing and made it across to the landing dock at the foot of the garden in record time—and he looked only three times across at the path where Marianne made her way around the lake back to the house.

THE TEARS HAD STOPPED BY THE TIME she reached the bottom of the garden, but Marianne went up the back stairs to her room anyway, not wanting to face any of the other guests. She knew she must look a fright, and she did not have the strength to deal with her impersonation of a lady at the moment.

A restorative cup of tea and an hour's reflection on the perfidy of men left her much calmer, if no less angry with Lord Lambeth. She put on her most attractive day dress and redid her hair, and when the fishing party returned, she went downstairs. She flirted outrageously with Lord Buckminster—at least when Lord Lambeth was in the same room.

He soon left, and then she launched into her role of spoiled, irritating *belle*. She treated Penelope like something of a servant, sending her first to fetch the fan she had left in her room, then, only a few minutes later, to bring down her light shawl. When Bucky expostulated, she merely gazed at him coolly and said, "Nonsense. Penelope loves to do it. It makes her feel useful."

She whined about everything she could think of, from the callous way Bucky had left her alone this morning to the temperature in the room, which was, by turns, too hot and then too cold for her delicate skin, to the lack of refreshment for her parched throat. When she was cold, she tried to persuade Buckminster to ask Lady Merridale to give up her seat by the sunny window to Marianne. When he stuttered that he could not do so, looking shocked, Marianne complained that he was not willing to do anything for her. Next she needed a stool for her feet and told Bucky imperiously to get one for her.

Nicola and Penelope were sitting with Marianne and Bucky when she demanded the stool, and Nicola had to put her hand over her mouth to hide her smile at her cousin's astonished face. While Bucky was gone to the other room, looking for a footstool, Nicola leaned over and squeezed Marianne's arm.

"Dear girl, you are wonderful! I have never seen Bucky look so indignant as when you sent Penny back up for that shawl."

"I hope it's working. I am running out of things to carp about," Marianne replied. She turned toward Penelope. "I hope I haven't hurt your feelings."

"Oh, no. I know you're doing it for me. It is just…" She looked a trifle sad. "I do so hate to see Bucky looking so crestfallen."

"Stiffen your spine, Pen," Nicola told her firmly. "Everything is going perfectly."

"Here he comes," Marianne, who was facing the door, said, quickly dropping her friendly manner. She smiled stiffly at Nicola and said, "Why don't you start a conversation about horses?"

Nicola grinned. "This should be a treat."

Bucky joined them, smiling determinedly, and set the stool down at Marianne's feet. She put her feet upon it and quickly decided that it was too close to her chair. It took several minutes of Bucky's moving it around before he achieved precisely the right spot.

Once he had resumed his seat, looking at Marianne somewhat askance, Nicola asked casually, "Did you ever buy those grays you were looking at, Bucky?"

He brightened. "Lord Pemberton's pair? Dash it, no! He decided not to sell, after all. I was a little miffed, I must say. I had my heart set on them." He turned toward Marianne, explaining, "They were beautiful steppers. I wish you could have seen them."

"Were they?" Marianne drawled in a bored voice.

He proceeded to enumerate their fine points. After a few moments Marianne cut in, saying, "Really, Lord Buckminster, such fuss over a couple of horses! After all, they are all pretty much the same, are they not? Let's talk about the ball your mother is giving this week. Who is coming?"

The conversation bounced along, with Nicola pulling the conversation back to horses, then Marianne dragging it back to her favorite topics—herself and parties. Nicola kept directing the conversation toward Penelope, as well, and each time Marianne quickly moved to shut the girl out. Marianne was afraid that perhaps they were being too obvious even for Bucky, but the growing frown on his face reassured her that they were not. Bucky's disillusion—as well as his protectiveness toward Penelope—was rapidly growing.

That evening, after supper, the guests were largely gathered in the music room, halfheartedly listening to Lady

Merridale play the piano. A few of the gentlemen had retreated to the card room—among them Lady Merridale's
husband, who had, presumably, heard her piano playing
often enough—but Mr. Thurston and his secretary, Mr.
Fuquay, remained, as well as Lord Buckminster and Lord
Lambeth. Lady Buckminster pressed Penelope into singing
some popular songs.

She looked quite pretty, Marianne thought, slim and
dainty in a sky-blue gown from Marianne's closet.
Marianne glanced sideways at Lord Buckminster, who was
watching Penelope, a faint smile on his face. She smiled
to herself and glanced at Nicola. Nicola, too, had been observing Bucky, and she smiled and nodded to Marianne.

Marianne let him watch for a while, but then she
whipped her fan open and held it up before her face,
leaning close to Bucky. "I think I shall scream if I have to
listen to another insipid recital this evening."

Bucky glanced at her, startled. Marianne dimpled at
him, wafting her fan in front of her face with practiced
grace. "Let us escape, shall we?"

His eyes widened at the audacity of her suggestion. A
young woman did not normally leave a room of chape-
rones, although at a more informal gathering such as this
it would not be an absolute scandal. And married women
were allowed a trifle more license than an unmarried girl.
But it was nothing short of bold behavior for a woman to
be the one to suggest departing.

Bucky cast a quick glance around. Marianne tapped his
wrist playfully with her fan. "Come, come, Lord Buckminster, don't tell me you are a *cautious* man." She invested
the word with a wealth of scorn.

"It is just—" he cast a glance toward the piano, where

Penelope still stood "—well, it might seem a bit rude, don't you think?"

"Penelope won't mind," Marianne said with a dismissive shrug. "It is only a little song, anyway."

She gave him a dazzling smile, and he stood up reluctantly. Casting another look toward Penelope, he followed Marianne out of the room. Most of the people, watching the front of the room, did not see them slip out the door, but Marianne saw that Lord Lambeth's sharp eyes followed them. She glanced back to see him glowering blackly at her. She raised her eyebrows lazily at him and swept out the door.

"Isn't this nice?" she asked, linking her arm through Lord Buckminster's.

"Quite." He grinned foolishly back at her, his recent doubts overcome by the beauty of her smile.

"What treat do you have planned for us tomorrow, Lord Buckminster?" she asked gaily, knowing full well from Nicola that they planned a hunt.

His grin broadened. "A hunt. Nothing big, of course. Not really the season, but it seems a pity to waste the opportunity."

"A hunt!" Marianne drew her mouth down into a pout. "Oh, no, really, that is too bad. Don't tell me that you are going to go haring off tomorrow and leave me all alone again!"

"You must come with us."

Marianne groaned. "Another ride! Yesterday was bad enough! Going all that way on horseback just for those silly Falls. But to dash all over the countryside, jumping over hedges and such—it is really too much. Why can't we do something else? Something fun?"

Buckminster stared at her in dismay. "But—but—I can't call it off now, Mrs. Cotterwood. Everyone is expecting it."

"But you don't have to go," Marianne pointed out. "You

could stay here with me." She smiled brilliantly at him. "Wouldn't that be more fun?"

"Stay here?" he repeated faintly. Marianne had to bite the inside of her lip to keep from giggling at the dismayed look on his face.

"Why, yes. Everyone else can have their fun, and you and I shall have our own private tête-à-tête."

"Ah, well, there will be some others here, of course. Lady Merridale, I believe."

"Then that will take care of propriety," Marianne pointed out.

"But, truly, I could not miss my own hunt," he protested, looking rather queasy at the thought. "It—it just wouldn't be the thing."

"Lady Buckminster will be there. Isn't that enough?"

"Well, but, Marianne…" He looked pained. "It is a highlight of the visit."

"You would rather go than be with me!" Marianne cried, her eyes flashing. "You care for me so little? I can see how much all your fine protestations of respect and affection are worth. You have no regard for me at all!"

"No! No, that isn't true!" Buckminster assured her earnestly. "My regard for you is the highest."

"Hmph!" Marianne turned away from him and began to walk briskly back toward the music room. Bucky followed her miserably.

"Please, Mrs. Cotterwood, listen to me. I assure you—"

Marianne whirled around. "Your assurances mean nothing. It is clear how unimportant I am to you."

"No, please, you mustn't think that!"

"What else am I to think? You prefer the company of horses and hounds to me."

"Never!"

Marianne used all the tricks she could remember the Quartermaines' daughter using to get her way. She stormed; she pouted; she sulked; she froze him out with icy silence, until finally, with a hangdog expression, Bucky agreed that he would stay with her instead of joining the hunt.

She had a moment's qualm, looking at him, but then she reminded herself that with any luck, this would be the final blow that would knock the young man out of his infatuation with her and straight into the arms of the woman who loved him.

She did not return with him to the music room, but, pleading a headache, went straight up to her room. She had no desire to be with him to hear the astonished comments and pleadings of his friends.

There was a soft tap on her door later, and when she opened it, Nicola and Penelope slipped inside. Penelope looked troubled, but Nicola was grinning.

"However did you manage that!" she exclaimed. "Bucky not going on a hunt is like—well, it's like nothing else. It's unimaginable."

"I played every trick I could think of. I was, in short, an unmitigated *witch*. I was beginning to think it wouldn't work, but then he gave in."

"He looked so unhappy," Penelope said worriedly.

Marianne smiled and put an arm around the girl's shoulders. "Don't worry. It will only be a little while longer. I predict that by the time you get back tomorrow, Lord Buckminster will never want to see me again."

Nicola chuckled. Penelope looked doubtful. "Do you really think so?"

Marianne nodded. "Absolutely. I intend to make sure

that he is immensely bored and thinking all the while of all of you out enjoying yourselves. Then, when you come in, he will want to hear all about it and, hopefully, want to pour out all his disillusionment about me into sympathetic ears."

"That's you," Nicola said, pointing a finger at Penelope. "What if I muck it up?"

"You won't," Nicola assured her. "That part is entirely natural to you. Just look at him as you look now, brimming with empathy and love. Listen to what he says, and agree and murmur encouragement. In scarcely no time, he will have forgotten all about Mrs. Cotterwood, except to be glad that his eyes were opened in time, and he will have realized what a splendid girl you are. It's perfect!"

"You might even suggest that he have another hunt the next day," Marianne added. "Then the two of you can enjoy it together, and he can be reminded of how well you suit each other."

"This is all working out perfectly." Nicola beamed and gave Marianne an impulsive hug. "I'm so glad I met you."

"So am I," Marianne returned honestly. She wished, with a pang, that she could be truly close to them, that she could tell them her thoughts and hopes and dreams. But the gulf between them was huge, she knew, and if they knew what she really was, she was certain that they would shun her. *Once they returned to London, what would she do?*

The other two went to their rooms, and Marianne turned to her bed, feeling immeasurably sad. It seemed to her that she no longer fit anywhere. All her old assumptions about the aristocracy had been shaken the past few days. She truly liked Nicola and Penelope and Bucky. But she was not really one of them; the life she lived here was a pretense. On the other hand, she felt separated from Della and the others;

they would never understand her reluctance to take property from these titled, wealthy idlers. Something in her rebelled at the thought of continuing to live the life of deception and criminality that she had been living. *But how was she to survive and provide for her daughter if she did not? And if she stopped working with the others, she would certainly never be able to afford to mingle with her new friends.*

Then there was Justin. Just the thought of him brought tears to her eyes. He desired her, but he did not love her, and even his pursuit of her was spurred by his belief that she meant to take advantage of his friend Bucky. He had no real feeling for her—and she feared that she was beginning to care all too much for him.

It was, she thought, all a terrible mess. She climbed into bed and pulled the covers up to her chin, closing her eyes on her tears. *If only she had never gone to Lady Batterslee's party.... If only she had never met Lord Lambeth....*

"YOU ARE LATE." LORD EXMOOR turned from his contemplation of the broad pond to face the man who had just entered the summerhouse.

"I came the long way, through the garden. I thought there was less chance of anyone seeing me that way. A boat is a trifle conspicuous on the pond at night."

"Are you sure it isn't simply reluctance? The same reluctance that causes you to make a mull of everything you try with Mrs. Cotterwood?"

"I don't know what you mean."

"I am talking about your latest pathetic attempt to get rid of the woman. Pushing her into the River Lyd? Really! Even if she had fallen in—which, I might remind you, she did not—the odds are that she would have done no worse

than get wet and acquire a few bruises. Besides, it was absolutely unacceptable to do it while I was there! That
defeats the whole purpose of the thing."

"Which is, of course, to protect you, and everyone else
be damned," his companion retorted bitterly.

"But of course." The Earl allowed himself a thin smile.
"Protecting me means protecting yourself, old chap, as
you well know, though I realize that you have become
such a paragon that it turns you quite queasy to think of
doing the woman in."

"I was *never* a murderer!" the other man snapped. "Not
even in my darkest, most wicked moments."

"I had some trouble with it myself…once," Exmoor
replied. "Fortunately, I overcame my inhibitions."

"Then why don't *you* kill her, if it is so easy for you?"

"We have discussed this before. It is your responsibility."

"She has seen me several times now, face to face, and
there has not been the slightest hint of recognition," the
younger man pointed out reasonably. "She has no memory
of me, and I am sure she has even less of you. There is no
possibility that she will turn either of us in."

"One never knows what might trigger a memory, especially if we allow the Countess to get hold of her. Her man
is looking for the woman, too. We are not the only ones. I
personally have no desire to bet my freedom against Mrs.
Cotterwood recovering her memory—or parts of it, at
least—when she meets her grandmother. Therefore, I
suggest that you finish her off before the Countess locates
her. It would be most unfortunate, don't you think, if
certain persons learned the full depths of your past?"

"I will do it. I have a plan. Yesterday was not planned.
I simply saw the chance and took it, knowing that it might

work and it might not. Nothing was lost by it. But I have a plan laid out, and I will take care of her. But have a care, my lord. This thing works both ways, you know. We both know that if you start spreading stories about me, I can reveal just as much about you as you can about me. I am sure the Dowager Countess would be quite interested in what I have to say."

Exmoor's eyes narrowed. "Are you daring to threaten me?"

"No threat. Simply a reminder."

"It would appear we are at a stalemate, then. Just remember that our interests lie in the same direction. Now, what is this plan of yours?"

The other man shook his head. "Let's let it be a surprise, shall we? So much easier for you to appear innocent, after all. Good night, my lord."

He turned and walked out of the summerhouse. The Earl watched him go thoughtfully. *The man could turn out to be dangerous. Perhaps, when the matter of the girl was taken care of, he might have to make certain that his accomplice would never talk, either.*

CHAPTER TWELVE

WHEN MARIANNE WENT DOWN TO breakfast the next morning, she found Lord Buckminster gloomily waiting for her. Lady Merridale, delighted to find a listening ear on a morning when she had thought to be left entirely alone, was happily describing to him her shopping expedition into the local village the day before. Bucky rose and greeted Marianne with great relief.

Marianne, suppressing her qualms, did not help him elude the talkative Sophronia, however. Much to Lord Buckminster's dismay, she engaged in an extended conversation with Lady Merridale on the merits of shopping in the village. After that, she regaled Bucky with several tales of buying this or that dress, or the great searches upon which she had engaged for exactly the right hat.

After breakfast, she turned down Bucky's suggestion of a stroll in the garden, declaring that it was far too warm. Instead, they joined Lady Merridale in the drawing room, where Marianne spent the rest of the morning in a verbal contest to see which of them could tell the most boring stories. Firmly she redirected every conversational gambit back to herself—her clothes, her many admirers, her home, her distaste for horses and for most forms of physical exercise. Even Sophronia, she was pleased to notice, could

not surpass her in banality, and Marianne felt she quite outstripped the other woman in terms of self-absorption.

Bucky, she noticed, had trouble keeping from nodding
off. When the hunting party returned, the relief on his face
was laughable. He jumped from his seat, sketching as brief
a bow to the ladies as courtesy would allow, and hurried
out into the hall. Marianne trailed after him to the door and
looked out. She was pleased to note that Penelope managed
to be the first person Lord Buckminster met, and the two
of them were soon engaged in an animated conversation.
Smiling, Marianne slipped away.

"YOU SEEM TO HAVE DONE YOUR job excellently," Nicola
murmured to Marianne, linking her arm through
Marianne's as she caught up with her in the hall after the
noon repast. "I noticed that Bucky did not look at you once
throughout the meal."

"He was probably terrified that I would break into
another account of one of my dresses, down to the last frill
and furbelow."

Nicola chuckled. "Oh, no, did you inflict that on the
poor man?"

Marianne nodded, grinning. "Yes. It was quite fun,
actually, to try to be a bore instead of trying to make people
like one. I think I may take it up as a hobby."

"I understand Lady Merridale joined you."

"Oh, yes. We had quite a little gabfest. I don't think poor
Bucky managed to get in more than a word or two all
morning. I concentrated on being egotistical and boring. I
think I've displayed my fangs enough—although, of
course, I did manage to slip in a catty remark or two about

Lady Merridale when she left the room. Of course, I was sickeningly sweet to her face."

"It sounds like a performance worthy of the stage."

"I hope so. With luck, this should be one of the last I shall be obliged to make. I expect Bucky to avoid me like the plague now."

"He talked with Penelope all through luncheon. Did you notice?"

"Once or twice. Between Mr. Westerton chattering in my ear about the ball Friday night and Sir William describing the hunt in exhausting detail, I had little attention to spare for anything else." She saw no point in mentioning that a great deal of her attention had been directed toward the other end of the table, where Lord Lambeth had sat chatting and laughing with Cecilia Winborne. "I did notice, however, that they left the dining room together."

"Yes. I think they were going to the conservatory."

"Ah. Then I think that we should turn toward the drawing room, don't you?"

"Absolutely."

They made their way to the drawing room, where Mrs. Thurston was in quiet conversation with Mrs. Minton and Mr. Fuquay. The occupants of the room greeted them with smiles, and they spent a few pleasant moments chatting about the beauty of the Buckminster gardens.

"I particularly like the rose arbor," Marianne admitted. "It's a very pleasant place to sit."

"Yes, indeed," Mrs. Thurston agreed. "But have you visited the summerhouse? The view is absolutely marvelous."

Marianne's hands clenched in her lap, and she hoped

that her face was not as flushed as it felt. "The—the summerhouse?"

"Yes, the charming little gazebo across the pond," Mr. Fuquay explained.

"Oh. Yes. Of course. No, I—I am afraid I have not been there." She hoped that no one had seen her returning from it the morning before. She simply could not admit that she had been there with Lord Lambeth; she knew that it would have been clear from her face exactly what had happened.

"Why, you should," Mrs. Thurston commented. "Nicola, you and Mrs. Cotterwood should persuade some of the gentlemen to take you there."

"I would be happy to accompany you," Fuquay offered politely.

"That is very kind of you. Perhaps we shall," Nicola agreed with a distinct lack of enthusiasm.

At that moment Sophronia Merridale sailed into the room, and it was all Marianne could do to repress a groan. She did not know how much more of the woman's company she could endure. But her dismay deepened when Cecilia Winborne followed the woman into the room.

The last thing Marianne wanted was to be stuck in a conversation with Cecilia Winborne. However, there was little way she could pop up and leave the moment the two women joined their group. Instead she smiled politely and started thinking about a plausible excuse to depart as soon as she could.

Unfortunately, almost immediately Miss Winborne turned her attention to Marianne. "I have been so looking forward to getting to know you better, Mrs. Cotterwood," she said, her thin mouth curving into a perfunctory smile.

"Really," Marianne replied lamely. *What could she say—that she didn't believe the woman for a second?*

"Yes. My friends speak so highly of you—and I believe you have quite captured my poor brother's heart." She waggled a finger at Marianne in a ghastly attempt at playfulness.

"I have?" It was all Marianne could do not to gape at her. She had caught Fanshaw Winborne looking at her a number of times, but he had barely spoken to her. The one time they had been in any sort of close proximity, he had stood looking down his nose at her and saying nothing in a way that made her highly nervous. If asked, she would have guessed that the man looked upon her with contempt, not admiration.

"I don't believe we have ever met before, have we?" Cecilia went on.

"No. I have not been much in Society, I'm afraid. The last few years I lived in Bath."

"Bath? Then you must know Lady Harwood."

"I have met her, of course." Marianne was relieved that Cecilia had chosen someone who spent all her time sitting in the Assembly Rooms; everyone who had spent any time in Bath would know who Lady Harwood was. "I am sure she would scarcely remember me."

"Her companion—what is that silly woman's name? Fifi?"

"I believe that is Lady Harwood's dog," Marianne responded coolly. *Cecilia was trying to trip her up.* The awful corollary to this idea was, of course, that Cecilia somehow had guessed she was a fake. "Her companion is Miss Cummings, I believe, but the time I spoke with her, I found her quiet and grave, rather than silly."

"I must be thinking of someone else. Mrs. Dalby, perhaps."

"I don't know Mrs. Dalby. Does she reside in Bath also?"

"Why, yes."

"Oh, no, I think you are wrong," Nicola chimed in. "If you are talking about Mrs. James Dalby, I am rather certain she lives in Brighton."

"Yes, of course, you're right." Cecilia smiled grimly at Nicola.

"I doubt I know a large number of your friends in Bath." Marianne decided to go on the offensive. "I have been in seclusion since my husband's death three years ago, and before that, he was ill for some time."

"I see. What part of the country are you from?"

"Yorkshire." It was the story she had decided on before she came to this party; it was as far away as she could think of from where they were.

"Oh, really? I am afraid I'm not terribly familiar with Yorkshire."

"Indeed? Where are *you* from, Miss Winborne?"

The other woman raised her brows a little, as if surprised that anyone would not know where the Winborne family lived. "Why, Sussex is our family seat, of course."

"Of course." Marianne's gaze fell upon Nicola, who rolled her eyes expressively, and Marianne had to press her lips together firmly not to laugh.

"And I am from Buckinghamshire originally," Nicola offered gaily, "since we are discussing our origins. What about you, Lady Merridale?"

"What? Oh, where am I from? Well, Sir George and I live in Norfolk. That is his family's home. I was born near Newcastle."

She proceeded to tell them in much more detail than anyone wanted to hear about both her ancestral home and the Merridale house, much of the wood of which was having to be rescued from dry rot. From the look on Nicola's face, Marianne suspected that she regretted the teasing question she had asked. Marianne thought that perhaps her own eyes were glazing over, and she waited for the woman to draw a breath so that she could take her leave of the group.

But when Sophronia at last paused in her monologue, Cecilia Winborne stuck in quickly, "What part of Yorkshire did you live in, Mrs. Cotterwood?"

Marianne was surprised by Cecilia's taking up the subject again, but she had prepared herself for being asked about her background, so she replied easily, "Why, Kirkham, Miss Winborne. It is a small place, not too far from York."

"And is that where your late husband's family was from, as well?"

"No. Actually, he was from Norton." Marianne replied in a cool tone that suggested that the other woman's questions were becoming impertinent.

"Ah, I see. So it is your family who lives in Kirkham."

"Yes, except that I am afraid that my parents are no longer living."

"I am so sorry. But no doubt you have brothers and sisters to give you comfort. What did you say your maiden name was?"

"It was Morely, Miss Winborne," Marianne said sharply, "and I have no siblings."

"Really, Cecilia," Nicola commented, "you sound like the Grand Inquisitor."

Cecilia cast Nicola a venomous look. "I am sorry," she said stiffly. "I did not mean to pry, Mrs. Cotterwood. I was merely looking for some common ground on which to base an acquaintance. Pray forgive me."

"Of course. But I am afraid I must leave now. I promised Lady Buckminster that I would help her with preparations for the ball Friday evening." Marianne rose with a smile toward the general company.

Nicola bounced up right after her. "I'll come with you. I am sure Aunt Adelaide could use an extra pair of hands. If you'll excuse me, Cecilia…Lady Merridale."

Marianne left the room with what she hoped did not appear to be undue haste. Nicola was right on her heels. The two of them glanced at each other, and a smile twitched across Nicola's face, but she remained determinedly silent until they were far enough down the hall that the occupants of the room they had just left could not hear them.

"I wasn't about to let you leave me in there with Cecilia and Sophronia Merridale!" Nicola exclaimed. "I don't know whether I would have been driven first to murder or to suicide!"

Marianne chuckled. "Miss Winborne obviously dislikes me. Why was she asking all those questions?"

"Cecilia is a witch. You must not let her bother you. I am sure she is hoping that you will say something about your background that will reveal how perfectly unsuitable you are for Lord Lambeth. She has seen how he looks at you."

"Don't be absurd." Marianne was vexed to feel her cheeks grow hot at Nicola's statement. "He does not stare at me."

"He does not hang about staring at you like a moon-struck calf," Nicola admitted. "Justin is far too sophisticated for that. But when he looks at you, there is something quite different in his eyes. I have noticed it myself."

"I am sure you are mistaken."

"Don't you dare go all prim and proper on me, Marianne Cotterwood. You know that Justin's interested in you. Why else would Cecilia go to the trouble of annoying you?"

"I cannot understand how you can say that their future marriage is purely a business arrangement," Marianne went on. "At least not on her part. She wouldn't be jealous of me if it were."

"You would be surprised at the depths of Cecilia's ill nature," Nicola retorted. "She does not love Justin, if that is what you're thinking. She loves the title and the wealth that will be hers. But she knows better than anyone that that is not a sure thing, for if Justin should fall in love…"

"There is little danger of that," Marianne said caustically. She glanced at her friend, realizing that perhaps her response had been too emotional. "I mean—I think you are mistaken if you are hinting that he is in love with me. His interest is the sort that men often have in a widow, and it does not end in marriage."

"Marianne! How cynical you are."

Marianne shrugged. "Aware of the ways of the world is more like it. The future Duke of Storbridge is hardly likely to marry plain Mrs. Cotterwood from an obscure village in Yorkshire."

"I think you do Lord Lambeth an injustice. I have always thought he was a man who did exactly as he wanted."

"I am sure he does—but I am also sure that what he wants is a wife with status equal to his own…and a mistress on the side for enjoyment."

Nicola's eyes opened wide, and she giggled. "For shame, Marianne. You say the most shocking things."

"He as much as told me so on the ride to White Lady

Falls." Marianne paused at the stairway. "Well, now that we have made our escape, where shall we go?"

Nicola considered, then smiled. "Let's look for Penelope and see how our scheme is working."

"Excellent suggestion."

They strolled down the hall and into the conservatory, a sunny room filled with plants. At the far end was a conversational grouping of wicker chairs and couch, and it was here that Penelope and Lord Buckminster sat, their heads close together, talking. Marianne and Nicola glanced at one another significantly, and Nicola pulled Marianne behind a tall palm.

"It looks as if everything is progressing rather nicely," Nicola murmured.

Marianne nodded. "Yes. I wonder...perhaps another dose of the 'wicked widow'?"

"It would make a nice contrast," Nicola agreed.

Marianne winked and sailed forth. Nicola stayed behind the tall palm, prepared to enjoy the scene about to unfold before her.

"May I hide, too?" a man's voice murmured in Nicola's ear, and she turned to find Lord Lambeth beside her.

"Justin, you startled me," she whispered, taking his arm and pulling him behind the palm. "Watch. This should be a treat."

"My lord!" Marianne's voice emerged in an annoying whine as she approached Lord Buckminster and Penelope. "There you are! I had wondered where you had gotten to. Sitting with Miss Castlereigh—how nice of you."

Both Penelope and Bucky started and looked up a little guiltily. Marianne bared her teeth at Penelope. "How are you, Penelope? I hope that Lord Buckminster has been keeping you entertained."

"Oh, yes. I mean, it was very kind of him to keep me company," Penelope's look of dismay was quite real. She had been having such a pleasant time with Bucky that she had forgotten all about their scheme, and she hated being brought back to it.

"It was quite unfair of you, Lord Buckminster," Marianne told the man archly. "I have been pining away for you."

She settled onto the cushioned wicker couch with a litany of complaints and requests, asking Bucky to fetch a stool for her feet, then pillows to make her more comfortable on the couch, most of which she pulled out again almost immediately. They were too soft, too lumpy, too hard, too much, or not enough.

Behind the palm, Nicola had to clap her hand over her mouth to keep her giggles in, and Lambeth stared in amazement.

Finally, with a sigh, Marianne settled back against the cushions and said, "I am so dreadfully thirsty, Bucky, dear."

"What? Oh. Certainly," the harassed-looking man answered. "Wait. I'm sorry. The conservatory doesn't have a bellpull. I cannot ring." He paused, then offered, "I shall go to the hall and ring for a servant."

"Heavens, no," Marianne answered, her hand on his arm to keep him seated. "I am sure Penelope would be happy to do it."

Bucky gaped at her. "You're asking Penelope to fetch you a glass of water?"

"Why, yes, dear. I am sure Penelope doesn't mind, do you, Pen, darling?"

"No. No, of course not," Penelope answered; it had taken all her ability not to laugh during Marianne's superbly carping performance, and she would be frankly delighted to get away where she could let a grin escape. She jumped up and hurried away.

Buckminster gaped at Marianne. "I say, Mrs. Cotterwood, that's a little, well, high-handed, don't you think? Sending Penelope to get refreshment, as if she were a servant."

Marianne looked at him with wide eyes. "I am sure Penelope does not mind. She is such a dear creature."

"But that is all the more reason not to take advantage of her."

"I could think of no other way to get you alone. She has occupied your attention all afternoon!" Marianne snapped. "It is quite clear to me what is going on, even if it is not to you!"

"What the devil are you talking about?"

"Don't play the innocent with me. It is clear what you and Penelope have been doing. I have eyes. I can see."

"Are you implying that I—that we—" Buckminster goggled at her.

"I am not naive, Bucky," Marianne said severely. "It is obvious that you find Penelope attractive. It is equally obvious that you and she were hiding from me. Did you kiss her?"

"Mrs. Cotterwood! How can you say such a thing? Penelope would never—"

"Ah, I notice that you say *Penelope* would never. No such assurance that *you* would not!" Marianne surged to her feet while Buckminster simply stared at her, his mouth opening and closing like a landed fish. "I should have known that you were playing fast and loose with me." She whirled and started toward the door leading out into the garden.

"But…but…Marianne! That is, Mrs. Cotterwood, you have it all wrong!"

Marianne whipped back around to face him, her expression cold, her back straight. "Have I? I think not. I suggest you search your conscience, Lord Buckminster. Can you honestly say that you have no feeling for Miss Castlereigh?"

On that parting note, she turned once again and strode out the door. Buckminster stood looking after her for a moment, then sank down on the sofa, staring thoughtfully at the floor.

"Oh, masterful!" Nicola whispered. "Well done, Marianne, well done, indeed!" She turned to Lambeth and took his hand, nodding her head toward the door behind them. She tiptoed to the door, Lambeth following her just as stealthily.

"What the devil was that all about?" Justin demanded as soon as they were out of earshot, walking along the hall toward the stairs. "What does she think she's up to? That is scarcely the way to capture Bucky's heart."

Nicola shot him an odd look. "Capture Bucky's heart! Is that what you think Marianne has been trying to do?"

"Why, yes, of course."

"Honestly, Justin…men can be so thickheaded."

"What else would I think? She has clung to his arm the past few days, flirting and laughing and—"

"And keeping him with her instead of going hunting this morning. Flirting heartlessly with all the other men, as well. Complaining incessantly. Let's see, what else? Oh, yes—filling his ear with boring stories about herself and her clothes and the many men who admire her. Making rude remarks about Penelope—and planting it in his mind that he is interested in Penelope!"

Lambeth stared at her. "But why?"

Nicola rolled her eyes. "Why, to nip his infatuation in the bud, of course. 'Tis much more effective and far less likely to bruise his heart to see that his goddess has feet of clay. Plus, it gave her an opportunity to angle him in Penny's direction. We made sure that Penelope was there, handy for him to commiserate with or to ride with when Marianne was a slug on horseback or, like this afternoon, handy for him to sneak away with to avoid spending the rest of the day with Marianne. I added my own bits of subtle nudging, of course."

She grinned smugly. Justin studied her.

"So this was a scheme that the three you of you cooked up together."

"Yes—well, at least the details of it. Marianne came up with the idea."

"When?"

"In the carriage on the ride down here. It was obvious that Bucky was head over heels about Marianne, and of course Pen was being quite resigned about it, but Marianne told us what she meant to do."

"That little minx," Lambeth murmured.

"What?"

"Nothing. Just talking to myself." He stopped, turning to face Nicola. "Where did she go, do you think?"

Nicola gave him a long, considering look. "I'm not sure. Perhaps to the rose arbor. She likes to sit there, she said."

"Thank you, Nicola. Now, if you will excuse me…"

MARIANNE SIGHED AND SAT DOWN on the wooden bench that stretched beneath the arbor. Roses grew thickly over the latticework, shading the area below with green coolness and perfuming the air with their heady scent. She closed her eyes, contemplating with a certain smug satisfaction the scene she had just played. She had, she thought, taken care of the problem of Lord Buckminster.

There was the crunch of boots upon the gravel path, disturbing her contemplation, and a moment later Lord Lambeth appeared around the side of the arbor. He stood for a moment, silhouetted against the light, his expression unreadable. Marianne rose to her feet slowly, as if pulled up by invisible strings. He came toward her, his hand going to her arm. He pulled her forward, and she had a glimpse of his face, eyes blazing with some unidentifiable emotion. Then his face blocked off all vision, and Marianne closed her eyes as his lips sank into hers.

He kissed her hungrily, deeply, with little of the practiced artistry with which he had kissed her in the summerhouse. Yet this kiss was even more stirring, and Marianne found herself leaning into him, her arms sliding naturally around his waist.

At last he pulled his head away and looked down into her dazed face. "Why didn't you tell me?" he asked fiercely. "Why did you lead me to believe—"

Then he kissed her again, cutting off his words. She wasn't sure what he was talking about—or of much of anything else, except that her world was trembling and tilting upon its axis, as wildly out of control as the breath in her lungs. His arms were around her like bands of iron, squeezing her hard against him, yet she wanted to be even closer, to melt into him. She strained against him, and he ran a hand down her back, pressing her more tightly to him all the way up and down.

He broke the kiss to rain more kisses over her face and up and down her throat, mumbling broken words of endearment against the tender flesh. Marianne's heart thrilled within her at the sound of the words. She was trembling with passion. Justin sat down on the bench, pulling her into his lap, and continued to kiss her, his hand roaming over her breasts and stomach. Heat blossomed in her wherever he touched, and she arched back, a groan of desire escaping her.

He cupped her breast with his hand, teasing and caressing it through the cloth of her dress. The nipple pointed, pressing against the material, arousing him further. He buried his face in her neck, drawing a deep, shuddering breath.

"God, if we keep on, I shall take you right here," he groaned.

Marianne did not think she would mind, but she could not form a sentence coherent enough to express the thought. She sat for a few moments, wrapped in his arms, her head against his chest. Gradually the tumultuous pounding of his heart began to slow a little.

"Why did you not tell me?" he asked again, pulling back a little to look down into her face.

"Tell you what?" She gazed back at him in a dazed lack of comprehension.

"About your scheme regarding Bucky. Worse than that, you made me think that you were trying to catch him!"

"Oh. That. How did you find out about that?"

"Nicola enlightened me. Why would you want to make me believe that you were a heartless, conniving little baggage?"

"You already thought that!" Marianne retorted with returning spirit and hopped off his lap, turning to face him. "I did not have to make you believe that. You *accused* me of it. If you will remember, you warned me away from him. I had never had the least intention of trying to ensnare Lord Buckminster's heart. But you believed me so lacking in honor, so…so willing to sell myself that I—" She broke off, remembered fury surging up in her again.

"So you decided to confirm my misconception?" he asked in amazement.

"I was angry."

"But why didn't you tell me the truth? Set me straight?"

Marianne cocked one eyebrow. "You think you would have believed me? You had already made up your mind about me. Nothing I could have said would have changed it." She shrugged. "I decided it would be much more fun to tweak your nose a little bit."

"Fun!" he repeated, slack-jawed, rising to his feet. "You call that fun? Making me suffer the—" He stopped abruptly, and a momentary confusion came over his face.

"Suffer what?"

"Nothing. It does not matter." Lambeth knew that he had been about to say "suffer the pangs of jealousy," but the idea rocked him back on his heels. He had never been jealous over a woman in his life. He had, frankly, rarely had cause to be, for it had usually been he who ended his *liaisons* and who had been diligently pursued by marriageable maidens. But, more than that, there had been no woman about whom he really cared enough to be upset if she decided that she preferred another man. It would have been a blow to his masculine pride, but nothing more, easily assuaged by the company of some other bit of muslin.

Had it been the fires of jealousy that had eaten at him these past few days, not a desire to protect his friend?

He turned away, his mind racing. Jealousy was an emotion for love-struck fools, not for men such as himself— worldly wise and logical, in control of themselves.

"Justin?" Marianne asked uncertainly. *Was he angry*

with her again? She had had to express her dislike of the assumptions that he had made about her, but she realized that she did not want him to turn against her once more. "What is the matter?"

"Nothing," he replied quickly, turning back to her. "I am simply, well, astounded. It is a lot to assimilate." He smiled crookedly. "I had thought you scheming, but obviously I had no idea how complex your schemes were. I mean, deceiving me into thinking you were after Bucky, and all the while deceiving him into believing that you were not the woman he wanted."

"I know. Thank goodness you are both men and therefore easier to deceive." She grinned impishly. "You will notice that I told Nicola and Penelope the truth."

He snorted. "Because you needed their help. Honestly, don't any of you have any compunction about manipulating poor Bucky like that?"

"Poor Bucky! You think he has cause for complaint—being turned in the direction of a woman who adores him?"

"But turned away from a woman whose beauty and wit surpass those of any woman here," he countered, his smile slow and sensual.

His words left Marianne breathless. "You have a pretty way with words."

"It is far more than pretty words." He moved closer. "You are unlike any woman I have ever met."

"You must have lived a sheltered life."

"Perhaps I have." His voice was low and husky, his body so close to hers that she could feel its heat. "Everything I have done with you has turned out wrong; I haven't felt so clumsy and inept in years."

"Surely that is not my fault." Marianne could not keep

the unsteadiness from her voice. Her lungs felt as if the air were being crushed from her.

"Ah, but it is." He smiled faintly. "It is easy to be practiced and assured when it does not matter if you fail. It is far more difficult when the outcome is so important."

Marianne could not have said anything if she had tried. She simply gazed up at him.

"I have tried the past day to stay away from you, but it has been damnably difficult. I told myself that you were wicked, that I was better off without you. But the fact is that I have thought of you every minute. I haven't ceased wanting you."

He took her hand in his and raised it to his lips. Silently he kissed each of her fingertips. "Will you forgive me for the things I said to you? The things I thought?"

"Then you have decided that I am not a thief?" Marianne struggled to keep her voice light despite the weakness his feathery kisses was causing all through her body.

He chuckled. "I realize that you are not the sort to try to trap Bucky, that you are, in fact, a good friend and a woman with a kind heart. I was wrong to assume you were an adventuress. As for thievery…" He shrugged. "I am finding more and more that I simply do not care."

He tilted up her chin, gazing seriously into her eyes. "Say you will give me another chance. Tell me I have not burned all my bridges with you."

"No, you have not," Marianne admitted softly. "I— perhaps you are a trifle hard to forget, as well."

He grinned. "What lovely words, Mrs. Cotterwood." He bent and kissed her lips lightly.

Marianne pulled away from him. "But I—I feel I must be honest with you, as you have been honest with me. You were right…about what I did. What Piers and Harrison have done. For the past ten years that is how I have lived." She raised her chin defiantly. "It was wrong, perhaps, but I do not regret it. I took only from people who would scarcely miss what I stole. And it was the only way I could find to support Rosalind and myself in any kind of decent life. I couldn't bear to let her grow up hungry and poor— not when I could give her the things she deserved. There was no other way I knew to do that except to sell my body, and I refused to do that. I owed Harrison and Della a great debt. They had saved my life, and Rosalind's. How could I not do everything I could to repay them?"

"You do not need to justify yourself to me. Heaven only knows, I am no saint." He paused, then said, "But it is a dangerous life to lead. What if you were caught? What would happen to your daughter then?"

"I know. And I—I am not certain that I can do it anymore. These past few days, everything has been so different. I have come to care—I mean, I do not think I could do something that would hurt Lady Buckminster. She has been quite kind to me." She grinned. "Even though I am a poor rider."

"No doubt she hopes to reform you." Lambeth reached out and took her hand again. "Will you overlook my past mistakes? May we start again?"

"I—I am not sure what you mean," Marianne hedged. "I don't know what you want from me." *Was he offering again to make her his mistress?* She had sworn she would never settle for such a position. It was far better to be her own woman—and she refused to make her daughter live under such a cloud. Yet she knew that there was no possibility of marriage with a man destined one day to be a duke.

He grinned. "A chance, that's all. Right now I ask only that you save a waltz for me at Lady Buckminster's ball Friday."

"That is a promise easily enough given. But what about after that?"

He shrugged. "Then we shall see. Right now, that is enough." He lifted his eyebrows quizzically. "Well? What do you say?"

"I will save you a waltz," she agreed, hoping she was not making a terrible mistake.

CHAPTER THIRTEEN

MARIANNE DID NOT SLEEP WELL THAT NIGHT. Her thoughts were too full of Justin. After their talk in the rose arbor, he had not tried to kiss her again. He had been lightly flirtatious the rest of the day, and although he did not make an obvious point of it, he had managed to spend a good deal of the evening by her side. He was subtly courting her, she knew, but she also knew that his courtship could lead nowhere except to a life she had promised herself she would never lead.

She lay awake for a long time, thinking about what had happened that afternoon in the rose arbor, going over in her mind every word, every gesture, every shade of meaning. *Would he come to her tonight?* Her nerves were on edge, waiting for a tap at her door.

She did not want Justin to visit, she told herself. An affair with him would mean nothing but pain. Still, she could not stop thinking about what would happen if he did come to her room. She tossed and turned, remembering the scene that afternoon, and when she finally slept, she woke up two or three times to find herself twisted in her sheets, damp with sweat and thrumming from heated dreams that she could not quite recall.

When she awoke the next morning, she was heavy-eyed

from lack of sleep. Stretching, she climbed out of bed, aware of a certain sense of piqué that Justin had not come to her room. Her eyes fell on a square white envelope lying on the rug just inside the closed door. Her heart picked up its beat. She hurried over and picked it up. Her name was on the front. She opened it quickly.

The note read:

Dearest Marianne,

    I shall be waiting for you this morning at 11:00 at the entrance to the abandoned mine that we passed the other day on the ride to the Falls. Wheal Sarah. Pray do not tell anyone.

Yours,
Justin

As if she would reveal to anyone that she was having an assignation with a man, she thought. But it was somehow endearing to see this bit of nervousness in a man otherwise so sophisticated. She smiled to herself. Obviously the place had some special significance to him because they had seen it together and talked about it on their ride. And just as obviously, his not coming to her room last night had had to do with discretion, not lack of desire.

It would be foolish to go, she knew. He could want to meet her at such an isolated spot for one reason only, and she was fully aware of the dangers of having an affair with Lord Lambeth. Yet she found herself pulling out her riding habit from the wardrobe. It might mean emotional disaster for her, but she realized in that moment that she did not care. She wanted only to lose herself in Justin's arms.

She dressed quickly, not waiting for the maid to help her.

A quick twist and pinning of her hair would hold it under her hat, and she needed no more than that. Within minutes, she was ready, and she left her room.

Hoping to avoid meeting anyone, she ran lightly down the servants' staircase. Only Lady Buckminster and her friend Mrs. Minton were up this early and seated at the breakfast table, and Lady Buckminster said only, "Ah, going riding, I see. Good idea. Be sure to take a groom with you."

"I will," Marianne replied mendaciously and tucked into her breakfast.

Lady Buckminster and her friend carried on their conversation regarding the ancestry of a particular horse that Mrs. Minton was considering buying and that Bucky's mother considered a bad bargain. Marianne could understand only about a third of what they said, but that was fine with her, for she had no interest in trying to carry on a conversation this morning.

As soon as she had stuffed down enough toast and tea to satisfy her stomach, she excused herself and slipped away to the stables. It was some distance to the mine entrance, as she remembered, over an hour at least, and she did not want to be late.

She had a groom saddle a horse, then set out at a smarter pace than she had the day they had ridden to White Lady Falls. She drew a deep breath, admiring the landscape around her. The looming moor seemed beautiful today, no mist hanging over it, the sky blue against its bulk. Even the gray upthrusts of broken granite, called tors, added a certain stark appeal to the scene.

She had worried that she might not remember the way, but as it turned out, it was not difficult. The path was clearly marked, and she remembered without hesitation which way to turn when she reached the place where the path crossed with the one from Exmoor House. She rode on, the path climbing, until at last she saw the mine entrance in the distance. It was set into the slope, and beside it lay a tumble of huge rocks. She turned her horse—not an easy task, as it had its own mind about staying on the well-worn path—and started toward the rocks.

There was no sign of another person around, and Marianne realized she must have arrived early. She sighed. It would not do to appear too early, but she did not see how she could avoid it now. There was no room in which to loiter until the right time, not even a tree behind which to hide. She dismounted and, holding the reins in her hand, she walked up to the dark square of the mine entrance. Large timbers stood on either side and across the top of the rough doorway, which seemed to open into the side of the hill itself. A little timidly, she moved forward, peering into the gloom. The doorway was not tall. She had to duck her head to look inside.

The inside was as black as a pit to Marianne's sun-dazzled eyes. She leaned in farther, one hand grasping the rough timber beside her, and waited for her eyes to adjust to the lack of light. Still, she could see nothing, and she was just about to withdraw when something hit her hard in the small of her back and she tumbled forward, hitting the ground with enough force to knock the air from her lungs. An instant later, something crashed into the back of her head and everything went black.

JUSTIN FINISHED HIS SHAVE AND turned away, wiping the remains of the soapsuds from his chin. Whistling, he went to the window and looked down from it onto the yard below. His window lay on the side of the house, and from it he had a clear view of the stables. He considered the possibility of convincing Marianne to go for a ride with him today, and the thought made him smile.

Then he saw the object of his thoughts walking across the yard toward the stables, and he had to blink to convince himself that it was really she. It seemed bizarre that she would be up so early—or going to the stables, given the quality of her riding. But it presented a perfect opportunity. If he could catch up with her, they could go for that ride he had been contemplating. He grabbed a cravat from his drawer, wrapping it around his throat and tying it with a haste that would have made his valet blanch. Shrugging on his jacket, he hurried out the door and down to the side yard.

He was too late. In the distance, he could see the trim figure of a female rider on a horse taking the trail around the lake. Striding into the stables, he ordered one of the grooms to saddle his horse. He intended to catch up with her, but as he stood, waiting, he began to wonder more and more why she was heading out alone at this hour of the morning.

"Did Mrs. Cotterwood say where she was going?" he asked the groom as the man finished cinching the saddle on his horse and stepped back.

"To meet Miss Winborne, she said, my lord."

Justin stared at him for a moment in blank surprise. It was ludicrous to think that Marianne would go riding with Cecilia. He frowned. *Unless Cecilia had some plot in mind...* But, no, he could not believe that Marianne would be so naive as to trust anything Cecilia said. Marianne must have lied to the groom. It was then that it occurred to him that she was sneaking out to meet one of her confederates.

His lips tightened at the thought. *Perhaps that Piers*

fellow had come into the village and was staying at the inn. Marianne could be slipping him some message so that he could more easily rob the house. The idea made him frown. Marianne was engaging in activity that was far too dangerous. She was going to get herself into serious trouble if she did not exercise greater care. *And he did not like her spending time with that damned rascal Piers.*

As soon as he mounted his horse, he set out after Marianne. He was careful not to overtake her, for he wanted to find out where she was going and who she was meeting. He followed the prints her horse's hooves made. Now and then, when he topped a rise, he caught sight of her. But when she started the climb up toward the moor, he had to hang back for a long time, not wanting to expose his pursuit on that long stretch of treeless ground. He waited in a copse of trees until she was completely out of sight, then started forward. In the distance he heard a loud noise, something like thunder, but shorter, and his horse shied, pricking up its ears. He urged the steed to a faster pace, an undefined worry beginning to niggle at his brain.

There was no sign of Marianne in the distance, and that increased his uneasy feeling. Given the fact that he had roused his horse to a trot and that Marianne's mount was unfailingly slow, it seemed to him that he should be able to see her in the distance. *Could she have turned off somewhere?* At that moment he noticed that a horse had turned from this path and struck out through the bracken and gorse toward the mine. Suspicion sizzled through him. The mine would make an excellent secluded spot for a secret meeting. He started forward, then came to a dead halt as his brain registered what his eyes were seeing.

The dark doorway of the mine was no longer there.

Where it had stood, empty, was now a jumbled pile of timber, rocks and dirt. The mine entrance had collapsed.

LAMBETH DUG HIS HEELS IN, AND HIS horse bounded forward. Close to the entrance, he flung himself off the animal, dropping its reins, and ran to the collapsed entrance, shouting, "Marianne! Marianne! Can you hear me?"

Frantically, he began to dig at the rocks and dirt that lay on top of the fallen timbers. Behind them was a hole, where two timbers had fallen at angles to each other and crossed, leaving an empty space above them. He climbed up, the smaller rocks and dirt sliding from beneath his feet, and threw one leg over the fallen timbers. He eased his way onto the crossed logs, and there was an ominous creaking, but nothing gave way, and he slid through.

Once past the barrier, he could stand almost upright, though the timbers above his head sagged, and one had snapped almost clean through. He looked around. There was enough light coming in through the hole he had created that he could see the few feet around him. Farther on, everything dissolved into darkness.

But Marianne lay only a few feet away from him, clearly visible. With a soft cry, he went down on his knees beside her. She lay on her stomach, her arms flung above her head.

"Marianne?" Panic seized his chest at her stillness, and he bent close to her face. His heart was pounding so hard in his ears that he could hear nothing else, so he held his hand beneath her nose. A warm breath brushed his finger, and he relaxed. "Thank God!"

He sat down, his muscles suddenly trembling so that he

could not maintain his position. He pulled up his knees, bracing his arms on them, and dropped his head, drawing in steadying breaths. He could not remember when he had felt such an avalanche of fear pour through him. For an instant he had been certain she was dead.

Wiping his hands down his trouser legs, he blew out a breath and turned to examine Marianne. This was no time to give way to emotions. Another creak from the timbers above him reminded him that quick action was necessary. With gentle hands, he made his way along her arms, then down her neck and back, ending by pressing his fingers into her legs all the way down to her feet. Nothing seemed to be broken;

nor was her neck at an odd angle. The only injury he could find was a lump on the back of her head. He thought it would be all right to move her.

He turned her over. Her face was streaked with dirt, but there was no blood, nor did any stain the front of her riding habit. Justin slid his arm beneath her shoulders and raised her to an almost sitting position, braced against his chest. "Marianne. Can you hear me? You need to wake up."

He glanced at the hole he had made in the rubble. It would be difficult to push her limp body through the opening. It would be much easier if she were conscious and able to help. He chafed her wrists and continued to say her name, wishing that he had brought some water to put on her face. There was an eerie groan above his head, startling him, and suddenly a shower of dirt poured down on a spot two feet away from him.

"Marianne! Wake up! We've got to get out of here."

He could not straighten up enough to carry her well, so

he hooked his arms underneath hers and pulled her the short distance to the opening. He coughed, the dust that lingered in the air clogging his throat.

He said her name again, and finally her eyelids fluttered. After a moment, they opened, and her eyes wavered around before focusing on his face.

"Justin? Oh, thank God!" She went into his arms, her face pressed into his jacket and her arms wrapped around him. "I didn't know—I couldn't see you. Were you in here? Who pushed me?"

"What?" He stared at her. She was obviously very befuddled. "No. I wasn't in here. I just got here, and I dug a hole in the rubble to get in. I—I feared you might be inside when I saw that the entrance had caved in. And what do you mean, who pushed you?"

She stared at him, blinking, as if trying to pull her thoughts together enough to make a coherent sentence. Justin went on quickly. "Never mind. The important thing is to get out of here. I don't like the way it sounds."

A loud crack made Marianne jump and bury her face in his chest again. "What was that?"

"I think it's the remaining timbers. I fear that the rest of the ceiling is going to cave in, as well. That's why we need to get out of here. You will have to crawl through the hole I made. I'll help you."

He pulled her to her feet and turned her toward the breach in the barrier of rocks and timbers. He put his hands at her waist, steadying her, and Marianne stepped up onto a fallen timber to climb over the rocks to reach the hole. Another loud crack sounded, followed by a low groaning, and suddenly dirt began to pour down upon them.

Justin let out an inarticulate yell and, wrapping his arms

around Marianne, threw both of them onto the ground. The timber above them snapped and came crashing down, followed by rocks and dirt.

The noise was deafening. Dirt rushed over Justin's body as he lay atop Marianne, protecting her, his arms crossed over both their heads. Rocks pelted his body, and something hit a glancing blow on one leg and bounced off. Another rock struck his cheek sharply, and he felt blood start to ooze from a cut. A roaring filled his ears.

Then it was over, except for the soft susurration of some last trickles of dirt. The air was thick with dust, and the darkness around him was stygian. Beneath him, Marianne wiggled and made a noise of protest.

Justin started to rise and found that he could not. A timber was holding him down, though he realized when he moved his legs a little that the wood was not pressing into his flesh but merely lying too close to him to allow for upward movement.

"Crawl forward," he whispered to Marianne, starting to do the same thing himself.

Together they wriggled and squirmed into the darkness in front of them, pushing through dirt and pebbles and twisting around larger rocks, until finally there was enough freedom of movement that they could crawl on hands and knees. They pulled themselves free of the timbers and tried to stand up, but it was impossible to do more than stand crouched over.

The darkness was not complete. When Justin turned around, he could see little cracks and pinpoints of light piercing the dark wall, creating a dimness in which they could at least see one another as their eyes adjusted to the darkness and the dust settled to the floor.

"Are you all right?" he asked Marianne, then smiled derisively. "Sorry. Idiotic question. Is anything broken?"

"I think not." She coughed. "My shoulder is wrenched, but I think that's all." He could see the faint gleam of her teeth in the darkness. "Except for being squashed flat, that is."

"I beg your pardon." Humor tinged his voice. "I shall try to do better next time."

"Good Lord, what a thought. I sincerely hope not to go through this again."

They crept nearer to the barrier and began to gingerly pull away rocks and debris, keeping a wary eye on the walls and ceiling around them. Justin struggled to roll away a large rock, and the timbers and other stones settled a little. They waited for a long, expectant moment, but nothing else happened. However, it soon became obvious that no matter how much they pushed and pulled away, the exit was still blocked by timbers and stones far too heavy to move. The second collapse had virtually sealed them inside.

They continued to work for some time even after it became obvious that their efforts were not going to win them their freedom. Finally, however, Justin sank down with a sigh, arching his aching back, and Marianne plopped down beside him.

"It is hopeless, isn't it?" she asked in a small voice.

"Nothing is hopeless," he replied staunchly. "But, yes, I doubt that we shall be able to dig ourselves out. Still, they are bound to search for us when neither of us returns. Did you tell anyone where you were going?"

Marianne cast him an odd look. "No. You told me not to."

Now it was his turn to look at her strangely. "What do you mean, I 'told you'?"

Marianne wondered if the cave-in had given him a concussion, though he had not seemed to black out. "In your note," she explained warily. "You told me not to tell anyone."

He looked at her for a long moment without speaking. "Note?"

"Yes. Note. Justin, what is the matter with you? Did you strike your head? I am talking about the note you sent me."

"I sent you no note."

"Of course you did." She frowned at him, frustrated. "Where is it? What did it say?"

"I don't have it. I tossed it into the fire before I left. But it said for me to meet you here. I thought you—"

"You thought what?"

"Never mind. It isn't important. Do you mean to tell me that you did not send me a note?"

He shook his head.

"Then why are you here? I thought you must have already been inside when I was push—" She stopped, her puzzlement changing to cold fear. "I was pushed."

"What?" That was the second time she had said something about being pushed. Justin's alarm climbed.

"I looked inside. I thought maybe you were in here. But it was far too dark to see anything, and I didn't want to come inside. It was too eerie. Then something pushed me, and I fell inside on the floor. And next there was a tremendous pain in my head, and that is the last thing I remember until you were saying my name."

"'Something' pushed you? You mean 'some*one*'?"

Marianne nodded weakly. The idea seemed too horrible to voice out loud.

"It wasn't just your horse nudging you in the back?"

"No." Her voice was quiet but decisive. "It was too hard

for that, and besides, it was smaller and—well, it felt like two hands at my back, giving a hard shove."

"And the pain in your head—did you hit the ground with your head?"

She thought for a moment. "No. I came down on my stomach, and my hands went out in front. It knocked the wind out of me but did not hurt my head. That was an instant later, and it was a sharp pain across the back of my head." She raised her hand to the spot, exploring, and winced.

"Yes," he agreed. "I felt a knot there. So something—someone hit you on the head from behind after he shoved you inside."

"That sounds absurd."

"Yes. But no more absurd than your receiving a note from me when I never sent one."

Marianne's hand went to her stomach. "I feel sick."

His arm went around her shoulders, and Marianne leaned gratefully into his side. *Someone had tried to kill her!* She could not quite absorb the idea.

"But wait—this cave-in—how did it happen? Why are you here if you did not send the note?" She turned to look at him, her eyes searching his face in the dim light.

"I followed you. I happened to see you walking across to the stables this morning, and I—" He stopped, looking a trifle abashed. "I thought perhaps you were meeting one of your confederates, and I decided to follow you."

"Then you must have seen what happened!" she exclaimed.

He shook his head. "No. I stayed well back, not wanting you to see me. I let you get out of sight, then followed. Your horse left tracks that veered off the path. I started in that direction. That's when I saw the mine entrance and realized that it had collapsed. Your horse was nowhere in sight any longer—I guess it must have run away at the noise of the cave-in."

"Or someone led it away."

"Yes." He paused, then went on. "Anyway, I dug a hole through the debris, and I saw you inside, so I climbed in to get you. You were unconscious, and I couldn't get you out. Then you woke up, and you know the rest. That is when the entrance collapsed again. Now it's more solidly blocked than it was before."

They were silent for a moment, both of them lost in their own terrible thoughts. Finally Justin said, "I heard a noise—a sort of roar. I didn't know what it was. When I saw the mine, I assumed it must have been the entrance collapsing. Now I think it was explosives. This person must have made it collapse on you."

"But why?" Marianne whispered, tears welling in her eyes. "Why would anyone want to kill me?"

His arms went more tightly around her, holding her to him. "I don't know. You must have angered someone very much. Or frightened them."

"Frightened them? Why would anyone be scared of me? I have no power. I am no danger to anyone!"

"Perhaps it is someone you—well, that you played your little charade for."

"What are you—oh. You mean someone who had things turn up missing?"

"Exactly."

"But how could they know that it was I?" Marianne asked thoughtfully. "I can assure you that nothing went missing at any party I attended."

"*I* figured it out. Why couldn't someone else? Perhaps

they saw you, as I did, or—" He shrugged. "I don't know. It makes no sense. Why not force you to give it back if they knew it was you who had done it? Why not turn you over to the constable?"

"They would have had no proof," Marianne pointed out. "Just as you have no proof."

"That is true. Perhaps it would not be enough for the law. Still…it seems a bit extreme to try to kill someone for stealing your property, even if it was something precious." He thought for a moment, leaning his cheek against Marianne's hair; it was, he discovered, a very pleasant position. "What else could it be? Jealousy? Do you have a lover who fears you are unfaithful to him?"

"No! I have no lover—have never had a lover. The only jealousy going on around here is on the part of your fiancée."

He stiffened and pulled back from her. "I have no fiancée."

"Indeed? That is not what I have heard. Even you admitted that it lay in your future."

"I did? Well, she is *not* my fiancée." His mouth quirked a little in amusement. "Nor can I quite envision Cecilia being jealous. It seems far too much emotion for her."

"Well, she has some sort of emotion brimming in her. It comes out as venom, and she has directed it at me. She is quite capable of strong emotion, I assure you."

"Not to the point of killing someone," Justin said decisively. "God knows, Cecilia can be poisonous. I have been on the receiving end of some of her remarks. But a physical attack? I think not."

After a moment, Justin asked, "Has this person tried anything else?"

Marianne hesitated, looking at him, then went on tentatively, "Well, there was that moment the other day when I slipped and almost fell into the River Lyd."

His eyebrows vaulted upward. "Are you saying you didn't slip?"

"I—I thought I felt someone give me a shove."

"Why didn't you say something?"

"What should I have said? It seemed absurd. I was sure that I must have imagined it. If *I* felt that way, you know how everyone else would have responded."

"Mmm. You're probably right." He sat back, hiking up his knees and resting his elbows on them thoughtfully.

"I am not sure even now that it was intentional. Perhaps it was just a stray elbow, an accident."

"And perhaps not. Anything else?"

"What do you mean? Any other attacks? No." She shook her head, then stopped short as she remembered something. "Although…no, it's unlikely."

"What?"

"Before this party, when I was back home, one evening a young woman was attacked just down the street from our house. He did not try to have his way with her. Apparently he leaped out, grabbed her from behind and began to choke her. He was frightened away. It was a most unusual event. It is a respectable neighborhood."

"Yes, I know. However, that doesn't necessarily mean that it is connected."

"No. It may not be. The only thing is…well, this girl had been visiting with Piers and the others. She had just left our back door. And her hair was red-gold."

"Red?" He looked at her sharply. "You mean, like yours?"

"No. It is not nearly so dark, but at night it would

probably look darker, and if someone did not know me, only that I was a redhead..."

"I see your point. Then this attacker followed you here from London?"

"Maybe." Marianne shrugged. "But it seems unlikely. How would he know about this mine if he were from London? And how would he know that you and I—well, that a note from you might bring me here? Most of all, how would he be able to sneak into Buckminster House and slip a note under my door without detection?"

"Valid points all," Justin admitted. "In that case, it appears that the would-be murderer must be a guest at Bucky's party. He is one of us."

CHAPTER FOURTEEN

MARIANNE AND JUSTIN LOOKED AT EACH OTHER, both of them reluctant to accept such an idea.

"I don't know," Marianne whispered.

"Let us say it is a possibility—a strong possibility."

"All right." She hesitated. "There is another odd thing. I am not sure that it is related, but it happened recently, and it was so unsettling.... There has been a man asking about me."

"What do you mean, asking about you?"

"Well, first he went to—to where I used to live. He was trying to find out where I live now, but no one knew, at least no one who would tell him. Or that is what I thought, but later, only days ago, a man showed up near our house, asking questions of one of our maids. He asked if a red-haired woman lived at our house. Unfortunately, Rosalind told him that her mother had red hair. After that, we saw him watching our house."

"This was before the attack on the other woman on your street?"

"Yes."

"This whole affair becomes murkier by the moment. There is someone from your past looking for you."

"Not someone I knew in my past," she corrected. "It was obvious that he did not know what I looked like. He asked only about my name and my hair."

"As if he was going on a description he was given."

"Yes."

"So there is someone who has been looking for you, knowing your name and hair color, but you have no idea who or why." He raised one finger, as if ticking off the item, then added a second. "A girl with your color hair was attacked close to your home. Again, no one knows by whom or why. Next, you may have been pushed into the River Lyd. And lastly, someone lured you to this mine, using my name, then knocked you unconscious and apparently caused the mine entrance to collapse, sealing you in."

"It sounds bizarre, I know."

"Also rather ineffectual. I mean, really, some fellow chokes a girl, not even being sure that it is you, and then is frightened away before he finishes the job. Next he gives you a shove into a river that is not particularly deep, although it is damned rapid and could, I suppose, have swept you away and drowned you. But what a time to choose, when you are with a large group of people and the chances are that someone would rescue you before you could drown. Now, when he knocks you out, he does not finish you off but collapses the mine entrance, sealing you in—once again leaving you available for rescue."

"Perhaps he meant for the cave-in to crush me. I mean, he set off explosives, so he might have thought that the whole thing would cave in, not just the entrance, and I would be crushed. After all, the second cave-in came close to killing us. If one of those timbers had actually fallen on us, we might both very well be dead now. Anyway, if I was not rescued, I would eventually die of thirst and hunger."

"I'm not sure. I was able to dig a hole and crawl through. If you had awakened here by yourself, you might very well have done the same thing from this side. It was the second collapse, which *I* caused, that sealed us in. And what if someone rescued you?"

"He couldn't have guessed that you would follow me."

"No, but they would have known that something was wrong when your horse returned to the stables. Since it is no longer here, that is probably what happened."

"Unless *he* took the animal with him so that it would *not* go back to the stables."

"Even so, eventually everyone would realize that you were missing, and at some point they would ask whether you had taken a horse. The groom would say when you had ridden off. Search parties would have been sent out. No doubt one of them would have passed this way and seen the collapsed mine entrance and investigated. There were tracks outside. You would have been found before you could starve to death."

Marianne looked at him. "Is that what you expect will happen with us?"

He smiled. "I jolly well hope so. Don't you?"

"Yes. But I am afraid I am not quite so optimistic."

"It will probably take longer for them to set out looking for us. Since both of us rode out, they will probably assume that we were together, and they would not worry so quickly as they would about a lady alone. It might appear scandalous, but not life-threatening. It may be nightfall before they grow anxious, and then it will be too dark for a rescue party to be effective. They will start out at first light tomorrow, however." He did not mention what he feared might happen—that before a rescue party could find them, there could be another collapse of the remaining timbers, and they might be buried beneath them.

Marianne shivered. "I don't relish spending a night in this place."

Justin squeezed her tightly and kissed her forehead. "Neither do I. However, I doubt that it will kill us. They'll find us. They will spot my horse, for one thing. He is well trained. He'll stand where I left him."

"That long?"

He shrugged. "I have never tested him to that extent. But my guess would be that he won't wander far off. Unlike your mount, the stables here are not his home. I think there is a good chance he won't return there but will stay in the vicinity."

Marianne leaned her head against his chest. It was amazing how comforting it felt to be held by Justin.

"Do you think that this person did not mean to kill me, then?"

He shrugged. "I'm not sure. It is possible, I suppose, that he is trying to threaten you, terrorize you, but if so, he is doing it in a damned roundabout way. Attacking someone else, asking questions about you, even that shove into the water. What if you had assumed that someone had merely stumbled into you?"

"It seems to me that he is trying very hard to make it look like an accident. Not the first one, of course. But these last two times—slipping and falling into a river, a mine collapsing on me. If either attempt succeeded, it would have appeared to be an accident, not murder. A knife in the back would be more certain but would obviously be intentional. The only logical reason anyone would want so badly for it not to appear as murder would be that the killer is someone here at the party."

Justin sighed. "You're right. If you had been murdered, the only suspects would have been the other guests."

"Not the only suspects," Marianne corrected. "Someone staying with Lord Exmoor could have done it."

Justin sat back, cocking an eyebrow at her. "Are you still thinking it could have been Cecilia? Marianne, I tell you, it won't wash. I have seen Cecilia when she's furious, and God knows it isn't a pretty sight. She can be mean and vindictive, but the type of revenge Cecilia seeks is social. She might ostracize you, but kill you?" He shook his head. "I don't think so. Nor can I imagine her brother doing it. Fanshaw's much more likely to try to seduce you than kill you. Now, the Earl is someone I could picture as a murderer. But why? You don't even know the fellow, do you?"

Marianne shook her head. "I have barely spoken two words to him. But I don't know most of the people here! Other than Penelope, Nicola, Buckminster and, of course, you, I never met any of these people before I came here. And who here *would* seem capable of murder, anyway? Mr. Thurston? Mr. Westerton? Sir William Verst?"

"Mmm. You have a point. It is a singularly innocuous lot, isn't it?"

"Indeed."

"So what is our conclusion? If the man searching for you and the incidents here are connected—and it would seem awfully coincidental if they were not—then the suspect is a guest here and is also somehow connected to your past. But he or she did not know you by sight, before this visit."

"True. I do not think he had information on me any more recent than ten years ago. That is where he was looking."

Justin frowned. "It makes no sense."

There was a faint groan from the timbers, and another cup or two of dirt trickled down off to the right. Marianne glanced toward it nervously, then back at Justin. She huddled into her arms, trying to control the shudder that shook her body.

"What—what if the other timbers collapse, too?" she asked softly. "What if it's not over?" She could imagine the stout wooden logs bending under the weight of the hill above them, could picture the tons of dirt and rocks that pressed down on the severely weakened structure.

"Don't think about that," he told her, moving over to her and pulling her into his arms again. "There's no point in it. Let's just concentrate on the possibility of getting out."

"I hate feeling so helpless!"

"I know. I do, too." It was not a position Justin was accustomed to finding himself in. He wrapped his arms more tightly around her, settling her so that she was sideways to him, her bottom between his legs, his knee cocked behind her to support her back, and her legs and skirts crossed over his other leg.

In this way, his warmth and strength enveloped Marianne, and she found it comforting. Gradually her shivering stopped, and she relaxed against his chest, letting her head lean against his shoulder. When Justin held her, it was easier to believe that it would turn out right somehow, that rescue would come before the mine collapsed on them.

She released a soft sigh and snuggled closer, her arms slipping around his chest. He could feel the side of her soft breast against his chest, her rounded derriere against the very center of his desire. He realized how sexual their position was. The darkness was velvet around them and utterly silent. With little to stimulate his sense of sight and sound, he found his other senses stronger. He could smell the scent of lavender soap that clung to her skin, could feel the satiny texture of her hair beneath his cheek. Heat flared at every point where her body touched his, building and pulsing deep in his abdomen.

Marianne felt the fire in him, the throb of his desire against her hip, and a shiver of an entirely different sort shook her. She, too, was intensely aware of every point where their bodies met; her nipples seemed suddenly swollen and extraordinarily sensitive. Desire welled in her, drowning out the tingles of fear. She wanted Justin. She wanted to feel his hands on her, his mouth. She wanted to run her own fingers over his body, exploring the wide chest and muscled shoulders, the curve of his buttocks.

Her breath rasped in her throat, and Marianne blushed in the dimness, embarrassed by her own reactions. *How could she feel this way at this time and place? Trapped, facing possible death at any moment...yet her thoughts turned to carnal lust!* She told herself a gentlewoman would be praying now.

Yet she knew that if she were to die, she wanted to know Justin's lovemaking first. She was, after all, no gentlewoman. And in the face of death, all her reservations and hesitations seemed silly and pointless. She had never known lovemaking, only the hurried and brutal coupling that Rosalind's father had forced upon her. She had never given herself, only been taken advantage of. *Was she to die without ever knowing real passion? Why did she deny herself what she wanted for the sake of the rules created by a Society that despised her?*

"Justin." She breathed his name, lifting her eyes and searching his face in the faint light.

She heard him draw in his breath sharply, and his arms

tightened around her. He looked down at her, his face turned stark and hollow-cheeked by the heavy shadows. But there was no mistaking the desire that widened his mouth and gave his eyes a heavy-lidded look.

He brought up his hand to cup her cheek, his skin faintly rough upon her softness; the contrast stirred her in a deep, visceral way. He slid his fingers down over the elegant column of her throat to the hard base of her collarbone. Her pulse fluttered in the hollow of her throat, and her flesh trembled faintly beneath his touch. Justin bent to kiss her, his mouth moving slowly and tenderly over hers.

Marianne gave herself up to the pleasure, her worries and doubts slipping away in the warm dark. This moment was life itself, vibrating with hunger and delight. Her body was alive to each sensation, each taste and touch and change.

She sank her fingers into his hair, reveling in the feel of it upon her skin, sliding tantalizingly. Her lips moved against his; their tongues entwined, moving in an erotic dance. The scent of him filled her nostrils, and she felt almost dizzy with desire. They kissed over and over, hungry to know each other to the fullest extent. His hands slid down her body, caressing her breasts and stomach and legs. Marianne's flesh tingled beneath his touch, and she wanted to rip away the barrier of her dress and feel his fingers on her skin. Her breasts were full and aching deliciously.

Her hands went to the buttons on his shirt, undoing them, then sliding beneath to feel the flesh, searingly hot, smooth skin stretched over hard muscle and bone. She brushed her fingers lightly over him, then spread her palms flat and ran them over his chest and stomach. He jerked a little as the sensations exploded within him, and his mouth turned ravenous on hers. Reaching behind her, he quickly unbuttoned her dress and shoved it down. Only the berib-boned cotton chemise lay between him and what he desired. He jerked the ribbon to untie it and, sliding both his hands beneath the material, lifted the white globes free of their binding.

Her breasts gleamed palely, the pink-brown centers in dark contrast. He held them for a moment cupped in his hands and gazed down upon them, his eyes hot. "You are so beautiful," he murmured huskily.

"Show me," she whispered.

He was eager to oblige. His thumbs brushed over her nipples, rousing them to hard points, and circled the aureoles, the soft, rhythmic movements setting off pulses of pleasure down into her loins. Marianne swung around to face him, seating herself between his legs, her own legs wrapped around him, and pulled her chemise down and off, exposing her torso to him. With a low groan, he put his hands on her buttocks and shoved her tightly against him. He bent his head and began to feast upon her breast.

His mouth was hot and silken, pulling her nipple in and gently sucking on it. His tongue rasped over it slowly, then quickly, lashing and stroking and circling until Marianne was panting and moaning softly. She moved her hips against him as thick moisture flooded between her legs. His breath shuddered out, fiery upon her skin, but he did not stop what he was doing, only switched to the other nipple, arousing it to the same pointing hardness. Marianne's fingers clenched on his shoulders, digging into the muscles, and her hips circled in an age-old pattern.

Justin slipped his hand beneath her skirts and up her legs, finding the hot, wet center of her desire. The cloth of her undergarment lay between them, frustrating him, and with a low curse, he brought his other hand up and ripped the thin cotton garment apart. She was open to his fingers, hot and slick, the delicate nether lips engorged. As his mouth moved on her breast, his fingers stroked the tender folds, caressing and teasing, one moment soft and brushing, the next firm and urgent.

Marianne groaned his name, moving against his hand, seeking release. She had never imagined that anything could feel like this, that the world could roll and tumble around her and such heat consume her body that she thought surely she must go up like a torch at any moment. She could feel his manhood surging against her through the barrier of his trousers, and she set upon the buttons with fingers that shook. When she slid her hand inside and took him delicately in her fingers, he shuddered, letting out a low, animal noise.

Frantically, he tore off his shirt, popping the last few buttons, and laid it upon the ground, then bore her back onto the fabric. He could hold back no longer, and he moved between her legs, his maleness probing, then sliding into her slowly. He savored each increment as her femininity closed around him with almost unbearable heat and softness. A moan escaped him, and he began to stroke in and out, moving in a primitive rhythm that grew harder and faster. His heart was pounding, his breath rasping, as he drove into her and pulled back. Marianne sobbed, the pleasure so intense it was almost painful, and her nails scored his back. She released a cry as the pleasure exploded in her loins and rolled through her in a great wave. Justin smothered her cry with a kiss as his own climax seized him, and together they tumbled into a dark, whirling abyss of pleasure.

THEY LAY AFTERWARD IN LAZY CONTENT, arms around each other, blissfully drained. Marianne had never felt such closeness; she knew now that whatever happened, she would always be connected to this man, that he knew her in a way that no one else ever could or would again. She knew, too, that she could no longer allow any dishonesty between them. It was as if her soul had opened up, and it would permit no barrier.

"I was not always a thief."

"No?" He twined one of her curls around his finger. "What did you do before that?"

Marianne tensed. This was harder than admitting to thievery, as she had done yesterday. Anyone, even a person of genteel birth, could fall on hard times and steal things. Being a servant put her irretrievably in the lower classes, as far from a duke's son as she could possibly be.

"I was an upstairs maid," she said. "I worked for a family named Quartermaine. I went to work there when I was fourteen. I came from St. Anselm's, an orphanage. I am an orphan. I don't even know what my name is."

His arm tightened around her. "I'm sorry." Again his lips brushed her hair. "You never knew your family?"

"No. I went there when I was very young. I don't even remember arriving at St. Anselm's, except for some vague sense of being terrified. I sneaked into the office once and looked at my papers. It said under parents—*unknown*. I think the matron gave me a name. So you see, I have made myself up entirely. Even my name. I chose Marianne Cotterwood."

Justin smoothed his hand down her hair. "But what about your husband? The supposed Mr. Cotterwood?"

"I had no husband. Rosalind is—" She paused, feeling the tears gathering.

"A love child," he finished for her.

"No. There was no love involved." Marianne turned on her side, curling up facing away from him. Her voice was so low that he had to strain to hear it. "Her father is the Quartermaines' oldest son."

"And he made no provision for her?" Justin's lips curled in disdain.

"He did not acknowledge her. He—I thought he loved me. At first he flirted with me and said sweet things. I fancied myself in love with him, too, and I daydreamed—oh, idiotic things. I naively believed that he would elope with me. But he grew more and more…demanding, and when I continued to deny him, he got very angry. He said I was a tease. I told him that I was not that sort of girl, that I was good. He laughed—such an awful, nasty laugh—and said that I was good for one thing only. I began to cry. I said I thought he loved me, that he wanted to marry me. That afforded him great amusement. I was heartbroken, and I turned to run away. But he grabbed my wrist and pulled me back. He said I would not deny him any longer, and he began to pull and tear at my clothes."

"Oh, Marianne…" Justin turned, cuddling her to him, and kissed the side of her face. "I am so sorry. He took you by force?"

Marianne nodded, her voice too choked with tears to speak. The remembered pain and shame flooded her, and she began to cry softly. Justin held her tenderly, stroking her and kissing her hair, until her sobs subsided.

"I'm sorry," she said shakily. "It's been so long. I didn't think it hurt anymore."

"He was a scoundrel," Justin told her, his voice rough with fury. "He deserved to be whipped. What was his first name?"

Marianne let out a watery chuckle. "Why? Do you mean to defend my honor ten years later?"

"I wouldn't mind teaching him a lesson. It's no wonder that you distrust gentlemen, but I can tell you that he is not deserving of the name."

"I was fired when I began to show. I told the housekeeper what had happened, but she said that it was no use. I must go. I was so furious that I confronted his mother. That got me turned out without even a recommendation. I told her what her son had done, and she said that I had tempted him. That I was too showy in my looks, my hair too bright, that anyone could tell by looking at me that I was not virtuous. As if the color of my hair had caused him to rape me!"

"Stupid bitch." He squeezed her tightly to him. "I am sorry, so sorry. I wish there were some way I could change it, make it up to you."

Marianne smiled and turned into him, snuggling once again against his chest. "There's not, but thank you for wishing it. Perhaps you can see why I felt little compunction from stealing from such people as they."

"Yes. What did you do, take some of the plate and flee?"

She laughed. "No. I wasn't clever enough to think of it. I left, all right, but with only the clothes on my back and the few miserable coins I had managed to save up over the three years that I had been there—and the savings of my good friend Winny, another maid. I made my way to London, thinking that there somehow I would find a job. Of course no one was interested in a pregnant maid, even to work in the scullery. I would be a bad influence on the other scullery maids, you see. I was starving, no place to live, scared. Then I met Harrison and Della. They saved me—and Rosalind."

She told him about her first attempt at theft and how her future friends had rescued her from the fruit seller, then took her in. "I owe everything to them," she said quietly. "They fed me and clothed me, taught me how to talk and act. I can never repay them. They—I guess they are the closest thing I have to a family."

"Probably better," Justin commented wryly. "I think I would prefer to choose my family, if I could."

"Oh, easy to say when you can trace your ancestors back to the Conquest!" Marianne retorted, chuckling.

"Before that!" he protested with mock indignation. "Just ask my grandmother—she will be happy to tell you."

"Tell me about your grandmother. What is she like? Tell me about all your family."

He shrugged. "They are dead bores, frankly. My grandmother married a duke, and that was her defining moment in life. Everything she did before that led up to it, and everything since has been as a consequence of it. She walked and talked and ate like a duchess. She did not laugh loudly nor scream with rage nor walk fast, because all those things would have been unbecoming to the dignity of a duchess. She could trace all her ancestors, too, but she was prouder of my grandfather's, of course, since they were dukes. Everyone in the household, including my father, went in terror of her. Every week the family had to go to pay their respects to her at the Dower House—one of the primary reasons, I think, that my parents always spent half the year in London, where Grandmother rarely set foot."

"Oh my."

"I never saw my parents much. They were in London for the Season, and for much of the winter, too. Mother, particularly, hated the country. The children, on the other hand, always stayed at the home seat. Mother was a beauty—they say that is how she managed to snag a duke. Her birth was good, of course, but they were not wealthy. I can remember Nurse usually took us in to see her while she was engaged in her toilette before dinner. I can remember thinking that she was as beautiful as an angel, but I preferred Nurse, who would hold me when I hurt myself and light a candle for me at night if I had a nightmare."

Marianne smiled. "There was one of the women at the orphanage who was kind like that. She would come and soothe you when you had nightmares. But usually it was my friend Winny who did that."

"You had nightmares often?"

"When I was little. I don't remember them anymore. I think it was when I was first at St. Anselm's."

They were silent for a moment. Then Justin said thoughtfully, "This man who was trying to find you…do you think he knew you before you were given to the orphanage?"

"I suppose. If he had gone to the orphanage, they would have sent him to the Quartermaines. They knew I went into service there when I left. They would have had no knowledge of me afterward. But why would he want to kill me? And how could someone who knew me then be the sort of person who would be at Lord Buckminster's party?"

"Well, *you* are at the party," Justin pointed out. "He could have risen in life, too. Besides, why do you assume that everyone who was connected with you was not genteel?"

"A gentleman's child is not thrown into an orphanage.

There would be a relative who could afford to take care of them. Provision would be made for it."

"Ah, but might not a gentleman's *illegitimate* child be put in one?"

Marianne stiffened. "I had never thought of that."

"Say her mother died, and he did not want the responsibility of her. Did not even want to acknowledge that he had an illegitimate child. There are men who would do that."

"I'm certain of that."

"Or, perhaps even more likely, a young woman of good birth had a child out of wedlock. The family might very well have wanted to get rid of the evidence of her 'dishonor.' Several possible gentlemen could be involved there—the young lady's father, her brother, even the father of the child. It could even be that the woman—or man— of good birth married someone of whom the family did not approve, and he or she was cut off from the family. Then the parents died, the child was left, and the arrogant, stubborn relatives still refused to acknowledge it. There are any number of 'gentlemen' who could be involved there— brothers, fathers, cousins."

"You could be right." Marianne sat up. She had dismissed her former daydreams of highborn parents as folly. But when looked at in the light that Justin had shown her, it would not be that unlikely for a child, at least a bastard child, of some member of the upper class to be shunted off into an orphanage. "But why would any of those persons wish to kill that child when she was grown? Years and years after she was gotten rid of?"

"Perhaps you are somehow a threat to him. He might fear that you could figure out who he is and denounce him as a lecher, a seducer."

"How? I have no memory of my life before St. Anselm's."

"He couldn't be sure of that."

"Besides, even if it were known that he had an illegitimate child or seduced some innocent girl, would it be important enough to kill for it? Surely it would be a relatively small scandal in Society—illegitimate children are not uncommon among so-called gentlemen," Marianne pointed out scornfully.

"A man would not be ostracized for having an illegitimate child," Justin admitted. "But if he had acted dishonorably, it would be a scandal. It might be enough to throw real fear into a man standing for election to Parliament, say."

Marianne's eyes widened. "Mr. Thurston!"

"Or it might be enough to earn the enmity of one's very wealthy wife," Justin went on.

"Sir George Merridale. Oh, but, Justin…"

"I know. If Sir George were capable of killing, surely he would have done in Sophronia years ago."

Marianne had to smile. "One would think so."

She realized as she looked at Justin that it had grown much harder to see him. The dark was closing in on them. She cast a quick, frightened glance at the barrier formed by the cave-in. The light coming in the chinks and cracks was much paler, almost gone.

"'Tis almost night," she said, with an involuntary shiver.

Justin quickly took her in his arms again. "It won't be so bad. At least we are together. And it has been some time since I heard the timbers creaking. They are going to hold. Tomorrow they will find us. You can count on it."

It felt good in his arms. Marianne wanted to believe his words. She closed her eyes, shutting out the increasingly dim cave in which they sat. *What did it matter that the place would soon be utterly black?* Justin would be there, she reminded herself; she would have his strength and comfort.

Still, she could not completely repress the flutter of fear that moved through her as a darkness more complete than anything she had ever seen settled upon them. Justin, as if sensing her fright, launched into a long, amusing story concerning a trip to inspect a horse that he had once taken with Bucky. It had been, if he was to believed, a journey fraught with more silly mistakes and mishaps than would occur to most people in a year. She suspected that he was making large portions of it up, but she could not help but chuckle at the pictures he described.

Finally, however, the story wound down, and they settled into silence once again. Justin lay down, cradling Marianne in his arms, and she closed her eyes, hoping that sleep would take her away until light was once more filtering through the timbers.

But sleep did not come easily. Her body was tense, and the ground was very hard beneath them. Clods of dirt and little rocks that she had not noticed before now seemed to press into her flesh in many places. Worst of all, her stomach was rumbling with hunger, and her mouth felt parched. Another, more unmentionable, need was pressing her, also, and she had no idea what to do about it.

Suddenly there was a scraping sound outside, and Marianne shot up to a sitting position, all annoyances forgotten. "What was that?"

Justin sat up beside her, saying in a whisper, "I don't know."

Hurriedly they jumped up and began to dress. After

a moment, there was another noise, then the whinny of a horse.

"Oh." Justin relaxed, his voice disappointed. "'Tis only my horse. Well, at least we know that he has stayed put."

They were about to lie down again when a voice came from outside, muffled by the dirt and timbers, "Hallo! Is anyone there?"

Justin and Marianne turned toward one another, hope warring with fear inside them. *Had rescue arrived? Or was this the killer, returned to make sure that he had finished her?*

CHAPTER FIFTEEN

THE MAN'S VOICE CAME AGAIN, "Can you hear me? Is someone in there?"

It did not sound familiar to Marianne, but muffled as it was by the barrier between them, she could not be sure. Justin cupped his hands around his mouth and called back, "Yes. There are two of us in here!"

Turning to Marianne, he murmured, "I would rather face him, if it is the killer, than stay in here."

Marianne nodded in agreement.

"Say it again!" The voice was louder now, just outside the entrance. "I couldn't understand you! Are you inside the mine?"

"Yes! It collapsed on us!"

"Devil a bit!" came the answer, and there was the sound of shifting dirt and rock.

"Careful!" Justin shouted. "When we tried to dig out before, it collapsed on us a second time."

"I hear you. I will go carefully," the cheerful voice assured him. "Perhaps you might want to stand back a bit."

Justin pulled Marianne back, and they stood in a fever of impatience, listening to the sounds of the man digging. There was a loud crack, and they jumped back, glancing around them anxiously. They could hear the soft sound of dirt sifting down onto the ground, but in the stygian dark, they could see nothing. Marianne swallowed hard and grasped Justin's hand more tightly.

There was a scraping and a thump outside, followed by a muffled curse, then the voice said pleasantly, "Sorry! Rock fell on my foot."

More sounds of digging followed before a faint shape showed in the barrier, about a foot long, paler than the blackness around it. A moment later a face appeared at the hole, or at least the eyes and nose of a face, indistinct in the dark. It disappeared, and a moment later, a lantern was held up, casting in blessed light, and the face edged in beside the lantern.

"There you are!" A white grin split the man's face. He was a stranger to Justin and Marianne, a handsome man from what little they could see of him, with dark, merry eyes and a generous, mobile mouth. "There is a lady with you?"

"Yes. We're terribly glad to see you," Justin told him, stepping forward. "We tried to move these timbers, but they were too heavy. Perhaps if I push while you pull…"

"Of course."

Their rescuer set down his lantern, and the two men began to work together, their movements slow and cautious, mindful of the unstable quality of the barrier.

Gradually the opening widened, but it was still blocked by several timbers. There was some debate about which timber could be moved without bringing down the remainder of the entrance on their heads, and finally they settled on one, which was too heavy and wedged in too tightly for the two men to move it. The stranger left and returned a few moments later with a rope, which they lashed around the timber, and he used his horse to slowly pull the timber forward while Justin tried to brace the other timbers to make sure they did not fall, as well. There was an ominous crack as the log shifted suddenly and the timbers resettled. A few rocks tumbled down, and dirt spilled on the ground, but nothing came crashing down.

Justin breathed out a sigh of relief and turned to Marianne with barely suppressed excitement. "There is enough room now. Come."

He held out his hand, and Marianne went to him quickly. Her hand on Justin's shoulder to steady her, she climbed up onto another timber and slid her upper torso out the opened hole. The man outside pulled her the rest of the way out and set her on the ground, then turned to help Justin climb through. Marianne sank to the ground, her knees suddenly like water in the aftermath of fear and excitement, and watched as Justin's head and shoulders squeezed through the hole. His passage was more difficult because of his weight and the breadth of his shoulders, and a timber slanted across his body creaked and slid back several inches, causing a shower of dirt and pebbles to spill over him. But in the next instant he was clear of the debris, the stranger staggering back as he took most of Justin's weight.

The two men collapsed onto the ground beside Marianne, panting, sweat gleaming on their skin in the lantern light. Justin stretched out flat on his back, looking up at the night sky, where an almost full moon hung low on the horizon and bright specks of stars were scattered across the darkness.

"Nothing has ever looked as good as that," he remarked, and he reached out to take Marianne's hand and squeezed it.

Their rescuer grinned. "I'll warrant that's true."

He was a tall man, with long, muscled legs and shoulders as broad as Justin's. His hair, like his eyes, was black, and his face was squarish, with a strong jaw and razor-sharp cheekbones. He was dressed simply in boots, a dark shirt and trousers.

"I cannot thank you enough." Justin extended his hand to the other man. "I am Justin, Lord Lambeth, and this is Mrs. Cotterwood."

"My name is Jack," the other man replied briefly, reaching out to shake Justin's hand. "And you are quite welcome. It is fortunate that I happened by. I saw your horse standing loose, reins trailing, so I decided to investigate."

"Yes, it is fortunate. I wouldn't imagine that there is much traffic along here, especially at night." Justin watched the other man steadily.

"I'm sure not," Jack agreed pleasantly. "What happened? Were you exploring the mine? How did you get caught in there?"

"I'm not sure," Justin hedged. "Mrs. Cotterwood stepped inside—just barely beyond the entrance. Then the entrance partially collapsed, and when I went in to help her, the rest of it caved in on us."

"Never knew it was so shaky," the man said lightly, and his eyes returned speculatively to the fallen pile.

"I think it was helped along," Justin told him grimly.

The other man turned to him, eyes narrowing. "The devil you say! Beg pardon, Mrs. Cotterwood." He ran a hand back through his black hair. "What makes you think that?"

"I heard a bang as I was riding. I wasn't sure what the noise was, but after I saw the cave-in, I was inclined to think that it was an explosion I heard."

Jack's eyes went from Justin to Marianne and back. "Why would someone want to do that?" he asked quietly.

"We don't know. But it appears that someone was either very careless or wanted Mrs. Cotterwood to be harmed."

"Why would anyone want that?"

"We don't know. What do you think?"

The man's eyebrows vaulted upward in exaggerated amazement, and he grinned. "Me? Why, I have no opinion on it. How could I? I scarcely know the lady."

"Mmm. I thought you might have some familiarity with the mine," Justin responded. "I mean, considering that you were riding by it."

Jack's grin broadened. "It is on my way home. But I don't know much about it except that it has been abandoned for years."

"An abandoned mine could be handy," Justin commented.

Marianne looked at Justin in puzzlement. He seemed to be hinting at something, and the other man's watchful, amused expression conveyed that he, at least, had some idea what Justin meant.

"I suppose it could be," he replied. "I wouldn't know, now would I? But I seriously doubt that its usefulness would in any way endanger the lady."

"Well, I am sure there is no way of telling why it collapsed," Justin went on. "I wouldn't think it would be worth the effort of digging it out to investigate."

"I am sure," Jack agreed, his dark eyes dancing. "If by chance anyone should, I'm thinking there wouldn't be anything inside it."

Justin smiled. "I am sure there would not be." He rose, and Jack did, too. He reached out to shake Jack's hand again. "You have my eternal gratitude, sir. It would have been far easier, I am sure, not to stop and help us. I am staying with Lord Buckminster—we are good friends.

Should you ever have need of my help—or Lord Buckminster's—I assure you that you have it."

Jack gave him a brief nod. "Thank you. I will remember that."

"Now, I think, *we* should get back to Buckminster, and no doubt you have business you need to attend to, as well."

The man made a noncommittal noise and turned toward Marianne, who had stood up when the men did, aware of the strange undercurrents of their conversation but still unsure what had occasioned them. "Mrs. Cotterwood. It was a pleasure to meet you. I cannot imagine why anyone should try to harm you."

"Thank you." Marianne gave her hand to him and smiled warmly. "I cannot begin to express my gratitude."

He grinned and gave her an audacious wink. "Why, that beautiful smile is thanks enough."

With that, he turned and picked up his lantern. Blowing it out, he hooked it onto the saddlebags behind his saddle and mounted his horse. With a nod, he nudged the animal in the sides and was gone.

Justin turned and went to his horse, taking the reins and spending some time patting its neck and praising it. Marianne stood for a moment, looking into the dark where their rescuer had disappeared, then walked over to Justin.

"What was that all about?"

"All what?"

"Those odd comments you made. You and that man seemed to be having a second, silent conversation that I was not privy to."

"There is something havey-cavey about him," Justin replied. "Why would anybody be out here by Wheal Sarah at this time of night? And why did he carry a lantern with him? There's a full moon—plenty of light to pick one's way across the landscape. You'll notice he was not using it as he rode. He blew it out before he got on his horse."

Marianne frowned. "Perhaps he needed it where he was going."

"Precisely," Justin agreed. "And where was he going?"

"You think he was going to go into the mine?" Marianne guessed. "But why? Surely you don't think he is the one who pushed me in, do you? That he is the one who was asking about me, who has been trying to kill me?"

Justin shrugged. "It's a possibility, though I think it's unlikely."

"But he couldn't have pushed me into the river. And if he had knocked me over the head and made the mine cave in over me, why would he have dug us out?"

"I'm not sure. It seems unlikely that he could be the man we were talking about. But if you had happened onto something he wanted to keep secret, he could, in a moment of panic have knocked you out, then decided upon reflection that he had acted foolishly and would only bring worse trouble down on his head by killing you. So he returned to see if you had died and, if not, rescue you, thereby removing himself from suspicion."

"But why would I suspect him, anyway? I have never even seen the man before. And I didn't happen upon anything. I don't know what you're talking about."

"It is my guess that that man is part of the gang of highwaymen that Lady Buckminster and her friends were talking about the other day."

"Who? Oh! You mean when we went to the Falls! They were talking about a gang that has been preying on local travelers."

"Yes. And they call the leader 'The Gentleman.' He seemed rather a gentleman, didn't he? As well-spoken and mannered as you or I, but I know most of the gentry who live around here from having visited Bucky often, and he was no one I recognized."

"It was odd that he did not give his last name," Marianne commented, understanding Justin's reasoning. "And he was dressed all in dark clothes, quite appropriate for someone who does not wish to be seen in the dark."

"Did you notice his horse? Good horseflesh. I'll wager he's swift. But rather nondescript looking. Black without a single marking upon him."

"Again difficult to see at night…and difficult to identify."

"Exactly."

"Amazing. But I still don't understand what you were saying about his perhaps knocking me out—that I might have seen something—"

"It's my guess that his gang has been using that mine, probably to store some of their loot. It hasn't been used in years, no one has any reason to go in there, so it would be a safe place. If he came upon you and thought you were snooping around and had perhaps seen some of their things, he could have panicked and knocked you in the head. But I don't think that is the case."

"Not unless he happened to be carrying explosives around with him with which to make the entrance cave in."

"Good point," Justin allowed with a grin. "He was probably coming over here to check on their goods or add something to them. That would explain his carrying a lantern so that he could see inside the mine. When he arrived, he found—to his great surprise, no doubt—that the mine entrance had collapsed—and that there was a horse outside, indicating that someone had been inside the mine when it happened."

"That makes it rather noble to have dug us out, then, thinking that we might have seen what he had in there and would possibly report it to the authorities," Marianne remarked.

"I agree. That is why I told him that we were not planning on re-entering the mine to investigate. I wanted him to know that I intended to keep his secret."

"So he let you know, in turn, that he would get any evidence out before anyone could investigate, anyway."

"Yes."

"When you told him to call on your help if he was in trouble, you meant that if he were caught or something—"

"I would do whatever I could to help. I wanted him to know that he could use my name—or Bucky's, since he is better known around here than I."

"That was kind of you."

"I owe him," Justin told her simply. "And he is an essentially good man. I am not, you know, completely unaware of the inequities and injustices that drive people to crime. Nor do I assume that the rest of the world is dirt beneath my feet because I am a nobleman."

Marianne threw her arms around his neck. "I know. That is one of the reasons why I—" She stopped abruptly. She had been about to say that she loved him, but she had doubts as to how he would receive a statement like that. Instead, she went up on tiptoe to kiss him.

His arms wrapped around her, and they clung to each other for a long moment, a little giddy with joy, relief and excitement. Dusty, thirsty, hungry and tired as they were, everything at the moment was rosy-hued.

Finally they released each other and mounted Justin's horse, Marianne riding sideways in front of him, his arms curving around her. They rode for a few minutes in silent contentment, but after a while, Justin said thoughtfully, "Everyone will be asking us what happened."

"I know." Marianne frowned. "How can we accuse someone in the party of having tried to kill me?"

"It would be a trifle awkward," he admitted. "Blast it, Marianne, is there any possibility that someone did not push you or hit you on the head? Could you have stumbled? Knocked your head on a rock?"

Marianne sighed. "I wish I could say yes. But I distinctly recall the push in my back. And I know that something crashed down into my head. Besides, there was the note telling me to meet you there. How could that be an accident?"

"You're right. It is impossible any other way. But I would prefer it if our would-be killer did not know that *you* realize that. If he knows that you are on to him and are trying to figure out who he is, then he will be all the more eager to do away with you. If he thinks you don't know, he might even put it off until a less conspicuous time or place."

"How could I not know?"

"Let's try this story: You decided to go for a ride, you don't say why. Just an impulse. You saw the mine and decided to look inside. You don't remember anything after dismounting and walking toward the entrance. Blows to the head will often do that, you know. So you can't remember anything from getting off the horse until you woke up and I was there, and there was the second cave-in. I just happened to be riding along, saw that the mine entrance had collapsed and went over out of curiosity. When I saw the footprints, I realized someone was inside, probably a woman from the size of the footprints. Imagine my surprise when it turned out to be you."

"Why tell it that way?"

"Well, the killer will know that you were alone, so he will know it's a lie if we say we were together. But if I say that I followed you, I will not only look like an idiot for skulking along after you, the killer will also suspect that I saw him, which will make him all the more inclined to kill us, thinking that we can identify him."

"Mmm. I see your point. But will he believe that you didn't see him?"

"Probably. After all, he is bound to have looked around, and he wouldn't have seen me. Improbable as it may sound, he will think that it must be true, that I arrived some time after he left."

"And if they believe all that, what then?"

"Then we are going to figure out who among the guests could be the culprit."

"How?" Marianne asked flatly. "We can hardly ask them, and we have no idea why anyone would be trying to harm me. How would we even know what to look for?"

"I'll tell Bucky the truth. We will need his help, and I'd stake my life that he is not our culprit."

Marianne had a smile. "I agree."

"Bucky and I will question the stable boys. Whoever this man is, he must have left and returned to the stables if he is one of Bucky's guests. I will find out who else was out riding yesterday. He must have left before you and been waiting, hiding, close to the mine. It will narrow down the list considerably when I find out who rode out before you this morning."

"All right. What else?"

"I'm not sure. We can find out everything we can about the other guests. We are agreed, are we not, that it is a man?"

Marianne shrugged. "I don't know. I still like Miss Winborne as a candidate, but it was definitely a man who was asking about me and a man who attacked the maid."

"Then we will find out all we can about the male guests. Sophronia ought to be able to supply us with a good bit."

"If you can get her off the subject of herself," Marianne added. "I will question Penelope and Nicola."

"Discreetly."

"Of course. A widow could reasonably be interested in all the eligible young men she meets at a house party."

Justin grunted. "Not too interested."

Marianne chuckled. "I would think that you already know a good deal about the men, don't you? They are friends of Lord Buckminster's, aren't they?"

"I know the younger set, yes. I have known Verst for as long as I can remember. He's some sort of distant relative on my mother's side, in fact. As far as I've ever been able to ascertain, he is interested in nothing but horses, hounds and foxes. I cannot imagine anything that would spur him to try to harm any other person. I cannot even recall his ever having been in a fight."

"What about Mr. Westerton?"

"Well, he and Lord Chesfield are seemingly inseparable. Have been ever since Eton. They even dangle after the same girls. Chesfield's more of a horseman than Westerton—anyone would be. They have small but respectable fortunes. Chesfield came into the title a few years ago—his father broke his neck taking a fence. Westerton hasn't inherited yet, but he will one day, and his father is a generous sort. I don't think either of them has large gaming debts. And I cannot think how some missing female relative could affect them, anyway, especially if it were one born on the wrong side of the blanket…and that is the only reason I can imagine any of their relatives having been placed in an orphanage. Anyway, is it likely that it is one of the young men? They would have been mere boys when you were put there. What would they have had to do with it? It seems more likely that one of the older ones could be your father or your mother's brother or something like that."

"Yes, except it seems that an older man would always have known what had happened to me and would have taken care of me years ago if I were somehow a threat, whereas a young man might reasonably have only recently found out about what happened, whatever that may have been."

"Bloody hell!" Justin snapped. "This is impossible. We haven't the faintest idea what sort of clue we are looking for."

"Perhaps what we ought to do instead of digging into everyone's past is to observe them all closely. I haven't really paid close attention to anyone—you don't, you know, in casual conversation. But if we were to watch, we might see something in the way he looked at me or in what he did that would reveal that he is my enemy."

"We would see this guilt on his face?" Justin said skeptically.

"Maybe not his guilt, but perhaps a look of dislike or contempt or—oh, I don't know, something! Surely if you have tried to kill a person, you must have strong feelings about her."

"That may be true, but if a person has such a strong dislike of you that it is obvious, wouldn't you have noticed it already?"

"Maybe. Maybe not. I have had a few other distractions." Marianne shot him a wry look.

Justin chuckled. "All right. Point taken."

"What do you know about the older men?"

"Very little. None are great friends of Bucky's. The Mintons are Lady B's friends. I don't know much about them at all. They belong to the same older, horsey set that Lady Buckminster does. Gentry, but not very distinguished. Well enough off to buy good bloodstock. I'm not sure how Sir George and Sophronia got invited. It's quite possible Sophronia simply wore Lady B down until she invited her just to get her to shut up. I have seen him at my club and now and then at sporting events. I know that she is the one who has the money. His family is from the north somewhere. Their name is good enough. Alan Thurston…he's not a particular friend of Bucky's, either. I think, though, that Bucky is rather interested in his campaign. I believe he invited him at Nicola's party. It may have just been that Bucky was searching for guests. This party was a trifle, well, spur-of-the-moment. The only guest he was interested in was you. The others were just invited to make it proper."

"So you don't know anything about him? And what about his secretary?"

"Who, Fuquay? He seems a likable enough chap. Haven't talked to him much, frankly. As for Thurston, I scarcely know him. Someone was telling me the other day that he was a trifle wild when he was younger. Always kicking up larks, pockets to let, gaming and drinking, that sort of thing."

"That sounds like the sort of person who would get a woman in trouble," Marianne said, perking up.

"Maybe. I can't remember who it was that said that. But lots of men are a trifle wild when they are young. It doesn't mean that they're murderers."

They rode on, speculating about their villain, until Marianne, lulled by the horse's smooth gait, laid her head upon Justin's chest and fell asleep. Justin smiled, enjoying the feel of her in his arms.

It was quite late by the time they arrived at the house, but it was ablaze with lights, and several grooms came running at the sight of them, babbling their relief and thanks at the sight of them. Marianne woke up at the commotion, and Justin handed her down to one of the waiting grooms. Justin took her hand, and they started toward the house, but before they reached the front door, it was flung open and Lord Buckminster hurried out, his face creased with worry. His expression quickly changed to a grin.

"Justin! Thank God! And Mrs. Cotterwood." He rushed to Justin and pumped his hand heartily. "Penelope! Mother! Look!"

He did not need to draw the attention of the others, for both Penelope and Lady Buckminster were following on Bucky's heels, along with most of the rest of the guests, curiosity and relief mingling in their faces. Marianne saw the eyes of more than one of the guests go to Justin's hand, which was linked with hers. She had not even realized until that moment that her hand was in Justin's. She jerked it away hastily, blushing a bright crimson. For the first time, it occurred to her that the danger she and Justin had been in had not been purely physical. Social disaster loomed, also. They had been alone for hours, a rather scandalous proposition, especially when it included several hours of darkness.

"We were so worried!" Lady Buckminster cried, coming forward to take Marianne's hands. "You poor girl! What happened?"

"Poor Marianne!" Penelope wrapped one arm around Marianne's shoulder, leaning her head against her friend's. "I was so afraid!"

Justin launched into the story they had created on their way home. It sounded a trifle dodgy, Marianne realized, especially the part about Justin just happening to take the same route she had. But he could not change it now; it was too late.

"By Jove!" Mr. Minton exclaimed, thunderstruck. "Wheal Sarah caved in! It always seemed damned sturdy."

"The scandal!" Sophronia Merridale intoned, bringing her hands to her bosom in a dramatic gesture, her face gleefully horrified.

"Scandal be damned!" Bucky exclaimed. "They could have been killed."

Lady Merridale, caught up in the potential for scandal, ignored him. She leaned forward. "You have been gone for hours and hours! Alone together! And at night! There is nothing for it. You will have to get married."

CHAPTER SIXTEEN

THE CROWD OF PEOPLE WENT UTTERLY SILENT. Marianne stared in dismay at Lady Merridale. "But we—" She began, about to deny any wrongdoing. Then she remembered what had happened inside the mine, and she could not keep a blush from rushing up her neck into her face. "Nothing happened," she finished lamely, afraid that everyone must see the truth written on her face.

"Don't be a fool," Justin growled.

Lady Merridale gasped at the roughness of his tone. "Lord Lambeth!"

"Here now, Lambeth, I say," Sir George expostulated. "There's no need for—"

"It's your fault!" Cecilia Winborne burst out, cutting the man off, as she strode toward Marianne. "No doubt you arranged this 'accident' just so you could get your hooks into him."

"How dare you!" Marianne snapped back, her hands clenching into fists, and started toward the woman.

"Shut up, Cecilia," Justin said, his voice cold as ice, as he reached out a hand and wrapped it around Marianne's wrist, bringing her to a halt. "I am sure that everyone's tempers are frayed." He looked at Cecilia for a long moment, his eyes like marble, then turned the same look on Lady Merridale. "I have told you what happened, and I am sure that none of you would doubt my word."

His eyes moved over the other guests in a cold, flat interrogation. No one spoke, and Justin gave a brief nod. "Good. I thought not. There was no scandal. There will be no lying, malicious rumors, either. If there are, I shall know where to look." He cast a significant glance in Sir George Merridale's direction, and that man began to babble assurances as to the utter silence of himself and his wife.

"Well, if everyone is finished being nonsensical," Nicola said, moving up to take Marianne's arm, "I suggest that Mrs. Cotterwood needs something to eat and drink and a nice long rest."

"Absolutely," Penelope agreed, and the two of them whisked her into the house.

"Pay no attention to Cecilia," Nicola advised her, propelling Marianne up the stairs to her room. "No one else will. And Sophronia won't dare spread her gossip after the way Lambeth reacted. She is in great awe of him because his father is a duke, and her husband, I am sure, has sufficient respect for his aim."

"His aim!" Marianne exclaimed in shock. "Are you talking about a duel?"

"Of course. Didn't you realize that was what he was threatening? I am sure Sir George did when he looked at him that way."

"But I don't want him to fight a duel!"

"Don't worry. Sir George wouldn't dare. It may be the first time, but I feel sure that he will put a clamp on his wife's galloping tongue," Nicola laughed.

When they reached the room, Penelope rang for a maid and ordered a bath to be drawn and a tray of food brought to Marianne, both with the utmost haste. In the meantime, Nicola helped Marianne off with her clothes and wrapped her in a dressing gown, then took down her hair and began to run a brush through it.

Marianne sighed, her muscles relaxing. To her surprise, tears oozed out of her eyes and coursed down her cheeks. "I'm sorry," she murmured, sniffing, and wiped away the tears. "I was holding up fine until your kindness."

"No need to apologize," Penelope assured her, taking her hand and squeezing. "It must have been an awful experience."

Marianne nodded. "It was."

She longed to tell them the whole truth of the matter, but she managed to hold her tongue. She was sure that she could trust Nicola and Penelope, but she realized that it would be difficult to explain about the man's searching for her without revealing the truth about her past. That, she was certain, would be the last of their friendship. Lord Lambeth might accept her past with apparent nonchalance, but that was because he desired her. Gentlemen often kept lower-born women as their mistresses. But women of the nobility did not make friends with maids, no matter how advanced Nicola's views were.

So she merely smiled and thanked them for their kindness, and after a few more minutes of fussing, they left her alone to take her bath. She made her ablutions quickly, then crawled into bed, too tired to even think about the events of the day. Within minutes she was asleep.

"WHAT THE DEVIL HAPPENED?" Bucky asked, splashing a healthy amount of brandy into two snifters and turning to hand one to Justin. He had hauled Justin into his study after

Marianne went upstairs, and closed the door, cutting off everyone's eager questions. "Here. This will set you right up."

Justin took the glass he proffered and drank from it. He let out a sigh and sank down into a comfortable leather chair. "I wish I knew what happened, Bucky, I'll tell you that. The mine caved in, as I told you. The devil of it is why."

Bucky's eyebrows soared up. "You mean you think it wasn't an accident?"

Justin shook his head. "No. Someone lured Marianne out there."

Bucky stared. "Lured her! You mean, you and she weren't…" He trailed off, blushing faintly. "Sorry, old chap. I just assumed you were trying to salvage her reputation."

"I know. I am sure that is what everyone thinks. But she went there on her own. Someone sent her a note telling her to meet him there and signed my name to it. Then he pushed her into the mine, knocked her out and set off a charge to seal the entrance."

Bucky's eyes looked as if they were about to bulge out of his head. "The devil you say!"

"I heard the explosion. Of course, I didn't just happen by. I had seen her ride off, and I—well, I followed her, at a discreet distance, of course. Unfortunately, it was too discreet. I didn't see who attacked her. The rest of it is just as I said. I tried to dig her out, and in doing so, managed to bring the rest of it down upon our heads."

"But what—who—"

"That is just the question. I have no idea who or why, and Marianne doesn't know, either. The thing is, it must be someone here."

Bucky opened and closed his mouth, looking like a landed fish. Finally, he gasped out, "You're joking!"

"Trust me, being trapped, waiting for the rest of the timbers to snap and crush you, is no joke."

"But it couldn't—damn it, man, how can you think that one of us is trying to kill Mrs. Cotterwood? Why would anyone do such a thing?"

Justin sighed and leaned his head back wearily against the chair. "Sitting here now, it seems unbelievable. But it did happen."

Bucky sat down, too, shaking his head in stunned disbelief.

"The question is, who did it?" Justin went on. "I have to find out and stop him."

"Rather tricky, that," Bucky opined. "Can hardly go about asking everyone else if they tried to kill you."

"Yes, it could be a bit awkward."

Bucky thought for a minute. "Perhaps you ought to turn it over to the local magistrate. I know the fellow, of course. Squire Halsey. He'll be at the ball Friday. We could take him aside and tell him what happened."

"I don't want to involve the law unless I have to," Justin replied. His mouth quirked up on one side. "Anyway, have you more faith in the squire's ability to solve the thing than in mine?"

"No. You are more clever by half. The thing is, well, damn, Justin, it isn't really your concern, is it?"

Justin smiled faintly. "Oh, I think it is."

Bucky shifted uneasily in his chair. "I say, old fellow, you haven't gone and fallen in love with Mrs. Cotterwood, have you?"

"You know me," Justin replied noncommittally. "Have you ever known me to fall in love?"

"No, but…Mrs. Cotterwood is a different matter."

"Yes, she is."

Bucky cleared his throat. "Ah, Lambeth…"

"Yes?" Justin looked at his friend quizzically. "Out with it, Bucky. You are squirming like a schoolboy who just stole a quiz."

"I hope you won't take this wrong. The thing is… of course I have the utmost respect for Mrs. Cotterwood. She is a beautiful woman."

"I agree."

"But I'm not really sure you ought to get too, well, too deeply involved with her. Thing is, well, she ain't, you know…"

"No, I am afraid I don't. What isn't Mrs. Cotterwood?"

"Sometimes, well—" Bucky broke off, sweat popping out on his forehead. "She just isn't very nice!"

Justin chuckled. "'Nice,' my dear friend, is not necessarily the first thing I seek in a woman."

"Damn it, man, she wore my nerves to a frazzle. It is my belief that she's a nag."

"No!" Justin pressed his lips together to keep from bursting into laughter.

"Yes, and not only that, she said unkind things about Penelope, when she is supposed to be her friend, and she, well, she downright *forced* me to miss the hunt yesterday!" Bucky looked indignant even at the memory.

"I'm sorry. Thank you for your concern. I am sure that she could not measure up to Penelope in womanly virtues. But, frankly, I like a little spice in my life. I think I am able to handle her."

Bucky looked uncertain. "If you're sure…"

"I am." Justin drained the glass and set it down on the

table. "And once I come up with a plan to ferret out this scoundrel..."

"You can count on me," Bucky assured him. "Whatever you need. I'll back you up. Why, it's damned insulting that he thinks he can get away with something like that at my house!"

"You are a true friend." Lambeth started toward the door, then stopped and turned back. "By the way, if ever that gentleman highwayman gets caught, make sure he gets away. He saved our lives today."

"You're joking. I say, Lambeth, the oddest things happen to you."

Justin grinned and left the study, striding down the hall. Just as he reached the bottom of the stairs, he was stopped by a loud whisper.

"Justin!"

He turned, and to his surprise, he saw Cecilia Winborne step out from a doorway down the hall and walk toward him.

"Cecilia." Justin looked at her warily. "I would have thought you would have gone to bed by now. What are you doing here at Buckminster, anyway? I thought you were Lord Exmoor's guest."

"Surely you did not think that I could simply go back this evening with the others when I heard that you were missing!" She looked at him with wide eyes.

"I did not think about it at all," Justin admitted.

"I was worried sick. No one had heard from you or knew what happened to you, except that that *woman* was missing also." The curl of Cecilia's lip made clear what she thought of Marianne. "Lady Buckminster kindly offered me a room, so of course I accepted."

"That was good of her," Justin said noncommittally. "I

hope you are relieved in your mind now that we are back. Now, if you will excuse me, you can see that I am badly in need of a bath, and—"

"Wait. I must talk to you. I waited for you to finish with Bucky so that I could speak to you."

"Can it not wait until morning? I am excessively tired, Cecilia." Justin had the dismal feeling that whatever Cecilia had to say, it would be a scene, and frankly, he was in no mood to put up with it.

"No, it cannot wait." Cecilia's gray eyes flashed. "It is rather immediate."

"All right, then." Justin crossed his arms and assumed a posture of waiting, his elbow resting on the newel post of the stairs. "What is it?"

"You have no responsibility to that woman," Cecilia began heatedly.

"I beg your pardon? What woman are you referring to?"

"Mrs. Cotterwood." She injected the name with scorn. "Just because she trapped you into a compromising situation does not mean that you should be compelled—"

Justin gave a sharp shake of his head, raising one hand as if to stem the flood of her words. "Stop it, Cecilia. You ought to know as well as anyone else that I am never compelled to do anything. I did not ask your advice on this matter, and, trust me, I do not require it. Now, good night."

"I know you will not marry her," Cecilia said, reaching out and grabbing his sleeve. "You could not marry a nobody like that, no matter what these other buffoons might say about honor and scandal and such."

Justin cast a cold look down at his sleeve, where her fingers pinched the material. His expression as immobile as wax, he reached down and plucked her fingers from his sleeve. "I suggest we end this conversation right here, before either of us says something we shall regret."

"No! I will not! I intend to have my say. I am not some meek little woman you can marry and put safely on the shelf. I am not a fool, Justin. I do not expect fidelity from you after we marry. We both know why we will marry and what our roles will be. I don't rail against that. I expect you will have the usual sort of little flings that all men do— opera dancers or actresses or whatever Incognita you should happen to fancy at the moment. But I will not tolerate your flaunting an affair with another woman in my face! If you think that you can form an alliance with a widow who moves in our social circle and I will not object, then you are sadly mistaken! I will not stand for Mrs. Cotterwood. I will not—"

Justin stepped forward so suddenly that Cecilia jerked back, startled. "You will not? I will tell you what you *will not*, Miss Winborne. You will not marry me."

Cecilia's eyes widened in shock, and she stared at him, speechless.

"You seem to be suffering from the delusion that I have offered for you. But I have not, and I never will. You are a shrew, and I would as lief shackle myself to a lunatic as to you."

"But...but..." Cecilia sputtered. "We have always known. It was assumed—"

"By you, perhaps. By your parents. Probably even by mine. But none of you have the decision to make. It is mine. And it is my decision that we should not suit." He whipped back around and started up the steps.

"You can't!" Cecilia shrieked. "You cannot do this! Everyone knows—"

"If everyone thinks that we are to marry, then I assume that it is because you have been spreading that tale around, and you have no one but yourself to blame for that error. You know as well as I that we have never even spoken of marriage."

"We did not need to speak of it!"

"If it was something we intended to do, I think that, yes, we did. Oh, there were moments in my life, when I was feeling particularly low or cynical, when I would say that someday I would probably fall into marriage with you, simply for want of any viable opportunity. But having seen you the last few days, particularly this evening, I have realized that anything, even growing old alone and dying heirless, is preferable to being married to you!"

Justin turned and stalked up the stairs, leaving Cecilia staring, dumbfounded, after him.

HE STRODE DOWN THE HALLWAY to his room. What he wanted to do was to go to Marianne's room and see if she was all right. Truth be known, he would have liked to stretch out beside her in bed and fall asleep, cradling her in his arms all night long. But that was out of the question, of course, with Cecilia there watching him balefully.

It was all too likely that someone else might see him slip into Marianne's room, even if it was not Cecilia. There were still too many people up and around. For all he knew, given Marianne's frightening experience, Penelope might even decide to spend the night with her.

He was thoroughly disgruntled when he entered his bedroom, and he sent his valet away as soon as the man had helped him off with his boots, saying, "For God's sake, man, stop fussing. I am quite capable of undressing myself, and these clothes won't be any worse for lying on the floor for a night."

His valet turned quite green at the thought, but he left, his head resolutely turned away from the sight of Justin unknotting and ripping off his own cravat. Justin stripped quickly, dumping the filthy clothes in a pile on the floor and kicking it aside, then settled down in the tub that the valet had prepared for him. But even leaning back in the steaming water, he could not quite relax. His thoughts kept tumbling furiously. *Damn Cecilia for her insinuations!* It galled him to hear her speak about Marianne that way; he had wanted to take the witch by the shoulders and shake her 'til her teeth rattled. The fact that she had been right about his intentions toward Marianne did nothing to alleviate his anger.

No one should think about Marianne that way! He frowned, thinking how everyone had been quick to assume that her reputation was damaged. He had squelched it for the moment, but he knew that the doubts still lingered in everyone's minds. Even Bucky had assumed that he and Marianne had had an assignation and had simply gotten caught by the cave-in. He wondered if he had made the wrong decision in withholding the information about the man who had arranged the cave-in. He did not want to let the villain know that they were on to him—however much the fellow might worry and suspect it, he could not know for sure that they were looking for him among the guests. On the other hand, it made his blood boil to think of everyone here looking down on Marianne and assuming that she was a loose woman.

It occurred to him that if he set her up as his mistress, everyone would think of Marianne exactly that way. The thought of women like Cecilia snubbing her and gossiping about her, labeling her, infuriated him.

Of course, once she was set up as his mistress, she would not move in these circles; she would not have to see the stares or hear the gossip. She would not be attending the same soirees or balls as these women; they would have no chance to snub her.

But even as he thought the words, he realized, with a heaviness in his chest, that he did not want Marianne to be ostracized from such places. He wanted to be able to dance with her at balls, to drive her in his phaeton through Hyde Park, to squire her to afternoon calls and the opera. More than that, he suspected that Marianne herself would be miserable in such a situation. She had become accustomed to the social round; he thought she would miss it very much—just as she would miss her friends, Penelope and Nicola.

It occurred to him for the first time how unfair it was that he could keep a mistress without being spurned by Society, yet that same mistress would be cut dead. It would seem, then, that the only way to handle it was to see her in secret, to let her continue her life as it was and to sneak meetings together whenever they could.

He grimaced, sliding down in the tub to wet his hair, and began to lather and scrub with such vigor that his skin was soon quite red. The idea of carrying on a secretive affair did not appeal to him. He wanted to buy Marianne a pretty little house for her daughter and herself. He wanted to take her out of the dangerous criminal life and give her a life of ease. He wanted to see her whenever he liked, unbound by social conventions. He wanted, in short, to have her for his own.

Worst of all, how was he to protect her from this unknown enemy who threatened her? He had no right to do so as things stood now; his only obligation was that of the heart. And he was well versed enough in the rules of Society to know that if he appeared to take over such rights, that, too, would expose Marianne to gossip. Such gestures, assuming the rights of a husband, would indicate to the world that he intended to marry her. Then, when he did not, she would be shamed.

For just the briefest of moments, the thought of marriage skittered across his mind. He pushed it away and surged to his feet, grabbing a towel and beginning to vigorously dry off. He was a fool, he told himself, thinking with his loins. The Marquess of Lambeth, the future Duke of Storbridge, did not marry because he desired a woman. Marriage was a duty one performed for the sake of the family. One must produce heirs and assure that the legacy of the family would go on, and one's bride was chosen on the appropriateness of family, position and wealth. Bloodlines were important, but passion did not enter into it, not for people like him. Love was never even spoken of.

Justin shook his head, angry with himself. He was acting like a moonstruck fool—worse than Bucky, even, for he knew exactly what the situation was with Marianne. The future Duchess of Storbridge could not be a thief, a woman who did not even know who her parents were.

He flung himself on the bed, scowling, and wrapped the cover around him. It was time he stopped thinking such foolishness and concentrated on the matter at hand—how to catch the man who had almost killed them both. Everything else would happen as it should. As it must.

JUSTIN WAS AT THE BREAKFAST table the next morning, obviously dawdling over a finished plate of eggs and bacon, when Marianne came down, and he jumped to his feet when she entered. Their eyes met, and Marianne hastily dropped hers, feeling a flush creep up into her cheeks. Just the sight of him was enough to make her remember what they had done yesterday—and to make her want it to happen all over again. Hoping that the servants could not read her thoughts in her face, Marianne sat down, primly unfolding her napkin and laying it in her lap, smoothing and adjusting it until she felt she had her face sufficiently under control.

"How are you this morning?" Justin asked, his voice low. "Any ill effects?"

Marianne smiled at him, unable to tamp down the glow in her face. "No. None."

His eyes darkened, and he leaned forward, about to speak, but just at that moment Mr. and Mrs. Thurston entered the room, and Justin sat back. He struck up a conversation with them, and Marianne soon realized that he was trying as delicately as he could to find out something about the man's past. Marianne, for her part, tried to ignore her wayward thoughts and concentrate on reading Thurston's face for any sign that might show that he was her enemy.

Breakfast set the pattern for the day, which they spent largely conversing with everyone they could, sometimes together, but more often separately. Marianne often felt Justin's eyes on her from across the room, and she noticed that he rarely strayed far enough away from her that he could not see her. The few times he did so, she realized some time later, was when she was in Lord Buckminster's company. She realized, with a feeling of warmth, that Justin was watching over her.

Though it pained her to do so, Marianne spent a large

part of the day talking to Sophronia. Boring though she was, the woman was a veritable treasure trove of gossip. She was at first a trifle cool toward Marianne—whether for the scandal of Marianne's long day in Lambeth's company or for Lord Lambeth's set-down of her later, Marianne was not sure. However, the availability of a ready ear was more than she could resist, and she was soon chattering away in her usual manner. It required some skill and persistence to keep her talk from veering off onto matters concerning herself, but Marianne managed to do so and was rewarded with a wealth of information about almost everyone there.

At the end of it, however, Marianne was not sure that any of it was useful. According to Sophronia, practically all the men present had sown far too many wild oats in their youth, her own husband apparently being the exception. A few probing questions elicited the fact that several of the men had sisters, but Sophronia related no scandal concerning any of them. The more she talked, the more Marianne began to wonder if such information was going to be of any help to her anyway. The idea that she was the illegitimate offspring of one of the men or of his dishonored sister was, after all, merely supposition on their parts. Moreover, if they were right, it hardly seemed likely that the matter had been the subject of scandalous rumors, or her attacker would not be trying so hard now to cover it up. So it was not likely that they would learn the truth by digging up old gossip.

Discouraged and wearied by an afternoon spent listening to Lady Merridale, she went upstairs to dress for dinner. She opened the door and stepped inside—and jumped, barely stifling a scream, when she saw the man sitting waiting for her.

"Justin!" she hissed and quickly shut the door behind her, turning the key in the lock. "What are you doing here? You nearly scared me to death!"

"I'm sorry." He rose and went to her, pulling her into his arms. "But I thought I was going to go mad if I didn't have you to myself for a few minutes."

Marianne melted against him, more than mollified by his explanation, and raised her face to his. They kissed for a long, satisfying time.

"I wasn't sure how you felt," she murmured. "I was scarcely with you all day."

"I couldn't trust myself to be around you," he replied huskily, bending to kiss the curve where her neck joined her shoulders. "It would hardly have been discreet to do this in front of everyone."

He illustrated his point by sliding his hand sensuously down her back and over the curve of her hips. He kissed her again, pressing her pelvis into his, and she felt the sudden flare of heat in his body. Murmuring something unintelligible, he kissed his way across her face to her ear and nibbled at the lobe, sending sizzling darts shooting down through her, where they exploded into heat in her loins.

Marianne let out a moan, sagging in his arms, and his mouth left her earlobe and moved down her neck, coming to rest on the soft, quivering top of her breast. Wrapping his arms around her beneath her hips, he lifted her from the floor and walked her back to the bed. They tumbled down upon it, lost in the sudden inferno of their passion. Justin's fingers went to the buttons at the back of her dress.

"I want to see you," he murmured, punctuating his words with kisses across the tops of her breasts. "Not in the darkness." He raised his head and gazed down at her, his eyes burning into hers. "I want to see your face when your reach your peak," he said hoarsely.

Marianne felt her loins turn liquid at his words. He saw her response in her eyes, and he let out a soft groan and buried his mouth in hers.

A tapping at the door made them both start, and Justin raised his head, cursing softly. Marianne tried to speak and could not. She cleared her throat and tried again, "Yes? Who is it?"

"It is I, Penelope," came the reply. "I was going down to dinner and I thought I would see if you wanted to walk down with me."

"Oh. Ah, well, I would love to, but I haven't finished changing yet," Marianne replied, pushing herself up to a sitting position.

"All right. I'll wait," Penelope told her. "Nicola isn't ready yet, either. I will be in my room whenever you're ready."

"Fine. See you in a moment." Marianne glanced over at Justin and almost burst out laughing at the expression on his face. She leaned across the space that separated them and kissed him lightly on the lips. "I have to go," she whispered. "She will think it extremely odd if I don't. We have gone down to dinner together nearly every night. Penelope hates walking into a crowd of people by herself."

"How nice that she has appointed you as her guard," Justin retorted sarcastically.

Marianne chuckled and slid off the bed. "It won't hurt you to wait," she told him teasingly. Even though she, too, wanted badly to continue what they had been doing, there was a certain pleasure in seeing the frustration on his face and knowing how much he wanted her.

"That's what you think." He stood up reluctantly. "I suppose I had better wait until you've left with her."

"Well, if you're going to be here," Marianne told him, "you might as well make yourself useful and be my maid." She turned and presented her back to him, where a long row of tiny buttons marched down her dress.

"What are you trying to do, kill me?" he asked, but his hands went readily enough to the buttons and began undoing them.

It was pleasantly erotic to feel the whisper of his fingers on her back as he unfastened the buttons. Unconsciously Marianne smoothed down her dress, her hands sliding over her breasts and stomach. Justin bent and kissed the exposed nape of her neck, not pausing in what he was doing.

"May I come to your room tonight?" he murmured in her ear.

Marianne nodded, not quite trusting herself to speak. Justin hooked his hands in the neck of her dress and pushed it slowly down over her body, letting it fall to the floor. Marianne leaned back against him, her eyes closing in sensual pleasure. He caressed her body, his hands sliding over her breasts and stomach, as he trailed long, velvety kisses down the line of her neck and across her shoulder. A deep quiver ran through her, and she thought that if he asked, she would slide down on the floor and make love with him right then and there.

But after a moment he stepped back from her and pulled a dinner gown from her wardrobe. Carefully he lowered it over her head and began to do up the myriad small buttons in the back, his fingertips brushing now and again against Marianne's bare skin. When he reached the top buttons, he bent and kissed the skin that he would cover up before buttoning them. He looked up into the mirror, his eyes meeting Marianne's there. His face was softened by desire, his mouth wide and sensual.

"I won't be able to take my eyes off you this evening," he told her.

"Justin…" Marianne turned to face him, her hands going up to his shoulders.

"No. Don't make it any harder," he said, with a tight smile, stepping back. "I shall enjoy looking at you…and thinking about tonight." He nodded toward the door. "You had better go now."

ALL THROUGH SUPPER, MARIANNE was aware of Justin's eyes on her, as he had said. She barely paid attention to the conversation of her companions, merely sat, nodding and sipping at her wine or picking at the food on her plate. Afterward, sitting in the drawing room with the other women, waiting for the men to return, was almost intolerable for her. All she could think about was Justin. She wondered how soon she could make her excuses and go up to her room without it looking odd. *How long would it be before Justin came to her bed?* He would have to wait, she knew, until everyone else had retired in order to be safe. But, then, he obviously had boldly walked into her room this afternoon when there had been the chance of servants or other guests happening down the hall and seeing him, so perhaps he would take the chance and come earlier.

She waited in a fever pitch of excitement, not daring to look at him for fear everything she was thinking would show on her face. As soon as Mrs. Minton rose to retire, Marianne jumped up also, declaring that she was rather tired, as well. She walked upstairs with the older woman and went into her room, ringing for a maid to help her undress. The girl seemed to take forever to come, and while Marianne waited for her, she took down her hair and began to brush it out.

The maid arrived after a time and helped Marianne out of her dress and into a nightdress. It was the sheerest and least plain of any of the nightshirts Marianne had brought with her, but Marianne, looking at her reflection in the mirror, wished that she had brought something a little more exciting with her. A simple scoop-necked white cotton gown that tied with a ribbon was hardly what she would term seductive.

She poured herself a glass of water from the pitcher that stood by her bed and took a few nervous sips from it as she paced. After a moment, she turned down the bed and sat down to wait. She yawned. What seemed like only moments later, she jerked awake, glancing around the room in a startled way. *Surely she had not fallen asleep!* Given the state of her nerves, it seemed preposterous. But somehow she could not keep her eyelids open. They fluttered and closed, and in a moment she was asleep.

Marianne drifted in darkness. *She was a child again, and her father was carrying her up to bed. She smelled the scent of his tobacco and the wool of his coat. She smiled faintly and snuggled closer to him. Dear Papa! Now he was rocking her in the white rocker in the nursery, and she was swaying, swaying, and there was the rhythmic slap, slap, of the rockers hitting the floor. She wanted to open her eyes, but she could not.*

Then, shockingly, she was cold and falling.

Marianne's eyes flew open as the cold water hit her face and she went down into the darkness, unable to breathe, and the water closed over her head.

CHAPTER SEVENTEEN

INSTINCTIVELY MARIANNE BEGAN TO STRUGGLE even as she sank beneath the water. Her mind was not really quite conscious as she scissored her feet and dragged her arms down, shooting her head up above the surface of the water. She flailed around clumsily, gulping in air, her mind groggy. Slowly she turned in a circle, blinking the water from her eyes. She saw a small boat, a dark figure hunched over in it, rowing rapidly away from her. She drew a breath to scream at him to stop, but at the last moment something stopped her, and she made no sound.

Nothing made sense—she did not even know where she was—and it was a great effort to think. Her body took over, making the movements to keep her afloat, movements that she had always seemed to know. She had been one of the few children at the orphanage who had known how to swim. She had not known when or how she had learned; she had simply enjoyed the few hours she could steal in the summer when she could go down to the river and swim. Somehow it had always made her feel better. It had been years now since she had done it, but the knowledge came back easily, without even thinking.

She started to swim after the boat, arms and legs moving a little jerkily, but then, with animal cunning, she stopped swimming, drew a deep breath and stretched out into a float, her face in the water. She held her breath as long as she could, then rolled to the side, gulped in another deep breath, and returned to her motionless float. She continued the process for three more breaths before she lowered her feet and began to tread water as she looked in the direction of the boat. Pale moonlight spilled over the water, faintly illuminating the small dock in the distance and the rowboat beside it. She could see no person anywhere about.

Marianne rolled onto her back, floating, looking dazedly up at the stars and the almost full circle of the moon. Her brain still felt fuzzy and slow. But at least she now realized where she was. She was in the middle of the large pond at Buckminster. If she turned around to face in the other direction, she could see, almost equidistant from her, the small white summerhouse where Justin had taken her. Both the dock and the summerhouse were a long swim away, and she was terribly weary. She wanted only to sleep, and her water-soaked nightgown was heavy, pulling her down.

She turned onto her stomach and began to swim toward the dock. She made slow progress, and her mind kept drifting toward sleep. She came to each time she sank into the water, and she fought her way to the surface, spluttering and splashing. The nightgown was weighing her down, she knew, so she began to struggle out of it, treading water until finally she managed to pull it off over her head. She released it, feeling lighter now, and began to swim again, heading toward a lower part of the yard that was closer than the dock. Her mind was somewhat clearer, and she swam with more coordination, but the water was chilly, and the cold seemed to penetrate her bones. Her teeth began to chatter. She wanted warmth; she wanted to sleep. Her arms and legs ached, and she began to fear that she would not make it to the shore.

She thought about Rosalind and what she would do without her, and it gave her renewed strength. She continued kicking, her arms cutting through the water, fighting off the demon of sleep. The shore gradually grew closer. Her movements slowed, her eyes began to close, her legs began to fall beneath her—and her shins scraped dirt. The water had gotten shallow this close to the edge of the lawn. Clumsily she staggered to her feet and lurched the remaining few feet to shore. The slope rose, and then she was on a stretch of mud, out of the pond. She managed a few more steps, then fell heavily onto her knees in the grass. Shivering and naked in the cool night air, she pitched forward and sank into unconsciousness.

"MARIANNE! MARIANNE!" JUSTIN'S voice pulled her from her sleep. She opened her eyes and looked up at him.

"Justin," she breathed. He was beside her on his knees, and had pulled her up into his arms, her head on his chest. Marianne leaned weakly against him and began to cry, unable to do anything but say his name.

"Hold on, love," he said and laid her gently back on the ground. He pulled off·his dressing gown and lifted her again, wrapping the heavy robe around her. Justin sank down on the grass beside her, holding her to him, his chest heaving. Marianne could hear the rapid pounding of his heart beneath her ear. The warmth of his dressing gown and his arms enveloping her was delightful, reviving her a little.

"Thank God," he murmured over and over, raining kisses over her hair and face. "I thought you were dead. When I found that note—I've never been so scared in my life."

"I don't—" Marianne struggled to organize her thoughts enough to speak. "I can't think—I'm sorry."

"It's all right. Don't worry. Nothing else will happen to you. I swear."

He picked her up in his arms and carried her across the lawn and through the garden. He whisked her into the kitchen and up the servants' staircase to her room. Once there, he set her down long enough to turn the key in the lock behind them. Then he pulled off the dressing gown and wrapped a blanket around her. After putting her into her bed, he climbed in beside her and held her, pulling the cover up over them both.

"Why...am I ...so cold?"

"Shock, I think. And the water's cool at night, even though it's summer. Don't worry. It will pass."

He was right. The heat was gradually penetrating her bones, and her mind was becoming somewhat clearer. "But what happened? Why was I in the lake?"

"Someone put you there," Justin replied grimly. "And I intend to find out who it was and stop him."

"But how—why—"

"Shh. Don't worry about it now. We'll talk tomorrow." Justin kissed her hair, smoothing it back from her face. "Damn! I should have had Penelope or Nicola sleep with you. It was my selfish lust that left you open to this. If your door hadn't been unlocked so that I could get in, this would never have happened." He released a few more heartfelt oaths.

"'S all right," Marianne reassured him sleepily, her eyelids drifting closed despite her best efforts to stay awake. "I love you," she murmured, then turned over and fell immediately asleep, leaving Justin awake and gazing into the dark, slightly stunned.

IT WAS STILL DARK WHEN JUSTIN shook Marianne awake. "I have to leave now," he whispered into her ear. "The maids will be up soon, and I can't let one of them see me leave. Can you lock the door behind me?"

Marianne nodded and crawled out of bed, following him to the door. She locked it behind him, then returned to her bed and was asleep as soon as her head hit the pillow.

She continued to sleep until long after the sun was up and sneaking in around the curtains. When she did finally awake, she sat up gingerly, realizing that there was very little about her that did not ache. Her eyes felt swollen, and the light hurt them. Her head was pounding. And every muscle in her body seemed sore. She sat for a moment, head hanging, trying to recall exactly what had happened. The effort was too much, and with a groan she sank back into the cushions.

It took an hour—and the help of the maid, who brought her a pot of tea and stayed to help her dress and comb the tangles from her hair—before she was able to leave the room and go downstairs in search of some answers. The only thing she was certain of was that she had almost drowned in the Buckminster pond last night.

She had barely reached the bottom of the stairs and started her search for him when she saw Justin striding purposefully down the hallway toward her. She raised her brows in faint surprise.

"There you are. I was just coming to look for you," she said.

"I paid the maid to come tell me when you left your room," Justin explained. "I could hardly lurk around outside your door without arousing comment, but neither was I going to allow you to roam around by yourself."

"Tell me what happened. I know nothing from the time I lay down on the bed until I was in the water, drowning."

"Let us go for a walk," Justin suggested. "I have no desire to talk in here, where someone might overhear."

So Marianne got her hat, and they went outside, taking a leisurely stroll down the long driveway, which was lined only with a series of tall trees spaced evenly apart, affording little opportunity for anyone to hide and eavesdrop.

"You were drugged," Justin said, scowling, as soon as they left the house. "That is the only explanation. Otherwise he could not have hauled you out to the pond without your awakening."

"Of course. That would explain my grogginess and how difficult it was to swim, too. I guess the shock of the cold water woke me up."

"Thank heavens you are a good swimmer. And perhaps you did not ingest all of the drug."

"How could anyone have drugged me?"

"It would not have been hard," Justin said. "They could have slipped something into your food or drink at the dinner table last night. Who sat beside you?"

"Well, Mr. Westerton was on one side and Mr. Fuquay on the other." She thought back, trying to remember. "I believe Mr. Minton was seated across from me, his wife on one side and...oh, Mrs. Thurston on the other. Do you think it was one of them?"

"Not necessarily," Justin replied in a disgruntled tone. "Someone could have entered the dining room a trifle early, I imagine, and put something into your glass. A few drops of liquid or a little powder in the bottom of your glass probably wouldn't have been noticed by the servants. The place card would have shown where you were going to sit.

And if they made a mistake…well, no harm done other than giving someone else a good night's sleep. Or the drug could have been in something else. Did you drink or eat anything later in the evening?"

"No. Oh, wait, I did have a glass of water before I went to bed."

"In your room?"

Marianne nodded. "Yes. From the pitcher there."

Justin looked grim. "It would have been absurdly easy to go into your room at any time during the evening and dose your water. The odds are you would take a drink sometime during the evening. And since the servants always put a fresh pitcher in the rooms late in the evening, he would have known when to do it. There's no way of telling when he did it, and anyone could have slipped away from the rest of us for the few minutes it would take to do that."

"How did you know where to find me last night?" Marianne asked. "How did you know he was trying to kill me?"

"It was pure luck." He shook his head. "I went to your room—I could not make myself wait as late as I should have. And I saw, of course, that you were not there. There was a note on your bed."

"A note! This man seems to specialize in that."

Justin nodded. "I suppose it would have passed for your note under normal circumstances. It looked like a woman's hand, and none of us would have known your handwriting well enough to say it wasn't authentic. But I knew, of course, that you had not written it. You don't make an assignation with someone for a romantic meeting, then run off and kill yourself. "

"Kill myself! But of course. That would be a handy way to get rid of me without casting suspicion on him. But why?"

"In the note, you apologized to Lady Buckminster and begged her pardon for putting this burden on her. But, you said, you could not live any longer with the stain upon your reputation, the cloud of scandal for having been trapped alone with me in the mine for so long. Since I refused to marry you, you were going to put a period to your existence. Fortunately, the note made an allusion to Ophelia, so I guessed that he meant to drown you. I ran to the pond…and the rest you know."

"What am I to do?" Marianne asked, anxiety welling up in her. "Perhaps I should go back to London."

"No." Justin shook his head firmly. He looked at her and smiled, his lips curving up in a way that made her heart beat faster. "I say that not just because I don't want to be without you the rest of the week. I think you would be in even more danger in London. Oh, perhaps not this week, for he could not leave without making it obvious who he is. But next week, in London, he would have much more opportunity to harm you than he does here. Any time you went out on the street, he could seize you, and you could not hide in your house forever. Whereas here, I can make certain you are protected. Penelope can sleep in your room at night— and you can lock the door. You were exposed to danger last night only because of me. If you hadn't left the door unlocked for me…"

"You can't blame yourself."

"I can and do. But it won't happen again. Bucky or I will make certain that we are with you every minute of the day—or at least that Nicola or Penelope is. He wants it to appear an accident, so I don't think he will do anything when anyone else is present. He will wait 'til you are alone, or he'll try to lure you away—which you will not allow to happen." He gave her a stern look.

"No, I won't," Marianne agreed fervently.

"Good girl. It will be easier to catch him here, too."

"I don't see how," Marianne said, a little hopelessly. "We haven't a clue who he is. At least, I don't. I didn't learn anything yesterday—except a lot of useless gossip about people I hardly know. And it seemed as if the harder I studied people, the less I could tell about how they regarded me."

"I didn't have any luck, either," Justin agreed. "You were the first person any of the grooms remembered saddling a horse for. So it would seem that our man saddled his own. They remember several men going and coming during the day—practically every man here, it seems. And as for learning about their pasts—it's like looking for a needle in a haystack. But I'm going to put a stop to it. I'll be damned if I'll let him hurt you again. Next time we might not be so lucky. I've come up with a plan."

"What?" Marianne turned toward him, hope rising in her.

"We shall trap him instead. We won't have to try to figure out who he is. We shall set out bait for him, and when he takes it, we'll seize him."

"You mean we'll make it appear easy for him to get me, and when he tries—"

"We shall get him. Exactly. Except, of course, that it's not actually going to be you. I am not going to expose you to that kind of risk. I will pretend to be you."

Marianne began to laugh. Justin looked at her indignantly, which caused her to giggle even more. "I'm sorry. It's just—really, Justin, how could you possibly make him think you are me? You are several inches taller and rather too wide across the shoulders. And if you're planning to try dressing up in my clothes, I can tell you right now I won't allow you to rip any of my dresses at the seams trying to get into them."

"Don't be absurd," Justin said with great dignity. "I had no intention of wearing your clothes. I shall wear something of Lady B's—she's larger than you, and it won't matter that she's shorter, because he won't be able to see my legs. Stop that!" He struggled to keep his own lips from twitching into a smile, but finally gave up the struggle and gave way to laughter, too. "Well, better me than Bucky."

The idea of his friend, who was quite barrel-chested, cavorting about in a dress pretending to be her sent Marianne off into fresh peals of mirth. Finally she subsided, wiping away the tears that laughter had brought to her eyes.

"Now," Justin said, giving her a stern look, "if you could kindly refrain from vulgar amusement until I have finished explaining…."

Marianne nodded, though her eyes still danced with merriment. "I will. I promise."

"All right. Bucky and I have it all planned out. We shall do it tonight at the ball. Bucky was planning to have fireworks shot off over the pond at midnight. It will provide the perfect opportunity to have all the guests out on the terrace at the same time, to look at the display. Now, we will assume that our culprit will have his eye on you. He must be getting more and more desperate, as he has failed several times now. Doubtless he will want to get it over with here. Going back to London would complicate matters. So I think he will be watching you, looking for an opportunity to do you harm, and then try to make it look like an accident or suicide or whatever."

"I agree."

"Now Bucky and I will have made it a point to stay with you all day, giving him no opportunity to get at you. Even tonight, when you're getting ready, Penelope or Nicola will be in the room with you. But then, while everyone is watching the fireworks display, you will separate yourself from the crowd. You will loiter there a little while, allow him to see that you are without an escort, and then you will stroll down from the terrace into the garden. Bucky will have flares lit along the pathways to provide light for the guests, but it will not be enough to make everything bright and clear, of course. Here's the important thing. You will wear a shawl that's easily distinguished and some sort of thing in your hair, a spray of jewels or flowers, something noticeable. You will start along the path, going toward the rose arbor. We'll enlist Nicola and Penelope's help. By the end of the day, they will have made sure that everyone knows how much you love to sit in the rose arbor."

"Shall we tell them the whole story, then?"

"I don't see why not. They're hardly suspects."

"No."

"You will take a path that we will go over beforehand. Right after the loveknot of flowers—" He looked at her questioningly to make sure she knew the part of the path he meant.

"I know where you mean," Marianne assured him. "The little circle where the path splits around—there's a loveknot of peonies planted there."

"Exactly. Right after it, you'll turn to the left, and for the next few yards, you will be hidden from the rest of the path by that high hedge." Marianne nodded again. "I will be waiting there, wearing a dress of similar color to yours, and a wig—not quite the same shade of red, but close enough. It's an old moth-eaten thing that Bucky and Nicola dug out of the attic that the girls used for dressing up. And I will have a similar spray of flowers or whatever it is that you have in your hair. You will hand me the shawl, which I will wrap around my shoulders. Bucky will be there, too, and he will whisk you down a different path, while I hurry to the arbor. I will sit down there, and when our man turns the corner, what he will see is the rear of the rose arbor with a woman sitting in it, her back to him—a woman in your shawl and with similar hair. In the dark, with only the light of the moon and the torches, it will be enough to fool him."

"Then he will attack you," Marianne said. "What's to keep him from killing you?"

"You think I can't defend myself?"

"Not if he has a gun and shoots you in the back."

"He won't do that. It couldn't be passed off as a suicide or an accident. Besides, he will believe that I am a woman and weaker in strength. He will try to hit me or strangle me or something, and I can subdue him. Bucky will be there to help, in any case."

"I should be the one to sit in the arbor. You and Bucky could hide nearby and seize him when he tried to do something to me."

"You think that I should hide behind a bush while you accept all the danger?"

"*I* am the one he is trying to kill. There's no reason for you to risk your life."

"There is every reason."

Marianne frowned. "I don't want you hurt on my account."

Justin smiled and, heedless of the house behind them, pulled her into his arms. "It's sweet of you to worry, but quite needless, I assure you. *I* will not be the one hurt."

"But he might suspect something if it is you. Even in dim light, I fear he will not think you a woman."

"I will not allow you to take the risk," Justin said firmly. "There is no point in talking about it. Your only choice, my dear, is to help us or not."

"Of course I will help you," Marianne replied in a vexed voice. "I can hardly refuse, but I warn you, if you get yourself hurt…"

"You may scold me all you wish," he promised, catching her hand and bringing it up to his lips.

THE PLAN WENT OFF MUCH AS JUSTIN had outlined it. Marianne strolled through the garden with Bucky and Justin in the afternoon, quietly noting where they would effect the exchange. They took Nicola and Penelope into their confidence about their plan, and Nicola agreed to slip a statement about Marianne's love of the rose arbor into a conversation with the largest group of guests she could find. The remainder of the day Marianne spent in either Bucky's or Justin's company, and Penelope and Nicola joined Marianne in her room while they dressed for the ball.

As they dressed, Penelope chattered confidingly about the attentions that Lord Buckminster had been paying to her. Blushing, she related that he had held her hand as they walked this afternoon. Marianne smiled and did her best to enter into the conversation with the other two women, but she had difficulty keeping her mind on the subject. Her stomach was tied up in knots, thinking of the evening ahead.

Marianne put on her most elegant gown, a deep emerald green velvet evening dress, with a short train falling from the back of the high waistline. She arranged her hair in a smooth, upswept style, with a distinctive spray of silver and rhinestones pinned in back. Nicola had provided the spray; she had a matching one with false amethysts, which they agreed would look the same from a distance. She and Marianne tugged and pinned the ratty old wig Bucky produced into an approximation of Marianne's hairstyle and fastened the similar spray in back. The three women stepped back and considered the wig. It was a garish orange color, faded through many years from its original red, and up close in this light no one would mistake it for human hair, let alone Marianne's vivid auburn coiffure.

"Perhaps in the dark…" Nicola murmured doubtfully.

"It will look fine," Penelope said stoutly. "In the dark, it will be indistinguishable from red, and all you will really see is the glitter from the spray of stones."

Carefully covering the wig with a scarf, Penelope carried it down the corridor to Lord Buckminster, who was waiting with a sack that contained an old green gown of his mother's. He would add the wig to the sack and later place it in the garden behind the hedge, where Justin would assume his costume.

Marianne pulled on her long white gloves, and the three of them went down the stairs to the ballroom. The large room, with its long outside wall of French doors opened to admit the evening air, was festooned with greenery and roses, and sparkled under the lights of its huge chandeliers. Justin waited for Marianne there, dressed in elegant black-and-white evening clothes. His manner gave nothing away, but Marianne could see the suppressed excitement glittering in his eyes. He led her onto the floor for the first dance and later for a waltz, but for propriety's sake, Marianne had to give the rest of her dances to others.

She also had to make polite conversation with the other

guests without betraying her nerves, all the time wondering if this person or that was the one who was trying to
murder her. It did not help any that Cecilia Winborne was
there and kept shooting her venomous looks.

"I'll cast my vote for Cecilia as the villain," Nicola told
Marianne in an undertone. "If ever anyone looked capable
of murder, it is she. Deborah tells me that she has been
seething the past two days."

Nicola had visited her sister, Deborah, Lady Exmoor,
twice during their stay, and Deborah had attended the ball this
evening, sitting quietly talking with Nicola or one of the older
ladies. Her figure was still slender, but Nicola intimated that
she was in the beginning stages of pregnancy. It was her third
attempt to have a baby, the first two both having ended in mis-
carriages, and she looked quite ill, her face as white as chalk.

"I know he made her come," Nicola said in a hard voice,
staring across the room at her sister. "She should be home
in bed. She should not try to have any more children, but
of course Richard is determined to have an heir."

Marianne slipped her hand into Nicola's, roused from
her own anxiety by Nicola's obvious distress. "Perhaps this
time everything will go better."

"Thank you. I hope you are right." But Nicola's eyes
were troubled and stormy. "She asked me to come stay
with her during her confinement. She is so frightened."

Marianne looked across the room at Lady Exmoor, a paler,
less attractive copy of her sister. She certainly looked less than
well, Marianne thought, but she did not voice her opinion. "I
am sure your presence would make her feel better."

Nicola's jaw tightened. "Yes. I shall have to go. I had
sworn I would never set foot in that house, but..." She
shrugged. "I must, if it will give Deborah any comfort."

"Of course. I know you dislike the Earl very much."

"It is far more than dislike," Nicola replied bitterly, and her face was suddenly bleak and older than her years. "He killed the man I loved, and I shall never forgive him for that."

Marianne stared, stunned by the woman's words. "Nicola! He murdered him?"

Nicola shrugged. "I don't know. He was furious with him. They were fighting. He said it was an accident. It could have been. I don't know. But he is still as lost to me."

"That is why you would not visit your sister there?"

Nicola nodded.

"I am so sorry." Marianne took Nicola's hand. "No wonder you were so unhappy that your sister married him."

Nicola squeezed Marianne's hand. "Thank you. Do you know that I have never told anyone else that, even Penny? You are very easy to talk to. I feel as if I can tell you anything."

"You can," Marianne assured her. "I just wish that there were something I could do to help you."

"It has been a help just to be able to air my feelings." She released Marianne's hand, giving her a slightly tremulous smile. Her eyes moved past Marianne. "Would you look at that? Penny seems to be walking on air."

Marianne turned in the direction of her gaze and saw their friend, strolling around the perimeter of the dance floor with Lord Buckminster. The two of them were engrossed in conversation, and Penelope's face shone with happiness. A few feet from them, Bucky parted from Penelope with obvious reluctance, raising her gloved hand to his lips for a courtly kiss. Penelope turned and floated toward her friends, her eyes sparkling.

"You are looking," she whispered when she drew up with them, "at the future Lady Buckminster."

"What!"

"Penny, are you serious? He asked you to marry him?"

They spoke in excited whispers, mindful of the other ears around them. Nicola took Penelope's hand and drew her toward a small, unoccupied alcove. "Tell us all about it."

"We went for a stroll in the garden, and he asked me to marry him. He said he loved me."

"Of course he does. We knew that all along."

"He has to ask Father, of course, but I am sure Father will not refuse."

"Lady Ursula is none too fond of Bucky," Nicola reminded her friend.

"No. But she is much more frightened of my turning into an old maid. Much as she cherishes hopes that Lord Lambeth will offer for me, she is much too realistic to believe that it will ever really happen," Penelope replied. "She won't object."

"That's wonderful." Marianne hugged Penelope. "I wish you very happy."

"I will be. And thank you. I can never hope to repay you for what you've done."

"Nonsense. Bucky would have realized that he loved you at some point. We just gave him a little push."

The evening wore on. Finally it was almost midnight, and Lady Buckminster stopped the band and announced that everyone should go outside onto the terrace. Marianne had made sure that she was near the doors when the announcement was made, so that she could slip outside and take up a position exactly where she wanted to. She stood at the top of the steps leading down to the garden, leaning against the pillar. She had slipped the lacy cream-colored shawl around her shoulders, as if against the cooler evening air. She saw no sign of Bucky or Justin; they should already be in their places. Marianne's hand knotted around her fan. She forced herself not to turn around and scan the crowd. She must not seem as if she was looking for anyone or as if she was suspicious. She could hear the crowd building up along the terrace and knew that she simply had to hope that her attacker was there and watching her.

The first fireworks went off with a boom, bursting in a shower of light over the pond. The guests on the terrace let out an exclamation of delight. Marianne waited through two more rockets of light, then moved down the steps and onto the grass, standing to the side of the garden path and away from the steps, where she hoped she was clearly visible. She also hoped that her movements would have caught the villain's attention and roused his curiosity. She waited for another burst of color to light up the sky, then, for good measure, let another one pass.

Finally she started off, walking neither quickly nor slowly, winding her way down the garden path until she was out of sight of the terrace. She walked more quickly then, but she was careful not to hurry. She must simply look like a woman going for a stroll alone, enjoying the beauty of the rose-scented night and the fireworks. Her ears were attuned to the slightest noise, but she heard nothing—no crunch of pebbles, no sliding of a shoe along a path. The back of her neck prickled, and her heart was pounding double-time. She felt terribly vulnerable and exposed.

Ahead of her she saw at last the corner of the hedge behind which Justin should be waiting. She did not even allow herself to think of what she would do if Justin was not there or not ready. With even steps she approached the hedge and rounded it. With relief, she saw Justin waiting at the end of the hedge, where the path turned to head toward the arbor. He was a strange figure, tall and broad-shouldered in a woman's evening gown that ended absurdly a few inches below his knee, exposing his trousers and polished black evening shoes, and with an ill-fitting wig perched on his head.

With the hedge blocking her from her pursuer's eyes for a few precious moments, Marianne flew to Justin, taking off her shawl. She handed it to him, and Bucky, standing behind Justin, grabbed her hand and pulled her quickly around the end of the hedge and into another row of bushes. Bending over so that the shorter bushes would conceal them, he led her around first one corner, then another. They were able to straighten up then, concealed behind another high hedge, and they tip-toed quickly along it. Bucky peered around the hedge carefully, then stepped back and motioned Marianne forward so that she could look around the corner of the hedge.

When she did so, she saw Justin, now seated on the small bench in the rose arbor. His back was toward the path he had taken, and he was facing forward at a slight angle to Marianne's sightline. She could not see his features in the shadow, but she could see the pistol he held ready in his lap.

Then, on the path behind him, moving quickly toward the arbor, came the figure of a man. It paused for an instant, looking at Justin's back, then started forward. Marianne's hands clenched at her sides, and she waited tensely, hoping that Justin was aware of the man's approach. She could hear Bucky's quickening breath behind her as he peered around the hedge above her head.

Justin had indeed heard the sound of feet on the graveled pathway, and he turned his head to the side, away from the direction from which the man would approach, so that their prey would not catch a betraying glimpse of Justin's masculine features until he was into the arbor.

"Mrs. Cotterwood," the man said as he stepped into the entrance of the arbor, and Justin whipped back around to face him, bringing up the pistol in his hand to level it at the other's chest.

The other man stopped abruptly, a gasp torn from his throat. He stared at Justin, surprise, then fear, flashing across his face.

"Good God!" Justin burst out. "Winborne! It's you?"

"Winborne!" Marianne and Buckminster repeated in unison and started out from their hiding place toward the tableau in the rose arbor.

Justin leaped to his feet and reached out to grab Fanshaw Winborne's arm, but Winborne jumped back agilely and took off at a run up the path. Justin tore off after him, pistol in one hand, holding up his skirts in the other, so that they would not hamper his running. Lord Buckminster flew after him, with Marianne bringing up the rear. They tore through the garden, dodging around bushes and trampling through flowers. Justin and Buckminster were shouting at Winborne to stop, and Winborne was yelling also—it sounded to Marianne as if he were calling for help.

On the terrace, the guests turned their attention from the finale of the fireworks show to see the strange chase through the garden. Winborne was heading around the side of the house toward the front driveway, and the crowd moved along the terrace in the same direction.

Justin was almost on Winborne. Dropping both his skirts and his gun, he made a flying leap and crashed into Winborne, knocking him to the ground. In an instant Buckminster joined them, pulling Justin, who was seated astride Winborne, pummeling him, off the other man. Then he reached down to haul Winborne up, too.

In the night air, Lord Chesfield's voice carried clearly from the terrace. "I say, why is Lambeth punching Fanshaw?"

"What I want to know is, why the devil is he wearing a dress?" came Mr. Westerton's rejoinder.

Marianne was some distance behind the men. She stopped to catch her breath at the edge of the garden, watching the show, as was everyone on the terrace. She started forward, and at that moment, an arm wrapped around her waist from behind, lifting her off her feet, and a man's hand clamped over her mouth.

"You're a very difficult woman to catch, Miss Chilton," he growled and hauled her back into the gardens.

CHAPTER EIGHTEEN

THEY HAD CAUGHT THE WRONG MAN! Marianne struggled against her attacker, kicking back with her heels and wriggling wildly. *Justin and Bucky would go on arguing with Cecilia's brother, and all the while the real attacker would carry her off and dispose of her!*

The man grunted as her heels connected with his shin, and his hand tightened involuntarily against her mouth. The movement pressed her lips painfully against her teeth, but Marianne saw her opportunity and sank her teeth into the fleshy area beneath his thumb. He cursed and jerked his hand away, and Marianne let out a scream.

Justin whirled around and saw what was going on. Understanding flashed across his face, and he dropped his hold on Fanshaw Winborne's shirt front. "Fuquay!"

He started toward Marianne and Reginald Fuquay, in whose grasp Marianne was held, but Fuquay whipped out a small pistol and placed it against Marianne's temple. Justin came to an immediate stop.

"Fuquay, what the devil are you doing?" he asked. "Don't make things any worse for yourself. Put down the gun."

"That's right," Marianne said. "Everyone has seen you now."

"I want a horse," Fuquay told Justin. "I will exchange her for the best mount in Lord Buckminster's stables."

"Of course," Bucky agreed. "Whatever you say. I will give you my own horse." He turned and shouted to one of the servants, who had by that time come out the kitchen door and were gaping at the spectacle before them.

One of the footmen took off at a run for the stables. Justin took two steps toward Marianne.

"Stop! Unless you want to see her dead!"

Justin raised his hands placatingly. "Of course not. I'm not trying to hurt you. I want to talk to you. Where will you go, Fuquay? Are you going to become a fugitive, running from the law? No one has been hurt yet. Maybe we could still work something out. None of us wants a scandal, after all. Perhaps if we talked… Why don't you put down the gun? Tell us why you have been making these attacks on Mrs. Cotterwood."

"Oh, God!" Fuquay cried, his breath catching in a sob. "I'm ruined anyway."

"It isn't the worst yet, though," Justin assured him. "If you put down the gun, we can talk. But if you harm Marianne, I won't rest until you are hanging from a noose. Think of your parents, man, your family. Save them the humiliation of that!"

Fuquay let out an inarticulate noise. Marianne felt his arm loosening around her, the gun falling away.

There was a loud crack and flash from the terrace. Fuquay cried out and released Marianne as he fell to the ground.

Marianne shrieked and bolted toward Justin, who was beside her in an instant, pulling her into his arms. They clung together for a moment in relief, then turned back to Fuquay. He lay crumpled on the ground, blood covering his face.

"Oh, God," Marianne whispered, covering her mouth. Her stomach turned.

"Wait here." Justin set her aside and hurried to the man, going down on one knee to take up his wrist and search for a pulse.

Marianne followed him. "Is he…?"

"He's dead," Justin replied grimly, rising to his feet and turning toward the terrace.

The Earl of Exmoor was walking toward them, carrying a pistol. Justin's face flushed with fury, and he started toward the Earl, fists knotting at his sides.

"Why the devil did you shoot him? You could have hit Marianne!"

"Nonsense. I had a clear shot, and my aim is excellent. Mrs. Cotterwood was never in danger," Exmoor answered coolly. "That is why I aimed at his head, so it would be clear of her. Pity."

"Pity? That's all you can say? Good God, you just killed a man."

"A man who was about to shoot an unarmed woman."

"He wasn't," Marianne protested. "He was letting go of me. I felt it. Justin had persuaded him to release me."

"Now we will never know why he attacked her!" Justin followed his words with a hearty oath.

"Yes. I am sorry for that," Exmoor agreed and walked over to look down dispassionately at Fuquay. "If the light had been better, I might have been able to wound him without endangering Mrs. Cotterwood. But with only the torches and not being familiar with this pistol—I grabbed it from the wall in the study—well, I could not take the chance. Odd that he should attack you like that. I suppose some men are unable to contain their lust. He was rather wild when he was young, but he seemed to have settled down in recent years."

"It wasn't lust," Justin told him flatly, still seething. "He had tried to kill Mrs. Cotterwood before, and we have no idea why."

"Kill her!" Exmoor ejaculated with an amazed look. "How very peculiar. Well! I should think you would be grateful to me for shooting him before he could be successful at it." He cast an assessing glance at Marianne. "And you have no idea why?"

"No."

"You were not close to him, Mrs. Cotterwood?" Exmoor asked.

"No. I had never met him until I came here this week."

"Strange."

"My dear, my dear." Lady Buckminster came bustling up to them, followed by Penelope and Nicola.

The older woman folded Marianne into her embrace, hugging her to her ample bosom. "What a terrifying experience for you. You should go back to the house and rest. Tom is the magistrate, so he can take care of this."

"Yes," Penelope agreed and slipped an arm around Marianne's waist when Lady Buckminster let go of her. Nicola fell in on the other side, linking her arm through Marianne's.

They walked back into the house and went into the drawing room. Most of the men remained outside. The Squire's wife had a fit of hysterics and had to be escorted to the sitting room to lie down by the vicar's. The rest of the women drifted into the drawing room. It was a trifle small for the crowd, but no one seemed inclined to gather in the festively decorated ballroom.

They said little, seemingly stunned by the events of the evening. Finally Mrs. Thurston said tearfully, "I don't understand. Mr. Fuquay was always such a nice man. I never even heard him raise his voice. What could have brought him to this pass?"

Marianne felt as if they were all looking at her. "I don't know," she said. "He didn't say. I didn't even know the man! I mean, except to chat with at dinner and such."

"He must be mad," Sophronia Merridale declared flatly. "What else would cause him to act so bizarrely?"

"But he was so sane, so rational, so hard-working," Mrs. Thurston protested. "My husband had known him for years and years."

"Had he seemed troubled recently?" Penelope asked.

"No, not that I had noticed. Well…sometimes he fell into silences, but he was prone to do that. He thought a lot. Perhaps he had done it a trifle more often the past couple of weeks. I'm not sure."

"I am sure Mrs. Cotterwood knows why," Cecilia Winborne said venomously, rising to her feet, her eyes fixed on Marianne. "There is more going on here than meets the eye."

"Cecilia!" Lady Buckminster exclaimed. "What a thing to say!"

"It's true! She's hiding something. Just look at her!" Cecilia pointed her forefinger at Marianne.

Marianne stared at her, so surprised she could think of nothing to say.

"You are being rude," Lady Buckminster told Cecilia sharply.

"I am being truthful. She is an impostor!"

Marianne felt sick to her stomach and was sure that the color had drained out of her face. *Would they all see the guilt in her face?*

"I don't know what you're talking about." She was glad that her voice sounded calm, even though her nerves were jangling inside.

"I talked to the squire's wife today. She is from Yorkshire, the very area, in fact, where Mrs. Cotterwood claims to have grown up. Both she and her conveniently deceased husband. Mrs. Halsey had never heard of any family named Morley or Cotterwood in the area. It is clear that she is only pretending to be genteel. Who knows where she comes from or who she is! I should not be surprised at what sort of connection she really had with Mr. Fuquay or why he wanted to kill her."

Everyone stared at Cecilia in stunned silence. Marianne could think of nothing to say; her brain seemed frozen. All she could think was that now everyone would know. *They would all look at her in disgust and contempt, even Nicola and Penelope. She would have to leave the house in disgrace.*

Then she heard Nicola's voice saying coolly, "Really, Cecilia…such high drama. What else was the poor girl to do when you were subjecting her to such an inquisition? One would have thought you were a court of law. 'Where were you born? Who were your parents? Where did your husband live?' I would have told you a lot of nonsense, too, if you had tried to interrogate me that way."

"But—but—" Cecilia sputtered, looking confused. "It isn't the same. I know you."

"And I know Marianne," Nicola replied, rising to her feet. "Her family is friends with my aunt in East Anglia."

"That's not true!" Cecilia lashed out bitterly. "I don't know why you are defending her, but I know that you didn't know her before this week. She is an adventuress!"

"Are you calling me a liar?" Nicola responded, raising an eyebrow.

The other woman's face contorted. "*She* is!" Cecilia cried, stabbing a finger in Marianne's direction. "She has taken you and everyone else in."

At that moment a man's voice came from the doorway, slicing through the room like a knife. "I would be careful what I said if I were you, Cecilia. You might find yourself in the embarrassing situation of having to take back your words."

Everyone in the room swung around to look at the doorway, where Justin lounged, his shoulder negligently propped against the doorjamb. As they watched, he straightened and sauntered into the room. "That is not the sort of slander that I take lightly when it is applied to my future wife."

If the room had been quiet before, it was now virtually tomblike. All the women, including Marianne, stared at Justin as if they had been poleaxed.

"You—you can't be serious!" Cecilia gasped.

Justin raised an eyebrow at her as he walked across the room. "I did try to caution you the other night, you know." He stopped beside Marianne's chair and looked down at her. "Are you all right, my dear?"

Marianne nodded speechlessly.

"The magistrate would like to speak to you. Do you feel up to it?"

"Yes. Of course."

"Good. If you will excuse us, ladies?" Justin cast an impartial smile around the room and offered Marianne his arm.

The room remained hushed until Justin and Marianne were several feet past the door; then the women broke into a babble. Justin smiled faintly. "I seem to have created something of a stir."

"Justin! Why did you say that?" Marianne gasped.

Justin looked at her. He was a trifle surprised at his own actions. He had not thought about marrying Marianne until that moment, when he had stepped into the room and heard Cecilia reviling Marianne. An anger fiercer than any he had ever felt had swept over him then, and he had said the one thing that he knew would stop her words. But now, gazing at Marianne, he realized that marrying her was precisely what he wanted to do.

"How will you explain it when we don't get married?" Marianne went on.

"Who said that we are not?" he answered.

Marianne stopped in amazement and stared at him. "You're joking!"

"I would hardly joke about a thing like that," he replied.

"But it's impossible!"

He quirked one eyebrow. "Are you saying that you refuse to marry me?"

"No, of course not," Marianne answered truthfully. The fact was that she loved him; she had known it since the day in the mine. And when he had told Cecilia that she was his fiancée, she had been filled with a rush of pleasure so great that she could hardly contain it. She wanted more than anything to marry him—to be with Justin always, to share his life, to bear his children.

"Then it's settled." He smiled at her and reached out to open the front door.

"It is not settled." Marianne caught his arm. She knew that it would be low of her indeed to take Justin up on his offer. She glanced around, then pulled him into the music room, which was unoccupied. "You can't marry me!"

"Indeed?" Justin gave her a quelling look. "And here I thought I was free and over the age of consent."

"Don't try that frosty aristocratic stare on me. It won't work," she said flatly. "You know as well as I do that you aren't free, not really. The future Duke of Storbridge cannot marry a nobody—worse than a nobody, a thief!"

"I do agree that we should keep quiet about your present occupation," Justin agreed. "And perhaps we should find your 'relatives' less larcenous methods of making money."

"It would take far more than that to make me respectable, and you know it. The truth will come out. Someone—most probably Cecilia—will start to dig into my past and will find out that I used to be a servant. It will ruin you!"

"Hardly that."

"It will be a blot on your family's reputation. Your parents—"

"I do as I wish," Justin told her flatly. "My parents do not make my decisions for me."

"But why?" Marianne asked almost desperately. "You do not have to—"

"I know I do not 'have to.' But when I heard what Cecilia was saying, I knew I could not allow you to be subjected to such remarks. I don't want people gossiping about you, speculating on whether you are my mistress."

"Oh, Justin!" Tears filled Marianne's eyes, and she threw her arms around him. "You are so good."

He smiled at that and bent to press his lips against her hair. "I suspect that there are those who would dispute that."

"Well, they would be wrong," Marianne said staunchly, going up on tiptoe to press her lips against his. "I love you."

Justin made an inarticulate noise and buried his lips in hers.

It was sometime later that he finally released her and stepped back. "If we go on, I shall never take you out to the magistrate," he told her hoarsely. "And he is waiting for us."

Marianne nodded. She could not let Justin make this sacrifice for her. But he was right; they needed to deal with the magistrate now. Later she would think about what she had to do.

The magistrate was a white-haired man whom Marianne had met earlier in the evening. He was the local squire, an amiable sort of man who apparently enjoyed Lady Buckminster's fondness for horses. Marianne suspected that around here he had few occasions to deal with deaths such as this one. He looked decidedly uncomfortable and a trifle in awe of Justin, who did not leave Marianne's side during his questions.

The questioning took little time as she had very few answers. *No, she barely knew the man,* and *No, she had no idea why he would wish to harm her.*

"I am sorry to be of so little help," she apologized.

Squire Halsey smiled on her benignly and patted her arm. "There, there, my dear, he was clearly a madman. Their ways make no sense. Don't worry about it."

"I just wish I knew why he—" Justin began, then broke off, grimacing. "I suppose I really cannot blame Exmoor. If I had had a gun at that moment, I might very well have done the same thing."

When the interview was over, Marianne left Justin with the magistrate and went up to her room. She had a great deal to think over. She had, she knew, unwittingly brought a great deal of trouble to these people. She did not know why Mr. Fuquay had tried to kill her, but now he was dead, and Lady Buckminster and Bucky had the scandal of it happening there at their party to deal with. If Cecilia or someone else did manage to find out about her origins in the orphanage and as a servant, then Nicola would seem to the others in the *ton* at best a fool, for being taken in by Marianne, at worst a traitor to her own by attesting to Marianne's nonexistent status. And Justin! It would be the worst for him, if he married her.

He was a proud man, and his pride would be destroyed if everyone learned that his wife was low-born. He would be held in amusement and contempt. His family would be furious. And there would be a blot on his family's name that could never be erased.

Marianne wanted to be his wife more than she had ever wanted anything in her life. It filled her with joy that he had wanted to protect her from people's gossip. But he had said nothing about love. And she could not let him throw away his life just to save her reputation. She could not marry him.

The only thing for her to do, she realized, was to leave this place as soon as possible. Once she was out of Justin's life, Cecilia would not bother to dig up Marianne's past. No one need ever know that Nicola had lied for her; Justin would not be burdened with an embarrassment of a low-born wife.

She would go home. Her heart swelled with love as she thought of being with her daughter again. Rosalind would help to take away the pain in her heart. She would tell the others that she could no longer continue in her role. Then she would take Rosalind, and they would go to some other city—Manchester or Leeds or some other growing metropolis where there were newly rich merchants who would be willing to pay for lessons in language and deportment. She would be able to make a living for her and her daughter…and if her days looked unremittingly bleak, at least she would have the memories of this week with Justin.

Justin would be angry at first, she knew. There was even the possibility that he might follow her and try to persuade her to change her mind. But, with a little luck, she would escape him. And in time he would be glad that she had not taken him up on his offer. He wanted her, and he had been too honorable to make her his mistress, but he had said nothing to her about love. She knew that he did not even believe in the emotion. Desire would fade, and reason would replace it. Then he would be relieved.

Marianne dashed away the tears that the thought brought to her eyes and set about carrying out her plan. She went to Lady Buckminster's room and found her still up, so she launched into the tale she had prepared: she was so shaken by her experiences of the evening that she had determined to return home first thing the next morning, and she would appreciate it if Lady Buckminster would let her take her carriage to the inn in the village the next day, so that she could get the first coach to London.

Lady Buckminster was all sympathy, though she at first tried to convince Marianne to accept the use of the carriage all the way back to London, as well as one of the gentleman as an escort. It took some time to talk her out of that idea, and then the lady insisted that she must take the post chaise. Traveling by coach was simply too slow and tiresome. Marianne also knew, though the older woman was too polite to say so, that a lady would not travel alone by coach, so Marianne finally agreed to hire a post chaise, knowing that when she got to the inn, Lady Buckminster would not know that she took the mail coach instead.

After getting Lady Buckminster to swear that she would not tell a soul where Marianne had gone, she returned to her room and packed her trunk and smaller suitcase. Finally she sat down to the hardest part: penning a letter of explanation to Justin. First she wrote a note to Nicola, thanking her for her help the evening before, as well as notes of thanks to her hostess and to Penelope. Then, unable to avoid it any longer, she wrote Justin. She shed more than a few tears over the missive, but she sternly forced herself to finish it.

She had just finished the letter and sealed it and the others when there was a soft tap at her door. Surprised, she slid the letters into a drawer and went to open her door. Justin was standing there.

Her eyes widened in surprise, but she stepped back quickly so that he could enter.

"Everyone else is in bed," he told her. "I couldn't sleep."

He reached out and took one of her curls in his fingers and began to toy with it. His eyes were hot and dark, his mouth heavy. "I had planned not to risk coming here tonight. I could wait, I thought, until our wedding day." His mouth curve sensually. "But I quickly found out how wrong I was."

He bent and kissed her, his mouth slow and velvety on hers. Marianne held herself stiff for a moment, then gave in. She deserved this one night, she told herself. *She was, after all, giving up a lifetime with him. Surely it would be all right for her to steal this one night to cherish as a memory.*

Justin raised his head and looked down at her quizzically. "Have you been crying?"

Marianne nodded. She should have realized that he would notice her reddened eyes. She wracked her brain for some explanation.

But he had already jumped to his own conclusion. "Poor girl. It's no wonder, after the night you had." Justin cradled her in his arms. "I should have stayed with you. Bucky could have handled it all."

Marianne let out a little sigh of relief and snuggled into his chest.

"Here. Let me take care of you," he said gently and began to take down her hair.

It fell, heavy and soft, over her shoulders, and Justin picked up her brush and began to pull it through her hair with long, smooth strokes. Marianne closed her eyes, luxuriating in the soft, sensual pleasure. With each stroke, her loins grew warmer and heavier. Finally he laid the brush aside and began to unbutton her dress, pausing halfway down to kiss the smooth skin of her back as the two sides of her dress fell away from it. Then he continued undressing her, letting her dress and petticoats fall in a pool on the floor.

When she was clad only in her chemise and pantalets, he led her to the bed and sat her down on it, then knelt in front of her and began to unfasten her slippers. He drew each slipper from her foot, rubbed her feet, easing away every bit of pain and tiredness. Next he slid his hand up her leg until he found her garter and pulled it down, following it by rolling down her stocking. Marianne shivered at the exquisite pleasure of his slow, delicate touch. He did the same thing with the other garter and stocking, and by the time he was through, Marianne was pulsing with desire.

"Make love to me," she murmured, sliding her hands up his arms and onto his chest.

Justin smiled and kissed her. "I will. Believe me, I will. But first…"

He pulled one end of the ribbon that tied her chemise until the bow fell apart. Then he slipped his hands beneath the top of the chemise and slid it down over her breasts, his hands cupping and caressing the heavy orbs as he did so. He untied the ribbon at the waist of the pantalets and removed them in the same slow, caressing manner.

Gently, taking his time, he kissed and stroked her, arousing her to an ever higher desire. He made love to her with his mouth, kissing her breasts and stomach and making his way down to the hot center of her passion. Using his tongue, he ignited her, and Marianne moaned, writhing and digging her hands into the bed beneath her.

Finally he stood and ripped away his clothing, then moved between her legs. Lifting her buttocks, he slid into her, filling her, and Marianne wrapped her legs around him. He thrust and retreated, thrust and retreated, until Marianne convulsed around him, pleasure rushing through her. He let out a hoarse cry and muffled it against her neck, shuddering as he poured his seed into her. Marianne wrapped her arms around him, clinging to him with all her might, as tears leaked from the corners of her eyes.

JUSTIN LEFT HER ROOM EARLY THE next morning. Marianne sat up as soon as the door clicked shut behind him. She had not slept the entire night, but had lain awake listening to him breathe and feeling the steady beat of his heart beneath her head. She had not wanted to miss even a moment of this last night with him. It would have to last her a lifetime.

Now she rose and washed, then dressed quietly and swept her hair up into a simple bun. She wore a traveling suit, made of dark, durable material, with a light jacket to protect against the dust of the road. Her bonnet was equally plain, and she looked, she thought, rather like a governess. However, that was what she wanted—to be as little noticed as possible. If Justin should come looking for her, she did not want people remembering that she had passed by.

She rang for the maid and found that Lady Buckminster had already ordered the carriage to be brought around for her. The maid went back to the kitchen and brought her up a light breakfast of tea and toast. Shortly after that, a footman came in and carried her trunk of clothes down to the carriage. Marianne handed the letters to the maid, asking her to deliver them to the appropriate people later in the day. She was hopeful that Justin would arise late and might not even notice her absence until the afternoon.

The sun was just beginning to come up when she walked out the door and got into the carriage. Tears filled her eyes as the coach rolled away. She turned her head from the view of the house and blinked her tears away.

The drive into the village took almost thirty minutes, and by that time, she had overcome her tendency to cry. The coachman carried her trunk into the inn for her. Marianne went inside the inn to inquire about the next mail coach and learned that it would be almost thirty minutes before it arrived. She strolled back out into the yard.

A large, expensive carriage rolled down the road past the inn, not turning in, but the rider on horseback that followed right behind it did enter the yard. The rider, a rounded fellow who rode clumsily, slid off his horse with obvious relief, shouting for an ostler.

"Here, she's thrown a shoe," he complained. "I need to get it put back on right away."

The ostler explained that the blacksmith next door already was working on previous orders, and the two exchanged words for a few minutes. The rider took off his hat and brushed the gathering sweat from his forehead, and Marianne drew a sharp breath.

The rider was the man whom Rosalind had pointed out to her across the street from their house—the man who had questioned Rosalind and the maid in the park!

Marianne quickly stepped back inside the doorway and watched the pair from the window, taking care to stand well back so that he could not see her. *Who was he? Had he followed her here?*

It seemed too strange a coincidence that he should happen to turn up in this town when she was visiting a house only a few miles away. He must have tricked it out of Rosalind or one of the others. *Was he even now headed for Buckminster? Thank heavens she was no longer there.* Marianne did not know what he wanted, but she did not think it could be anything good. He must, she thought, be somehow connected with Mr. Fuquay—his accomplice, or perhaps his employee. She had thought herself safe now that Fuquay was dead. *But what if this man now tried to finish off the job?*

Clearly he would enter the inn once he had transacted his business with the blacksmith, and Marianne wondered how she would manage to avoid him until the mail coach arrived. She watched as he walked away with the ostler to the blacksmith's, leading his horse.

Marianne slipped out the front door and ran across the yard. She stopped at the gate and peered cautiously out. The ostler and the rider were disappearing into the shop next door. Marianne let out a sigh of relief and started down the street in the opposite direction. She had not gone twenty steps when she heard a voice raised behind her.

"Wait! Stop!"

She whirled around and saw the man, now standing in the doorway of the blacksmith's, looking at her. She whipped back around and set off at a rapid pace. Behind her, the man shouted out her name. "Mrs. Cotterwood! Stop!"

She heard his footsteps running after her, and Marianne picked up her skirts and broke into a run. She darted up the street and ducked into an alleyway. She was going to run through it to the street beyond, but then she saw a stout plank of wood lying discarded on the ground, so she swooped down and picked it up. Stationing herself at the entry to the alley, she waited, listening to the man's running footsteps. He slowed and turned into the alley, and Marianne swung the board with all her might, catching him square in the stomach and knocking the air out of him.

He doubled over, gasped for air and staggered back out into the street. Marianne raised the board and brought it down again. She had meant to strike him in the head, but at the last second she could not bear to do that and she pulled back, hitting him in the back and sending him sprawling to the ground. She looked up and saw a man in a landau a few yards away. He had stopped his vehicle and was watching her with interest. His eyebrows shot up as he recognized her.

"Mrs. Cotterwood!"

"Lord Exmoor!" Marianne did not like the man, but at the moment he looked like a godsend. Jumping over the man she had hit, she ran toward the landau. "Can you help me?"

"Mrs. Cotterwood, every time I see you, someone is attacking you. You lead a highly unusual life."

"This isn't how it is normally, I assure you," Marianne answered breathlessly, reaching up a hand. "Will you help me?"

"Certainly." He reached down and took her hand, helping her up onto the seat beside him. "I take it you need to get away from that man. Shall I take you back to Buckminster?"

"No!" Marianne cast a panicked look over at the man,

who was now staggering to his feet and coming after her. "Oh, dear. I was going to take the mail coach back to London. But now I can't. Not with him here."

"That does present a problem," Exmoor agreed. "I tell you what. I shall drive you to Exeter myself. You can catch a coach more easily there, anyway."

"Would you?" Marianne looked at him hopefully. She did not relish being alone with this man for several hours, but she had to get away from her pursuer—and she was determined not to return to Justin.

"Of course. I am always happy to help a lady in distress." Exmoor gave her a cold smile and slapped the reins. The horses set off smartly.

They were driving straight toward her pursuer. Exmoor slapped the reins again, and the horses broke into a run. The other man waved his arms, shouting at them to stop, but he jumped out of the way at the last minute, and the landau whipped past him.

Marianne twisted around in the seat. The man clambered to his feet and lumbered after them, shouting and cursing and shaking his fist. It was, of course, a pointless effort, for they soon outstripped him. Marianne turned back around, and Exmoor's vehicle rolled through the village and onto the road to Exeter.

CHAPTER NINETEEN

THEY BOWLED ALONG FOR SOME MINUTES in silence before the Earl slowed the horses. Exmoor cast a sideways glance at his companion.

"Who was that fellow?" he asked.

"I don't know," Marianne admitted.

The Earl raised an eyebrow. "Then why was he chasing you?"

"I don't know that, either." Marianne sighed. "My life has gotten...very strange lately."

"I have to agree. Two mysterious attacks in the course of two days would seem somewhat abnormal."

"I know. But truthfully, I have no idea why either of them was after me. I presume they were somehow connected, but I don't know how. Nor do I know why anyone would want to kill me." She looked at him. "Do you believe me?"

Exmoor shrugged. "Yes. Why would you think I don't?"

"I don't know. I felt last night that everyone must think I knew something and just wasn't revealing it."

"Perhaps you know something and don't realize it yet. Had you thought of that?"

"Or perhaps they think I know something when I do not. I think...I think it might have something to do with my childhood."

His hands tightened on the reins. "Indeed? Why do you think that?"

"Because that is the main area of my life that I know nothing about. And that man back there—he was searching for me earlier."

"Was he?"

Marianne nodded. "Yes. He went to where I lived when I was young. So I thought it must have something to do with that time in my life. I can remember almost nothing before I was seven or eight."

"Have you tried to remember? Tried casting your mind back to that time, dredging up any lurking memory?"

"Oh, yes, many times. And not just since this trouble started. For years I have wished I could remember when I was a little girl. But it is all very murky."

"I see." After a moment, he went on, "Was Mr. Fuquay someone you knew as a child?"

Marianne shook her head. "If he was, I don't remember him. He never seemed familiar to me. It is all so senseless. I suppose we shall never know."

"Mmm. I suppose not." He paused, then asked, "Was your friend back there the reason you are running off to London?"

"I'm not running," Marianne protested automatically. Exmoor quirked an eyebrow without saying anything. Marianne sighed. "All right, yes, I am running, but not from him. I didn't even see him until I reached the inn to catch the mail coach. I—it just seemed better not to stay any longer."

"Because of the incident yesterday with Mr. Fuquay."

Marianne nodded. That seemed as good an excuse as any, she thought. She had no desire to reveal the real reason.

"What will you do when you get to London?"

"I'm not sure. I—I have been thinking of moving."

"Indeed? Why?"

"I have a daughter." Marianne smiled as she thought of Rosalind. "Sometimes I think it would be better for her to grow up somewhere else. Somewhere smaller. And the appeal of the Season has began to pall."

"Perhaps you could return to your parents," Exmoor suggested.

Marianne shook her head. "No. They are both dead."

"I am sorry to hear that."

The conversation lapsed after that, and they rolled along in silence. Marianne's head ached from crying and from lack of sleep, and she felt quite miserable. Even the prospect of seeing her daughter again did little to cheer her up.

The landau came to a stop, and Marianne's head snapped up. She realized that she had actually dozed off. She blinked and glanced around her. "Why are we stopping?"

The Earl glanced at her. "I was thinking of turning off onto this road." He pointed toward a lane that branched off from the main road. "It is, I believe, a shortcut to Exeter."

Marianne looked down the peaceful lane. Hedges grew on both sides of the road, and trees arched over it, creating a dappled shade. It was a lovely and secluded spot, but it scarcely looked to be a road that led much of anywhere, let alone a major town.

"It is?" she asked somewhat doubtfully.

Exmoor chuckled. "Yes. I know it looks like any country lane, but it intersects with a larger road."

Marianne felt strangely uneasy. There was an odd, considering look in Exmoor's eyes as he watched her. She straightened.

"Actually, you do not need to drive me all the way to

Exeter," she told him. "I have put you to far too much trouble as it is. I am sure that I would be able to catch the mail coach from a nearer village."

He started to answer her, but the sound of hooves on the road behind them caught his attention, and he turned to look. Marianne twisted around in her seat, also. A man on horseback was approaching them, and as they caught sight of him, he kicked his mount into a run. Marianne's heart leaped in her chest. The rider thundering down upon them was Justin.

He pulled to a halt beside them. He was scowling and without hat or coat. Marianne noticed that a pistol was stuck into his belt.

"What the devil do you think you're doing, Exmoor?" Justin growled. "Adding abducting young ladies to your bag of tricks?"

"My dear Lambeth," Exmoor replied smoothly, "you wound me. I was, in fact, rescuing Mrs. Cotterwood."

"Rescuing!"

"Yes, he was, actually," Marianne put in. "A man was chasing me, and Lord Exmoor helped me get away."

"Good God, Marianne! The minute my back is turned you are running off and being chased or thrown into mines or some other improbable thing." He swung down off his horse and came around to Marianne's side of the landau. "Get down, Marianne. I am taking you back."

"I don't want to go back. You cannot make me."

Justin drew his brows together. "Damnation! Am I so fearsome that you must sneak out of the house in the middle of the night to avoid marrying me? All you had to do was refuse my proposal. I will not force you to the altar."

"You know it was not like that!" Marianne retorted hotly.

"I know nothing of the kind. All I know is that I was

awakened early by some sort of fuss downstairs, and when I asked about you, Lady Buckminster told me that you had left before dawn! What else would you call that?"

"I left a letter for you. I told the maid to give it to you later."

"Well, it is sooner, and I want an explanation from you. I will not keep you if you want to go, but first, blast it, you will talk to me and tell me why you refuse me." He turned to glare at the man beside her on the seat. "I don't need your presence, Exmoor."

"I confess I do feel a trifle *de trop*," the Earl commented dryly. "However, I cannot desert Mrs. Cotterwood."

"No, go," Marianne said. "Justin is right. I owe him an explanation. And it would be beyond enough to embroil you in this." She held out her hand to Exmoor. "Thank you for your help, and I apologize for putting you to so much trouble and wasting your time."

"I am always glad to help a lady in distress, madam," Exmoor replied, taking her hand. "But of course I would not wish to intrude on your privacy. If you are quite sure that it is what you want, I will leave you with Lord Lambeth." He raised his eyebrows in mute question.

"Yes, thank you, I think that would be best."

Exmoor tipped his hat to her, and Marianne climbed down from the landau. With some delicate maneuvering of the vehicle, he turned it around without landing in the ditch on either side and started back in the direction from which he had come. Marianne turned to face Justin.

"All right," he said. "Tell me why you ran away from me."

"I wasn't running away from you. I just saw that it would be best all around if I disappeared. Cecilia would not look for information to discredit me and make you a laughingstock. You would not have to marry me."

"I do not *have* to marry you," Justin pointed out sharply. "I *chose* to. Obviously, however, I forgot to ask if *you* wished to marry *me*."

"It is not a matter of not wanting to marry you. Of course I want to."

"Indeed. Your behavior is scarcely that of an eager fiancée."

"I did not want to have to argue with you!" Marianne snapped back. "I tried to tell you last night why we could not marry, and you wouldn't listen. It will ruin you! Your family will be furious. Everyone has told me how proud they are, how proud you are. What will happen to that pride when everyone finds out that you have married a girl who not only cannot trace her lineage back eight generations, but doesn't even know who her parents are?"

"Do you think I care about what my parents say? I will marry to please me, not to please them. And I don't give a damn about your parents—or eight generations of ancestors, either."

"You once did. You told me that marriage for you was a business proposition, that you would someday marry someone of proper lineage like Cecilia and produce an heir, as was your duty."

"Bloody hell! Don't throw my words back up at me!" Justin's hand lashed out and grasped her arm. "I am well aware of the sort of idiotic things I have said in the past. But I had never been in love then. I did not realize what it would be like to live without it. But I understand that now, and I will be damned if I shall cut myself off from the woman I love to please my family or Society."

Marianne stared at him, the blood draining out of her face. She felt suddenly light-headed. "The woman you love?"

"Yes. Of course. Why else would I ask you to marry me?"

"Why, to save my reputation. You said that when you heard Cecilia, you realized that you didn't want people gossiping about me, that you—"

Justin let out an oath. "Of course I did not want people gossiping about you. I love you far too much for that. I don't want you for my mistress. I don't want to spend only stolen hours with you. I want to live with you. I want to be with you all the time, to dance with you at balls—every damn dance, if I want, to wake up in the morning and see your face. I want to look at my children and see you in them. I want to watch your belly grow round and know that it is my seed inside you. I don't want a dalliance. I want to marry you."

Marianne swayed on her feet. "You—you did not say then that you loved me."

"Good Lord, don't faint on me now," Justin commented, wrapping one arm around her to hold her up. "I would look like a right ogre."

He swept her up in his arms and carried her across the road to a low stone wall. He set her down on the wall and went down on one knee in front of her. Taking her hand, he looked into her dazed blue eyes. "Of course I love you, you goose. And I refuse to suffer the rest of my life without you for the sake of pride or family or anything else. The only way you can get rid of me is to tell me that you do not love me."

Tears filled Marianne's eyes, and she let out a watery little chuckle. "You know I cannot do that. I love you more than anything."

"Good. Then will you marry me? And promise not to run away again?"

"Yes." Marianne's smile was sunny. "I will marry you, and I shan't ever run away!"

She threw her arms around his neck, and he kissed her. They stayed on the low stone wall for a few more minutes, kissing and murmuring sweet words of love, until the sound of a cart down the road recalled them to their surroundings.

"I suppose we had better return to Buckminster," Justin said with some reluctance. "Though how we are to explain this latest escapade, I don't know."

Marianne giggled. "We shall say I was terrified by my experience last night."

"So terrified that you neglected to inform your future husband that you were leaving this morning?"

"I was hysterical."

"Mmm." Justin cocked an eyebrow. "I think we will have to come up with something better than that."

He helped Marianne up onto his horse and mounted behind her. Taking up the reins, he commented, "I am getting quite used to traveling this way. Perhaps I won't even buy you a mount. You can just ride pillion with me."

They started down the road at a slow pace, nodding at the driver of the farm cart as if nothing was unusual about their mode of conveyance. They talked and laughed and spun silly stories to explain Marianne's bolting from the house that morning.

After a while, Justin spotted a figure riding toward them in the distance. It resolved into a rather rotund rider on a shabby mount, plodding determinedly toward them. "I say. It's that fellow," Justin said, nodding toward the rider. "The one who told me which way you had gone."

"What?" Marianne, who had been leaning against Justin with her head on his chest, now straightened and turned to look forward. "Who?" Her eyes narrowed. "But that's the man! The one who chased me!"

"What? What are you talking about? *He* chased you?"

"Yes. Lord Exmoor helped me get away from him. It was that man!" She explained about seeing him at the inn that morning and recognizing him, about fleeing from him and his giving chase—until she laid him out with a plank and escaped to Exmoor's vehicle.

Justin began to chuckle, and Marianne fixed him with a cool stare.

"It wasn't funny," she protested.

"No? It sounds it." Justin struggled to pull his mouth into a sober line. "I would say that I will make short work of the chap, but it seems as if you have already done so."

His expression turned thoughtful as they rode nearer. "Dogged fellow, isn't he? Well, I think it's time we had a talk with him. Perhaps we can find out some answers."

As they approached the other man, Justin reached into his belt and took out his pistol. He pulled his mount to a halt and swung off him, raising the pistol and pointing it at the other man. The man's mouth fell open, and he raised his hands quickly.

"'Ere now, no call for that!" he exclaimed. "I don't mean you no harm."

"Off your horse," Justin demanded. "I have a few questions for you."

"Of course. Of course." The man smiled and dismounted with none of Justin's grace. He faced Justin, still smiling. "I'll tell you anything I know. Like I said, I don't mean you no harm." He shot a wounded look at Marianne. "You hadn't ought to hit me with that wood, miss. I was only trying to talk to you."

"Well, you have your chance to talk now," Justin said grimly. "Who are you? And what connection are you to Fuquay?"

"Who?"

Justin's eyes narrowed. "I might remind you that at this range I could scarcely miss you. In fact, I could pick or choose exactly where I want to hit you. So unless you would like a ball in the knee or—"

"I don't!" the man assured him hastily. "I'll tell you anything I know. I just don't know any Fuquay. My name is Rob Garner, sir. I—I'm a Bow Street Runner."

"A Runner?" Justin asked scornfully. "You expect me to believe that? A Runner, and you're stalking Mrs. Cotterwood like a hunter after a doe?"

"I *am* a Runner, sir. I swear it! And I wasn't stalking her. That is, I was hired to find her, sir."

"By whom?" Marianne slid down off the horse and came closer. "If it was not Mr. Fuquay, who was it?"

"It were the Countess of Exmoor. That's who hired me."

"The Countess of Exmoor!" Justin exclaimed, and in his astonishment he lowered his pistol.

"Yes, sir."

"Nicola's sister!" Marianne exclaimed. "Why would she want to hurt me? I scarcely met the woman."

"It's the Dowager Countess I'm talking about, miss, and, Lord luv ya, missus, she don't want to hurt you. I wouldn't a hurt you neither. I was trying to talk to you! Only no one would let me near you. You ran away when you saw me, and them servants at your house were the most close-mouthed lot I ever did meet."

"My God!" Justin exclaimed quietly, the first glimmer of understanding beginning to dawn in him. "Is that why the Countess came to Buckminster this morning?" He glanced at Marianne. "It was her arrival this morning that created all the stir. But I didn't speak to her. I assumed she had come to get Penelope."

"I don't understand." Marianne looked from Garner to Justin and back. "Who is the Dowager Countess of Exmoor?"

"Penelope's grandmother," Justin answered for the Runner. "But I think this concerns another matter, doesn't it, Garner? Her son's children?"

"Yes, sir." Garner nodded and smiled at Justin. "You're a downy one, you are." He turned to Marianne. "First, I got to ask you a question, Mrs. Cotterwood. Are you Mary Chilton?"

Marianne sucked in a breath. She had known that somehow all this was connected to the man searching for her at the orphanage, yet the confirmation was still chilling. "Yes," she replied, lifting her chin up almost defiantly. "I used to be called Mary Chilton."

"Bloody hell," Justin murmured.

Marianne glanced at him. "Why do you say that? What do you know about this?"

"And were you at the orphanage of St. Anselm's?" Rob Garner went inexorably on.

"Yes, I was." Marianne turned back to him, though she continued to glance uncertainly at Justin.

"And do you remember anything about your life before you were at the orphanage?"

"No," Marianne answered truthfully. "I'm not even sure if my name was my own or one the matron gave me. Why are you asking me all these things? What does it mean?"

"The Countess asked me to track you down and bring you to meet her. It—it is possible you may be related to her."

"What!" Marianne gaped. She turned toward Justin. "Justin, what is he talking about? How could I be related to a countess? Do you know what he's talking about?"

"I have heard gossip," Justin admitted. "I think what he's saying, Marianne, is that there is some possibility that you are the granddaughter of the Countess of Exmoor."

"IT'S ABSURD," MARIANNE SAID. She was once again seated on Justin's horse in front of him, and they were moving at a swifter pace back toward Buckminster. They had already outstripped Mr. Garner, but he had assured him that taking Marianne to the Countess was far more important than his being there when the two met.

"How could I be a countess's granddaughter?" Marianne went on. "Noble children are not stuck in or-phanages. I don't know why anyone would even think it."

"I'm not sure," Justin replied. "Obviously if the Countess's grandchild were put in an orphanage, it must have been some kind of mistake. I don't know much of the story. But that last name—Chilton. Lord Chilton was the Countess's son. That was the title he carried while his father, the Earl of Exmoor, was still alive."

"The Earl of Exmoor! You don't mean the one who shot Mr. Fuquay, surely."

"No. He is some sort of cousin to them. The old Earl, the Dowager Countess's husband, has been dead for a long time. The Earl you know came into the title upon that man's death. You see, right after the old Earl died, their son, Lord Chilton, and his wife and children were killed by the Mob in Paris. It was during their Revolution, you see, and Chilton and his family were unlucky enough to be caught there. I believe his wife was French. So Richard acceded to the title, and that was the way things remained for twenty-two years. Then, a few months ago, an American woman showed up in London. Took it by storm—she is a beauty. All of a sudden, the Countess announced that this woman, Alexandra Ward, is actually her granddaughter, Lord Chilton's youngest daughter. It turns out that she was not killed after all, but had been rescued by some American woman who adopted her as her own daughter."

"My, what a story."

"I know. It sounds rather like a novel, doesn't it? But I did not realize that they thought the other children might be alive, as well."

"How many children were there?"

"I'm not sure. Three or four, I think. Alexandra and a boy and at least one other girl, or the Countess would not be looking for a granddaughter."

"But if this child was supposedly killed in France…"

"Yes, it does seem a bit unlikely that she would pop up in an orphanage in Britain. Perhaps Lady Exmoor is grasping at straws. No doubt having retrieved one grandchild, she hopes to recover the others, as well."

"Wouldn't I remember?" Marianne asked. "How could I have forgotten living that way? How could I have forgotten how to speak correctly?"

"What do you mean? You speak perfectly."

"Yes, after Della *trained* me. I didn't before." But Marianne could not help remembering how impressed Harrison and Della had been at the ease with which she had picked up the high-toned accent and speech patterns. And she knew that her speech was better now even than her mentor's was. There was a certain indefinable style that delineated the speaker as a member of the *ton,* something that went beyond the proper grammar or accent, and she had conquered that as Della had never been completely able to.

"I don't know whether you would remember much of your childhood or not. I don't, at least not until after I'm eight or so."

"Yes, but don't you think a war would be something you would remember?" Marianne asked. "Mobs rioting and trying to kill you?"

"Sometimes things are too painful to remember. And sometimes children are protected from the harsher realities."

Unconsciously Marianne's hand stole up to her neck, where her cameo lay against her skin beneath her dress. *Was it possible that the elegant man and woman in the portraits really were her parents, as she had believed when she was a child? If she showed her locket to the Countess, would she recognize them? Or would she crush all her childhood dreams, once and for all?*

"It is odd," she said. "This is what I always dreamed of when I was a girl at the orphanage. I would tell myself that my parents were beautiful and wealthy, a lord and lady, and that I had been stolen from them. They would search for me and find me, and I would be restored to my family." She smiled a little crookedly. "And now, here it is—sounding just like my dream. But instead of jumping for joy, I feel— I don't know, scared, I think. What if I am the Countess's granddaughter, but when she sees me she is disappointed? Or what if she realizes that I am definitely not related to her at all? What if she says it's obvious that I am common?"

Justin kissed her on the forehead. "Don't worry. The Countess would never say that, even if it were true, which I can assure you it is not. You are definitely uncommon. Besides, I will be right here with you—whether you are the

Countess's granddaughter or merely an orphan with a co-incidental name."

Marianne smiled up at him, her heart swelling with happiness. He was right: whatever happened, the important thing was that Justin loved her and would be with her always.

When they arrived at Buckminster, the first person to greet them was Penelope. She came rushing out of the drawing room, her hands extended to Marianne.

"Isn't this marvelous?" she cried. "I can scarcely believe it! To think that all the time they were looking for you, you were right here."

Penelope's cheeks were a rosy pink with happiness, and she looked quite pretty. "It's the luckiest thing in the world that you should be my cousin. Wait until you meet Alexandra—they are back in England, you see, Thorpe and Alexandra. They came with Grandmama. Alexandra is so eager to see you. They are out in the garden, but they should be back soon. And I sent a servant up to Grandmama's room as soon as I saw you come up the drive."

A little dazed by all this information, Marianne said weakly, "But what if I am not the woman for whom you're searching? I don't see how I could be. "

"Oh, I am sure you must be," Penelope protested. "It makes sense. I liked you immediately and felt so relaxed with you. I am usually quite shy; it takes me a while to warm up to people. But we must have sensed the relation. Don't you think?"

At that moment, the door to the drawing room swung open and Marianne turned toward it, her heart pounding in rising hope. *Would she recognize this woman and know at once she was her grandmother?* An older woman, using a cane, walked at a dignified pace into the room. It was obvious that she had once been a great beauty. Though her white skin was wrinkled and creased, the bone structure of her face was elegant, and her blue eyes were bright. Her thick white hair was swept up and anchored on the side with a diamond spray. Her gray silk dress was in the latest mode. She carried herself with a regal confidence that would probably have rendered Marianne awestruck, had it not been for the merry twinkle in her eyes.

She paused, looking at Marianne. Finally she said, "So you are Mary Chilton."

"Yes, my lady. But I am afraid that you have the wrong person." Marianne sighed. "I had hoped that I would have some recognition of you, but I am afraid I do not."

The older woman smiled. "Well, you are a very honest, if rather blunt, young woman—a quality, I might add, that you share with Alexandra." She came closer. "I will be honest, too. I am no more sure than you are." She stopped, gazing into Marianne's face. "You have the height of our family. And Marie Anne's hair was red, though of a lighter shade than yours. But it is not uncommon for one's hair to darken as one grows older. There is some similarity in your face to my son's…."

She paused, studying Marianne, then said, "Excuse me, I forget my manners. Please sit down."

Marianne sank into a red velvet chair, and the Countess sat down across from her. Marianne realized with a fierce ache how much she would like for this woman to be her grandmother. "It is your name, you know, that is the most convincing. I suppose Mr. Garner told you that my son's name was Chilton. And Mary—so close to Marie. Now, he tells me, you call yourself Marianne—we usually called my eldest granddaughter Marie Anne."

A little chill ran down Marianne's spine. She had been called Mary as long as she could remember. *What had caused her to choose Marianne as a name? Could it have been a long-buried memory? Or was she grasping at straws because she wanted the story to be true?*

"You were the right age when you were left at the orphanage. My Marie Anne was five then, as well. One of the women who worked there said she remembered that the matron had told her you were brought in by a 'gentleman.' The matron apparently assumed you were some high-born man's by-blow."

Marianne's cheeks colored. "That could well be the case, my lady. I remember almost nothing before my time at the orphanage. I have racked my brain, trying to remember, but…the only thing I recall with certainty is being terrified."

She knew that she should show the Countess her locket. It might clearly prove or disprove the Countess's hopes. But she found herself afraid to put it to the test. She did not want to find out that this sudden new possibility of a family was just as abruptly gone.

"Five is a terribly young age," the Countess said. "I doubt many of us have clear memories before that age. If one was completely cut off from one's former life, it seems that the memories might fade more than they do normally, for there would not be the constant reminders of family and places."

"I don't understand, my lady!" Marianne burst out at last. "How could your grandchild have been put in an orphanage? Why would you not have known?"

"I was deceived by someone close to me," the Countess said sadly. "Mrs. Ward—the woman who raised my granddaughter Alexandra—brought the other two children,

Marie Anne and John, to me, but I was laid up in my bed in grief, seeing no one. My companion—and cousin—met with the woman in my stead and took the children. She never told me. Instead she turned them over to the Earl."

The older woman's lip curled in bitter distaste. "He got rid of them. My cousin told us that on her deathbed. She said that he put you in an orphanage, and that my grandson died."

"Richard?" Justin asked. "Are you saying that Richard got rid of your grandchildren?"

"I believe so, yes, but I have no way to prove it."

"Good God!" Justin looked struck by this news. "Is this all tied up with Fuquay then? Is that why Exmoor shot the man?"

"Shot who?" The Countess looked from Justin to Penelope. "You didn't tell me anyone had been shot!"

"I'm sorry. I didn't even think about it. Your arrival and this news drove it completely out of my head. Richard shot a man yesterday, Reginald Fuquay. Mr. Fuquay had a gun to Marianne's head, and then Richard shot him, and—"

"Reginald Fuquay!" The Countess was suddenly charged with excitement. "Reginald Fuquay was once a friend of Richard's."

"What?" Everyone stared at her.

"They acted as if they hardly knew each other!" Penelope exclaimed.

"Oh, they knew each other, all right. Richard always seemed to have a number of wicked companions, most of them young. He corrupted them—I suspect he delighted in it. Reginald Fuquay came from a good family. He had a reasonable inheritance, but he squandered it all on riotous living. I have heard that he was an opium-eater. He was under Richard's thumb. No doubt he owed Richard money, since he had run through his own fortune." She paused and looked at the others significantly. "It seems to me that it would not have been odd if Richard had gotten Mr. Fuquay to do things for him, certain things that perhaps he did not have the stomach for."

"You mean, killing one child and carting the other off to an orphanage?" Justin asked.

The Countess nodded. "Exactly. You know, it was around that time that Fuquay split from Richard. I had heard that they quarreled, but no one knows what really happened. Neither of them ever said. But they stopped being friends, and Mr. Fuquay began to pull himself out of the mire into which he had sunk. Of course, he could not recover the lost fortune. That is why he had to work as Mr. Thurston's secretary. But he recovered his good name."

"He certainly did," Justin agreed. "I had no idea that he had been wild in his youth."

"'Tis a common enough thing, and they often straighten out as they get older. Still…"

"I agree, Grandmama," Penelope said breathlessly. "It is highly suspicious. If Mr. Fuquay were about to reveal why he had tried to kill Marianne, and if Richard knew that he, too, would be ruined by Fuquay's confession, it would be no wonder that he shot him."

"A very effective way of stopping his mouth," Justin agreed.

Marianne said nothing, her thoughts in a turmoil. She knew that she must tell them about the locket now, must show them the man and woman inside. She could not let her fear keep the Countess from learning the truth.

She cleared her throat. "My lady, I have something that might help to clear—" She was interrupted by the clatter of footsteps in the marble hallway outside, and everyone turned toward the doorway.

A man and woman entered the door. The man was tall and dark-haired, with an angular face. The woman on his arm was a statuesque beauty. Her complexion was strawberries-and-cream, her large, fine eyes a dark brown, and her thick black hair, swept up and caught at the crown of her head, spilled down from the knot in a riot of curls.

Marianne sprang to her feet when she saw her, her face white as a sheet of paper. "My God!" she gasped, and every eye in the place turned to her.

"Marianne!" Justin jumped up and put his arm around her waist. "Darling, are you all right?"

The Countess rose, too, her eyes fixed like a hawk on Marianne's face. "What is it, child?"

They stood fixed for a moment in a frozen tableau, Marianne's and Alexandra's eyes locked on one another.

"I—I'm sorry," Marianne breathed and sat down, her knees no longer able to hold her. "It is just—you look so much like the lady in the picture."

"Picture?" The Countess and Alexandra chorused sharply. Alexandra crossed the room to Marianne.

"What picture?" the Countess pressed.

"I—the one in my locket." Marianne raised wondering eyes to the young woman before her. "I was just about to tell you—I have a locket with pictures of a man and woman—" She reached inside the neck of her dress and caught the chain, drawing out her locket and opening it. "You see? I have had it since I was little. I have always thought that they were my parents, but…I was going to show you and ask you if you recognized them. And then—then she came in and—"

She stumbled to a halt, numbly looking from the Countess to Alexandra. Alexandra went down on her knees in front of Marianne and took the locket in her hand. "It is just like mine!" she cried, tears welling in her eyes.

"I gave them to you both when you were little," the Countess explained, her voice thick with unshed tears. "Yours has an *M* engraved on the front." Marianne nodded. "And Alexandra's has an *A*."

"Mimi," Marianne said suddenly, then stopped, looking surprised. "I'm sorry—I don't know why I said that. It just popped out. When you said that about the locket, I thought 'Mimi.'"

The Countess did break down into tears then. It was a few moments before she was able to say, "That is what John and Marie Anne called me—'Mimi.'"

"We are sisters!" Alexandra exclaimed, smiling and crying all at the same time. She opened up her arms. "Marie Anne. Sister."

Tears sprang into Marianne's eyes, and she threw her arms around Alexandra.

DUSK WAS CREEPING THROUGH the garden as Marianne sat in the rose arbor, thinking. The remainder of the day had been filled with tears and laughter and the joyous telling and retelling of the Countess's news to the other guests. Marianne had to confess that she had felt more than a little wicked pleasure at the expression on Cecilia Winborne's face when she learned who Marianne really was.

Then she and Justin had spent part of the afternoon making plans for how they would take care of the family she had thought of as hers for so long, so that they would no longer have to worry about money or being captured by the law and thrown into Newgate. Della and Harrison and her parents could retire from "the business" and settle down in the cottages Justin would buy for them. Piers could be set up in some sort of business, and Winny would be more than content with just having her own pleasant little house and a small stipend to live on.

It had been a busy day, and she had finally retreated to this spot to think. All her life, she had wanted a family. She had developed a sort of family with Della and Harrison and the others, and she would always love them. But there had also been, deep inside her, a hollowness at her separation from her blood relatives. She could not help but wonder why they had deserted her, could not help but feel as if a part of her was missing. But now here they were—the most wonderful family imaginable! Her sister was warm and funny. She could not imagine a more perfect grandmother than the Countess. Why, even her cousin was already a friend. She would be able to introduce Rosalind to them.

But even more than that, she loved and was loved by a wonderful man.

This morning her life had seemed bleak, something she would have to endure without the friends she had made or the man she loved. And now, here she was, with everything she wanted. Even the mystery of Mr. Fuquay's attacks had been solved. Only two things lay like stains on her perfect happiness: the fact that they would never come to know their brother again, and the fact that the Earl of Exmoor was alive, unharmed even by this new development. She was certain now that he had been the guiding force behind the attacks on her. It explained the halfhearted way the attacks had been carried out. Obviously Mr. Fuquay had been forced by the Earl into getting rid of her, but deep down he had not wanted to do it. Then the Earl had effectively silenced the one man who could implicate him, all the while making it look as if he were saving her.

Marianne grimaced. She wished there was some way to bring Exmoor to an accounting for the evil he had done. She wondered what would have happened this morning if Justin had not caught up with them. *Would Exmoor have seized the opportunity that fate had dropped into his lap? Would he have taken that other road and hidden her lifeless body somewhere along its secluded path?* Marianne remembered the chill she had felt when he had sat there, watching her and talking about the other road. She thought now that he had been trying to decide whether to do away with her.

"I thought I would find you here." Marianne looked up to see Justin walking toward the rose arbor.

"You know me well."

"Not as well as I hope to." He entered the arbor and bent to brush his lips to hers. "I am afraid that now that the Countess has the bit between her teeth over this wedding thing, I shall have to suffer through a number of long, lonely nights. She will have you trapped in that house of hers as if in a fortress, while she makes wedding plans."

Marianne chuckled at his downcast expression. "Mmm. Well, it is rather special, having two granddaughters marry at the same time."

"It lightens my spirits only a little knowing that Bucky will have to suffer, too." He gave her a teasing smile. "It is also rather lowering to know that now everyone will assume that I have married you to form a suitable alliance. I have lost all chance of being a romantic hero."

"Not to me," Marianne answered, reaching out to take his hand. "I will always know that you wanted to marry me when I was penniless and nameless, ready to face down Society and your family. Whatever others may think, I will always know that ours is a marriage made only for love."

"It is indeed." Justin smiled and pulled her into his arms.

HQN™

We *are* romance™

From *New York Times* bestselling author

CANDACE CAMP

No longer quite young, Miss Constance Woodley could scarcely imagine why one of the leading lights of London society should take an interest in her. But under her benefactor's guiding hand, she was transformed into a captivating creature who caught the eye of the handsome and ever-so-slightly notorious Lord Dominic Leighton. The "nobody" and the rakish viscount showed that even in the heartless world of the marriage mart, when love was at stake, all bets were off....

The Marriage Wager

Don't miss this charming Regency tale, the first in Candace Camp's new series: The Matchmakers.

Available in September

www.HQNBooks.com

PHCC243

HQN™

We *are* romance™

Will fate bring two lost souls together?

From *New York Times* bestselling author

BRENDA JOYCE

Lady Blanche Harrington has everything a woman could want—wealth, independence, grace and beauty. But none of these allow her to feel genuine emotion. The victim of a childhood tragedy that she has yet to recover from, Lady Harrington is forced to find a man to marry after her father passes away. She has a bevy of suitors to choose from, but there is one man she has not seen—the reclusive Rex de Warenne, a dark and brooding war hero. When fate intervenes to bring the two together, will they be able to overcome their pasts and create a future together?

The Perfect Bride

Catch the fifth book in Brenda Joyce's captivating de Warenne Dynasty series. In stores today.

www.HQNBooks.com

PHBJ244

REQUEST YOUR
FREE BOOKS!

2 FREE NOVELS
FROM THE ROMANCE/SUSPENSE
COLLECTION PLUS 2 FREE GIFTS!

YES! Please send me 2 FREE novels from the Romance/Suspense Collection and my 2 FREE gifts. After receiving them, if I don't wish to receive any more books, I can return the shipping statement marked "cancel." If I don't cancel, I will receive 4 brand-new novels every month and be billed just $5.49 per book in the U.S., or $5.99 per book in Canada, plus 25¢ shipping and handling per book plus applicable taxes, if any*. That's a savings of at least 20% off the cover price! I understand that accepting the 2 free books and gifts places me under no obligation to buy anything. I can always return a shipment and cancel at any time. Even if I never buy another book from the Reader Service, the two free books and gifts are mine to keep forever.

185 MDN EF5Y   385 MDN EF6C

Name	(PLEASE PRINT)	
Address		Apt. #
City	State/Prov.	Zip/Postal Code

Signature (if under 18, a parent or guardian must sign)

Mail to **The Reader Service:**
IN U.S.A.: P.O. Box 1867, Buffalo, NY 14240-1867
IN CANADA: P.O. Box 609, Fort Erie, Ontario L2A 5X3

Not valid to current subscribers to the Romance Collection,
the Suspense Collection or the Romance/Suspense Collection.

Want to try two free books from another line?
Call 1-800-873-8635 or visit www.morefreebooks.com.

* Terms and prices subject to change without notice. NY residents add applicable sales tax. Canadian residents will be charged applicable provincial taxes and GST. This offer is limited to one order per household. All orders subject to approval. Credit or debit balances in a customer's account(s) may be offset by any other outstanding balance owed by or to the customer. Please allow 4 to 6 weeks for delivery.

Your Privacy: Harlequin is committed to protecting your privacy. Our Privacy Policy is available online at www.eHarlequin.com or upon request from the Reader Service. From time to time we make our lists of customers available to reputable firms who may have a product or service of interest to you. If you would prefer we not share your name and address, please check here. ☐

BOB07

HQN™

We *are* romance™

**A flick of the dice won her his body…
and wagered her heart.**

From award-winning author

helen kirkman

A princess of the defeated English kingdom of Mercia,
Rosamund had lost all hope of a future, until she
stumbled across a chained Mercian prisoner. Drawn
by Boda's brute strength and the defiance in his closed
fist, she impulsively wagered her safety for his and won
him from their Viking captors. But Rosamund's risk is
great. Though she yearns to trust Boda's honor and
lean upon his strength, the scars of war run deep,
and betrayal may be the price of love….

Captured

Be sure to catch this captivating historical romance
in stores now.

www.HQNBooks.com

PHHK237

CANDACE CAMP

77136 A DANGEROUS MAN   ___$6.99 U.S. ___$8.50 CAN.
77135 AN UNEXPECTED PLEASURE   ___$6.99 U.S. ___$8.50 CAN.
77097 AN INDEPENDENT WOMAN   ___$6.99 U.S. ___$8.50 CAN.

(limited quantities available)

TOTAL AMOUNT $ _____
POSTAGE & HANDLING $ _____
($1.00 FOR 1 BOOK, 50¢ for each additional)
APPLICABLE TAXES* $ _____
TOTAL PAYABLE $ _____

(check or money order—please do not send cash)

To order, complete this form and send it, along with a check or money order for the total above, payable to HQN Books, to: **In the U.S.:** 3010 Walden Avenue, P.O. Box 9077, Buffalo, NY 14269-9077; **In Canada:** P.O. Box 636, Fort Erie, Ontario, L2A 5X3.

Name: _____
Address: _____ City: _____
State/Prov.: _____ Zip/Postal Code: _____
Account Number (if applicable): _____

075 CSAS

*New York residents remit applicable sales taxes.
*Canadian residents remit applicable GST and provincial taxes.

HQN™

We *are* romance™

www.HQNBooks.com   PHCC0807BL